GHOSTING ACADEMY

Book 4
The Limerent Series

LS Delorme

For the people who have travelled through time with me and who are unafraid of intensity and a wide spectrum of emotion.

You are my "pod"

Author's Note

Ghosting Academy is a cross genre book.

I would describe it as a psychological thriller with elements of dark fantasy and spy fiction. It also has an element of horror. As such it contains graphic violence, explicit language, psychological manipulation, drug use, and references to mental health struggles and chronic pain.

The novel explores both individual and organizational power, delving into the morally ambiguous actions of its characters. As a result, it does not shy away from depicting intense and challenging situations, because they are integral to understanding the complex nature of the characters and the high-stakes environment they operate in.

So, as always, reader discretion is advised.

Chapter One

Decorating a White Room

Amelie was sitting in a white room—a white room with white walls and a white ceiling. There was no furniture in the room other than the rectangular white table she was sitting at, and the three white chairs surrounding it. The room reminded her of the sanatorium where she had been sent as a child ... and this was not a good thing.

It was an interview day for her. The interviewee in front of her was a fairly normal recruit for them, with her gleaming, perfect blue hair, rehearsed tough-girl slouch, and endless stream-of-consciousness babble.

Amelie's hand was snapping and unsnapping the holster of the gun that was strapped to the underside of the pristine white table. She was weighing the pros and cons of just shooting this girl in the head.

The pros were that it would shut the girl up, clear Amelie's schedule for the day, and no one in the Academy would question it. In fact, she would bet good money that this girl wouldn't make it through the interviewing process and would therefore end up dead anyway. She would be saving somebody else work. Plus, her bladder was cramping, and it would mean she could go back to the pod and get some pain meds.

The cons were that tiny shred of a conscience that she still had left after all her years at the Academy. The one that said, *Is this girl really so different from who you were when you showed up here eighteen years ago?*

It was this voice that always gave her pause. It hadn't always prevented her from shooting someone early in the recruiting process, but sometimes it had. Of course, probably the real reason that she hadn't shot Alt Girl yet was that there was another recruit sitting right next to her.

This one was a dark-haired, tanned boy of about sixteen. He had said almost nothing so far but had watched the whole process with a calm demeanor and

1

unusually alert eyes. He might have a shot at getting through, and Amelie shouldn't fuck that up for him.

"So, can you elaborate a bit about what you think about the concept of 'the end justifies the means'?" Amelie asked, interrupting the girl's tale of how misunderstood she had been in high school. She was probably only nineteen now, so she was not long out of high school, but she was putting on an air of jaded sophistication.

"Oh, I completely believe in it. People are shit. No, people are like viruses. They've taken over the earth and they're destroying it. Best thing that could happen is if there was a huge plague that wiped out half the population."

"Would you be willing to be part of the dying fifty percent?" Amelie asked.

"What?"

"If it was for the good of the planet, would you be willing to be part of the fifty percent that dies?" Amelie asked again.

The girl's tiny round eyes narrowed for a moment, assessing whether Amelie was serious or making fun of her. Amelie knew her face would give away nothing. She had years of practice in hiding her feelings—even before she came to this place.

"Yeah, sure. I would be willing to do that," the girl finally lied. "I mean, it's not like life has been a fun ride for me anyway, so leaving it wouldn't be so bad. Life's meaningless in the end anyway, and then we die."

"So you are a Hobbesian sort of girl?"

The girl looked at Amelie blankly, obviously not familiar with Thomas Hobbes or his famous quotes about man unfettered by a social contract.

"You believe that men's lives, or their natural ones, are 'nasty, brutish and short'?" Amelie asked.

The girl beamed and nodded her head; apparently this was something that resonated with whatever alternative lifestyle persona she was adopting. She was wearing a wildly ripped and ragged offensive gesture T-shirt over a black bustier. Her pants were leather and tight, and she wore a proliferation of jewelry in her ears, on her neck, on her fingers, through her eyebrows, and through her nose. She was probably pretty minus all this, but as it was, her attire screamed of a pathological need for attention.

Real freaks don't go around advertising themselves, Amelie thought to herself for probably the millionth time in her life as she switched legs and put one foot under her opposite hip. Thank god she only had to do these sorts of interviews a couple of times a year.

2

She unsnapped one of the leather straps holding the gun under the table but left it unsnapped this time. She then caught the eye of the boy, who was watching her intently, and stopped. She knew that she was being more reactive to this girl because she was irritable. And she was irritable because she was just back from a mission and was in pain.

This pain was different from the pain she had endured during much of her youth—the IBS, the arrhythmia, the headaches, the joint pain. All of that, all her chronic pain, had disappeared after that one memorable night on the beach when she was eighteen. She had waited for years for it to return, but it hadn't. Now the only time she had pain had to do with sex. Every time she had sex with someone, her immune system went insane and began attacking her own body, particularly targeting the nerves around her bladder and vagina. "Autoimmune disorder" was what the Academy doctors said, but this felt very different from the autoimmune disorders she had when she was young. Now it happened when she had sex, and only when she had sex. But, as most of her missions revolved around having at least a fair amount of sex, this meant that she managed it the best she could in the field with an overuse of anti-inflammatories and pain pills. After a mission it usually took her a few weeks to a month to get her immune system calmed down, so right now her bladder was cramping, and she was itchy enough to want to strangle someone.

"There are lots of sacrifices that people have to make to be here. You have to give up ties to your outside world. You have to cut yourself off from loved ones," Amelie began.

"I don't love anyone, so that's not a problem," the girl said, in a tone that said she thought this was something to be proud of.

"No?" Amelie asked.

"Love makes you weak," the girl responded, rolling her eyes.

"I see," Amelie said, still toying with the gun. She wanted rid of this girl with her horrible attire and predictable attitude but killing her was still probably unwarranted for the moment.

"So, do either of you have any questions for me? Anything I can answer, that is. I won't give you any specifics about the Academy just yet, but anything else?"

"Yes, what do *you* actually do here?" asked the girl, with a little smirk.

"I told you that I can't tell you that," Amelie said, putting her hand around the butt of the gun.

"I think she might have been asking if you could elaborate about what circumstances and talents brought you here," replied the boy, large dark eyes

3

connecting directly with hers. "I would be very interested in that as well, assuming you are allowed to discuss it."

Amelie nodded and leaned back in her chair, pretending to ponder the request to give herself a moment.

It was a smart question that showed emotional intelligence. Also, what teen boy uses the word *elaborate*? This one was the one to watch here.

She took a moment to open her inner eyelid. The colors around the girl were what she would have expected. Reds, oranges, a bit of gray and black, but all pale and watered down. Pretending colors. The boy, on the other hand, was a different story. There were very few colors around him, as if he was blocking, but occasionally a flash of brilliant color pulsed from him in indigo, pink and gold.

That one could be special.

"I was born a seducer," Amelie finally said. The girl's eyes widened for just a moment.

"You mean you have to fuck people?" she asked, not able to keep an element of disdain from her voice. The boy leaned back in his seat, eyes firmly on the girl, not Amelie.

"No, I mean I can seduce people," she said.

"But that means you have to fuck them, right?"

The boy sighed audibly.

"Comparing sex to seduction is like comparing a paintbrush to a fully completed portrait. The paintbrush is only a tool to get you there," he said, smiling slightly.

Amelie felt herself smiling, despite the pain in her abdomen and her rising irritation.

The girl snorted and glared at the boy, who only smiled more broadly and leaned toward her a bit.

"Any other questions?" Amelie asked. She wanted this over with and to get back to her room. The dry, reconditioned air in the interview room was making her eyes sting.

"Yes," said the boy. "If you were in our shoes, would you choose this same path again? Do you have any reservations about the choice you made?"

"No," Amelie replied without reservation or complicity. "This place is my home. These people are my family."

The girl's face suddenly took on an ugly look of superiority. It was the look of a person who believes that all human ties are a form of weakness. It made Amelie want to bitch-slap the smile off her face. Instead, she continued coolly.

"And I cherish my family."

4

Amelie heard a familiar laugh from behind her. It was James, her most annoying podmate, who had obviously finished his interviews. He was dressed in the combat pants and leather jacket that he favored, but had added a fedora to the mix. God, the man had the worst fashion sense.

Despite his dress, the girl eyed him with obvious approval. James wasn't good-looking in any traditional sense. He was fairly short, his nose was too big, his skin too pale, and he had mouse-brown hair that he had cut at the cheapest barber he could find. He also had numerous twitchy mannerisms. On the other hand, he was nicely built, and he had the bluest eyes Amelie had ever seen on a human. Add that to the fact that he oozed charisma and a palpable sort of charm, and Amelie could understand why the girl in front of her was now leaning forward.

The boy had no reaction at all to James's sudden appearance, other than nodding ever so slightly.

"You should take Amelie's statement very seriously," James said to the girl, winking. "If you make it to training, she will be your big sister. She has a hundred percent clearance rate on all the candidates she puts forward ... any idea why?"

The girl shook her head, now leaning onto the table to put her breasts on display.

"As her podmate, I can tell you that Amelie has a hundred percent clearance rate because only about twenty-five percent of her trainees make it past her."

The girl's snake eyes were back on Amelie, slithering over her face.

"What does that mean?" she asked.

"It means she kills seventy-five percent of her candidates," James said, smiling and raising his eyebrows.

"James is prone to exaggeration," Amelie replied, hand still on the gun.

"Okay, okay, thirty percent make it through," James said, coming and putting a hand on Amelie's shoulder. He had clocked her hand on the gun under the table.

"The actual number is thirty-four percent," Amelie responded lightly.

"And right now, she's got her hand on a gun that is strapped to the underside of this table," James said.

The girl's eyes flew wide and she lunged across the table toward them.

Instantly, Amelie pulled the gun from under the table and shot Alt Girl in the middle of the forehead. The girl was thrown backward into her chair by the impact of the shot. The chair absorbed the blow easily, as it was bolted to the floor. For a moment Alt Girl's body hung on the chair, spine balanced against the back of it. Then her body slid sideways toward the floor, landing with her head and torso on the ground. One leg was on the ground, the other still stuck

5

in the plastic slats of the chair. Blood was splattered across the floor behind her body.

James flung his hands out to either side of him.

"Jesus, can you give some warning before you are going to do that?"

"You provoked it," Amelie said quietly.

"I was checking her judgment," James said.

"She failed," Amelie replied, putting the gun back in its holster.

"So shooting her was the answer? And in the white room? Why not the green room or the red room? They are much less messy."

"I don't interview in the red room," Amelie said quickly. A vision of a balding man with a comb-over inserted itself in her head and she immediately blotted it out.

James rolled his eyes.

"Red, green, whatever. Anything but white. You know the custodial staff here hate you, don't you?"

"The custodial staff don't know me," she muttered.

"Oh yes they do. They know you by name. And they hate you. I've heard them talking about it. You don't have to shoot people. You could just wait and let the chem department take care of them," James said.

"That wastes people's time," Amelie said, shifting in her seat.

"It did seem a bit harsh," the teenage boy suddenly said. He was leaning forward now, looking at her intently. It had not escaped Amelie that he barely flinched when she pulled out the gun. In fact, he barely blinked when she fired.

"You see, you freaked out the recruit," James said, nodding at the boy. "Now we won't get a reliable read for the rest of the day."

"We don't need the rest of the day," Amelie said, switching to put her other foot under her other hip. "He passed."

"Oh, and are you going to be the one to tell the OCD freaks in psy ops that he can skip all the rest of the psychometric tests?"

"No, of course not. But he's in my candidate stream, so I have the final say. Let him go through the tests, but I'm making the call now. He's on board."

"He has a name, you know," said the boy, with a slight smile.

"Sorry. Amelie had a bit of a tough weekend of potentially abnormal sex, you must forgive her," James said.

"My name is James Nightshade," James said. He paused for a moment. Amelie knew he was searching the boy's face for his reaction to James's over-the-top, designed-to-annoy last name, but his face remained placid.

"You have met Amelie," James continued, extending his hand.

6

"Caio Silva," said the boy, taking James's hand with a smile that looked disturbingly genuine. For a moment, Amelie questioned her decision. Then the smile was gone, replaced by that calculated calm he had displayed since entering the room and she felt more comfortable again.

Her bladder chose that moment to mimic labor and she winced.

James looked at her and his expression changed. It softened and his brows knit.

"Okay, dear heart, Widget has prepared a nice, organic, flavor-free lunch for you. I am guessing that you are a bit low blood sugar. So why don't I take it from here?"

Amelie nodded and stood up slowly, the muscles in her pelvis spasming as she did so.

Caio stood up and extended a hand to her; such antiquated manners from a teen. When she took his hand, she found it warm and more calloused than she would have expected for his age.

James motioned her toward the door, concern once again flickering across his face.

It would be good to go back, have some lunch, and take a nap. But she made a mental note not to shoot her next recruit. She didn't want to prove James right.

When Amelie got to the building in Covent Garden where she lived with her podmates, she didn't immediately go to their rooftop flat. Instead, she took the stairs to the basement. At the bottom of the stairs was a large, rusty metal door that looked hundreds of years old and immovable.

As she pushed her weight against it, it opened easily enough into a large, dimly lit room. What light was present was the soft illumination coming from lamps and computer screens that were scattered around the room. A single giant table was covered in test tubes and microscopes. On the wall there were counters with various other lab equipment: Bunsen burners, a couple of handheld spectrophotometers. In one corner was a massive computer, with some sort of weird chemistry graphics program that threw up 3D images of organic compounds.

This was Widget's playground. There were a lot of toys but not a lot of space to move around in.

Widget kept one small corner for a living area. Here he had a couple of lounge chairs and a hammock strung up between two water pipes. Which is where he was now, lying in his hammock. She suspected he was waiting for her.

He had an almost uncanny ability to know when she had had a more difficult assignment.

She went to him, and he opened his arms, welcoming her. She curled up next to him in the hammock.

"It was bad this time," she whispered, hesitantly. She didn't like admitting to this. She didn't like admitting that her assignments affected her at all.

There was always physical pain with these missions, but that would be gone soon enough. The worst part was that they always triggered memories. It didn't matter how hard she blocked them. It didn't matter how quickly she suppressed them. The memories were always there, brought naturally by comparison. Oh for the days when she had felt nothing but physical pain. That gift had been stolen from her—stolen and incinerated. Now she felt every emotion in sharp, painful detail. She existed, she moved, she ate, she slept, she laughed, but the emotional pain inside her was constant. She could not escape it, so she had developed ways to live with it. She supposed it was a bit like how she had learned to live with chronic illnesses in her youth. One just had to readjust what one considered normal. There was always some pain, but some days were better than others. The irony was that the physical pains that had plagued her most of her life disappeared at the same moment that her emotional pain began.

"I had to get in closer than I wanted to," she whispered to Widget.

She stopped and listened to the sounds of the machines. She felt Widget nod. He could hear just fine but he couldn't speak. She didn't know why, as he had never disclosed a reason.

Widget took her chin and looked into her eyes. His smile was soft. It was strange to see such a giant man look so gentle. Widget looked like some sort of nerd Viking. He was easily six foot five and was all lean muscle. He could have been a male model but for the awkwardness in his stance and movement. She often thought he looked like he was trying to sort out a foreign gravity. In the beginning, she had nicknamed him Clark Kent. Majo had shortened it to Kent. She thought it was James who had changed it to Kenti, and then on and on until it finally somehow settled on Widget, which stuck.

"I want to go home. I just want to go home," Amelie muttered softly.

It wasn't home she wanted, and they both knew it. She had never had a real home or a real family. Her real family were in this building now, with her. But she couldn't say what she really wanted … who she really wanted. She couldn't say his name out loud again. Tears welled up in her eyes.

Here it came again. It wasn't always like this, but sometimes, after a particularly difficult assignment, it came crashing down on her … for a bit.

"I thought I would get over it," she said weakly to Widget, to herself. "Not immediately, but eventually, I thought I would get over it. People say time heals all things, but people are wrong. I let him get so connected to me—no, I did that. I sewed him into my own soul. When I had to let go, it meant ripping those sutures open. My heart almost bled out. Over time, it did scar over but the rip is still there, so I will never be the same. When I move the wrong way, it tears open again."

She could feel Widget nod again. She didn't know exactly what Widget had lived through, but she knew it had been bad. His empathy level was extraordinary in moments like these. She circled her arms around his neck.

Widget held her head close to his heart. She heard the deep, comforting swish of blood flowing through his chest. It sounded like it was being pushed by a heart that was the size of an elephant's. Her tears were wetting his shirt. She tried to weep quietly in these moments. At least she could aim for that level of decorum. Widget never seemed to mind. His arms were strong and true, and totally without passion. His touch felt like that of a father, or a brother … a real one.

"I don't know how to let go," she said softly, her mouth wet with tears and spit. Widget kissed the top of her head, and began to rock her. Back and forth like a child. They had been through this before. And she knew she would cry herself out and fall asleep in his arms. Later that night, when the others were asleep, he would carry her up to her bed and tuck her in.

And tomorrow they would act like none of this happened.

Chapter Two

The Real Meaning of Worm Hole

The first sign he had of consciousness was the feeling of being on fire—on the inside. A storm of flame was spinning inside him, melting him, unmaking and remaking him simultaneously. The pain was excruciating, but it wasn't the worst. What was worse was an overwhelming feeling of horror—and loss.

His eyes snapped open, expecting to see smoke and flames and perhaps his own burning flesh. Instead, he found himself standing in a sunlit courtyard, looking up at a small castle. It was not much bigger than the plantation houses that could be found in the Deep South. It might have even been smaller but what it might have lacked in size, it made up for in glitz.

He was in Disneyland, and almost as soon as he recognized it, he remembered he had been here before, and he had been happy. In front of him, he could see a girl with wheat-colored hair wearing a Minnie Mouse wedding veil headband. His heart screamed inside him. Then the fire on his insides flared, and the scene around him was burned away, as his own body burned away.

The smell of the sea washed over him. He found that he was standing on pale sand. The sun was setting over the ocean, lighting the waves with flashes of rose, violet, and orange. He knew this place. Behind him, he heard someone cough. He turned to find himself staring at a young girl dressed in rags, but she did not see him, she was watching a young man in the waves.

He shouldn't be here; this was a major scene. He had told someone that. Someone important. He heard a soft sob and turned to see a young man with wings on his knees. In front of him was a girl, but she was fading. As he watched, he saw the girl's form disappear. The boy let out a sob and put his face down into the sand. He knew this boy. Wait, this boy was him. He looked up just in time to see the tidal wave approaching. There was no time to run. He was caught by the huge wave and pulled beneath the surface of the water. He struggled for the surface, but he could not find it. Finally, the fire in his lungs forced his mouth open, and all became blue and dead. He was dead.

The smell of magnolia brought him back. He was standing on a bridge that crossed a small stream just next to a country fair. He saw an unnaturally beautiful woman facing an equally beautiful young man. The woman was wearing a thin dress that left nothing to the imagination.

"I will never be able to forgive you if I discover that you are willing to do for that girl what you would never do for me."

"What is that?" said the young man in a bored-sounding voice.

"Break all the rules," the woman said.

"So you will spend lifetimes wasting your time chasing a woman you claim not to care about just because you are jealous that she stole your lover?" the boy said.

"No. A lover I can stand losing. But what I couldn't stand was losing my son."

At those words, rips began to appear in everything around him—the grass, the earth, the sky. He looked down and saw rips beginning in his skin as well. The pain flared as pieces of him were yanked from his body and his soul was torn from him and thrown to the wind. He screamed but his tongue was taken. Before his ears were removed, he heard the woman say, "I protected you. You can't be possessed by more than one demon at a time."

The words entered his ears and seared them shut. His eyes were pulled out in strips, and everything went white. He was gone.

Except he wasn't. He was somewhere, surrounded by white. He could feel no ground beneath his feet. He could see no sky or building above him. He existed in a milky space, free-floating and suspended in a white nothingness. He couldn't even determine the orientation of his body. But he knew that he had a body—because he was in agony.

The pain felt as if his body had been split, torn apart, and smashed back together with all the delicacy of a toddler having a tantrum. The pain at the ripped edges was almost unbearable. He was covered in a clear, slimy, sticky substance that both burned and cut into him if he moved or shifted. The substance that masqueraded as air around him was acidic and smelled of ash and burned metal. It stung his lungs and eyes. If that had been all, that would have been too much. But there was also the pain he felt from the parts of him that were now missing, like the pain from a phantom limb. Or in his case, the pain of a phantom self. He didn't know his name, who he was, or where he came from. He suspected that that he had existed in other places and that parts of

11

him, the stolen and ripped-out parts, might still exist in these other, cleaner, places.

Occasionally, as if to torment him even more, he saw actual flashes of these other, more wholesome, places. Warm, dark rooms. Sublime skies. Pools of water filled with colorful fishes and flowers. Cheery pink castles. But such flashes came and went in milliseconds and were always accompanied by increased pain. And then he was back here in this sickly white space.

The contrast between these wholesome places and here added grief to the pain he was experiencing. In his here and now, nothing had understandable shape or substance. All was a white murk that undulated and bulged. Occasionally this murk would begin to roll and boil. In those moments, it would bulge, blister, and pop, spewing forth flocks of monstrous albino monsters that had the color and smell of curdled milk. He had learned to clamp his eyes closed whenever he saw these things emerge. The mere sight of them added nausea and vomiting to his list of physical ills. They had no form that he could describe. They had no design that was comprehensible. He suspected that they had different dimensional elements that his mind could not process. Seeing them made him feel sick, weak, and lightheaded, on top of the slicing pain across his chest and the burning of his skin.

He sometimes told himself that he must be in hell, but he knew this was wrong. He knew that he still had a body, or at least part of one. He knew this in the way he knew that he had been ripped apart. He knew it in the same way that he knew that he was simply a part of a larger whole that was spread across … what? Planets? Worlds? Galaxies?

And there was one more thing that he knew. The thing that brought him despair, confusion, panic, and the occasional sliver of hope.

He knew, for some reason that he could not remember, that he had chosen to be here. Even worse, he knew that somehow this was home.

Chapter Three

Morning Obsessions

It was early morning and Amelie was curled up on the couch in their living room, staring a bit blankly at the TV on the wall. She was watching a movie that came out more years ago than she wanted to think about, with a plot she already knew by heart. In truth, she didn't care about the movie or the plot. She was watching it because of the actor starring in it. Her night had been disrupted with bad dreams again, and sometimes watching this guy helped.

Her surroundings would take the edge off most people's problems. This penthouse flat in London was her home and it had been for thirteen years now. Their pod had been together for longer than that, which was extremely long by Academy standards. And now she had grown accustomed to, if not exactly comfortable with, her life here.

During Amelie's first two years with the Academy, she had been in the Paris hub, training in the basics of espionage, risk assessment, psychology, psy ops, and a bit of weaponry. It had been quickly decided that this last was not her forte. Her forte was in getting people to fall in love with her, or more accurately, to make them believe they had fallen in love with her. What she actually did was to incite obsession, but most people couldn't tell the difference. The fact that her impact on people could last years, or even their entire lifetime, made it even harder for her targets to see the difference. For this reason, Amelie preferred it when her targets were either eliminated or killed themselves. Those that were still out there had to be added to the growing list of potential future stalkers. Of course, the Academy kept track of all these people and changed her legal identity often enough for this to rarely be an issue, but it still felt messy to her.

Of course, messy was a major element of most of her jobs. Her last assignment had been to seduce the ethically challenged operations manager of a giant tech firm. There had been more sex on this mission than was usual. She could sometimes get through her assignments and complete them without actually having sex with someone. On even better assignments, she might have the sex but with minimal to no emotional connection. But she had not been so lucky this time, either physically or emotionally.

Leaning back into the sofa, with one leg curled under the other, she looked around the quiet flat. There could be a lot worse surroundings in which to recuperate. Their flat was more than comfortable, it was luxurious. This city could be dreary in the wrong sort of apartment, but the view from the windows and balconies had various views of the London Eye, the West End and the Thames. There was enough neon light coming from their surroundings to brighten up even the drabbest of evenings.

In the very worst weather, she could just curl up inside. She and her three podmates each had their own large bedroom and bathroom along with the communal eat-in kitchen and an open living/dining area. The living room was huge and decorated in tones of natural wood, white, and black. The kitchen was almost as big. The walls and ceilings were white and there were hardwood floors throughout, covered with the occasional exotic rug. The kitchen and living room both came equipped with fireplaces.

The fireplace in the living room had already been lit when Amelie stumbled down this morning. Amelie deeply appreciated this. It was mid-October and the days were getting grayer and shorter in an exponential fashion, and the smell of fire had always calmed her. Widget had probably lit it, as he was the only one who got up earlier than she did. But for the moment he was nowhere to be seen. This was a bit of a relief, as she always felt sort of stupid and guilty the day after going to him for a cry.

Amelie focused on the face of the actor in the movie. He was ridiculously beautiful but in an exotic, otherworldly sort of way. She felt a warmth in her chest, as she watched him turn, smile, and laugh on the screen. She sighed and closed her eyes. If only the other one had been an actor … how much easier that would have been. Instead, he had turned out to be the only person she had ever loved or would ever love, but he had not returned her love. He had manipulated her for the sole purpose of injuring her. On the positive side, all this had made her unusually fearless and that was a great asset to the Academy.

Just at that moment, there was the sound of a door being thrown open and footsteps pounding down the stairs. It could only be James, who was the most annoying of her podmates. First, he was ridiculously noisy. He was a non-stop talker. He talked to other people, he talked to himself, he talked to the kitchen appliances. On those rare occasions when he wasn't talking, he was either watching TV with the volume up too high, playing an old beat-up saxophone, or trying to "help" in the kitchen by unloading the dishwasher in such a manner that Amelie was always amazed that there were any dishes left unbroken. Second, he had a very bad habit of picking up women and then talking about it. She had to admit, he wasn't one of those "conquest" guys who bragged about sleeping with women per se. In fact, he had never brought anyone back to the flat, unlike Majo, but his tendency to rhapsodize about the beauty of the girl he met the night before somehow always ended up feeling insulting.

If he had slighter fewer irritating habits, Amelie might have found him attractive in an everyman sort of way. She had always liked his nose. It looked like it might have been broken a couple of times. It was a strong, blue-collar kind of nose. Which was, as far as she could tell, a fairly good summary of James himself. A scrappy kid from the council houses of Glasgow who had somehow talked his way into a world way beyond what he could have predicted for himself, but while she kind of admired him, she still found it hard to be around him alone for extended periods. The noise was just too much.

"Who's on the agenda this morning?" James said, as he entered the room, plopping down on the couch next to her and throwing a Nerf ball in the air.

"Oh god. Not him again," he said when he saw the actor's face.

"James. Leave her alone. She can watch whoever she wants to," came a soft voice from the kitchen. It was Majo, who had managed to get up and past Amelie without her even noticing. This was even more impressive given that Majo had the kind of unique beauty that stopped people in the street. She had Asian bone structure but Nordic coloring. That would have been enough to turn heads, but she also had a deep scar that ran across her cheek, just below her cheekbone. Rather than hide it, Majo had chosen to accentuate it by having tattoos of flowers running along each side of it, as if it were a flowering vine. This made the scar an accent to her beauty. All this made her ability to enter and leave a room unnoticed all the creepier. She was the one who had recruited Amelie all those years ago. She had saved her life on that same day. After eighteen years, Amelie thought she would have discovered the reason that Majo saved her and the circumstances surrounding it. But she hadn't. Neither Majo nor the Academy worked that way.

"I just don't get what she sees in that guy," James snorted. "He can't act. He takes horrible movie roles. And he's supposedly a total arsehole. So why get obsessed with him. And she doesn't even watch the new movies, just his old, boring ones."

"Hey, I like watching certain actors too," Majo said, coming into the room with two cups of tea. She handed one to Amelie.

15

"Actors are at their most interesting at that moment just before they become famous," Majo said, sipping her tea. "When they have that spark that you know everyone will discover soon but it hasn't become common knowledge yet. And you know that once they become famous, they will be lost to the three Ds."

"What are the three Ds?" Amelie asked, being drawn into the conversation despite herself. It was Majo's voice. Her voice was as soft and compelling as her face was cold and beautiful.

"Drained, degraded or dead," Majo responded. "Fame is a vampire. Once it has you, it leaves you drained, degraded or dead."

Amelie nodded and sipped her tea. It was a warm, not hot, jasmine tea with a coma-inducing level of sugar added, just the way Amelie liked it.

James suddenly threw the Nerf ball at the TV screen, hitting the actor on his enlarged face.

"Amelie, you could have that guy if you wanted him. Just show up at some function he attends and there you go, he's yours."

Majo turned and glared at James. Strictly, they were not supposed to discuss either their gifts or their missions, but Amelie's particular gift could be hard to hide—she gave Majo a small smile and shrugged.

"She could, though," James said to Majo, ignoring her glare.

"I know, but I don't want to," Amelie muttered, yawning.

"Why the hell not?" James said.

"God, James, are you that much of an idiot?" Majo said.

"Most of the time, yes, but I don't see how I am an idiot on this one."

He looked at Amelie, but Majo was the one who spoke.

"Well, think it through logically, if you can. What's the best that could come out of seducing him? One, she has sex with the guy, and it doesn't live up to her fantasies. Which means one night of average sex costs her multiple nights of masturbatory fantasies. Two, she has sex with the guy and it's great sex. Well, even if she could have a relationship with him, he is unlikely to be interested in long-term commitment."

"Ouch," James said. Majo shot him a nasty look.

"I'm not questioning your attractiveness, Amelie," Majo said, turning back to her, "but narcissism is a job requirement for actors. He will never want you for you, so you would have to constantly use your energy to keep him."

Use it? I don't use it. I suppress it. I control it. Maybe it would be nice just to let it go with someone.

Outwardly, she only shrugged. Majo turned back to James.

"If the encounter ends this way, then Amelie will have solid proof that he is a dick. So again, she loses the masturbatory value. Third, they fall in love or something. And, well, that would just end in misery for everyone. So all of us handle this differently. You have your bar girls. I have my pick-ups. Amelie has her celebrity crushes, which makes sense given that sex is so much a part of her job. I don't know what Widget does, but I doubt he is celibate."

James raised his eyebrows. "Well, I would bet he doesn't settle for nights alone with his hand," he said.

Amelie settled back down into the couch. James was starting his argument with Majo about average flesh being better than beautiful fantasy, which was a common debate for them. This took Amelie off the hook. She tuned them out and focused on the actor on the screen. If she squinted, it could be him. She had dreamed about him last night. Of course, she dreamed about him, or dreamed about searching for him, almost every night. In that way, mornings were always hard. But mornings after particularly draining assignments were worse.

"I hear you have a new trainee," Majo said, breaking into her reverie.

"Yeah," Amelie muttered. "I got him yesterday. Young kid, but weirdly mature."

"Is he a nouveau or a transfer?" Majo asked.

"Oh, he's a total transfer," James replied. "He didn't even blink when Amelie shot the other recruit."

"You shot *another* recruit?" Majo asked.

Amelie nodded.

"You're becoming worse than me."

"You should have seen the mess. It was in the white room—" James started, but Amelie interrupted him.

"Look, there's another outbreak," she said, pointing to the TV. A warning was flashing across the bottom of the screen.

Dog flu virus mutation outbreak reported in Spain. Vaccinations should be available by end of week. Avoid any outside activity or unnecessary contact with strangers until you can be vaccinated. If you develop symptoms of fever with euphoria, decrease of inhibition or exaggerated sex drive seek immediate medical attention, the red bar advised.

"Another fucking mutated outbreak. How many is that this year?" James said.

"Since January—nine," Majo replied.

"Nine in as many months." James whistled. "Seems to be getting worse. We only had eight all year last year."

"The bugs must be getting smarter," Majo said. "Pity people aren't."

"At least we can stay ahead of them with vaccines," James said.

"For now."

17

A rabbit ran over Amelie's grave at those words, and she turned to scan Majo's face. It was impassive, as usual.

As if on cue, the elevator opened at the back of the room and Widget entered. Widget had the ability to make even the largest rooms seem small. Today he was wearing a gray tracksuit and carrying a tray of needles. They had all had their weekly blood draw on Monday, so it was too early to be that.

"What's up with the syringes?" James asked, swiveling on the couch, and bumping into Amelie in the process. Amelie's pelvis cramped and she glared at him.

Widget nodded toward the TV screen as he put the tray on the glass dining room table.

"You saw the news, right?" he signed.

Everyone nodded.

"So these are the vaccinations."

"We had new vaccinations last week," James said.

"The *new* new ones," Widget signed. "And some vitamins of my own design."

"It said on the news that the vaccines wouldn't be ready until the end of the month," James said.

Widget rolled his eyes and Majo openly snorted. It was a stupid comment. They all knew that the Academy was light-years ahead of the general population in just about everything. It was likely that they had this vaccine in the vault before the outbreak. And, as Widget was in the biological sciences unit of the Academy, he would be one of the first to have access to it.

Widget picked up a needle and motioned to Amelie. She grimaced and shook her head.

"I hate these things. Vaccinations are the worst," she muttered.

"No, death is the worst. This is just a little prick in your arm," Majo said.

"So can I assume you have already signed up for Evermore then?" James asked with a smirk.

"What's Evermore?" Amelie asked.

"Do you never read the news?" James said.

"Not unless it's pertinent to my job. Why?"

"It's been all over the news lately," Majo replied. "There is a company that claims to be able to move your consciousness from your body and into a virtual world that they have created."

"Created to your *specifications*," James added, getting up as Widget nodded to him.

18

"So they say that they can identify and isolate your actual soul, and move it?" Amelie turned to face James, who was stoically getting his vaccination.

"Oh, they don't mention souls at all," Majo said. "They only discuss consciousness."

"And they know it works?" Amelie asked.

"The gamers who did the beta testing all came back singing its praises and wanting to go back in," James replied. "Who knows, maybe the human race has finally found a way to cheat death."

"I would never do that," Majo muttered.

"Why not, if you hate death so much?" James asked her.

"Because I don't believe that they can do it, despite what anyone says," Majo replied. "And if they can, I don't trust the result. If they can isolate your consciousness and transfer it into a computer network—well, that's playing with the natural order of things in a way that is destined to go wrong."

"Did you actually say 'playing with the natural order of things'?" James laughed. "That sounds about one step away from 'we might anger God.'"

"Well, I'm sure if there is a God, then playing God would anger it," Majo replied. She stood up and walked over to offer her arm to Widget. "And I wouldn't want my soul to be stuck in a computer if said deity decided it was time to become offended."

"Do you believe in God?" Amelie asked, a bit shocked. She had always assumed Majo was an atheist.

"Do I believe in God?" Majo mused. "If there is a God, then it created death. And it created us to be creatures that are aware of our own mortality. What kind of being gives its creations sentience of its own death and then forces them to die. So, while I think there is something out there, I prefer to think of it as only indirectly involved. Because if there is a God, or a being that is an active participant in this whole setup, then I hate it in the same way that I hate death."

Just then Widget jabbed Majo's arm with a needle and she gasped.

"What about you? Would you consider something like Evermore? Or are you worrying about offending God too?" James asked Amelie, as he walked to the kitchen and grabbed some leftover tortilla chips from a bowl on the counter.

"I don't know," Amelie replied, turning to stare out of the window. "I think it's logical that there is something out there greater than us. It seems improbable the design of the universe was just an accident. So I think I would agree with Majo. It feels like taking a serious risk to play with that."

"A greater risk than just dying?" James said through a mouthful of chips. "You know, a lot of their clients are in critical condition. With a few exceptions, I think most of them are unlikely to live out the year. I'm guessing when they are faced with death, the fear of death becomes greater than the fear of technology."

"Fear is an excellent driver," Majo said, sipping her tea. "And they have an elegant business model. They charge clients different amounts based on their ability to pay. They advertise that as if they are doing something charitable when, in fact, they are simply charging the client the most that they can."

"What about you?" Amelie asked James. "Are you saying that you would do it?"

James's face became unusually serious.

"No, I absolutely wouldn't," James said, with a little sigh. "I understand why people would do it. But to me, living forever is a very unattractive prospect."

Words came into Amelie's head unbidden.

I don't think about it. I concentrate on the moment … live in the moment. If you live in the moment, or in the very near future or past, then life can still be sweet.

Her eyes began to well up. It had been almost twenty years and remembering his words could still bring her to tears.

She quickly turned toward the TV screen and focused again on the face of the actor there.

Close it down. Close it down. Close it down.

She was focusing so hard, she didn't even notice when Widget jabbed the needle into her arm.

Chapter Four

Adolescents and Interns

Amelie's morning mood passed in the same fashion that it always did. She was miserable until about 10 a.m., and then the memories of her dreams faded, and she became fully immersed in her physical life. The rhythm of her life was now completely opposite to what it was when she was a girl. When she was a girl, she had feared her physical life. Her most precious time had been when she had been out of her body. The times when she flew in her sleep. Later, her life revolved around her moments in the hallway. Then, after one night of bliss, that had all been ripped away from her. Maybe she had given it away. She didn't really know. What she did know was that from that point on, she could no longer fly in her sleep. She couldn't get to the hallway anymore, even though she had spent years trying. So all she had to cling to in those early years was her own physicality. This had hurt her, but it had also sustained her. The illnesses and chronic problems that she had always associated with her physical body had largely disappeared. She learned to trust her body for the first time and to use it. It had become her tool and her altar. This physicality was now precious to her, as she knew how untrustworthy and unstable non-physical things could be.

"Goddamn it!"

James was in the living room playing Verite on the big TV. From what Amelie could gather, the game had some sort of new tech that was supposed to respond to a person's vital signs. As a result, one played the game wearing a stupid-looking tight black outfit. It looked a lot like padded long black underwear. James said that it inserted tiny microfibers into your skin to collect and relay information about you. But, as he also said that the suit had microneedles that administered electric shocks when you did something wrong, Amelie thought he was probably just fucking with her.

"I don't know how he can stand that thing," Amelie said to Majo and Widget.

They were sitting outside on the patio, which was facing Victoria Embankment. They were curled up in padded armchairs and the girls were having a brunch of soft-boiled eggs and soldiers. It was starting out to be a rare day for October. The clouds and mist of the morning had lifted, and the sky was Indian-summer blue with a few misty white clouds clinging to the horizon. The air was cool and fresh and smelled of the coffee and pastries that were being sold on the streets below.

"You mean Verite?" Widget signed.

"Of course," Amelie responded.

"Well, get used to it," Widget replied.

"What does he mean, get used to it?" Amelie asked Majo.

"He means that it's now the most popular game in the history of games. Half the kids under eighteen spend seventy-five percent of their waking hours with their heads in those absurd helmets."

"Yeah, but how old is James? Thirty-eight? Thirty-nine? Surely old enough to outgrow that, right?" Amelie asked.

Majo shook her head sadly. "Amelie, gamers don't outgrow gaming. Not serious ones. It's more addictive than smoking. And this game, even more so. It uses actual physical stimuli to affect you in the game. The lighting affects your nervous system. Somehow the suit checks you for what causes your heart rate and blood pressure to go up. The helmet assesses the dilation of your pupils. The game uses that to learn what you like, what you don't like, what excites you, and so on."

"That could be powerful," Amelie mused. "I'm surprised the Academy hasn't gotten into that yet."

"Have they used those applications for porn yet?" Widget asked, with a sly smile.

"Well, actually—" Majo began.

"I don't want to know," Amelie said, shaking her head.

"Ignoring these things won't make them go away," Majo laughed.

"What am I missing?" James asked, appearing at the sliding glass door with his hand shoved in a box of Frosted Flakes.

"Conversation about tech and porn," Widget signed.

"Goody," James said, plopping his box of cereal down on the table, causing a not insignificant amount of it to be released into the air before it scattered in all directions.

Majo gave him a death stare.

"I can't do anything right with this one," he said nodding at Majo, he then bent down and gave Amelie a quick hug, which she immediately squirmed out of.

"Okay, right then," James said, backing away and holding up his hands. "I'll just move away before I get frostbite."

He grabbed his cereal and sat down on the wooden floor.

"I know we aren't supposed to know the nature of your assignments and everything, but how can you do what you do, when you can barely stand being hugged?"

"A hug is much worse than sex," Majo said. Her face was back to its normal calm.

"Pardon?" James asked, raising one eyebrow.

"Sex, you can prepare yourself for," Majo said.

"Not always—" James began, but Majo cut him off.

"Yes always. Even in the worst of circumstances, you have a few moments to put up energy barriers, if you can keep your wits about you. But a hug can catch you completely off guard, particularly if the person is brave or foolish enough to touch you heart to heart. They can connect to you before you have the chance to stop it."

"We'll agree to disagree," James replied.

"I'm not looking for your agreement, I'm stating a fact—a basic truth," Majo replied.

"Enough of all this, back to my game. I've almost seduced the princess," James said with an exaggerated wink.

"That answers the porn question," Widget signed to Amelie.

"Pornography is boring," Majo said, as she dipped a piece of toast into the runny yolk of her egg.

"You find sex boring?" Widget asked. There was no sign of judgment in his expression. He was sensitive enough to know that Majo's mood had moved away from teasing.

"No, I find pornography boring," Majo replied. "Machines don't have the chemicals needed to make sex interesting. I'm attracted to people's chemicals but maybe that's just me."

She turned to look at Amelie.

Amelie shrugged.

"I don't know what I'm attracted to and, given everything else, I'm not sure it matters."

"It matters," Widget signed. "You are a person, not just an operative."

"Don't let the Academy hear you say that," Majo muttered.

23

Just then there was a knock at the door to their flat and for a second the three of them froze. In reality, someone knocking meant that they had got through the burly security guy downstairs, had the code to get into the elevator, and didn't mind having their hand scanned for recognition. The likelihood that a problem would knock at their door was unlikely, but everyone always tensed anyway.

"I'll get it," Majo said. "The addict won't hear it."

Majo got up and headed to the door. A few minutes later, she returned with Amelie's new recruit, Caio, in tow.

"Amelie, your trainee has been sent to see us," Majo said, sitting down at her place. Widget motioned for Caio to take his place at the table, while he moved to the small couch that was situated just next to the sliding glass door.

"You mean he has been sent to see me," Amelie corrected.

"No, the agent who dropped him off specifically said he is here to meet us," Majo said. They caught each other's eye. This was more serious. They might be considering introducing him as a member of their pod. If that was the case, there was also a possibility that it meant one of them would go.

Shit. Go or be eliminated. Neither option was good.

"So, would you like something to eat? Some coffee?" Amelie asked Caio.

"Some coffee would be nice," he replied. He was dressed casually in dark jeans and a sweatshirt. His hair was a bit long in the front, like it had been a while since he had bothered with a cut. His body stance was relaxed but Amelie could see tension in the muscles in his neck, arms, and thighs.

Widget got up before Amelie to get the coffee.

At that moment, James burst through the sliding glass door.

"So nice to see you again. Caio, isn't it?" James asked, extending a hand.

"Yes. And you're James, right?" Caio took the outstretched hand. Their handshake was short and non-aggressive. That was a relief.

"So, as they are sending you to us on the weekend, I am guessing we are supposed to fill you in on the basics," James said, then turned around. "Oh, I forgot my manners, which I usually do. You know Amelie, who is your sponsor. This beautiful woman is Majo and the Norse god getting you coffee is Widget."

"Widget?" Caio asked. "Is that a nickname?"

"Yeah," Amelie said, more curtly than she intended. "Oh, and you should also be aware that Widget is mute. But he isn't deaf, so keep that in mind when you are speaking."

James sat down on the couch and turned to face the table.

"Amelie, do you want to give him the summary talk, or should I?" he asked.

"You are much better at it than me, so feel free." Amelie didn't mind training this guy, but she was unsettled by the fact that he had been sent to her pod, not to the offices.

"So the general rule is that you will be told what you need to know when you need to know it. That's true for most of the facts and activities. But there are a few basic facts and ground rules that you need to know at the start."

James leaned forward. He was the only member of their pod who seemed to enjoy this little song and dance. Amelie found it monotonous, Majo found it hypocritical and, as Widget was excused from these exercises, it was inconsequential to him.

"How much have you been told about the Academy and what we do here?" James asked.

"Nothing so far," Caio replied, his eyes directly on James but Amelie noticed a slight tic in his lower eyelid. A tell.

"Okay, well that means I don't have to worry about cleaning up someone else's informational fuckup. So, first, the history. The Academy is old."

"How old?" Caio asked.

"Well, we know it has existed at least as long as the Masons, although we're not connected to them in any way. But I, personally, believe that the organization is much older than that."

James stopped for a split second and just for that second, his face shadowed inward into itself. But just as quickly, the expression was gone.

"But how old the organization is doesn't really matter much. I only brought it up because people always ask. What really matters is what we do, which is to nudge the course of global events."

James paused, as if waiting for a question from Caio, but none came. He just sat regarding James with his cool brown eyes.

A transfer for sure.

"Our job is to bank negative trends before they get out of hand," Amelie interjected.

"What do you mean by negative trends?"

"There are lots of people here with lots of gifts," Amelie replied. "You must have some as well for you to have been recruited. So some of the people in the Academy have the gift of foresight. Some have the gift of exaggerated analytical intelligence. Some have the gift of reading people. And on and on. These folks are usually part of our strategic arm. They have files and assessments of everyone that has or could have global influence, from babies to old age pensioners. If it is determined that someone can move the world in a positive direction, we do things to help that along. If it is determined that someone has the potential to become a global threat, we try to eliminate that threat."

"How?" Caio asked.

"One way is by eliminating them. Another is by recruiting them." This time it was Majo who spoke. She was drinking her tea, with her bright blue eyes scanning Caio.

"And who determines what is a positive direction for the world, or what is a threat?" Caio asked, eyes locking with Amelie.

"The Academy," she replied. "There is a subdivision of the strategy group that works with the global mission. They all have the ability to predict multiple futures. And they work with the Director regarding direction and focus."

"Do you all work with the Director?" Caio asked.

"No," James responded quickly. "Our pod is not with the strategic arm of the Academy. We are operatives. And that's what you will be. You will carry out local missions designed to promote the Academy's overall mission."

The patio suddenly became silent. All eyes were on Caio, but he was calm and cool. His file said he was seventeen but that had to be wrong. No seventeen-year-old was this composed.

"That's it? That's all I need to know?" he asked.

"Nope. Not all," James said. "That's the history. Now, the rules. We don't have a lot of rules but the ones we have are not to be broken. If you break them, there is a high possibility that you will simply disappear."

Amelie waited for Caio to flinch, but he did not.

"And those rules would be?" he asked.

"First, even though we are all in a pod together, we are not to discuss each other's gifts or talents in detail. We will obviously have some basic idea of everyone's role here, but we don't discuss the specifics of why we were chosen for those roles or how we use them. I can mention that Majo works with identification, selection, and IT, but I can't ask her about why she was chosen for identification, selection, and IT. I know that Widget works with the chem arm of the Academy, but I can't ask about how that intersects with operations or what he does there. Do you get the difference? We don't want to know the details of each other's gifts and the Academy does not want us to know. Clear?"

Caio nodded.

"Second, we don't ever discuss where we are going when we leave, particularly when it comes to going on assignments."

The corner of Caio's mouth turned up ever so slightly. "A bit like Cowslip's warren?"

"What?" James asked.

But Amelie was the one who responded, as she seemed to be the only one to catch the reference to *Watership Down*'s unnatural and sick warren.

"The third rule is that we don't question the Academy, its rules or its motives," she said sharply. "This may be the one day you would be allowed to do so."

Caio's eyes widened just a bit.

"So I would be careful about what allusions you make from this point onward. Most of us are very smart and there are a few who be very unhappy with that kind of reference."

"Understood." Caio nodded at her.

James looked back and forth between the two of them, then shrugged.

"Also, you should remember that Amelie is your sponsor here. So you'd be off your head to get on her bad side," James said. He actually said something like "eff ur heed." This told Amelie he was getting a bit pissed off. His Scottish accent only came out when something had annoyed him or made him uncomfortable. Most of the time, he sounded English.

Caio nodded again. "I'm sorry. I intended no offense by that. It just came to mind and then out of my mouth. Lesson learned."

Intended no offense. Again, the phrasing was not a teenage boy's phrasing. *Something is not quite right about this one. Need to watch him.*

There was another sudden knock at the door. Again, they all tensed, all but Caio.

"I'll get it," James said. Something about this kid was bothering him too, Amelie could tell.

"Next week, they should start you on weapons training and probably psychology," Amelie said, turning to Caio. "You will be living in the dorms, but I will be taking you on at least one training mission per week. Or that's how this usually works. We will find out the details when you show up at the training compound on Monday."

"Where is that?" Caio asked.

"I'm not sure. They change it all the time. But they will send you the information on Sunday night. I'll tag in with you on Monday—"

She was interrupted by James who returned to the patio holding two envelopes made of thin tissue paper.

"Amelie McCormick. Majo Petrov." He handed the envelopes to them.

Amelie took hers and gently pulled it open. Inside, it read:

Update on DC assignment: Meet the following at Hay-Adams hotel bar at 7:30 Tuesday night. Goal: Discovery of personal and professional passions, above and beyond that on record. Appropriate photos, based on character analysis. Timeline: Report due 7/11 p.m. Recruit to report to other pod members for first week.

"I'm on assignment," Amelie said. "You all are on point for training Caio."

James turned to Caio. "It looks like you will be spending today with me. I am guessing Amelie and Majo will both be gone for the evening."

"Actually, according to this, it looks like he will be reporting here to you guys for the next four days. I should be back by Wednesday morning," Amelie said. She heard James's sigh as she turned to go upstairs and pack her bag.

On the way, she stopped in the restroom and flushed the envelope down the toilet.

Chapter Five

Inviting Azazel for Dinner

The Off the Record bar in the Hay-Adams hotel was striking, even for a DC hotel bar. The walls, sofas, and barstools were all crimson, while the ceiling was golden and embellished with crests and clover shapes. From these ceilings hung golden chandeliers. The walls were decorated with more gold, this time in the form of wall lamps interspersed between historical sketches and documents. The flooring was some dark wood, and it was littered with oriental rugs. Amelie was unsure if it felt more like a British private men's club or a bordello in hell—or maybe that was the same thing.

If the decor was devilishly striking, the man in the navy suit standing at the bar was more so. He was tall and well built without looking bulky. He had dark hair, lightly streaked with gray, and eyes that were large enough and blue enough to be noticed from halfway across the room. He was speaking with a red-haired beauty in a forest-green suit. For a moment, Amelie tensed. Red-haired women were a trigger for her. But then the man saw her, smiled, and waved. He turned from his companion with little more than a nod of his head and moved toward Amelie.

They met in the middle of the room.

"Elizabeth Freeley?" he asked.

Amelie nodded.

"I'm Jeffrey Paul, you can call me Jeff," he said, moving forward to give her a slight hug—nothing impolite or improper, no touching below the shoulders. She had worn a conservative navy silk dress. Conservative but very thin, so that her body could be felt beneath the fabric. As he hugged her, she let her shields down ever so slightly and gave off the slightest pulse of energy. When he pulled back, his eyes were a bit wider. He felt something, and he was shocked. People usually had one of two facial expressions upon meeting her under these circumstances: either shocked or dreamy. Dreamy was much easier to deal with. Shocked meant they recognized something in her energy. So his expression of shock meant she might have to push him harder and, to safely do so, she would need to get him alone.

"I'm so glad to finally meet you," he said, with a smile that managed to look both confident and boyish. Demons usually had charming smiles. "Ricky tells me so many good things about you and the work you are funding."

Of course he does. She had established contact with Representative Ricky Jordan over eight months ago, for the sole purpose of getting to this man. After this much time with her, Ricky, a devout Christian Congressman with a strain of misogyny as wide as his out-of-date tie, was happy to model adult diapers as she photographed him. He would cut off his own testicles if she asked him to do so.

"Yes. I was so thrilled to get to know him, and to contribute to some of his noble causes. His commitment to preserving life, for example, is so admirable," she said, as she cocked her head to the side, and leaned on one leg. She managed to say this without a trace of sarcasm. Ricky was a warmonger pining for an opportunity to show the world how big his dick was by getting his country into another war. He also happened to be pro-life.

"Isn't it, though," Jeff replied.

"Absolutely. But to be honest, and direct, I am looking to expand my contributions from just Ricky's causes to broader and more far-reaching projects. Ricky suggested that you might be just the man to speak with about such options. He says that you are very forward thinking on such things, and that you are quite passionate about turning the world around for the better."

This was laying it on a bit thick, but Jeff beamed.

"I don't know if I would go so far as to say all that, but I would be very happy to share with you some of the projects I am most passionate about—tax reform, health insurance … Second Amendment rights," he said.

"I would love to hear about that. I don't know about you but I feel like so many people are not taking responsibility for themselves anymore. They are simply expecting the government to fix all their problems for them. This just promotes laziness and sloth," she said, with a calculated sigh.

"I couldn't agree more," he said, nodding solemnly. "But I feel like a cad, standing here with a drink while you have nothing. Would you like a drink?"

"Oh, I don't drink," replied Amelie.

"I don't either," he laughed. "This is just water."

Amelie laughed back and switched her weight to her other hip.

"To be honest, I don't drink but I am a bit hungry. I suppose I could get a few appetizers here, but I don't really like eating in these sorts of places," she said. "I prefer places a bit more casual."

Jeff raised his eyebrows. For a moment, his eyes changed color ever so slightly, from blue to a silver-blue. Amelie blinked and the image was gone.

"Well, we could go for dinner somewhere else. What would you prefer?" he said this with a concerned little smile and nod of his head.

"I know a small Vietnamese place up the street that's really very good."

"Then by all means, let's go there. I love Vietnamese food."

She nodded and, as she walked toward the door, she felt his hand on her middle back, as if gently guiding her. Yes, she was having dinner with the devil—again.

Amelie watched Senator Paul over dinner. He was jovial, polite, and charismatic and more courteous than most people she interacted with daily. His accent had just a trace of Southern in it, giving it a musical lilt. That made it even more horrific to hear the things he had said in public broadcasts and on the Senate floor.

This man had promoted bills to cut funding for education, senior citizens, medical outreach programs, needy children, the homeless, refugees, and the Paralympics. He was only missing babies and puppies in his all-out attack on the vulnerable. At the same time, he had hiked up taxes on the lower and middle classes, he pushed through a bill that eliminated inheritance taxes for the wealthy and gave big tax breaks to the largest corporations. It was also known that he personally contributed money to hardcore right-wing advocacy groups that targeted and attacked abortion clinics. What was less known was that he had also anonymously funneled money into Vanguard American, Identity Europa and even a Klan fringe group that had bragged about "re-instituting lynching." He did all this, while still managing to hold out a moderate, well-reasoned Boy Scout image.

She knew she was hitting a nerve when she talked about personal responsibility. She had done her homework. Jeffrey Paul came from a white, middle class Christian family with a squeaky-clean public image. But, as was often the case, behind closed doors things were very different. His father was a drunk. He was also abusive and beat his son with leather straps for even the most minor infractions. There was also more than a little evidence to suggest that his father had used sexual abuse as another form of discipline. So little Jeffrey grew into a

31

man who didn't drink, didn't swear, but was likely to have some nasty sexual hang ups—if the psych department was on target.

The additional files that had come through a scrubbed server as she landed in DC had indicated to Amelie possible misappropriation of funds and campaign finance violations. She was supposed to probe for evidence of this before she really used her gift to gather more personal and damning evidence. Once she had targeted him with that energy, she would not be sure of the validity of what he told her. He would say anything just to make her happy, regardless of the truth. So, for now, she needed to make herself over in line with his ideologies to keep the conversation going.

"I suppose Ricky told you that I inherited a great deal of money from my parents," she said.

Jeff looked up, surprised.

"He did mention that your father was in oil and finance, I do believe," he replied, leaning forward ever so slightly.

"Yes, that's right. So, to be blunt, I am quite wealthy, and I would like to use my money to help make the world a better place."

He had probably already checked this, but would have only found just what she told him. God bless the efficiency of the Academy.

She almost smiled, but banked it.

"But what I wanted you to know, is that I don't believe in being a spoiled trust fund baby, who only spends her time with charities. So I have a day job as a risk consultant, for which I am paid a substantial amount. Working is important to me. I don't believe in being idle or pampered. I don't like that sort of life, a life of idleness. And I don't like seeing others living that sort of life."

His eyes had widened and when he smiled it was genuine.

"I believe that is probably the most admirable thing I have heard today." He bit into an egg roll. "Ricky didn't share that with me."

"To be honest, I may not have mentioned it to him, but you seem like a man who is not put off by someone who likes to work," she said with a little shrug.

"Indeed, I am not. There is a lot of work to do."

"What would you do, if you had all the money in the world?" she asked.

"Well, money can't get you everything you want—" he began, eyes narrowing slightly.

"No, of course not, but it can help. Personally, and I know this is both impossible and not popular, but I have always dreamed of being able to live in a crime-free world of Christian values. I think these personal differences are what creates the tension in the world. If we believed the same things, then there would be less tension."

"Not a lot of people would agree with you," he said quietly.

"Oh, I know. And I know it's not the politically correct thing to say. Maybe I am just tired of all the fighting and discord. I know I should say that differences are good, and they make us strong and that's what makes our country different, but I am having a hard time believing it these days. To be honest, when I watch TV, it just seems like things are becoming sleazier and people are getting stupider."

The best lies contain a grain of the truth, and it would be good to get him to say something, as she was taping this conversation for later analysis by psy ops.

But he only nodded.

"It's like with gun ownership. Everyone blames the gun. No one blames the person holding it. Where is the personal responsibility in that?" she said, shaking her head.

"You're right. You're absolutely right," Jeff said. "It's been one of my major concerns for years. We need to teach responsible gun ownership and not simply take people's constitutional rights away from them by restricting guns."

Amelie nodded.

"The NRA is not the bad guy here, they are trying to help educate people," said the man who was receiving massive donations from the NRA.

"I know. It's enough to make people afraid to do anything. It seems like you can hardly move these days without being accused of being racist, or sexist, or some other '-ist,'" she said.

He chuckled.

"I understand. It can be very frustrating. But there is work you can do. There are ways you can help. I can have my admin send you a list of charities that would benefit from your support."

"That would be wonderful. The more expansive the list, the better," Amelie said. "I am contributing to Ricky's mission in both my name and the name of my father. He would be pleased to know that he was contributing to the greater good. If there is anyone or anything else you would suggest, I would be very appreciative."

She said this quickly and quietly. She was waiting for him to flinch, as she knew contributing in the name of another person was a violation of campaign finance laws, but no flinch was forthcoming. Instead, his eyes crawled over her face. Amelie returned his gaze openly.

"Good," he said, with a nod. He then picked up his phone. "Let me AirDrop something to you."

Amelie took out her phone and opened it. The document appeared almost immediately after she accepted the notification. When she opened it, she saw that it was indeed a full list—full of some of the nastiest right-wing players out there. There were also some people who had ties to public trusts and public land.

Bingo.

"Wonderful," she said. "Should I run my contributions through you or directly?"

"Just let me know which ones interest you," he replied. "I can organize the best way for your contributions to have the most impact."

He was just finishing his meal and she needed to get him alone for the second part of her assignment, but without being noticed.

She sighed and dropped her head into her hands, taking deep breaths.

"Are you okay?" he asked, reaching out to touch her hand. She shot him with a tiny burst of energy.

"I feel a bit nauseated. It's probably because I flew directly from London to here. I haven't done much besides drop my bags off at the hotel and meet you. I'm so sorry. I will be fine. I probably just need to lie down."

"Of course," he said, signaling the waiter. He paid the bill and walked around to pull her seat back.

As Amelie stood up, she wobbled a bit and fell into him. She shot more energy, directed lower on his body. His energy field was now glowing red.

"I'm so sorry. I really do just need to rest."

"Let me get you a taxi," he said.

"Not necessary, my hotel is really just up the street."

"Then let me walk you, to make sure you are all right," he said, taking her arm.

"I should say I don't need help, but to be honest, I think I might. I am feeling quite lightheaded," she said in a breathy voice.

He walked her to her hotel, and then to her hotel room. And with very little push from her, this Christian, married, father of two came into her hotel room for a nightcap.

***

Less than six hours later, she had all the information and photos that the Academy had requested. She had made copies of the contents of his wallet and his pockets. She had also uploaded the contents of his phone to the Academy's server and had given access to the IT guys to implant a trojan horse. She had recorded their conversations at the restaurant and hotel room for later analysis. She had also taken skin samples, urine samples and semen samples.

Looking at the man's sleeping form lying atop the king-sized mattress, she realized that she had changed her opinion of him. He wasn't the devil per se. He was just weak. His opinions formed as a result of a childhood abuse and a deep-seated fear of inadequacy. This knowledge changed her opinion of him, but it didn't soften it. Weakness was no more forgivable than pure evil. In fact, a weak person often did more harm than an openly evil one. If you are smart, you can see evil coming. The evil that came of weakness could sneak up on you. And this man's actions, based on his weakness, had resulted in hungry children being hungrier, and monsters being allowed weaponry. No, she felt no pity for his weakness.

For the photos, she had made sure that his current attire accurately reflected that weakness. After a session of normal-ish sex, she had thrown her energy at him hard. And he had rolled over like a puppy, willing to do anything for her. So he was now dressed in a leather outfit with obvious crop marks on his well-toned buttocks. Of course, she made sure that his face was clearly visible for the photos. It was also important that he be photographed doing something that he probably wouldn't have done if he had not been directly under her influence. It was not enough to be caught in a sex act that could damage his career. No, to blackmail him most efficiently, there needed to be a strong element of shame. For him personally, this would be more than highly shameful as it would trigger emasculating memories. Perhaps he could be removed from his position before he destroyed the lives of anyone else.

Amelie moved quietly about the room, picking up and cleaning anything that might have left a trace of her. She didn't know if this man was her final target or just another step on the ladder to reach someone else. In the end, it didn't matter.

She just wished she could be there to see his expression when he was sent the pictures.

Chapter Six

Celebrity Skins

Amelie got a text as she was boarding the plane home in DC. She was to attend *Empire* magazine's awards ceremony in London the following night, the night of her return. Three assignments in as many weeks. This was almost unheard of at the Academy. Sometimes she went weeks without so much as a peep of an assignment. Her longest-running dry spell was three months. While she some-times liked time off, Amelie preferred to stay busy. But this was a bit much. She had just come off two highly sexual assignments. She was tired, jet-lagged, and sore. She needed a break, but she wouldn't have time for one. When she got home, she would immediately have to drop her belongings and go out shopping for what she would need. Her target had specific tastes—but they always did.

This also meant she would need to stay on pain medication for another few days and endure the side effects of it.

When Amelie finally made it through customs, immigration, and a particu-larly slow taxi ride, she found their flat to be unusually quiet. No one was home. Apparently, this was a busy week for the Academy. She quickly scanned the information she had been sent again, dropped her bags in her room and headed out to the shops for what she needed.

That night, as Amelie stepped out of her taxi and approached the crowds gathered at the front of the famous Grosvenor House, she avoided the red-carpet entrance. Her tickets allowed this, and while no one would know who she was, she didn't want to risk being photographed. Her job was to be largely inconspicuous—to everyone but one person. She wore a plain, olive green, silk wrap dress that was classy but not particularly inspired or noteworthy. Her hair was pulled back in a conservative fashion, much like the wives of many of the studio execs here. Her shoes were simple strap sandals—all very nice but unob-trusive. She didn't want to be mistaken for a celebrity. Once again, that presented the danger of a photo being taken. Her cover here, if asked, was that of the wife of a journalist. She was going by the name of Ivy Fitzpatrick, also only if asked. On the carpet, various celebrities were being interviewed in between posing and preening for cameras. The truth was that in this shrine to narcissism, Amelie would probably have to walk the red carpet naked to garner any attention whatsoever, but it still paid to be diligent.

As she walked into the hotel via the non-celebrity entrance, she scanned the paparazzi to make sure that there was no one she recognized. As her pod had lived in London for years now, she had met some journalists during other assignments. It was a hazard of the trade. But, for the moment, she saw no one she recognized.

The inside of the hotel was like many other luxury hotels she had been in, and she had been in quite a few. It was opulent in that old building, old money way that was so typical of London society events. This was exactly the sort of place where so many of her assignments ended, if not began. Luxury hotels meant little to Amelie. In the end, a bed was a bed, no matter how posh the surroundings.

After being directed through a few hallways and down a few sets of stairs, she came to the hotel's ballroom. At the entrance, she was stopped by a security guy, who took her ticket and marked the back of her hand with an invisible pen, just like old Disneyland. Amelie smiled to herself. Whenever she attended such events, she found the comparisons to Disneyland were numerous. The similarity between the event and a Disney character meal was particularly apt. There would be people wearing costumes that were designed to hide who they really were. There would be a meal, which no one would pay much attention to. There would be entertainment. There would be celebrities/characters who would make the rounds of the tables, chatting and being photographed. And there would be celebrity/character handlers never too far away. The main difference was that, at a Disney event, the rules and expectations were clearly defined. At awards shows there were confused messages and alcohol. This meant that it would be relatively quiet in the beginning, and through the awards themselves, until the booze kicked in and stupid people started acting even stupider.

The room where the event was being held was on two floors, with the tables and stage on the lower level, and a mezzanine overlooking the lower floor. Here were several bars, a few small tables, couches, and several "interviewing areas" complete with professional lighting and cameramen. She was walking by one of these when a tall, pale young girl with long red hair almost ran her over in her rush to be interviewed. She was dressed in a white dress with ruffles and an apron, kind of like some cross between *Alice in Wonderland* and *Little House on the*

37

Prairie. Amelie knew her to be a baby actress, daughter of another actress and a producer.

"Excuse me," Amelie said.

The girl gave Amelie a haughty look, dismissing her clothes, her shoes, her hair, her life as unworthy of the effort of basic manners. Her boyfriend was a European gigolo stereotype—handsome, olive skin, his long hair filled with product. He looked at Amelie as if she were dirt. No, like she was worse than dirt, because underneath the look was something sexual. He viewed her as beneath him unless he had the potential to use her to entertain himself. Amelie found herself subconsciously twirling the small silver ring that she constantly wore on the index finger of her right hand. The one that, if she pressed hard on a very particular spot, would trigger a small switch, causing a needle-like spike to emerge at the opposite side of the ring. This spike contained a small mixture of curare and tree frog venom. Widget had made it for her, to protect herself when people tried to rape her—not if, but when. This happened to her monthly, if not more. Anytime she slipped up, it was possible. In those moments she didn't feel any more provocation than she did just now, and it would be easy enough to walk by and scratch both. The venom didn't always result in death, but it usually did. But if she did this here it would cause a scene. There would be doctors and ambulances and security people rushing in. All of this would make it harder to attract her target. Maybe later. Yes, maybe later she would run into them again. There was some good that came out of this encounter. It reminded her of why she did what she did and the value of the Academy.

The room was filling up now. She noticed that there was another interviewing area directly in front of an open bar. Amelie assumed it was to encourage the celebrities to drink a bit before the interviews, maybe in the hope that they would make asses of themselves. She didn't know this to be true but there was a lot of hatred between journalists/promoters/businesspeople and the celebrities. When the alcohol hit it could be a very thinly veiled hatred. As she wandered to the bar to get a Diet Coke, she noticed that her target had already entered, and was being interviewed by an *Empire* magazine journalist. He looked cool and collected, dressed in a casual brown suit, navy shirt, and tie.

Okay, he's clearly not a fashion guy.

He had light brown hair and a matching beard. This guy looked more like a middle manager than an actor, except for what seemed to be an exceptional build, even if on a small frame. He also looked benign. Actually, he looked blank.

Not for the first time, Amelie wondered about this assignment. It had come so quickly on the heels of her other assignments, and she was simply supposed to make contact with him. There had been no directive to collect particular information or any information at all. There had been no comment on taking photos or directing the conversation toward anything in particular. Except for the fact that this man was a celebrity, this was a bland assignment. This was a "newbie" assignment, and she was far from a newbie. No, this was an "untalented newbie" assignment. She was a senior operative at the Academy. The arrival of Caio into their pod arrangement once more entered her mind.

She accepted her Diet Coke from the bartender, cocked him a knowing grin, turned her back. She was targeting the barman rather than her target directly. As her target had already glanced longingly at the bar a few times, his eyes would be directed to her by the barman's stare. Sometimes this secondhand approach was safer until she knew what she was dealing with. If she had been sent on this baby-doll assignment, it must be more than it seems, so she would have to make an even greater effort not to be sloppy.

She slowly scanned the room for others who might be of interest. One never knew if there were connections that needed to be picked up on, but it seemed to be a normal sort of upper-class dinner gig. Amelie thought a bit about her last assignment, which had been a typical assignment for her. Although the interaction with the senator had been a quickie, it had been yet another step in an extended and ongoing assignment. This, this showing up at an awards ceremony just to case someone, was really below her, and it was vague. There must be something here she was missing, or the Academy had lost faith in her somehow. The consequences of that were unthinkable.

She turned her eyes back to the man in question. He was standing near the balcony now, in mid-banter with a corpulent magazine reporter. She tried to read the air around him. The whole place would become a jigsaw puzzle of symbols and lights if she opened her brain up too far. So she had to focus directly on him. What she found was quite odd. While the interviewer was pulsing with color waves of dark green envy and pink admiration, the air next to her target was blank. It was almost as if she were seeing him with a soft-focus lens.

She focused a bit harder but still nothing. Perhaps this guy had some sort of shields. If that was the case, this could be why she was sent in. Maybe this would be more interesting than she initially thought. She pushed just a little harder to see more, and suddenly he looked right at her. Not in her general direction—at her. His eyes went directly to her eyes—and his eyes were bright green, like a traffic light. She had never seen anyone who naturally had that eye color before. Wait, what? There was no way she could see someone's eye color from this distance. She blinked and he was looking back at the interviewer and gesturing.

Had she made that up? She doubted it. Now she WAS intrigued. That moment felt almost like a *glamouring*.

Damn.

She pulled her energy back in fast. She would need to rethink and take this a bit more seriously.

As he was finishing up his interview, Amelie moved toward the stairs that led down to the dining area. She stopped for just a moment in front of a mirrored column and slowly began adding some lipstick, not because she had any need but because she realized her target was walking behind her and she wanted to test something. She aimed one little laser stroke in his direction. A gentle, soft one. Sure enough, he slowed his step as he walked by, slow enough for her to know that he had felt it. That was good. She was able to affect him. She caught snippets of conversation he was having with another, very drunken, man and a less drunken woman, both of whom seemed to be in his party.

"… enough whiskey," the drunken man was finishing. It seemed it was his brother.

"No worry there," the woman laughed. Not her target's wife but his sister. Ah, that made things easier.

She moved into the dining room to take her place at her own table. The lighting was green and rose, an odd combination. Odder still was the use of a haze machine to create a fake smoky environment, that looked like nothing so much as a pub filled with smokers. On the stage was a podium situated in front of a large screen. For the moment, the screen saver was rolling through a list of sponsors. Amelie was a bit surprised to see the name "Verite" pop up. She was more surprised to see it flash and glow in yellow and green. Amelie closed her inner eye, and the name became plain white. There was something with the name Verite.

Amelie moved through the tables quietly and quickly. She took her seat at table 23, which was in the second row of tables from the stage. At the Academy she had asked them to arrange that she be seated just in front of her actor but facing sideways. This way he could see her, but she could also see him without having to turn around. She didn't want to be facing him directly, she wanted him to feel free to look at her without worrying about her watching him back.

Throughout the course of the Award ceremony, she learned a few things about this man from her tablemates and from her own talents. Much of it was knowledge she already had, and that was easily attainable with a short Internet search. His name was Ossian Reese. He was Welsh. He was thirty-five. He came from a working-class family and had two brothers and one sister. He was estranged from his mother for reasons unknown. He was generally known to be

a "nice guy" by fans but also had the reputation of being hot-headed with journalists and reporters. He was married and had a child from a previous
relationship, which he did not discuss with journalists. He was a "thinking
woman's sex symbol" according to magazines. This was a way of saying that he
was short and not traditionally handsome, but charismatic anyway. He was also
known for his breadth of roles. He had successfully played comedy, drama, and
even science fiction. But he was predominantly a British star, and still largely
unknown to the US audience. These were the facts that were easily attainable.
What she learned from her tablemates, during their random discussions about
celebrities present, was that it was rumored that, of all the award shows, he only
ever attended this one. He refused to attend the BAFTA awards or the Oscars.
The word on the street was that he found them snobby, but that rang false to
her, even given hard dry facts. The truth was that he was never nominated for
industry-driven awards, so she suspected that it had more to do with ego than
principle. There were other bits and pieces but nothing much of note. What
continued to be fascinating to her was that she could not get even the slightest
whiff of information about him, from him. No information was forthcoming,
despite that fact that she could feel his eyes crawling on her for most of the
evening. When she allowed herself to gaze across him, she noted that he was
staring at her with a great deal of intensity, and not hiding it.

She did, however, glean some information from the energy around his sister
and brother. His brother was an unsavory character. He had done time for man-
slaughter, yet he was intimidated by his actor brother. There was no sense of
violence between them, but there was an intense discomfort, a wariness. The
problem reading the brother was that he was an alcoholic as well, and already
quite smashed. This made her read unreliable. Ossian's sister was easier. She was
infatuated with her brother, to the point of it being unhealthy. As she got
drunker, her energy took a definite sexual turn regarding him. Amelie was certain that their relationship had been of a sexual nature at some point in their
shared past. Amelie found herself recoiling from this woman's energy. It was
not the incestuous feelings that caused this; she was used to reading these. Humans hid a lot—most of all from themselves. So no, the sister's incestuous
feelings were not what bothered her. What bothered Amelie was the power in-
equality existing between sister and brother. She thought of her brother as a
god, and she viewed herself as even less than mortal. It was a little too *Story of
O* for Amelie's taste or tolerance. It also meant that any data gleaned from the
woman would have to be analyzed and filtered in light of this.

At some point, a lifetime achievement award was given for a well-known US
actor. He was sitting two tables behind her and had to walk past Ossian to get

to the front. Ossian made a big production of bowing to him as he went by. This was one of the few times she got any real read from him. He hated this other actor. He hated him deeply and passionately. She filed that away for future use and investigation. Toward the end of the night, the award for Best Picture was given. Several big Hollywood blockbusters were nominated, but so was a smaller, British, film starring Ossian Reese. Against all odds, his film won. This should have been an ecstatic moment for him, and a narcissistic one, but he used his walk up to the podium as a moment to walk by Amelie and brush his wrist against the side of her breast. This was not accidental. She knew that. Okay, this was getting weirder. If he had been already glamoured by what energy she had sent, his actions would be more clumsy, less designed. Instead, his touch was subtle, gentle, and yet purposeful. She was being assessed just as much as she was assessing here.

Shortly afterward, the ceremony finished, and the food was served. During this, Ossian kept his eyes on her as he chatted with people who came up to congratulate him. Amelie realized that this was not the place to get in close. So she stood, and as she did so, she sent out a gentle wave of energy. He turned to watch her, along with many other people. Amelie caught his gaze briefly, hit him more directly with a single jab of energy, sighed and then walked past him. She felt him watch her go.

As she was waiting in the queue for a taxi to the Italian restaurant that was the location of the after-party, she kept glancing back. She had expected him to follow her out, but so far there was no sign of him.

Damn, am I losing my touch?

She had thought that she had hit him hard enough to bring him begging, but no joy.

As Amelie reached the front of the queue, the red-haired baby actress she had seen earlier appeared at the exit, in the midst of an argument with her boyfriend. She charged toward the line of taxis, pushing past Amelie roughly, glaring at the concierge who had opened the taxi door. Instinctively, Amelie flipped open her ring and grabbed the girl by the wrist.

"Please, feel free to take this taxi," Amelie said sweetly to the girl, pulling her hand loose, with a slight squeeze to make sure that the needle in her ring had scratched the surface of the girl's skin.

The actress's eyes widened slightly but she was quickly bundled into the taxi by her boyfriend. The poison would take two to three minutes to have an effect, and they would be well down the road by that point. The news of her illness might not make the news, but her death would hit the media within an hour or two.

Amelie smiled to herself.

The next taxi arrived. As Amelie got in, she saw Ossian Reese standing just outside the exit of the hotel. He was smiling at her and clapping his hands. *He knows what I've done.* Her intuition and the symbols and glowing letters around her told her that.

This man was definitely not what he seemed. This could make for an interesting night.

Amelie's shoulders relaxed and she smiled as the taxi pulled into traffic.

Chapter Seven

In the Flesh

She was one of the first to arrive at the after-party, which suited her. She found a quiet, dark place in the corner from which she could observe people. People began to arrive in groups of twos and threes. These started with the backers and businesspeople. Eventually, some of the more confident, coupled, celebrities appeared. It took about two hours for the other celebrity groups to begin to arrive.

But still no Ossian Reese. Amelie was getting concerned that she might have missed him somehow, when she saw him walk up toward the bar. He was alone. He had dumped his brother and sister.

Amelie decided it was time to be seen. She strode purposefully from her dark corner and out onto the dance floor. She shot little lasers of energy at the people around her. Heads turned. The eyes of the men locked on her, even if they were already with beautiful celebrity partners. Amelie was nowhere near as pretty as these women, nor was she famous, but it didn't matter. This was the fun part of her power. It was nice to be able to take a few well-deserving people down a few pegs.

She began to sway with the music. It was dumb, standard dance fare, but it didn't matter. She could find the sexual intent in the bass line and work that. Before long, she found people trying to dance close to her. Not with her, mind you, but close to her. She didn't really dance, instead she moved in time with the music and that was enough.

Before long, she noticed Ossian Reese was dancing just behind her. She did not look at him but sensed his movements. It was drunken dancing ... but it wasn't. She felt purpose behind his exaggerated moves. It was an attempt to get attention, and she knew from whom. What was strange was that she still couldn't get a read on his purpose or intent. She could read his actions but not his energy patterns. This was highly unusual for her. After a few more songs of dancing in uncomfortable heels, and getting nowhere in terms of gathering information, she went back to her dark corner.

She sat down on her little bench next to the toilets and took off her shoes. She rubbed the bottoms of her feet, where she was developing blisters. Back on the dance floor, people were bouncing, shaking, and grinding. The dancing itself was entertaining but the music got boring after a while. The beat never changed. She dug in the bag she had been given at the awards show—she had seen some plasters buried in there at some point. She had just opened one and was curling her feet to one side to get it into place when someone slid up next to her.

"You have dancing feet then, Miss Ivy?" Ossian smiled at her. She was startled. She hadn't seen or felt him coming.

"Oh, yes. I'm a real tenderfoot in heels." She smiled back. Wait. He said "Ivy."

"How did you know my name?"

"Oh, I'm an actor you know. So I'm not just a professional liar, I'm also a professional researcher. I saw your name posted on the seating list."

"Really, so you memorized the whole seating chart and everyone on it before you even sat down. That's impressive!"

"Oh no. I'm too lazy for that. Actor, remember? I couldn't be arsed to get a real job. I saw you sitting in front of me, so after I won the award and spoke with all the required industry executives backstage, I went upstairs to check the chart before I came back to my seat. Easy-peasy."

"Easy, but still a lot of trouble for a girl you don't know." Amelie smiled at him and consciously licked her lips. He watched her tongue before answering.

"Men must go to a lot of trouble. Women don't appreciate that." The smirking smile vanished for a moment then reappeared. "You should be flattered, right?"

"But of course, unless you are a stalker or some other sort of freak," she teased.

"I can be whatever you want me to be," he said softly. This should have sounded like the cheesiest and most painful of come-on lines, but he delivered it with a strange flatness, and then he looked away from her and out onto the dance floor. His face had a strange, conflicted look, and for the first time, something broke through the psychic shields he seemed to have in place. It was a clear sentence sent directly from his brain into hers: *Get away from him now. I can't—*

This alien thought was abruptly cut off.

Amelie shook her head.

45

Get away from "him." Who was "him"? Amelie thought. *Was it someone else? Was he referring to himself in the third person?*

Okay, Amelie had occasionally referred to herself in the third person in her own head, but it was a weird trait. She didn't have time to concentrate on that for long, though, because when he turned his gaze back to her, his focus was unnerving.

"… whatever you want me to be, Ivy," he repeated, smiling this time. He moved closer to her and nodded to the dance floor. "I would ask you to dance, if the dancing were different. I do like dancing, but I miss the days when you could dance close to someone. You know, when dancing was just an excuse to hold someone, and you had to win her permission to do that. That's so much more erotic than grinding up against some random stranger's ass. And that's pretty much all that is happening out there right now."

She tried not to look surprised at his invasion into her previous thoughts.

"But we can give it a whirl, if you want to."

Amelie nodded assent and he smiled. His smile was crooked. His top teeth were set a bit to the right when he smiled. It made him look a little crazy and more intense.

"Okay, then. Are you ready to have a go at dancing with a drunken Welshman?"

Completely out of the blue, Amelie was sexually attracted to this man. It came on about as gradually as being pulled under by a riptide. Suddenly, she wanted to touch him, to share the alcohol he had consumed in the taste of his tongue, to feel him pressed up against her and to know, without question, that she had affected him. There was nothing affectionate or caring about this feeling. It was like hunger or anger. It was a primal sort of desire. Of course, she had felt desire during assignments before. There were times she did her job so well that her magic bounced back and she glamoured herself, at least for a short while. This was not that. It wasn't secondhand. This was a drug coming from him and she was mainlining it directly from the source. She felt the heady chemical mixture of lust hit her brain.

He's glamouring me.

This thought brought another type of excitement as well. The only person that had ever been able to glamour her, was her. Except for—

Stop. Don't go there. She banked that thought and refocused.

If this guy could do this, then he might be something special and the Academy would want him, surely. And the line about getting away from him—that was not how normal people's brains worked. What were the possibilities here? He could be clinically schizophrenic. He could be possessed. He could be a

46

potential recruit. Or he could simply be unusually conflicted. But all of this meant that he was NOT the normal target. She felt herself relax even more. Although it would likely be more difficult, difficult was her norm. Things were back to a steady state.

Ossian took her hand and led her to the dance floor. The DJ's choice of music had taken an industrial turn, and most people were kind of slamming themselves around the dance floor, but her partner had no intention of missing the chance for body contact. He pulled her in close to him and used his hips to sway her body. He was a good dancer. By the way he positioned one of his legs between hers and used it to sway and move her, she had no doubt that he would be a good fuck as well. They danced until both were sufficiently sweaty, at which point he walked her over to the bar to get a drink. As his back was turned to her, she focused her energy, trying to get a read—still nothing. It was like a fuzzy cloud was around him. She was definitely being blocked. She smiled to herself.

Okay, you want to play this game, I can play. No one blocks me forever, she said to herself. At that moment, he turned around to her with that off-set smile.

"Well, let's see then," he said.

Mind reader, she thought loudly.

"Yep," he said out loud. Amelie immediately banked all of her thoughts into the center of her brain, into a dark hole that had come to live there after—well, after she joined the Academy. The thoughts that she left on the surface were her reactions to the music, the ambient sensations, and her desire for him. Ossian leaned forward, his scruff scratching her face just slightly as his cheek touched hers.

"So would it be presumptuous of me to ask you if you would like to come back to my room?" he whispered in her ear. "Have I misread the signals? It can be hard to tell with an American."

"No, you read fine," she said back into his ear. She then tilted her head and kissed him slowly on the lips. He leaned in, opened his mouth, and let her taste him. He had been drinking a whole hell of a lot, but that didn't bother Amelie. In fact, it made him a bit sexier, somehow.

Ossian pulled back and took her hand. "Let's go before too many people notice and decide it's their business," he said.

***

They started making out in the taxi on the way back to his hotel. They stopped just long enough to walk through a very posh hotel lobby. Amelie noticed a stiff-looking concierge give her a disapproving look. She suspected she looked a bit more rumpled than would be considered appropriate by English standards.

47

Ossian didn't seem to be noticing anything. He had his arm securely around her waist.

When they got into the elevator, he pulled her back in for a kiss. By the time they got to his floor, her arms were wrapped around his neck and his hands under her dress. He picked her up and she straddled him as he carried her to the room. Somehow, he managed to get his key card out with one hand while holding her up with one arm.

He's much stronger than he looks, she thought, incoherently. She was still a bit in shock at the desire she felt. No, she was shocked that the desire was not self-manufactured. He shoved the door open and maneuvered them toward the bed, letting them both fall onto it.

Ossian pulled her on top of him, still holding the kiss he'd begun in the elevator. She spread her legs and sat on top of him so that he could feel her. They kissed for a few minutes before he rolled on top of her.

"I have something to confess," he smiled down at her. "Tonight was not the first time I saw you."

Uh-oh. Amelie's heart stopped briefly but she kept her face composed.

"Do tell," she replied.

"I saw you in New York last year. You were singing at some dodgy little jazz club. You did the most heartbreaking version of 'God Give Me Strength.'"

Amelie smiled, but her brain was racing. That was a mission where she was trying to seduce a musician to get information about the practices of some of his contacts in the music industry. Majo had coached her in singing. Shit. How would this guy know this? And there was no way that she would have missed this guy, even he was just a part of the audience. She caught herself and shoved these thoughts into the well.

"I'm impressed you remember that. That was something I tried for a while, but I wasn't very good at it." Amelie smiled and constructed a thought for his benefit.

I wonder if he thought I was good. If he thought I was pretty then.

"I think you were dating some slimy wop-looking guy," Ossian continued, his smile looking more like a sneer. Amelie's alarm system was blaring now, but she casually sat up and undid her hair.

"Do I hear a bit of jealousy?" she said teasingly.

That was when he slapped her across the face.

Chapter Eight

Not Quite Ossian Reese

The blow was hard enough to throw her off the bed and onto the floor. She was taken aback. Somehow, she had not seen this coming. Her face throbbed. She shook her head, trying to get her eyes to focus.

"Poor lamb, did you slip and hurt your face? There will be a bruise, but not to worry. We think it makes you look so sexy. Positively gorgeous."

We?

There was a smile in his voice as he swung his legs over the side of the bed and looked down at her.

"Looks like we are in for a fun evening," he said. She didn't need her colors and shining to tell her that she was in danger now. Common sense was enough. She had drawn a freak—but she had dealt with freaks before. She knew how to handle even the worst of them.

"I guess so," she said prettily, as she looked up at him, caught his eye and pushed as hard as she could. He probably didn't need that level of energy, but fuck him, he just hit her. Let him suffer.

For the briefest of seconds, his eyes widened and their color almost imperceptibly flickered.

"Oh now, you're not going to try to play that little game with me, are you, pet? Then you should know that I am, how do you say it, immune to those particular charms. But you have so many other charms that you hardly need that, do you? You certainly have my full attention already."

He came over to her in two strides and yanked her to her feet. This time, as she looked into his eyes, they full-on changed, turning from green to silver. And something moved behind them, inside them. Something that crawled and bulged.

She quickly flipped the ring on her finger around and raked the curare spike across his face. His eyes widened and he snarled, but he remained standing.

If it was possible, Amelie was relieved when he threw her against the wall, where she crumpled. It gave her a chance to recover from the mental shock. She was in serious trouble. She had handled freaks before, true. She had even handled possessed people before, or those who believed themselves to be. This was not that. She didn't know what he was, but the colors around him had turned green and black. A green smoke seemed to be seeping out of his mouth. And he was not affected at all by deadly poison. Senseless words and symbols lit up around her. The only messages she could read were from a tabloid on the nearby table. *Danger* and *alien.*

Yes, she was in trouble, and she should have been scared, but she wasn't. When his eyes had changed color, for just the briefest moment she had had a visceral memory of love. The thing in front of her might be housing a spirit, but it was nothing like the incubus she had known. To have that aching memory tarnished by violence from a stranger filled her with rage. A rage so deep, she could taste it in the blood that filled her mouth. It tasted sour and metallic.

She knew that she was no fighter, and her main weapon seemed to be useless against this thing, but if it wanted to take her down, she wasn't going down without inflicting some damage of her own.

She began to make soft snuffling sounds.

"Oh bless, it's not so bad," he said. "I promise that I will make you come. I always do."

She looked up and he had lost his clothes. To give him credit, his body really was magnificent. He wasn't tall, but he was perfectly proportioned, and very well-endowed. She felt a surge of pleasure, but not at his physical charms. The pleasure came from the fact that he was naked, and she was still wearing heels.

She fell over to her side and curled up in a fetal position, with her hands over her head and her back braced against the wall. As he moved closer, she waited until he was stooping down to grab her hair, and she kicked out hard with the heel of her foot toward his groin, where it would have had roughly the same effect as stabbing him with a knife. Her kick connected perfectly with his balls. This should have dropped him, it would have dropped any man no matter how strong or trained he was, as it had probably just ruptured one of his testicles. But instead, he just grunted and stumbled back a few paces, holding his hands over his crotch.

Fuck, this bastard is still standing, she thought.

At this realization, her anger was gone. It was replaced with real fear. She needed to get out of there. Amelie kicked off her shoes and made a dash for the bedside table. She grabbed a heavy brass lamp and yanked it from the wall. All around her the room was illuminated in a black and poisonous green light. There were lightning bolts of yellow that occasionally flashed through it. She had never seen this before. Not these colors or in these ways, and the symbols appearing around the room were of no language she knew. She heard movement behind her and as she turned, he lunged for her. She had just enough momentum, time, and adrenaline to swing the lamp, base forward. The brass hit the side of his head with a dull, sickening thud. Now he did crumple to the floor. The side of his head looked caved in and unnatural, but there was no blood.

What the fuck! There was no blood. There should be blood everywhere from that sort of blow. It was a serious head wound. For a second, she considered checking for a pulse, but then, insanely, he began to move. Amelie didn't wait to see anymore, she ran for the door, but not before she heard him call out.

"Well, well. You are turning out to be a lot more interesting than I expected."

She bolted down the hallway of the hotel and into the stairwell, where she ran directly into Majo.

"Thank god," she said, as Majo pulled out a gun.

"What happened—" Majo began, but Amelie grabbed her hand and said one word.

"Run."

Majo didn't speak but followed her. They had made it down roughly four flights when Amelie heard a door up above thrown open, slamming against the wall and echoing down the stairs.

"Are you down there, my sweet?"

He was actually able to make it to the door. This guy should be dead. Not walking dead but dead dead. She opened the door at the next floor she got to and pulled Majo after her. They ran down a long hallway and to a second set of stairs. They were old servants' stairs. They took these down another four flights before coming to an end. It was not the ground floor, though; it was a basement of some sort. There was an elevator at the other end of a long cement hallway.

"We can take that," Amelie said, pointing to the elevator.

"I don't think we should," Majo said. "He's likely to be coming down in the elevator by now."

"I don't think so. He would be too visible. I did some damage," Amelie responded between breaths.

Majo pulled the gun in closer to her body.

"You might as well put that away," Amelie gasped. Her ribs were hurting badly from how she had hit the wall. "Whatever that is, it is an 'it' not a 'he.'

51

Your gun may slow it down, but it won't stop it. It will just get us stopped. It's better to get away without notice and make sure we aren't followed."

"Isn't he a famous actor?" Majo asked.

"Yeah, but he's a non-human famous actor. So we need to get into a public space fast."

They hit the Up arrow on the elevator. Despite Amelie's warning about guns, Majo had hers drawn as the doors of the elevator opened. They breathed a sigh of relief when there was no one there. They got in and rode it to the lobby. Amelie knew that with her torn dress and bare feet it would be hard to go unnoticed. She just hoped that British reserve would prevent anyone from saying anything. She was wrong.

They made it halfway across the lobby before they were stopped by a concierge.

"Excuse me," said the concierge, "Mr. Reese called down and asked me to escort you back to his room. Apparently, you left with something that doesn't belong to you."

This was the same man she had seen before. He was a portrait of everything that is wrong with British culture. There was a battered woman in front of him, face bruised and swelling, shoeless, in torn clothing, and he was asking her to return to the room she had just left. This was because Mr. Reese was a person "of some importance" and she was—well, no one as far as this man was concerned. Amelie felt a regret that she had already used up the poison allotment in her ring earlier in the evening. Instead, she reached out and touched the man's arm and sent a surge of energy up it.

"Oh, he must be mistaken," she said and watched his eyes mist over and a dopey smile appear on his face. A face that looked like it was about to crack because it hadn't hosted a real smile in decades.

"Very well, my dear," he said, "but I will need to call Mr. Reese and tell him."

Duty before love, apparently. Her urge to torture this man was rising but she wasn't completely sure that Ossian wasn't able to spontaneously heal. So she just smiled, grabbed Majo's arm and turned for the exit.

"That's fine," she said to the grinning concierge, waving prettily at him, realizing how ghastly this must look to passers-by. A beaten-up woman and her friend flirting with a seventy-something grumpy concierge who was eating it up.

Just then the elevator door opened and out popped the man of the hour. Ossian had dressed but that was not all that was different. Her intuition had been right. His head looked completely normal. There was no sign of the damage she had inflicted. He saw her and strode purposefully in her direction, with a predatory smile. Majo reached inside her coat for her gun, but Amelie shook

52

her head. Instead, she pushed them through the revolving doors and out to the street.

A crowd of both fans and paparazzi had formed in front of the hotel. In the crowd, Amelie suddenly saw a familiar dark-skinned man wearing a stovepipe hat.

I know him. His name is Dante. He's dangerous. She had been told this in the past, and the voice she heard in her head was the voice that still caused her heart to ache.

Dante pointed behind her, and cupped his hands round his mouth as if he were yelling. Amelie turned to see Ossian charging out of the door and straight for her.

The meaning of the gesture came clear.

"Look, it's Ossian Reese," Amelie yelled, pointing backward. She then pulled Majo into the crowd of paparazzi and fans who had been waiting there just in case this moment presented itself.

Amelie and Majo ran to the zebra crossing. On the other side of the street there was a small chapel. The wind was picking up and the spire of the church was wreathed in low-lying clouds that looked silver-gray against the night sky. For just a moment, Amelie considered seeking refuge there, but then she remembered that churches were not sanctuaries from monsters anymore. They often bred monsters instead. That thing behind them would probably pull them apart and then sacrifice their entrails on the altar of whatever it worshipped, while the local priests watched on.

They were pretty far from a Tube, but they were in luck with the bus system, as a bus pulled up just as they reached the stop across the street. They got on quickly. Amelie looked back to see if they were being followed but Ossian was surrounded by his fans and signing autographs. She and Majo watched from the back window as they pulled away. Just as they were pulling out of sight, Ossian looked up and waved.

"How did you know to come?" Amelie whispered to Majo.

"Caio told us," Majo whispered back.

"Caio?" she started, but Majo interrupted her.

"What the fuck just happened?"

"I can't talk about it here. Let's get lost before we head home, just to make sure no one is tailing us."

"Can you do that, or do you need a doctor?" Majo asked, eyeing Amelie up and down. "Any broken bones?"

"I'm fine. Or fine enough to get home. Really the worst is an awful headache from getting smacked in the head. Widget can patch up the other bits when we get home."

They took four buses and a Tube train before they felt comfortable enough to go back to their flat. Despite what Amelie had said, she collapsed onto the couch the minute she made it home.

"What happened?" Widget signed to them later, after he had tended to Amelie's most noticeable wounds. He was now holding an ice pack to her face. It was uncomfortable but Amelie trusted Widget. He once mentioned in passing that he had trained as a doctor—a surgeon, even. He had patched all of them up at one time or another.

"Where is James? And Caio?" Amelie asked weakly. "I think I need everyone here for this one. Something happened and I need the whole pod to examine it."

"They went out," Widget said.

"They were looking for you," Majo said. "That's why I was there. Caio told me that you would need backup on this, so each of us was to take a different venue in which to watch you. James was outside the after-party. He called when he saw you leave the restaurant. He had found out what hotel Reese was staying in from a reporter outside. He knew it wasn't the Grosvenor, so he called me as I was closest. I found out the room you were in and had just made it up the stairs when you came out—like a disaster victim. Bastard. I should have shot him. I had a silencer."

"It's like I told you. It wouldn't have done any good, he wasn't human."

"It would have made me feel better," Majo replied. "And monsters are not immortal, just harder to kill."

Just at that moment, James burst through the front door. When he saw Amelie, relief flooded his face as tears filled his eyes. He ran to her and gathered her into his arms.

"Ow. Ow. Ow."

"Sorry. Sorry. Sorry." James said, gently putting her back down on the couch in the living room. "I was just so bloody worried. I couldn't get Majo on the phone, and by the time I got to the hotel everyone was talking about Ossian Reese. But one older photographer told me he had seen two girls come out first, and that one was in bad shape, like she needed a hospital. I knew it was you. So I looked everywhere. I texted Widget and told him to have you text me the minute you got in. I guess he forgot."

He glared at Widget. But Widget simply pointed to Amelie's shoulder, face, and leg then crossed his arms and glared back.

"So how are you?" James asked, turning his attention back to Amelie.

"Widget says that I have a tiny cheekbone fracture, but with no displacement, so I should be okay on that one. It feels like half my face is throbbing off, though. And I had a dislocated shoulder, which Widget already fixed. No concussion either. Otherwise just lots of bruises and scrapes. I should be okay in a few days but pretty sore until then, but we may have bigger problems than that."

"Tell me what happened," James said.

"Where is Caio?" Amelie asked.

"I'm not sure. But I sure as hell have questions for him when he gets back," James muttered.

"He knew I was in trouble?"

"Yeah, it was fucking weird," James replied. "He was on the terrace and suddenly he bursts back in and tells us that you are going into a trap. When I asked how he knew, he told me that if he took the time to explain, it might be the difference between life and death for you."

"And you believed him?" Amelie asked.

"We all did," Majo responded. "We knew he was telling the truth. That one is not a novice, and he's not a lightweight."

"Yeah, lightweight or not, he will be answering my questions when he gets back here," James said.

"Well, he might have saved my life, so don't kill him," Amelie said, with a dark little laugh.

"So what exactly happened?" James said, eyes softening as he touched her face.

So Amelie told them everything. From beginning to end. She left out the incubus references, but she was completely candid about everything else—including her belief that Ossian Reese was something not completely human.

There was silence in the room when she finished. James had his head in his hands. She could tell he was thinking, hard and fast.

"You think he was not human?" he said.

"No, she doesn't think he was not human. He wasn't human," Majo snapped. James snapped his head round to look at her sharply.

"Have you considered that you might have been administered hallucinogens?" James asked suddenly.

"What?"

"If the arsehole gave you hallucinogens that might explain why you think all this incredible stuff happened."

Amelie felt like she had been slapped in the face—again. She knew when her mind was on its game. She would know if she had been drugged.

Before she could say anything, Majo stood up from the couch where she had been sitting and walked over to James

"You think Amelie wouldn't know if she had been drugged?" she asked, her voice soft but with a sharper edge than usual. "Any of us would know those signs. Any first-year rookie would know if they had been drugged. You are suggesting that Amelie, who has a well-known and flawless completion record, would be incapable of recognizing that she had been drugged?"

James looked away for a moment, then he looked at Amelie.

"I think it may have been some new form of hallucinogen," James said, his accent becoming distinctly more Scottish than English. "Maybe it was something that we wouldn't recognize or haven't encountered. That would make sense. We get sent on a lot of drug runs. And it would explain why they sent Amelie and only Amelie. Maybe she thought she hit this guy with a heavy lamp, but maybe it was really a light one. She thought she kicked him in the balls, but she could have missed and hit his leg."

"What about me?" Majo snapped. "I saw him in the stairwell, and he didn't—"

"I think you didn't see anything," James interrupted.

For just a second James caught Majo's eye and she flinched. It was a tiny one, but Amelie had never seen Majo flinch before.

"All you saw," he continued, "was the aftermath and what happened to our podmate. So, if you were half as pissed off as I am, then you probably overlooked a lot and assumed more."

James was talking total trash. She knew it and so did Majo. What she didn't know was why. What he was saying didn't even flush with events. If Amelie had been drugged, it wouldn't have miraculously exited her system when she left the hotel room. And it wouldn't have only affected her perception of one person.

She was starting to get angry when James caught her eye. His demeanor was unusually calm and his voice thoughtful, but she saw that his pupils were approximately the size of saucers. She had seen James exhibit a lot of emotions over the years, but she had never seen this. He was shit-scared. And he was letting her see this for a reason. His eyes quickly flitted around the room, then back to her face.

"Okay," Amelie said carefully. "Look. I'm really getting tired. I don't know about the rest of you, but I don't think a clear answer is emerging here. And if there is no clear answer, then I would rather look at an unclear one with fresh eyes. Besides, we haven't gone through debrief yet, so maybe there is something that we just don't know. As crazy as this is, James might be right."

Widget nodded. She noticed that about a hundred small muscles in James's face relaxed.

Majo looked at each of them and then sighed. "Okay. Then I opt for bed as well."

With this she went to her bedroom and shut the door a tiny bit harder than usual.

"Ah, the joys of living with someone who hates you. Nothing like it to keep you on your toes. Most nights I wonder if I will wake up in the morning," James said, as he bounced a stress ball between the front and back of his hand. "I don't know about anybody else, but I'm hungry. Who's in if I make spaghetti and meatballs?"

Widget shook his head vigorously and signed that he didn't trust James to boil water and that he would make a quick dinner. He also signed that Amelie should go lie down in her room until dinner was ready. Just as Amelie was getting up to do as suggested, all the lights in the flat went out.

Chapter Nine

Nightmares Reinvented and Reborn

When the lights went out, Widget was at Amelie's side in a flash. He picked her up and silently carried her into the kitchen. On the way, she saw Majo exit her room, descend the stairs and crouch in the small alcove just behind the front door, gun in hand, completely motionless. Amelie had no idea where James had gone.

Once in the kitchen, Widget opened the broom closet. In it there was a large space at the bottom which held a broom, mop, bucket, and vacuum cleaner, and a smaller space on the top. It was much smaller, but big enough to hold a seated adult, if she were petite enough. Widget pointed to it and then lifted her up so she could crawl in. Widget pushed her further back once she got in and handed her a gun. He signed for her to shoot anyone who opened the door in the top of the head.

Amelie sat silent in the dark for what seemed like a small eternity. Her ribs ached and it hurt to breathe. Her head was also throbbing. Suddenly, she heard a sound to her right, coming from the door to the balcony. Then sounds that could have been footsteps, but that had the wrong cadence.

She closed her eyes and sent energy runners out like sonar. They bounced back off something heading toward her on the right. Something close. Something dark and malformed. When she opened her inner eyelid, she saw colors that were like the ones that she had seen on Ossian in the hotel room. The predominant colors were yellow and black, with a bit of greenish blue. It reminded her of a squashed yellow jacket.

She readied the gun and waited. There was a soft sound of scraping and scratching, as if something was feeling its way along the cabinets in the kitchen. When the scraping reached the broom closet, it stopped. All was still and quiet. Amelie could hear the soft sound of her own breathing and that was all. And then, there was the sound of creaking as weight was put against the closet door ever so slightly. Amelie readied her gun as dim light appeared in the crack of the door. But before she could see anything the door was slammed shut, and there were grunts and thuds followed by the sound of glass breaking.

Lights blazed through the cracks around the closet door and Amelie heard footsteps, followed by Majo's voice.

"Widget, get it around the right arm."

There was another thud and the sound of a something being smacked on the floor.

"For fuck's sake, don't kill him," Amelie heard James's voice. "Last thing we need is to have to cover up the death of a celebrity."

"I don't know what that is," Majo said, breathing hard. "But it being a celebrity is the least of our worries. Get Amelie."

The door opened and Widget quickly pulled her out of the closet. Majo was on the floor with one knee on the arm of Ossian Reese. Her other knee was on his stomach, and she had a gun pointed at his head. James was on his other arm and checking for a pulse. There was no blood, but Amelie guessed that the sound she had heard while in the cabinet had been Ossian Reese's head smacking against the floor.

"Is he dead?" Amelie asked.

"Doubt it," Majo muttered. "Hadn't seen anything that gross since I had nightmares from reading H. P. Lovecraft short stories as a kid. I doubt bullets would do much but lodge in this mess."

The others turned and stared at her, but Majo was still staring at Ossian. James leaned back on his heels.

"Well, from Majo's response, I am guessing that our friend Ossian Reese is possessed," James said.

Majo nodded.

"So what do we do? Call a priest?" Amelie said, trying not to get the giggles at exactly the wrong time, as she often did.

"No. We can't risk it," Majo replied, turning to look at James.

"Right," James said, and winced a bit. "I'm afraid that I know where this is going."

Ossian moaned a bit and Majo put her gun closer to his face. Widget's eyes bugged out.

"Not supposed to be waking up, is he?" Majo asked.

"No," Widget signed. "I gave him enough tranq to take down a man three times his weight. He should barely be able to breathe."

"Okay, we only got this guy down because we got the drop on him," Majo said. "If he wakes up, then I am afraid we may not be able to take him. So I say we take his head off. I doubt even he can come back from that."

"No," James said. Amelie shook her head to clear it. She was still feeling fuzzy, and she wasn't sure she heard him right. Majo's plan had seemed perfectly reasonable, and it wasn't like James had a weak stomach for killing.

"If he's possessed, we don't want to kill his body until we get the thing out," James said. "If we kill him, the monster inside him is still there and is likely to try to invade someone else. Like one of you."

"Of course," muttered Majo. "So we need to handle this another way."

"Like what? Call the Ghostbusters?" Amelie said, stifling a giggle again—laughing at funerals again. Her head felt a bit wrong. But the colors around her had calmed.

"I can take him," James said.

"What?" Amelie said and Widget signed at the same time.

"That's my gift. I'm a soul stealer," James said softly, looking around him. "Among other things."

The room around Amelie began flashing so many lights and colors that she couldn't begin to make sense of them. The last time she had seen this many images and colors had been many years ago when she was in a library and had first read—

"Amelie, did your gift work on him?" James asked. "Your seduction gift?"

Amelie looked at him hard. A suspicion was forming in her mind. Or a hint of one.

"No, it didn't. Or not in the normal way."

"Right. Whatever is in him isn't human and has never been human," James said.

"Our problem is, if he starts coming to then we won't know what we are dealing with," James continued. "We won't know if Ossian Reese or the thing possessing him is in charge, until it's too late."

"I'll know," Majo said softly. "I can see it."

"Widget, we are going to need some more tranquilizers. Do you have some?"

Widget nodded and left the room.

James looked at her and Majo.

"It would appear that we have a lot to talk about," he said softly.

Widget returned with a syringe, which he immediately jabbed into Ossian Reese's neck. The veins on Widget's own neck bulged and his eyes were narrowed to slits. He looked nothing like the normal, geeky Widget she knew and trusted. This Widget looked like a predator—an angry predator.

"Good," James said. "Now I can extract whatever is in him. It won't be pretty but that way we can just dump his body at a bar somewhere. When he wakes up, he will only be his human self."

"Assuming he has a human self," Majo muttered.

James shot a look at Majo.

"Even if he doesn't, I don't think the body will remain empty for long," James said. "Either way, he is unlikely to remember this or any of us, and we won't have a celebrity death to contend with."

"What will you do with it once it's extracted?" Majo said. She was staring at the man on the floor with open disgust.

"And how will you do it?" Amelie asked, now openly breaking the rule about not discussing their gifts.

"Don't ask now," James replied. "I can't explain it any quicker than you can explain how you can do what you do. But it will be inside me until I get to a place where I can get rid of it. The good thing is that I can control it, so even if I look weird to you, Majo, try not to shoot me."

Majo nodded. James leaned over the man in front of him and put his lips to his.

"Wrong spot," Majo said. "Soul enters at the back of the neck on this sort."

James looked at her with the beginnings of a smile.

He rolled the man over and then placed his lips to the spot of the top of his spine, just at the base of his head. Ossian's body started to tremble. Widget and Majo held him down as James appeared to breathe in. Then the body was still.

James leaned back on his heels, his face scrunched up and his hands in fists at the side of his head. He began to rock back and forth, moaning softly as he did. Amelie moved next to him.

"Are you—" she began, but he held up his hand. There were beads of sweat on his face and he started rocking harder. Then he put his forehead to the ground and slammed his fists on the ground, still moaning. She heard a snap and suspected that he had just broken at least one bone in his hand. Amelie looked up at Majo and Widget helplessly.

"Don't touch him," Majo said quietly. "He is referring the pain. God knows how much that must hurt. Give him time."

Amelie had had enough pain in her life to understand what this meant, so both she and Widget were still. But no one was as still as Ossian, who was gunning for the Oscar in the best-actor-as-a-corpse category.

After a few moments, James stopped rocking and moaning. He sat up and opened his eyes. Amelie gasped because his eyes were completely silver with no irises and no pupils visible.

"What do you see?" James asked.

"Your eyes, they're silver," she said. "Can you see?"

But James looked at the others.

"Is that what you see?" he asked. Majo's mouth was a tiny straight slit in her face. She was glancing back and forth between Ossian and Widget.

"No," she said. "But don't ask."

He looked to Widget, who looked a bit perplexed but signed that James looked just as ugly as usual to him.

"Good," James said. He was smiling but his face was beet-red, and he was still sweating. "We need to get this guy out of here before his own spirit, or another one, finds him."

Widget nodded, picked up the body and threw it over his shoulder. He then headed to the elevator.

"I need to go to the roof for a few minutes," James said, his hand on the back of his neck.

"Are you okay?" Amelie asked, moving toward him.

"Don't touch him," Majo said, grabbing Amelie's arm.

"Yeah, fine. Just give me a minute," James said. He took a few steps but then stopped and leaned over for a moment, hands on his knees. He then unceremoniously vomited on the floor. After taking a few breaths, he stood back up.

"When I get back, I think we all need to talk," he said, then quickly turned and headed for the stairs that led to the upper floor.

As he vanished from her sight, Amelie felt a wave of fatigue and pain hit her. It was all she could do to make it to the couch before she collapsed.

***

She woke up with the sunlight in her eyes. She was still lying on the couch and her body felt still and heavy. When she tried to turn, she found that someone had hold of her hand. She sat up and found that James was lying on the floor next to her. He was still asleep, but his hand was firmly grasping hers.

"Despite what Widget said, he was afraid you might have had a concussion, so he didn't want to leave you," said a soft voice. Amelie turned to find Caio sitting on the side chair, regarding her with a strange intensity.

"How are you feeling this morning?" he asked.

"My head and cheek hurt and my sides sting. I might have a cracked rib, but it could be a whole lot worse, I suppose," Amelie replied.

"Yes, it could have been," Caio said.

"When did you get back?" she asked, unsure of how much he already knew about the night before or how much information she should divulge.

"Just after you crashed on the couch," he replied. "And just in time to help Widget and Majo debug the house."

"We were bugged?" Amelie asked. Caio rolled his eyes.

"Of course you were bugged. Pods are experimental as well as functional, so they are all bugged. Video, audio, and biometric bugs. The blood you give every week is not just to test you for disease."

"What else do they test for?"

"Hormones, drugs, immunological changes … all sorts of things. They even collect your shit. It's collected in a holding tank and analyzed weekly. If you go on a diet or try a new bread, they will know."

Amelie gently extracted her hand from James's. He moaned a bit and rolled over on the floor.

"He's a deep sleeper," Caio said, looking at him.

"Yeah. Always has been."

"That's a bit unusual for an operative," Caio replied. Amelie was scanning Caio for body tells.

"How do you know all this about the Academy?" she asked.

"Because I have been in it for a long time. But you guessed that I wasn't a new recruit already, didn't you?" he said, smiling slightly.

"How can you have been with anything a long time? You aren't that old," Amelie asked, but Caio just shrugged.

"I am old enough to know a lot about what is going on," Caio said.

"What the fuck." James sat up and rubbed his head. "It feels like something crawled in my head and died last night."

"No, technically, something crawled in your head and, unfortunately, lived," Majo said, entering the room. Widget was following her carrying a tray and five cups, along with a new tray of shots.

"Right," James muttered and swallowed hard. "Sorry, hard night of vomiting."

He took a cup of tea from Widget, who then held out the tray to the rest of them.

"It's coming back in all its Technicolor glory," he said, as he sipped his tea.

"What did you do with Ossian Reese—I mean, his body?" Amelie asked.

"I took him to a bar," Widget signed, grinning. "I stayed with him in a booth until he started waking up. Then I suggested that he and I had slept together. He left quickly after that."

Amelie laughed out loud. It sounded strange after the events of last night and it made her head ache. It also felt good.

"So, James. We didn't know you were an exorcist." Widget sat down. James jerked his head around to stare at him.

"Are we safe for bugs?" James asked, eyes widening a bit.

"Yes," Caio said.

"When Amelie came in last night and started spilling her guts about her assignment, all I could think was that they would be showing up in minutes to take her away," said James. "She openly admitted to seeing and attracting a non-human. So I was trying to make up a reason that she might be acting so carelessly."

"That's why you said that I was affected by drugs?" Amelie asked.

James didn't answer but turned to Caio.

"Are you sure you got all the bugs?" he asked.

Widget touched James's shoulder.

"I checked everything, everywhere," Widget signed. "We found twenty-seven different forms of surveillance. I only knew about twelve of these. Caio found the rest."

"Caio did?" James asked, raising his eyebrows.

"You first," Caio replied.

James stared at him for a few moments before shrugging.

"I don't know why last night happened," James said. "But I know from the thoughts of the thing inside Ossian that it wasn't an accident. We were targeted. Or Amelie was targeted. I couldn't get why because the thing was even more immaterial and disjointed than most demons, if it was a demon. To be honest, I'm not quite sure what it was besides something without a body. I haven't encountered anything quite like that before."

"But how could you get it out of him?" Amelie asked.

Majo was strangely quiet, her eyes glued to James.

"I told you last night, that's my gift," he said softly. "That's why I am in the Academy. I can steal bits of people. Sometimes it's bits of their memories. Sometimes it's fractions of their souls. If the thing is not inherently physical, then I can absorb its whole soul for a while, like that thing last night. And yes, I was exorcist in a small town in Greece for a while. That was the first time I worked with Majo, after being the one who initially recruited her."

Majo smiled.

"And you all thought I was just here for my looks," James said, with a little smile.

"What does the Academy want with that gift?" Amelie asked.

"Information gathering," Caio said, before James could reply. James nodded.

"Mostly it was that. I steal people's memories of an event or a time and dig through them for information that the Academy wants. Mostly, I work with women, because I can more easily get into the brains of women."

"Why?" Amelie asked. James flinched ever so slightly.

"Because I am a man, I guess. I don't really know," James replied, looking away.

"So that was the purpose of your hook-ups, then?" Widget signed.

"Mostly they were missions, yeah," James said. "But it doesn't mean that I didn't find the women beautiful. That part of the missions has always been a joy."

James said this with a level of passion and gravity that was unusual for him, and in that moment, Amelie understood how his targets could find him attractive.

"You said that you were working with Majo in Greece, to exorcise people?" Widget asked.

James nodded.

A memory of the night before inserted itself into Amelie's brain. Majo, sitting on top of Ossian Reese.

"Last night, you said that you could see whether Ossian was Ossian or the thing inside him," Amelie said, looking at Majo.

Majo nodded. "I can tell the dominant personality in something. That's what I see. So I know if something is human or not."

"What do you see, when you look at it?"

"I see the difference between human and not human."

"Is that what you do for the Academy? Is that your skill? You see spirits?" Amelie asked.

Majo eyes met Amelie's. She then turned and looked around the room.

Finally, she sighed.

"Not exactly. The work I do for the Academy is usually just IT and operative work. When they paired me with James, my job was initially just to be the muscle—I was protecting him. But I stupidly let it slip that I was able to distinguish between a person who was really possessed and one who simply had a mental illness. After that, the Academy started sending me out on missions where I encountered possessed people and had to take them out. Sometimes the possession was so well hidden that no one else could have known."

"So you knew when you saw Ossian that he was possessed?" Amelie asked.

"Yes. And I knew that the thing possessing him was very strong and very dangerous," Majo said.

65

"How?" Caio asked. He was seated, leaning forward with his elbows on his knees. "How can you tell that someone is possessed? Do you actually see the entity? Can you distinguish what it is?"

Majo smiled gently, but before she could speak, James stood up and came to sit next to Caio.

"Before we go into any more details about that, I would like to know a little more about you, new boy," he said, smiling.

Amelie knew that smile. It looked genuine enough at first glance, but it was just a little sideways, slightly off-kilter. It was the smile that James used just before he was about to start a fight, physical or otherwise. James wasn't a fair fighter; he was someone who had learned to fight on the streets of Glasgow as a boy. He wasn't necessarily inclined to fight but he didn't shy away from it if he felt threatened.

Caio glanced around the room before shrugging.

"Well, I am guessing that James has already determined that I was sent here as a plant."

James stood, but Majo caught his eye and put up her hand. He sat back down.

"He was the one who told me about Amelie yesterday. She might be in a lot worse shape, if not for him," Majo said.

"Thank you," Caio said.

"How did you know that I was in trouble?" Amelie asked.

Caio sighed.

"The Academy knows about some of our abilities, but not all of them. The Academy usually sends me into pods to trigger situations that bring out people's gifts."

"Doesn't the Academy already know our gifts?" James asked.

"It knows the ones you have shown. It may not know gifts you are hiding, or ones even you don't know you have."

Majo and James exchanged glances. Widget came to sit next to Amelie and put a protective arm around her.

"So you were sent to see what gifts we are hiding?"

Caio nodded.

"The Academy already knew about James's ability to steal memories and Majo's ability to see non-physical entities," Caio said. "They knew that Amelie could attract people. They knew that Widget is uniquely gifted in chemistry. They have you working on biological weapons, right? Using tech-enhanced humans to spread computer viruses, right?"

"And vice versa." Widget nodded.

66

"Really? You're really doing that?" James began, but Caio cut him off.

"So the Academy knew you could do these things, but they must have had suspicions that you could do other things. That's why I was sent. And, sadly, last night will have confirmed that."

"In what way?" Majo asked. "We only exhibited the abilities that they already knew."

"No, not really. They now have two new vital pieces of information," Caio said, with a little laugh. "The first is that Amelie's ability to attract extends beyond attracting people."

Amelie felt her insides start to get cold … the tiny box that she kept inside her was sending out tendrils of ice through her body.

Don't react.

"Meaning what?" James asked.

"Meaning that she can, to some extent, attract non-humans," Caio replied.

"Like spirits?" Majo asked.

"That's one example but there are lots of types of non-humans," Caio said, momentarily glancing at Widget, whose hand briefly tightened on Amelie's shoulder.

"So that's one piece of information. You said there were two," James said.

"Yeah. I did." Caio took a deep breath. "The second one is me."

"You?" Majo asked.

"I was being tested here," Caio said. "That was the piece that I didn't expect. As I told you, I am usually sent in to shake things up in pods. I'm good at that, because I am not what I seem, and people know that, they can sense it. Just that puts people off their guard, and often triggers mistakes."

"In what way are you not what you seem?" Widget asked.

"I'm not young," Caio replied. "My gift, or curse, or whatever you want to call it, is that I don't age. That's what the Academy brought me in for, and that is what I utilize in my missions. I have more experience with people and life in general than most people around me, in terms of depth and breadth."

"How old are you?" Amelie asked. "And why don't you age?"

"How old I am doesn't really matter, and why is biochemical and something it isn't wise for you to know too much about, for your own safety. But the point is that *this* is the gift that the Academy knows about. But last night they learned something else about me—something I would rather they didn't know."

Majo closed her eyes and sighed.

"Of course, it was how you knew Amelie was in trouble," she whispered.

"How did you know?" Widget signed.

"A ghost told me," Caio said.

"Yeah, right, followed by a little bird," James snapped.

"He's serious," Majo said to James, then turned to Caio. "You're serious, right?"

"Yeah, I'm serious. I can hear ghosts. I don't see them, but I can hear them. Last night, someone came to me. I was playing James's game to see if it was what I thought it was, and I heard a ghost calling me. He said he was Amelie's friend or dad, or something, somehow he knew Amelie. His said his name was Ken. He told me that she was about to encounter a dangerous, possessed creature. He said that she would likely be killed if she wasn't helped. Even worse, he said she might become damned."

"What did that mean?" Widget asked.

"I don't know now, and I didn't know then, but I knew it was important that you find her. So, I told you," Caio said, turning to look at all of them. "And in doing that, I outed myself to the Academy."

"The bugs?" This was Widget, but everyone was already nodding.

"Why did you do that?" Majo asked.

"I don't know," Caio said. "I shouldn't have. I have other—well, I'm not particularly altruistic. So that bothers me too."

We are not particularly altruistic by nature, Clovis had said to me.

"Are you human?" Amelie found herself blurting out before she could stop herself.

Strangely, Caio smiled.

"I'm as human as any of you are," he said. "But there is something about all of you that has obviously become interesting to the Academy. From what information I managed to glean, there is something in our blood."

"Is that why we have had more blood draws since you came?" Majo said, but her voice suddenly seemed far away, like she was speaking from the end of a long tunnel.

Amelie looked around. The air around her was shimmering in a strange way. She tried to say something but her voice didn't work.

Something's wrong.

She threw her inner eyelid open. Her head was beginning to throb, and she was having a hard time remaining seated. Widget's grip on her arm was now so tight it was painful.

From the bookcase across the room, three letters from books lit up and reflected across the room.

G ... A ... S

Someone is gassing us, Amelie thought. She tried to get to her feet but stumbled and fell to her knees. Across from her, she could see Majo crawling toward the bedroom. Then her eyes ceased to work. Behind her she heard someone break-ing down the door, and the sound of a scuffle, and then it all went blank.

Chapter Ten

Refinding Wings

Amelie felt bliss. She was flying again. It was the first time in what felt like forever; the first time since she had lost the ability all those years ago. The sun was low on the horizon, and she could feel the cool, moist air against her skin. The gloaming was filled with the sounds of water and wind.

She was flying high above a green-gray ocean. To her right, she could see a landmass, dotted with large squares of dark green and smaller squares of red and white and gray. If her memory of past flights held true, the dark green squares would be fields or parks, covered in flowers and smelling of grass and dirt. The smaller squares would be houses, apartments, or businesses. These looked a bit ugly from the air but, in truth, much uglier from a ground view.

Just below, she could see what seemed to be an island. It was obscured by clouds and a mist that didn't move or drift or change. There was something unpleasant about the island and so Amelie turned her gaze away from it and up to the sky. As her head turned, the day flipped to evening. Above her, a million stars played peek-a-boo through wispy clouds and reflected off an ocean as smooth as glass. The sky that held court between the stars was blue, gold, lavender, and silver in patches. It was all beautiful enough to make Amelie forget her world. This is why she had always loved these flights. She closed her eyes and threw her hands outward. There was a niggle of concern in the back of her head. She suspected that she had come here from less than perfect circumstances, but she didn't remember it and didn't want to think about it.

She suddenly felt a tug in the center of her gut. She opened her eyes to find herself hurtling through space, stars and planets flying past her. This didn't disturb or startle her; it was customary for these flights, or it had been when she used to regularly take them. Eventually, she slowed, to find herself floating above an ocean of shooting stars. Silver streaked across the dark blue space like ripples in water.

Then, in the distance, Amelie saw a familiar sight. A single hallway floating alone in the emptiness of space. She focused on it and drifted closer. She remembered this place. All her instincts about it returned in a flash. She knew this place was dangerous and glorious and beautiful and destructive. Everything she had ever wanted she had found here, only to lose it in her own world. She knew she probably should avoid it, but she could no more do that than stop the beats of her heart.

She floated toward the hallway and dropped into the top of it like she had done so many times before. This time, it had taken an earthy form. The floor that her feet touched down upon was dirt, or maybe dark sand. But whatever it was, it was moist and stuck to her feet.

There was a door to her left. It was made of rain and though much was obscured, she could see the green of trees through it.

"Hello," a voice called from inside the door. She peered through, but she could see no one through the rain.

"Hello? Down here ..."

The voice was loud enough to hear, but shaky and weak-sounding. It sounded like an old man. Against her better judgment, Amelie stepped through the door and into the rain. She was standing on a wide, round patch of brown earth that was surrounded by forest on all sides. The forest was wet and lush with undergrowth of lacy shrubs and vines. As the rain began to dissipate, she turned around and saw that the door had disappeared from behind her.

The voice was coming from the hole in front of her—and it sounded cloyingly familiar. Amelie moved forward tentatively. She no longer believed that she could not be hurt in these places. History had taught her differently. While it may have felt like ancient history to her heart, her body still heeded its warning.

"Who's there?" she called.

"Caio."

Amelie stepped forward and looked over the edge of the hole. At the bottom of the hole, Caio lay in a puddle of mud. He looked awful. He was skeletal-skinny and covered in sores, most of which seemed to be open and oozing.

"Oh, it's you. I thought I had seen you before," he said with a tiny smile that just seemed grotesque and out of place on his tortured face. "You're Amelie, right? Your name is Amelie."

"Yeah, it's me. What happened to you?" Amelie said as she crouched at the edge of the hole. She reached down toward him even though she already knew

71

he was way too far down for her to grab. She would need get a branch or some-thing for him to hold onto. She looked around but she could see nothing in her immediate vicinity. In the distance, she saw trees, large trees, but they were de-void of branches most of the way up their trunks. The vines on the ground were probably her only shot.

"I'll be back—" she started, but Caio interrupted her.

"Wait. Stay."

"I need to find something to get you out with."

"You won't find anything and I'm too weak to pull myself out even if you do find something. Besides, you don't have much time." His voice was surpris-ingly calm, and much stronger than it had been moments before.

"What? Hold on, just wait—"

"No, you don't have much time before this vision fades."

"This isn't a vision," Amelie said. "It's a story."

But Caio shook his head.

"From my perspective at the moment, it's a vision, but that doesn't matter. I need to tell you something. I was put here by the Academy," he said.

"The Academy put you in a hole?" she whispered.

"No, the Academy owns—owned—the slave trade business that put me here."

"The Academy owned slave traders?"

"Yes. They did in your past and in my present—and they do in your present, but in much worse ways. You are in my present now but in your past. The me in your present got out of this hole. He is now part of the Academy."

"How do you know what you will do in the future?" Amelie asked.

"See these things on me," Caio said, pointing to his arm. As Amelie focused, she saw small white worms on his arms and a much larger blob on his abdomen. She first thought it was his engorged belly but now she realized that it was a large worm, partially buried in his skin.

"These things are switching DNA with me. They have DNA that is missing the code for aging, so some of these worms, like this one,"—he pointed to the one on his belly- "this one is probably thousands of years old. It is going to infect me with a virus that is infecting it. The viral DNA in that will stop my aging. It will also change my relationship with emotions and time."

"It changes your emotions? That helps you see the future?" Amelie was hav-ing a hard time concentrating on anything but the worm undulating on his belly.

"Yes, my emotions will atrophy but it's my relationship with time that allows me to see the future. Time is different for viruses. They can sometimes even cross stories. So the virus part of me has a different relationship with time and space. But this isn't what I need you to know. I need you to know two things. So listen carefully before you are pulled away."

Amelie nodded.

"First, you need to know that I will be, I am, a hostage of the Academy. The Academy knows about someone I love. The only person I love or will ever even be able to love. She is someone I saw in a vision when I was in this hole. The virus will take away my ability to care for anyone in the future. I can only love or care for people that I knew before I was changed."

"I don't understand—" Amelie began.

"You don't have to, you'll understand later," Caio said. "Just listen now. Her name is Sarah. You need to know that I will do anything to save her. I will sacrifice you, the pod, the Academy, anyone and anything to keep her safe. So there may come a time that you will need to kill me to save others. Do that if you must, I won't blame you."

Caio had turned his head up to look directly at her. His eyes were wide and clear in his wasted body, clear but tortured. He looked like someone waiting expectantly to embrace death. Amelie felt anger flood her body.

"I won't kill you," she said. "I won't let them make me do that."

"Yes, you will," Caio replied. "If it becomes necessary, you will. And that's okay. That's who you are. That's who you have become. Majo—her name is Majo, right?—she wears a coldness on the outside, but underneath there is fire. But you're different. The cold in you seems lighter at first, like a dusting of snow, but it goes deep, doesn't it? It can only go that deep if you freeze yourself. It only goes that deep if there are large enough holes inside you to hold the cold. I understand that, and I respect it. So you will do what needs to be done."

Suddenly, there was wind around her and she ceased to feel the rain. She could see it, but she could not feel it. She was fading.

"What is the second thing?" she asked.

"If you do need to kill me, it will be hard to do," he said. "I can't be poisoned or made sick. My body is a carrier for drugs and disease but doesn't succumb to it. The Academy knows and uses this as well. I have started more than one pandemic to destroy their enemies since I have been with them. And I recover from most wounds. To kill me, you will need to obliterate my brain, completely. One shot to the head won't do it, you will need to turn my brain completely to mush. Do you understand?"

Amelie nodded.

She felt herself becoming thin.

"Wait. Promise me one more thing before you go," Caio said. His voice was getting softer and harder to hear, but not so soft that she couldn't hear it quaking.

"What?"

"If I die. Remember … Sarah Baker. She lives in the Cloud on the Big Island of Hawaii. If something happens to me, find her, and keep her safe. Keep them safe, her and …"

His last few words were so soft they were hard to hear. She thought he said "my child."

Caio has a child.

***

Rather than waking, Amelie found herself flying again, over the same island that she had seen before she entered the hallway. This time, instead of flying over it, she began to descend toward the clouds that didn't move. The minute her foot touched the upper edge of one, she felt an electric shock run through her body. She felt her heart begin to palpitate even though she had no idea where her actual body was. The further into the cloud bank she got, the harder and faster her heartbeat. As if this wasn't enough, a wave of nausea hit her, and she began to feel lightheaded. She was beginning to worry that somewhere her body was entering heart attack territory when she emerged from the clouds. Immediately, the nausea abated, and her heart returned to its normal erratic beat.

Beneath her, an island emerged from the mist, if one could call it an island. It was tiny but mountainous. Looking at it, it was easy to be reminded that this was simply the tips of mountains that hid the greater part of themselves beneath the waves, like sleeping gods waiting for the great fire to wake them. Amelie felt a sense of dread and revulsion looking at it. She tried to stop her movement but could not. She looked up at the sky, as this usually drew her out of whatever world she was inhabiting, but not this time. Her body continued its course, dropping as she approached.

As she got closer, she saw a group of buildings that sat at the top of the island, nestled between two of the peaks. The shape of the island was like that of a wishbone or a horseshoe. On the outside of the horseshoe the jagged tops of the mountains descended sharply downward as if falling toward the water around the outside of the island. However, in the inner circle of the horseshoe, the one that formed the harbor, the slope was gentler and ended in a thin band of sand. It was toward this tiny beach that Amelie now descended. As she got a bit closer, she saw that there was a group of people huddled on the beach. About half of these people were adults. The children present seemed to range from as young as eight to gangly teenagers. There were also one or two much older adults. All of them seemed wildly underdressed for the weather. Most were wearing nothing but what looked like long black underwear. But as she got almost close enough to see the faces of these people, she changed direction and moved quickly toward the building at the top of the peak. She picked up speed as she went. As she sped the last few feet toward the building, she threw her hands out in front of her. Instead of feeling an impact, everything went black.

At first, she could neither see nor hear anything. The first thing she became aware of was flashes of images combined with sounds. A thumping at regular intervals along with a consistent swishing sound, like a river flowing. On top of these two sounds, there was an occasional sound of gurgling. It was the combination of these sounds that told her she was inside a body. She would never have guessed it from what she was initially able to see. Across the black sky of this person's insides there came flashing meteors that tore rips in the fabric of whatever soul lived here. Occasionally, there would be a burst of bright light that would blind her for a few moments. For all the world, these moments felt like a supernova. These moments were exciting and transcendentally beautiful in their way, but that beauty was destroying its own environment. Whenever a meteor passed, or a star exploded, it left behind a different type of darkness. One that was not simply the absence of light. It was a material that wasn't defined by something as simple as light and dark. The edges of the rips dripped red and white, combining to a pink color that looked less like valentines and more like milk and blood. Accompanying all this was pain. Searing pain. It was a pain that increased incrementally, second by second. It started as a simple burning in her heart but spread inside her, throbbing and cramping as it went. Amelie tried to pull herself out of this person, but she could not. This creature wasn't human and that seemed to make whoever it was immune to her influence. She turned her attention outward, and found that if she focused, she was able to tie herself to her host's senses.

She found that she was walking through an atrium, decorated with potted trees and plants of all varieties. Walking beside her was a breathtaking creature. He looked like a man, with wavy golden hair and fair skin. His face was a song with a straight, strong nose and high cheekbones but there was a sternness to his thin lips.

"So you got nothing from the girl?" he asked her.

"No, pet, I didn't say that I got nothing," replied her host. "I just didn't get the specific information that *you* were looking for."

"Which is what matters," the man said, turning to her. His eyes were the color of lapis lazuli, streaked with gray, like storm clouds over the Aegean Sea.

However, the glory of his eyes, of his face, was marred by the way his lips were pinched together, causing the corners of his mouth to be dragged downward. Almost as soon as Amelie noticed this, his expression lightened, and he shrugged.

"Well, let's see what we can find out now. And if we can't do it this way, there are other ways," he said, with a smile that dazzled.

"Of course, you are right, pumpkin, you always are," her voice said.

The man next to her beamed, and it was at that moment that she noticed that he had wings—snow-white wings with lavender tips.

An incubus. Shit.

Amelie tried to pull herself further back inside this person, for fear that he would see her or be able to influence her, but she couldn't. After a few seconds of panic, she realized that she could feel no sense of attraction resonating in the emotions of her host. The internal pain might have been blocking it, but it wasn't just that. There was an anger there as well, and a condescension.

The two of them entered what looked like a cross between a library and a foyer. At the opposite end, there was a doorway with a window to the outside.

The incubus stopped and turned to her.

"Did you have all the new recruits taken to the beach?"

"Of course," she replied.

"How many do we have?"

"Sixteen total."

"Have we placed them yet?" he asked.

"Of course. Four adults and four children for the beach matrix, two adults and two children to the sensory unit, and three adults to human resources."

"What level?"

"They're nothing special," she replied. "Except for the fact that all three have been heavy drug users, so easier to access."

The incubus nodded, then paused.

"That's only fifteen."

"True, I was waiting for you to decide what to do with the Chappell woman."

At that name, Amelie felt her blood run cold. Surely it was a coincidence.

The incubus smiled at her host.

"Ah yes," he said. "So what did you learn about her?"

"She isn't what you are looking for," her host replied. "At least, she has not collected enough of what you are looking for to get direct access. But she may have absorbed some pieces that would accelerate the overall substrate."

The incubus beamed.

"So I would advise that we send her to coding," her host said. "If that agrees with you."

"Exactly what I would choose," the incubus said. "Can you call coding and tell them she will be transferred promptly?"

"Of course."

The incubus turned toward the door, but her host reached out and touched his arm.

"I also think that it would be advisable to bring in our current catch, so that all the recruits can see."

"I don't mind, but why?" the incubus asked.

"It will cause a spike in neurotransmitters, which should make it easier for the human resources people as the recruits will be more malleable in their bodies and give us more interesting results from the beach matrix." A sharp flash of pain exploded in the space between and behind her host's eyes.

"Of course, I forget how important those little chemical agents are to un-boxing a human's junk DNA. That is what you are talking about, is it not?"

"Yesssss," said her host, using her breath to extend the word in a seductive way, even as a burning sensation flared in her chest. "As the Chappell woman is there, we may want to up the intensity even more."

"You have an idea?"

"Yes, you have suggested retiring a few of our current seers. You might do that, and let the recruits see."

The incubus laughed and clapped his hands.

"That would certainly be intense for a human brain," he said. "You will have one sent to the beach?"

Her host nodded. The incubus came to her and put his arms around her. Inside her, she could feel the revulsion this caused her host. For a moment, this feeling overwhelmed the pain, but just for a moment. It then layered itself between the other pains, adding to their horrific chorus.

"Beautiful and brilliant, as always," the incubus said, pulling back.

"I'll go get her," her host said.

As the incubus turned and walked out the door, Amelie felt herself yanked out of her host and thrown through the doors after him. The first thing she noticed was that the incubus no longer looked like an incubus. Instead, he looked like a medium-sized human with longish, light brown hair and an easy gait. Some of the incubus charisma clung to him, but it was like a faint and distant scent—forgotten but still capable of affecting mood and behavior. For a moment she also felt bliss. Her pain was gone, or the pain of her host was gone. It was only in its absence that Amelie realized the depth and breadth of the agony that her host was carrying. Carrying such pain should have been as unbearable as it was unimaginable. Yet her host had, and she had as well, if only for a few moments.

Amelie took all this in as she was drawn along behind him toward the beach, and the people standing there. There were the sixteen people that they had mentioned. There were six children and ten adults. She drifted toward a woman who was shivering in the cold, staring out across the bay to the sea. Whatever blissful, contented feelings she had felt evaporated as the woman turned toward her.

And she was confronted with the drawn and wasted face of Sophie Chappell.

Chapter Eleven

A Faith-Forgotten Land

Sophie was dressed in the same long black underwear as everyone else. She had pale blonde hair cut in a longish bob. When she looked up, Amelie saw the ruins of a face that had never been beautiful but was pretty enough to make a living in regional modeling for catalogs and such. It was older than when she had last seen it, and the years hadn't been particularly kind, but she could still see the remains of the Sophie Chappell she had known in high school.

Without slowing down, she felt herself enter Sophie's energy field and then her physical body. Immediately, Amelie's head was filled with sights, sounds, and smells. She could feel the cold wind on her bare arms. The smell of the ocean, that strange mixture of salt, fish, seaweed, and rot, assaulted her nostrils. The people around her looked equally cold and miserable but mostly they looked afraid. Sophie felt afraid too, but she was trying to control it.

How had Sophie ended up here?

The moment this question entered Amelie's brain, a series of images flashed through her head. Sophie leaning forward to kiss Amelie in her car on their senior beach trip. She saw her own face through Sophie's eyes and was shocked by how beautiful her own face had looked. It looked nothing like the face Amelie had lived with for all these years. She saw a boy, who looked a like an older, adult version of Charlie Danos, the musician that Clovis had once possessed all those years ago. He was now sporting a bit of a paunch and thinning hair. He was standing in front of Sophie with tears in his eyes, and a face full of rage. This image was chased away by bright light. When Amelie's internal eye adjusted, she saw lights, cameras, and naked people all around her. Visions of men and women's genitalia flashed through her brain with alarming speed and in equally alarming numbers. Then a vision of walking into a small office with an even smaller sign over the door that read Evermore. With all these visions came knowledge. Sophie had married Charlie, only to leave him. She had never felt any real desire with Charlie, so she went to try to find it with others. First, she tried the dating scene, then the bar scene, then the online scene, but none of these things matched what she had felt when she had looked at Amelie that first day of their senior beach trip. Eventually, Sophie had decided to get a job in the porn industry, in the hope of finding someone who might actually excite her. These were professionals at desire, but, without exception, all the people, all her encounters, felt lifeless and dull. Eventually she had become so depressed that she went to Evermore. While being tested for compatibility with the system, they had shown her a marketing video and Sophie had felt a wave of desire from watching it that she hadn't felt since high school. Immediately, she had signed whatever document they shoved in front of her. She had then gone to sleep in an odd, shaped pod and had woken up on this island.

That was two weeks ago, and she had seen enough already to know that this was a bad place—a very bad place.

"Hello everyone," the human form of the incubus said. "I hope that you are all getting a bit of fresh air. I know it can be a bit claustrophobic inside."

His voice was a soft Southern drawl and as he walked by one of the young girls, he placed his hand on her cheek. The girl looked up with a tentative smile but when she met the incubus's eyes, her face froze.

"Don't be afraid, my dear," he said to her. "It is from such little things as you that great things can be accomplished."

This time when he touched her face, she cringed and pulled away.

"Before anything else, let's see what our catch has for us," he announced to the group, signaling up and down the beach in each direction. It was then that Amelie noticed two machines at each end of the beach. Nets extended from each of these into the water. As if by the sound of his voice alone, these machines came to life and began pulling the fishing nets in from the murky, steely water.

"While we are waiting to beach our catch, let me organize you by group. You, you, you, and you are one group," he said, pointing to an oldish, gray-haired man, a young woman in her early twenties, and two girls that Amelie now noticed were identical twins.

"You will be part of our sensory unit. Someone from that unit is heading down in a few minutes to collect you," the incubus said. He was smiling but his expression was not friendly, it was closer to fierce.

As he said this, he pointed to a group of people who had now appeared on the beach and were walking toward them. They were all dressed in what looked like uniforms. There were seven in total but three of them were dramatically taller than the other four. These three stopped as the other four kept moving toward them. Amelie noticed that apart from being tall, the three were beautiful, well built and androgynous.

"You, you, and you," the incubus said, pointing to three adults. "You will be working in human resources, they are waiting for you, so go on now."

The beautiful people on the beach waved and the three adults that the incubus had pointed to quickly turned and ran up the beach with little hesitation. Amelie sensed that Sophie would prefer to be leaving the beach as well. There was something unwholesome in the air that everyone present seemed to feel.

As the androgynous staff members led the group of three adults up the beach, four more people were making their way down the beach. When they got a bit closer Amelie noticed a woman amid the four. Her face was covered in a white veil and two men were leading her.

The engines of the machines pulling the net toward the shore were grinding and whining. As the net was pulled closer, the sea in front of it began to bubble and churn, but not in a normal way. The bubbles came in waves that moved not toward the beach but away from it.

"These people work in the sensory unit, and they will escort you from here," the incubus said to the two adults and twins that he had separated out to one side. Two of these staff moved forward to take the hands of the twins and lead them up the beach. The other staff turned to follow but the incubus stopped them.

"Leave her," he said, indicating the veiled woman. The staff exchanged glances but nodded and led the twins and adults up the beach.

The woman in the veil stood still. Her arms were rigid at her sides but her hands were alive, clenching and unclenching, forming angles normally impossible for something with bones to achieve.

"She's smelling," the incubus said to the others. "Unfortunately, she is at an advanced age for her job, but I want to give her the honor of presiding over and contributing to a catch before she retires."

The woman cringed and fell to the ground in a crouching position, planting her feet in the sand.

"Let's not be childish at such a poignant moment," the incubus said.

"Don't worry, I can help her up," said a voice behind her. Sophie turned her head and Amelie saw what was probably the ugliest human being she had ever encountered. The owner of the voice was round, pasty, and covered not in warts, but huge, oversized skin tags. These skin tags were whiter even than her pale skin and Amelie noticed that they moved as she walked around Sophie and toward the incubus.

81

"Is the catch in?" The voice that said this was more feminine than masculine but not by much.

"Yes," said the incubus. "Our chaplain of the moment is just a bit reticent."

"Come along," the pale thing said. "I'll help you." Despite the horror of her appearance, when the creature touched the veiled woman, she relaxed. With help, the woman stood and let out a deep sigh that moved her veil for just a moment. In that moment, Amelie saw that the face beneath the veil was not a face, but what looked like a plate of solar panels. Amelie felt her stomach drop. Sophie must have seen this as well, because her legs began to shake.

The round woman led the veiled woman to the water but stopped at the waterline. The waves churned more, as if in anticipation. From the first step she took into the water, her flesh was surrounded by whatever fish were caught in the net. The water churned more, and the foam turned red. The woman didn't slow her forward motion but walked slowly and deliberately into the sea which was becoming more crimson by the moment. In mere seconds, the woman's head was completely submerged, but the churning did not stop. It increased. Fish were leaping into the air in a frenzy, some accidentally beaching themselves in the process.

The incubus clapped his hands and laughed.

"The rest of you here will be part of our beach matrix. So, if you don't mind, could you go in the water and help pull the rest of it out. Our machines are strong, but this end bit always requires the dexterity of human hands."

He reached his hand out to the young girl he had touched earlier. She shook her head.

"Come now, don't be difficult," the incubus said.

"I don't think she wants to go," Sophie said, stepping forward. Inside Sophie's head, Amelie heard her voice as if it were a gong.

"She doesn't have a choice and she should be honored to be part of this." The incubus looked around, but everyone was shivering in their spots, eyes down. They would have run if there had been somewhere to run to. The incubus nodded and smiled.

"What's in the water?" Sophie asked.

"Well, strictly speaking, here in the bay it isn't water. It's more like substrate," the incubus said.

"Listen, I know you are afraid, but nothing will harm you," he continued. Some of the injections that you have received since being here will protect you from harm by anything. What we are doing here is for you. We are working to give you, all of you, a place in eternity."

The girl moved forward, and the incubus gave her a hug. Then he took her hand and began to lead her toward the water. They had only taken a few steps when the little girl's eyes landed on one of the fish that had beached itself. She immediately began to scream and turned to flee. The incubus grabbed her by the waist and pulled her off her feet. He was about to throw her into the water when Sophie ran forward.

"Let go of her, I'll go in," she screamed.

She reached the incubus and pulled the girl away from him.

"Oh, no. We have something much more interesting for you," he said, putting his arm on Sophie's shoulder

Amelie felt the touch like an injection of dopamine. Everything felt okay suddenly. Sophie didn't move even as the incubus took the girl and threw her into the waves.

Sophie was numb to the screaming around her. Instead, she focused on the fish that had beached itself near her feet. There was something wrong with it. It took even Amelie's brain a few more seconds to register what it was.

The fish had tiny human arms.

That was when Sophie began to scream, and Amelie felt herself forcibly ejected from Sophie's body.

***

Amelie awoke to find herself lying on her back. She had just been somewhere, somewhere awful. Her body knew it as her heart was pounding and she was breathing fast. But her brain was clueless as to why she felt this way. She could remember nothing.

"Welcome to the Academy's Control and Integration Training Department," she heard a sing-song sort of voice say. "We call it ACID for short."

Amelie opened her eyes and immediately closed them. The light was too bright, and her eyes were too sensitive. She had apparently been drugged—no, gassed. They had been gassed in their flat

"What?" Amelie coughed out. Her vocal cords were sore and her voice weak. She opened her eyes just enough to let the slightest glimmer of light in, and that still hurt.

How long have I been out?

"Take a few minutes to adjust yourself. You don't have to rush things. Well, not too much," said the voice.

"What is this place?" Amelie croaked.

83

"ACID is the Academy's facility to train basic frontline operatives to become strategic operatives. In short, you have graduated into the big league now, lamb. Congratulations!"

The more awake she became, the more annoying this voice sounded. It was perky and nasal—a bad combination.

"Where is the rest of my pod?" she asked the voice, opening her eyes by fractions.

"They're just there," the voice said, pointing to her right.

As Amelie's eyes came into focus, she realized that she was lying on a stretcher in a large open room. It was a medical facility to be sure. It was sterile and white with fluorescent lights built into a gypsum acoustic ceiling. The walls were covered with clear plastic shelves and drawers. Each drawer was labeled with words that were too fuzzy for Amelie's post-drug eyes to read. The floors were predominantly white tile but interspersed with large blue rectangles every fifteen feet. On top of each of these rectangles was a stretcher, each complete with its own IV drip and crash cart.

Her podmates Majo, James, and Widget were lying on the three stretchers nearest her on the right.

Each of them was hooked to an IV and were not moving.

Where was Caio?

"So we were drugged, right?" Amelie muttered, blinking hard to try to get her eyes to water, hoping that might clear them. Right now, they were dry and gummy.

"You are fine. They are fine," the voice said, not answering the question. "Personally, I am so sorry for the forceful way they brought you in here. I hate that this is the way we treat our new graduates."

I … they … we. Lot of switching of personal pronouns is never a good sign. And being called a "graduate"? That rings edgy.

"What exactly is this place? It looks like a hospital." Amelie asked, turning to find that the owner of the voice was a white blob. A HUGE white blob. It took Amelie a minute to realize what she was seeing was the back of a very large someone in a white uniform.

Whoever this is either has a serious love of food or a glandular problem.

"This is the MAO, the labs arm of ACID," the blob said. "MAO stands for Medical Acute Orientation. We do some research but we're mainly the medical unit here at ACID. Right now, you are in our recovery room."

The voice of the blob was of such a pitch and register that made it impossible to determine whether it belonged to a male or a female. It probably would have been annoying in either gender. The difference was that she could push a male.

84

If it was a female, it would be harder, not impossible, but harder if no one else was around. She might have to find another way to get out of the situation if it turned bad.

"So why would you need to gas us to get us here?" Amelie asked, beginning to sit up. On a counter behind the blob, Amelie could see a knife sitting on a tray table. She was weak but she could probably grab it if she needed to.

At that moment, the blob turned around to reveal that the owner of the voice was a woman. A woman who, in today's vernacular might be called "beauty-challenged." She had a large, protruding forehead that sat just above a wide, fleshy lower face. She had so many chins that it was hard to discern where her head stopped and her neck began. Her eyes were tiny and hidden by bushy eyebrows and folds of fat. A strong nose might have helped her facial construction but instead she had a tiny button nose, the sort of nose one might expect on a toddler. She also had strange growths of skin tags on her cheeks and chin that looked like they might have been moles if they had been dark and regularly formed but instead, they were paler than her normal skin color and more bulbous than uniform. They looked like pustular acne's albino cousin. She was singularly unattractive and yet she seemed strangely familiar.

Where have I seen her?

She had a name tag printed with Academy insignia pinned on her expansive white shirt. It read *Camp*.

"The reason that the Academy uses the means it does to bring new recruits here is that we need to keep the location of this place secret to all, even those who are trained here," Camp said.

"Why not just tell us that and blindfold us or something?" Amelie asked, glancing quickly to see if her podmates were waking up. Not yet.

"It's quite simple. Some operatives have trust issues, and we understand that. Also, we bring people when they have exhibited or are exhibiting some sort of exceptional talent. Sometimes the discovery of that leads to psychological imbalance on the part of the person affected, at least temporarily. Finally, there are some people whose gifts we are just discovering because they have hidden them from us. So those people are not usually too happy to discover that we have outed them. Due to all this, it's believed that it is simply more efficient to gas you and bring you in, rather than to send in trainers to try to explain beforehand. We have lost quite a few trainers that way."

Shit. Were we still being bugged in the apartment after we removed the bugs? What did we say? Too much.

"So exactly what talents do you think we have that require you to drug us and bring us here?" Amelie asked.

85

Camp laughed out loud. Her teeth were actually white and straight, and her smile was warm. The contrast between this and the rest of her face ended up being alarming rather than comforting.

"I have no idea," Camp said. "I'm an underling here. My job is just to monitor you until you are stabilized enough to be taken to your apartments. Then I assist you throughout your training."

As she said this, a flume of green smoke fell from her mouth and began dripping on the floor.

Amelie started, before realizing that her inner eye was wide open, and she was seeing colors. This green smoke was a clear lie indicator. With that realization came the memory of flying. She had been flying. She hadn't been able to fly in years, but she had just done it. And then she had been somewhere bad.

Was it from the gas they gave me?

"Are you all right?" Camp asked. Amelie's face must have registered her shock. She needed to pull things in, and quickly, until she knew what was happening here.

"Yes," Amelie said. "Just a bit dizzy." She shut her inner eye down hard.

"Well, your vitals seem good, so I think it's okay to release you. You can rest up a bit more in your own room. It looks like your chariot is here anyway."

An unnaturally handsome young male orderly had arrived next to her stretcher with a wheelchair. He was wearing a name tag like Camp's that read *Lynche*.

"Hi there, new girl," Lynche said. "I'll be your escort to your new pad."

For the first time she noticed what she was wearing. Rather than the usual backless gown of hospitals, she was wearing what looked a long black underwear top and leggings. It was both soft and warm enough that she hadn't even noticed it.

Amelie exaggerated her wobble a bit as she stood up. Contrary to popular opinion, it was rarely a disadvantage to be underestimated—at least, not in her line of work. She made a slight show of righting herself and then obediently sat down in the wheelchair offered to her.

"Groovy, we'll just be one our way now," Lynche said.

Groovy. Pad. Strange word choices for a young person. Amelie adjusted herself in her seat again as an excuse to accidentally brush against his arm. Nothing. There was a strange lack of energy. No, it wasn't exactly a lack. It was weak energy fields. Crazy-weak energy fields.

Camp gently removed the IV drip from Amelie's arm and bandaged her.

"What about my podmates?" Amelie asked, nodding to the others. None of them seemed to have moved yet.

"Oh, you will see them at orientation this afternoon," the young man said, backing her up.

"And I'll see *you* in a couple of hours to take you to the orientation," Camp said, waving as the young man turned Amelie's wheelchair toward the door.

As the door opened, Amelie turned back—and saw that the trail of green smoke she had seen had not dissipated.

It had expanded and was now creeping across the room and covering her sedated friends.

Chapter Twelve

Game Theory

Lynche opened the door to Amelie's studio "apartment" with a smile. The room itself was small, in a mid-range hotel room sort of way. The decor was muted grays, blues, and purples. There was one double bed placed against the wall. In a small alcove next to the bed there was a kitchen area with a microwave and refrigerator along with a tiny glass table and two chairs. At the back of the room was a hallway leading to a bathroom with walls of smoked glass. There was nothing in the center of the room, giving it a feeling of spaciousness even though it was quite small. But what was unusual about the room was the fact that there were no windows. Instead of windows, all the wall space, from ceiling to floor, including the floor itself, was made of high-quality flat video displays.

"You can change your environment as you like," Lynche said, pointing to a small remote sitting next to the bed. "You can even have different settings on each wall, but I wouldn't advise that. It makes you dizzy." He said this with a laugh that was loud and clipped, more like a bark. "If you are okay, I'll go and fetch you some lunch."

Amelie nodded.

He left her still sitting in her wheelchair. As he walked away, she noted a jerkiness to his movements. It was slight, but noticeable to a trained eye. After he left, Amelie stood up quickly and immediately regretted it. She sat back down. Apparently, she hadn't needed to pretend to be dizzy. Her head throbbed.

How long was I out?

She stood up, gingerly this time. As she walked gently across the room, the floor, which had been projecting grass, changed. Instead of grass, she was now walking on a narrow old bridge over running water.

That's a bit sadistic, she thought.

Here she was, a person recovering from gas poisoning, and she was being subjected to feeling like she was walking on an unsafe bridge over rough water. If she hadn't felt any nausea before, she did now.

She made it to the bed and sat down. The walls around her were set to lush mountains. The ceiling showed blue sky and white clouds. All this was lovely.

But the bridge, is that a glitch … or is it on purpose?

She was just about to go check the toilet when Lynche returned with a tray of food. She was expecting bland. What she got was even blander, consisting of a ham sandwich with mayonnaise on white bread, fries, and a soft drink. The only splash of color in the mix was one tiny slice of tomato on the sandwich. Amelie knew that doctors tended to keep things bland for patients coming out from under sedation, but this seemed extreme.

Of course, bland lunches and sadistic interior design tech were the least of her worries. She was supposedly at an Academy facility, and she had seen subtle but numerous Academy insignia on people in the hallways, and on the objects around her. Still, just because she was in an Academy facility did not mean she was safe. If there was one thing she had learned from her time at the Academy and her trauma before it, it was that safety was something you provided for yourself. You could not expect it to be handed to you. Certainly, the Academy had no issues with "retiring" operatives that had become a threat, or simply less useful.

Most of what Camp had said to her in the recovery room had registered true. At least until she said that she was just an underling here. That bit was clearly a lie, but the rest of her words leading up to it didn't register at all, and Amelie had her inner eye wide open at the time.

That was the other thing. She had flown again and that was new and amazing. What wasn't amazing was what she had seen while she while flying, apart from the scenery she had flown over. Maybe that was all that had happened, but she didn't think so. There was a block, and a lingering current of uneasiness, when she tried to focus on what she had seen. She didn't know if that happened because of the gas, but somehow, she didn't think so. Of course, she had woken up with an IV in her arm, so who knows what they might have given her while she was out.

She wished that she could talk to one of her podmates.

There was a clipped knock at her door, followed by the appearance of Camp. Amelie glanced at the clock and two hours had passed without her realizing it.

"Hello there, lamb," Camp said. "I'm here to take you to orientation. Are you able to stand yet?"

"Yes," Amelie said, getting up. "But I don't have any other clothes."

"Oh, don't you worry about that. All the new recruits will be wearing the same thing," Camp said, holding the door open for her.

Amelie joined her at the door. In the hallway, another underwear-clothed older man walked by them. He smiled at Amelie sheepishly.

Camp and Amelie fell in step behind him.

"Where are we going?" Amelie asked.

"You have an orientation in the auditorium with the Director," Camp said. "He will explain everything to you."

"The Director? Which Director?" Amelie asked.

"THE Director."

"The Director of the Academy?"

"The one and only. Have you met him before?"

Amelie shook her head.

"Have you ever seen him speak?"

Amelie shook her head again.

"Oh, my lamb, you are in for a treat," Camp said with a laugh. "Everything out of that man's mouth is gold … and he's not hard on the eye either."

The openly hungry look on Camp's face was embarrassing to observe. Amelie made herself smile.

Camp shrugged.

"I probably shouldn't say that. Some people have a problem with acknowledging someone's attractiveness," Camp said, then leaned closer to Amelie and whispered in a new, completely different, honeyed voice. "But I am guessing you aren't one of those people, as those are your talents, aren't they, dove?"

"Hello there, Paul," Camp said suddenly to an orderly just in front of them. They had come to a door where various people dressed like Amelie were filing into a larger room.

"I'll just leave you here, my love," she said, turning back to Amelie. "Afterward, you can find your way back to your room, I suppose. You are in room 21b, first floor. They are coding a retinal lock just now, so that should be ready by the time you get back. But there is a cafeteria on the fourth floor if you don't want to hurry back. We probably won't start anything important until tomorrow morning, so just feel free to make yourself at home."

With that, Camp turned and swished away, leaving Amelie with a feeling of dark déjà vu.

***

The auditorium Amelie entered was large, and bright orange. The walls were orange, the carpet was orange, even the backs of the chairs were covered in

90

orange fabric. As Amelie was still a bit dazed, the effect of this was a cramp of complaint in her already acidic stomach. The bile-inducing impact of it wasn't that it was orange per se. It was the shade of orange, which was generally only found in fast food restaurant decor or processed "cheeze" spread.

The space was set up as an in-the-round sort of venue with seats on all sides of a central stage area. The seats themselves were in classic theater style, with an area for stalls and seats, as well as balconies. The bright orange ceiling had large hexagonal windows at every corner which opened to a deep blue night sky. This contrasted with the orange in a way that was almost beautiful. It was the first time that Amelie had gotten any sense of her external surroundings.

The hall itself looked as if it could possibly hold a couple of thousand people, but at the moment there were, at best, two hundred black-clothed figures arranging themselves in the first few rows in front of the stage. As Amelie walked down, she was met by a smiling female in a bright blue dress.

"You should move on down to the front. There aren't a lot of people here today, so we should just cozy up," she said, placing her hand on Amelie's lower back as she walked by. Once again, Amelie felt no energy whatsoever coming from this woman.

What is going on here?

Amelie found a seat on the far left end of the third row. As others filed in and took seats, she looked around for her podmates, but saw no one. It wasn't until they dimmed the lights and lowered a projection screen down over the stage that she saw Majo enter at the back. Her stance seemed relaxed, but Amelie felt her discomfort even from this distance.

As the lights went out, the screen lit up with images of people in what seemed to be various stressful situations. One image was of a man climbing up the outside of a building toward a child dangling from a ledge. Another showed a woman with a gun, surrounded by animals that looked kind of like bears but not exactly. Then with shock, an image of Caio flashed up on the screen. He was on the terrace of their apartment, grabbing his head with his hands. Over him was a dark cloud of something.

These are images of people in this room, Amelie thought. *How did they take these? Were we being photographed and videoed as well?*

When the video ended and the lights came up, a tall, lean man walked onto the stage. He was wearing jeans and a simple white long-sleeved shirt. His hair was light brown, medium length and messy in a rock star sort of way. It was thinning a bit at his temples, in typical male pattern baldness fashion. On his nose, he was wearing gold wire-rimmed glasses.

91

When he reached the center of the stage, he turned to face them. For a few minutes, his eyes scanned the audience. Amelie dropped her eyes. She had no desire to meet anyone's eyes until she knew better what was behind them.

"Survival of the fittest," he said, with a voice that was both soft and resonant. Amelie thought she caught the slightest hint of a Southern drawl. Something about his voice caused goosebumps to rise on her arms. It was both familiar and disturbing.

"This is an elegant phrase that came from an elegant mind," the Director said. "One of ours, I might add. But so many people misinterpret it. These people think that it means survival of the strongest but in truth it means, and has always meant, survival of the most adaptable. That is why all of you have been brought here. You were initially brought to the Academy because you were genetically gifted with certain abilities. And since then, those in this room have all proven yourselves to be among the most adaptable beings our world can produce."

The Director waved his hand in the air and smiled.

"But I am getting ahead of myself. Introductions are in order. My name is Taylor Nathan Thompson." He looked around at them and then chuckled. "And yes, yes, I am aware that my initials are TNT. Believe it or not, I was once young enough to be teased about it. But now that I am the Director here at the Academy, most people just call me 'Director,' a huge improvement, for me at least."

He said this with a small laugh. His tone and stance were more akin the lead counselor at a summer camp than a person who was the final authority of a covert worldwide organization.

"Some of you I've met before," he continued. "If I have, I am so pleased to be able to work with you again. For those I've not met, let me say that the honor is all mine. Also, here at the beginning, let me apologize for the way that most of you were brought in. The simple reason for this was that recent events made you more vulnerable to attack from our enemies. Also, recent events might have made many of you more vulnerable to disease, including the mental and emotional variety. So, we needed to get you into this facility quickly and without resistance on your part. Some of you were drugged, some of you were gassed— and a few lucky ones were simply nicely invited."

The Director shrugged and gave a sheepish smile. A few people in the audience laughed, but not many. The sound of the laughter gave Amelie an excuse to turn and look at the audience, scanning for familiar faces. But everywhere she turned, Amelie saw the flat expressions that she had come to associate with

Academy operatives: flat smiles, flat eyes, flat body stance. Besides Majo, she saw no one she recognized.

"But now that I have apologized for how you were brought here, let me explain *why* you were brought here," the Director continued. "Each of you was recently given a vaccine. We told you that it was an update on the dog flu vaccine, and it was, but that's not all it was. The shot you were given was loaded with a virus—a virus that we here at the Academy created."

There was a soft sound of intake of breath. A small puff of air drifted across Amelie's arms and caused the tiny hairs to tremble.

Then the Director laughed.

"Oh, don't get all panicked on me just yet. The virus that we injected you with was a dormant one. It was designed to be so. It was created to find and insert itself into the junk sections of your DNA. For those who don't have a science background, that means parts of your DNA that scientists think don't code for anything particularly useful. But here at the Academy we have a particular interest in these junk sections of DNA. We think that they may, in fact, be the area where some of your Cambion DNA resides. Your more human body walled it off inside you because it was deemed foreign."

Cambion. Amelie hadn't heard that word spoken aloud since she was recruited here all those years ago.

"As such, we think that the genesis of some of your gifts may lie in these sections of DNA. We created a dormant virus to attach to some of these sections of DNA. Each pod was given a virus designed to attach to different segments of this junk DNA. And then we watched."

"Watched for what?" someone asked from the back of the room. That was a shock, and an obvious plant. A trained Academy operative would not be speaking at this point.

The Director smiled.

"Good question. We hoped that the virus would act on the section of DNA like a grain of sand acts in an oyster, and force expression of something in those seemingly dormant genes."

He began to pace across the stage.

"After they were administered, we watched to see how you were affected. We tested your blood, your stools, and even the CO_2 output in your pods. Then we set about testing the effect on your respective gifts, at least the ones we knew about. Most of those testing scenarios did involve a certain amount of stress. I am sorry for that."

As he said this, he put his hands to his chest and bowed.

"We felt it was worth it because it allowed us to find *you*. For those who are now in the room, the virus produced exactly what we were hoping for. Some of you exhibited a sudden spike in your abilities. Some of you had dramatic changes in your blood work. Some of you had behavioral or personality changes that expanded your psychological repertoire. But whatever way it happened to manifest, it came as a joy to us here at the Academy, and we want to help you develop it and expand it. In short, all of you have now been promoted into the strategic arm of the Academy, with people who share your same unlimited potential."

Develop and expand? How does that work for someone who just showed a change in blood work? Something smells wrong …

She opened her inner eyelid and scanned the room. She found nothing. Not nothing interesting, she found nothing. The room did not change. There were no colors, no symbols. It was unusual to the point of freakish to have such little activity in a room filled with people.

"How will we do that? I mean how will you develop us?" asked one of the plants from the back of the room. The voice rang in her ears with a strange metallic growling quality. It sounded like one sound layered over others at different speeds.

Voices. She had never been able to assess voices before. Her assessment gifts had always been purely visual. If they were right about expanding their gifts, maybe this was something new.

"Well, that's the most exciting thing," the Director said. Amelie glazed her eyes and focused on the sound of his voice, the timbre and resonance of it. She had heard this voice before, she was sure of it.

"But it's not the only exciting thing. How many of you have heard about Verite? Anyone?" the Director asked, scanning the room.

Amelie had the sudden feeling of being assessed. While he wasn't looking directly at her, she felt his presence as if it were knocking at her brain. It was not aggressive; it was soft and seductive. It felt like cream or butter. But after a second of it, a taste hit the back of her mouth. Something bitter and metallic.

Taste now, too?

Some hands must have gone up behind her because the Director smiled and nodded.

"I see a few of you are gamers. For those who don't know, Verite is a video game. What is unique about it, is that it immerses the user completely inside the video matrix. It uses a biometric interface inside helmets and clothes to track people's physical and emotional responses to the game and changes the game experience based on these readings. It is a revolution in the gaming industry, and it has taken the gaming world by storm."

94

He stopped and smiled at them.

"And it was designed by us."

"For what purpose would you use this in the general population?" interrupted a new voice. This one was caustic and less shiny than the voices that had spoken before. Amelie would bet that this one was not a plant.

The Director shrugged slightly.

"To study people. To find people like you. The viral game interface that allows the game to learn and adapt to the user also collects biometric data on each gamer. That data is then collated and sent back to our mainframes. Being able to track this biometric data allows us the possibility to track people who have unusual neurotransmitter markers, unusual heartbeats or who have enough damaged DNA to be at risk of infection by new viruses."

"Why would you need to know this?" asked another shiny voice.

"Because if we know it, then it's likely that others know it as well. I assume most of you have heard of the office and the creatures that run it."

"Kara and Dante," said another shiny voice.

"Yes, Kara and Dante," the Director said, looking down and shaking his head. "I don't want to discuss them in detail right now, because this is a moment of celebration. But we collect information in the hope that we can find people like you before Kara and Dante do. If they find you, they won't take you in. They won't nurture your gifts. They would consider anyone as gifted as all of you to be a danger to their way of life."

"So they would kill us?" someone asked.

"If you are lucky, they would kill you. If you aren't lucky, they unmake your very soul. But let's not dwell on that. Here we will teach you how to avoid them, or even combat them if you are ever unfortunate enough to encounter them."

He shook his head.

"That wasn't a nice topic but at least you all understand how vital it is to get trained. Verite will help with that training."

The Director's voice had deepened and widened in response to the initial unintended question. But now his voice was back to a smooth, gentle cadence, like flowing water.

"Each of you will be trained in your particular gifts. Your body's ability to adapt to and integrate the virus that you were given is also an indication that you will be able to more completely integrate with the Verite system because this system uses a virus to perpetuate the interface."

There was another intake of breath from the audience. Amelie wasn't sure if it was audible to everyone, but it hit her ears like wind.

A virus as an interface. That can't be good. Who was it that told me recently that viruses can jump stories?

"This interface will allow you to fully expand and utilize your mental, spiritual, and emotional gifts in a safe, neutral environment." The Director continued in a voice that sounded like a song. "What is even more exciting is that it can also be used to train your physical self."

The Director crouched down in the middle of the stage. He rubbed his hands together as he stared out at the audience.

"You see, we have discovered that our interface with the game can be upgraded to impact the physical body in all sorts of ways. For example, if you build muscle in your mind by training your body in the game, that code for muscle building can be transferred to your physical body via the viral interface. It sounds complicated, and it is, but in short what it means is that if you get ridiculously fit in the game, your body can be told to do the same in life, without the work."

There was muttering in the audience.

"How? Training takes a long time, even in a game. So why is it any better to do it in a game than in the flesh?" said a shiny voice from the middle of the crowd.

"Ah, but that's the beauty of it," the Director said, his face lighting up as he stood. "In Verite, we have created an alternate time frame. You know how dreams seem like something that happen over hours but in reality is only a few moments. The same is true in Verite. You can spend hours, days, weeks inside the matrix when only minutes pass in your physical body. This is another advantage of using the program to train you. What would take years to train you on in our physical world can be done in weeks with Verite."

He beamed at the crowd.

"You will become more than you ever thought you could become ... maybe even more than you ever dreamed you could become ... and by doing nothing more or less than playing video games for a few weeks."

He laughed and a few laughed with him. Amelie forced herself to smile. She didn't feel like smiling. For some people, expanding their gifts might be appealing. For Amelie, her challenge had always been about *controlling* what she could do, not expanding it. Of course, expansion of her abilities had come as a natural part of the missions she did, but that felt evolutionary. This felt less like evolving to an environment and more like poking a hornet's nest.

"Does anyone have any questions?" the Director asked.

"How long will we be here?" someone asked.

"As long as it takes to train you—at most a month," said the Director.

"That's a relief. I'm not sure I could stand the food for much longer," the shiny voice said, and everyone laughed.

That was a planted comment as well, designed to ease the tension. It didn't do a lot to allay her concerns.

Amelie opened her inner eye again and focused on the Director. But the only colors that came from him were reflections of the room she was in—orange and blue.

She felt suspicion crawling up her back and taking up residence in her shoulders. She stretched her shoulders very gently, to avoid garnering attention.

Maybe she was wrong in her suspicions. After all, the Academy had been good to her. No, it had been more than good to her. It had given her a life, a home, and a family. It had given her a reason to live when she was sorely lacking one. Sure, she didn't trust the Academy per se, but she didn't really trust anything, including herself.

The Director took a few more softball questions and then clapped his hands.

"Okay then, I am sure you are all tired after your respective trips. So I will let you go and explore our little facility. Despite what was said earlier, there are several nice restaurants located on the fourth floor. We have a covered pool on the roof and a sauna. I would only ask that you refrain from going on any floors below ground. That is where we are conducting some of our microbiological experiments and we don't want any outside contamination or contamination of agents."

"We are allowed to go outside?" asked a non-shiny female voice.

"Of course. You aren't prisoners here. We are all still Academy operatives. This is an Academy facility. We are closed to the outside world by geography, as we are on an island, but our world here is completely at your disposal. Oh, and we have lovely tennis and basketball courts outside. There is a beach too, but I dare say it's too cold for swimming at the moment."

There were a few soft mutterings in the crowd. What energy flow existed was trending positive.

"Okay. Before I let you go to discover our cafés, there are some final housekeeping pieces," the Director said, clapping his hands again.

"Over the next few days, you will all begin your training on Verite. If you came with your pod, you will likely be kept with them. If not, you will be assigned to group work in accordance with your talent. I will personally meet with each of you at least once a week. I will meet with your groups once a week as well to give you feedback on your training modules. You represent the top one percent of operatives, so I want to be directly involved in your training. If you have concerns or questions, you can ask your attendant to contact me, and I will reach out to you directly."

"Who is our attendant?" a non-shiny voice asked.

"Oh. Were you not told?" The Director's brow furrowed for a moment. "Your attendants will be both the nurse and orderly who was monitoring you when you came in. You will find their names and numbers in a folder in your apartment when you return. So, before I let you go, let me say again how thrilled and honored I am to be able to work with a group of such talented operatives. I look forward to watching you grow and become."

He bowed.

"Now, go get some real food. The mush they serve you after you wake up is dreadful." He laughed, and walked off the stage.

The audience laughed as the lights came up.

Amelie was just standing up when she felt something like an electric shock hit her body from behind. She turned to find Caio standing about five feet away from her. He was just staring at her. Then his face came alive. So many expressions ran across it in the space of thirty seconds that it was impossible to read and painful to watch.

He took a step forward.

"Amelie?" he said. "It's you."

Of course it's me, you know who I am, Amelie thought. Then a scrap of memory returned to her from her flying. She had seen Caio. He had been in a hole. He had told her … what had he told her?

"It's you, right?" Caio asked. "It was you?"

Amelie nodded. She wasn't exactly sure which context this was asked in, but the nod seemed appropriate.

At that moment Majo came up to her.

"How are you?" Majo asked.

"Tired, dizzy," Amelie said.

"Oh, poor honey," Majo said, and leaned forward to give her an uncharacteristic hug. As she did so, she whispered in her ear.

"We can't talk here. Over half the people in this room aren't human."

Chapter Thirteen

Verite

"So this place is a trip, right? Decent coffee though." James sat down next to Amelie.

Amelie, Majo, and Caio had located Widget shortly after they left the auditorium. That wasn't hard, as he was always one of the tallest people in any given room. James was always easy to find as well, as he was usually the loudest. They had agreed to test the café on the fourth floor. It was located in a small nook tucked into one corner of the building. Plush sofas and soft lighting made it look cozy, welcoming, and discreet. None of them were fooled by this. Places like this were an attractive nuisance, promoting dangerous intimacy. So, as they chatted, none of them said much about anything of substance.

"I met a few interesting agents," Majo said, gently stirring her tea with a swizzle stick. "One was a lady that James and I met years ago. One of our exorcism patients from Mexico."

It was the lack of any sustained eye contact between James and Majo during this exchange that told Amelie that there was more to this story than was being presented. Majo would know that Amelie would notice, so it was probably for her benefit.

"That wouldn't have been Gabriella, would it?" James asked, sipping his coffee.

"Yes, it was," Majo said.

"Yeah, I thought I saw someone who reminded me of her. It's surprising, but it shouldn't be. She was very talented."

Majo nodded. She dropped her hand slowly down by her side, eyes focused on James now. Majo shook her hand gently, as if stretching it. As Amelie watched, she began to sign, her hand hidden from view by the two padded chairs.

"Gabriella was supposed to be possessed but it turned out she was a spirit in a non-human body," Majo signed. "I saw the spirit in another body."

A non-human body? What the hell was that? Amelie thought.

Widget sat back in his chair slowly and crossed one leg over his knee.

"Does Gabriella happen to speak in sign language?" Widget signed. "It doesn't seem that many people do."

"I wouldn't be so sure about that, mate." James laughed. "Besides, that shouldn't keep you from getting laid, you Viking god."

Widget smiled.

Caio had spent this time with his eyes on his coffee. He was much more tense than she had ever seen him before. Every now and then, he would sneak a glance at her. But now, he looked up at all of them.

"The Academy has more than a few mind readers in its ranks, so I'm sure you won't have trouble finding someone to communicate with," he said.

Shit. Mind readers. Of course they would have those here.

Amelie threw a cover of static thoughts over the top of her brain. She saw Majo blink slowly as she took a sip of her tea. Her energy pattern dimmed significantly. All around their table, their energy signatures changed. Everyone got the memo.

And Caio risked himself again by alerting us. Why would he do that? He told me that he wouldn't. Wait. When did he say that? He had been in the hallway. Shit, I was flying again. I was in the hallway.

Now that she remembered that, their conversation came flooding back. And he had known this when he saw her in the auditorium. Something had changed. But he hadn't known before, she felt sure of that. She needed to ask him, but they couldn't speak here. Amelie wasn't sure where they would be free to speak. She concentrated on the tea she was holding.

Amelie was sitting next to Widget, and she felt him move his thigh until it was touching hers. He was connecting to her, stabilizing her, so that she could read the room.

She opened her inner eye fully and the room around her came alive with colors, but only in small patches. Some groups in the coffee shop were buzzing with color and energy but others were barely registering. These had less energy output than hibernating insects. Amelie looked back to her pod.

James was unusually calm; he was not fidgeting or twitching. He was simply sipping his coffee silently. This meant he was on edge. Majo's eyes were flicking around the room. Widget was still but poised. Each of them knew a threat when they felt it, but they were at a loss to identify the exact nature of it or where it was coming from.

Only Caio sat with his head down. He was chewing his fingernail and not even trying to hide his discomfort.

"I see you found your friends," a voice exploded behind her. Amelie whirled to find Camp beaming at her.

James choked on his coffee and began coughing uncontrollably.

"Breathe through your nose," Majo muttered to him.

"What are you doing here?" Caio asked Camp sharply. His face was registering disgust, and he wasn't trying to hide it.

"I'm Amelie's training facilitator," Camp said, her smile broadening.

"So, you ... two know each ... other, then?" James asked.

"Yes, we've had the pleasure of meeting," Camp laughed. "I've been involved with some of Caio's training over the years. I try to keep my finger on the pulse of what's going on here, as difficult as that can be at times. If the walls could talk ..."

"They would probably scream," Caio said, finishing her sentence. Camp gave him a momentary look of shock but then laughed.

"But if there is one thing I always make a point of, it's getting to know all the attractive men."

"Counts me out," James muttered.

"Oh lamb, don't underestimate yourself. I certainly don't," Camp said, winking at James. The look on James's face wasn't hard to read. It was open disgust.

"Don't you have somewhere to be? I mean somewhere that's not here," Caio said coldly.

"Of course, I am just here to pick up Amelie to start her training," Camp said, motioning to Amelie. "Your facilitators will be along to collect you shortly."

"How do they know where we are?" Caio asked bluntly.

"Oh, don't worry. They can find you wherever you are. You have geolocation in your suits," Camp said, as Amelie stood up.

"Because there's no door or window you guys can't crawl through, right?" Caio said to Camp, but his eyes were on Amelie.

Door. When he said the word *door*, it was shiny in her ears.

"Come along, love. Let's introduce you to Verite," Camp said, taking Amelie by the arm.

Her touch felt unnervingly like Novocain.

***

Amelie was sitting on her bed. Camp had instructed her to make herself comfortable there while she set up Verite. Camp herself was now standing across the room, fiddling with a panel on the wall.

"What is that?" Amelie asked.

"This? Oh, this is just the game setting for your room. It makes sure to set the parameters of your game so that if you get up and move around, you won't run into anything. Walls and features will be set up in the game, so it will help you avoid them."

"Am I expected to get up and move around then?" Amelie asked.

"No, not yet and maybe not ever. It depends on how synched up you are with your physical body and how comfortable you are operating only inside your head. Some people tend to stand up and wander around. That's why, for this first test of Verite, we want you to be alone in your room. We want to see how you will react in an environment that is more contained and more personal. If you tend to start wandering out of rooms, it's good to know that now, while you are in a locked room," Camp said, as she finished adjusting the buttons on the panel and closed it.

Amelie heard a metallic quality to Camp's voice and opened her inner eye, but she saw nothing but undulating streams of gray and lavender. It didn't feel like a warning, but it didn't feel like assurance either.

"So how does this work?" Amelie asked, watching the energy pattern for changes.

"You will go into Verite, and the game will begin reading you. To be honest, the first few times people go in, it's usually boring. I think the game has to learn you. Someone said the first few times was like playing Pong but later it's like a whole new life."

"Does it read my mind?"

"No, lamb, it's not a mind-reading device," Camp laughed. "No one has invented a device that can read minds yet, only certain people can do that. What it does is analyze your body's responses, and sometimes that can indicate what you feel or think. So, if your pupils dilate, the camera in the mask will pick that up, and the game will know that you saw something you like."

"How will this train what gifts I have?" Amelie asked.

"I have no idea," Camp replied, but a cloud of dark lumpy light fell from her mouth as she said this.

"Have you been in the game?"

"Oh, I go in all the time," Camp said, with a huge crocodile smile. "Don't get me wrong, I'm not a big gamer but Verite is completely different, and the sex is great."

She crossed the room and handed Amelie what looked like long black underwear, exactly like what she was already wearing.

102

"What is this?"

"It's your digital interface with the game," Camp replied.

"It looks like what I am already wearing," Amelie said.

"Yes, we start you with a trainer suit. From this point onward, you will only wear the interface suits. We found that they are warm enough and comfortable enough to use as everyday clothes."

"Don't they get dirty?"

"Oh, you will have a new one every day." Camp smiled.

"You need to undress completely and then put the new suit on. I'll step out for a moment while you get into it. Just let me know when it's on."

Camp then stepped out of the bedroom and into the hall without another word.

Amelie studied the leggings and long-sleeved top she was given. It was light and silky. She couldn't see anything like wires or sensors anywhere in it. She sniffed it, looking for that metallic smell of technology but what she smelled was more like baby powder. She opened her inner eye but saw nothing. That wasn't terribly surprising, it was hard to get reads on non-living things.

She slipped out of her clothes and threw them on the chair in the corner. She had just put on the new clothes when Camp returned to the room. She was carrying something metallic silver in her hands.

"What's that?" Amelie asked.

"It's your interface helmet," Camp replied. There was a single circle of metal and from it smaller branches emerged and leafed out in multiple directions, connecting and reconnecting until it formed a light halo of metal around her head. Some of the branches wrapped around and supported eyeglass lenses. In truth, it looked disturbingly like a crown of thorns with goggles attached. It also reminded her of the deer head that used to hang in her family's living room.

"It doesn't look anything like the helmets I have seen people using when playing the game," Amelie said.

"It's the new model," Camp said.

Before Amelie could say anything else, Camp placed the helmet on Amelie's head. Given the size and shape of it, Amelie had expected it to be heavy at least and painful at worst. It was neither. The sharp edges were flexible and soft. They touched her at different spots on her head and forehead, but gently, without pressure or friction.

"It's so light," she commented.

"Of course. If you had to wear a heavy helmet, it would distract you from the game. And part of the point of the game is that you have to feel like you are really there. You know, I suspect that part of what they are doing with you in particular is testing how exactly you do the things they know you can do."

"You mean how I attract people?"

"Exactly."

"Great."

"Don't worry, they won't throw anything too difficult at you … particularly in the beginning," Camp said, as she checked bits of the helmet. "It's actually really creative. If you go in with the right mindset, you can help shape the world inside. But this first time, it's just about level setting. Of course, if you see anything interesting, we will want to know."

Camp smiled at her, and that taste hit the back of her mouth again—the metallic one.

"So in you go," Camp said, flipping a switch on the side of the goggles. This caused a film to cover the eyepieces. Then everything faded to black.

***

At first, Amelie saw nothing. Then she saw only white around her, as if she were staring at a blank movie screen. Normally, Amelie had an aversion to the color white. White was the color of snobbish swans, wedding dresses, and the teeth of TV weathermen. White was a cold color, like the light of distant stars. It was the color of things she never had, never was, and would never be.

Amelie looked down to find that she could see her body. She scraped a nail across the skin of her arm, and she felt it, just as if she was in her physical body. It was weird and unnerving.

She took a step forward. At first, she hadn't been sure that she could move in this space, but she could. She turned and looked around her. Everything looked white, except for one area. On her right, there was a rectangular space that was whiter than the white around it. As Amelie got closer, the difference between the shades of pale became more apparent.

It looked like a white door in the snow.

Doors. Caio had put emphasis on that word.

Amelie stepped toward it and, after a second of hesitation, through it. She wasn't sure what she was expecting, but the space she was in now was identical to where she had just been, except the white surrounding her now felt different. It felt less like a color and more like a template—like it was waiting to become something.

The moment this thought entered her brain, she felt a breeze ripple through her hair and with it came a familiar smell. It was the smell of tar and gasoline and pine trees, cut with a momentary scent of mown grass and flowers. It was the smell of summer. No, it was the smell of summer from her youth in North Carolina. The sound of cicadas followed next, filling the space around her with their longing, tragic song.

The white space around her then began to fill up with lines and colors, connecting and disconnecting with each other in no particular order or pattern, just a random jumble of shapes appearing and disappearing. Amelie walked forward among the splashes of color and sounds of insects. Something hit her arm and she jumped. A bloated gray line had fallen at her feet. As she watched, it filled out and twisted, adding more lines and blurry, interchanging shades of gray. The harder she looked, the more it took shape until she recognized it as one of the very cicadas she had been hearing. She laughed, and the sound of her own laugh in this space shocked her. When she looked up, she was even more shocked.

The lines and colors had now arranged themselves into an Escher-like depiction of her old high school. She was standing just in front of the landing, which was very present and quite solid. The building behind it needed some work. The entrance to the building was present and recognizable, if a bit blurry, and some of the windows were a reasonable facsimile of what they had been. But one window to the right looked like a white hole. Another to the left resembled a petaled flower, soft, fragranced, and alive, more than a window. Amelie smiled to herself. She preferred this flower window to the real thing. The moment she thought this, several more flower windows appeared in the building. They no longer looked exactly like biological flowers and more like the stained-glass equivalent.

As all this was taking place, the space around Amelie had filled up with individual streaks of color. If she looked at one streak long enough, lines would begin to fill in enough so that she could make out a person. Around her on the landing, she saw smear of pastel blue and brown. As she stared, she began to be able to make out skittering, frightened movements on the inside of this blur of color. Without knowing how, she knew that it was her schoolmate Elodie. Near her was another smear of darker blue and black in which sparkling bits seethed and rolled in the motion of a storm. Amelie knew this to be Judith.

Seeing any form of Judith was enough to get Amelie off the landing.

Despite what Camp had said to her about Verite not being able to read minds, it certainly seemed like the system was pulling this scene directly from her memories. Amelie certainly wasn't feeding it in any way ... or was she? Had something reminded her, ever so briefly, of her high school experience and that had triggered this? Maybe the sound she had heard when she first entered, the cicada sound, was not really a cicada sound. Maybe that was just the memory that it had invoked in her and this was what was coming from it. The more she thought about it, the more that made sense. If the interface was as elegant as they claimed, then it might be able to recreate her memories simply by using plus and minus biofeedback cues. That would be an incredibly elegant system, but the Academy was known for being way ahead of the curve in biology and tech.

Amelie decided to test this theory. As she walked toward the back of the auditorium, which was actually the entrance to it, she let her mind wander to-ward unpleasant memories. She thought of the horrible bestial look on Jack's face all those years ago, when he was holding her friend Hudson over the ledge of parking lot, above the thirty-foot drop. As these thoughts entered her head, color smears inserted themselves near the exact spot behind the auditorium where this had happened. She turned her head away from this scene, but not before the memory of the attack suddenly inserted itself in her head and in that instant a smear of multicolor appeared on the steps of the entrance to the audi-torium, a smear that was quickly assaulted by two other smears appearing from behind her.

They had pushed her up against the wall just there, just at the spot where the multicolored smear was now dimming.

"Enough," Amelie said out loud, and these images began to fade in front of her eyes, but not fast enough for her. There were too many memories in this moment for her ... too much mixed emotion.

Amelie walked quickly away from this place and toward the parking lot. Around her, more streaks of color roughly in the shape of people moved past her, as if they were being blown by a summer breeze. If she didn't focus on them, then that seemed to be what they remained, simply streaks of color.

Amelie rounded the far side of the auditorium. As she did so, she saw the fuzzy outline of a lone car parked in the teachers' parking lot. There was a figure sitting in the driver's seat. The figure was clearer and more defined than the other streaky figures around her. It was formed enough for her to see that it was Mr. Sawyer. She moved toward him, despite herself. The closer she got, the more he materialized. At first, she could only see his outline and basic shape but as she stepped closer, features began to appear on his face. They were indistinct at first but with each step they came more into focus. She was so busy watching this clarity of features appear that she failed to notice his expression until she was already almost upon him. His eyes were closed, and his mouth was open. In horror, she turned away but not before seeing that his hand was moving frantically in his lap.

Amelie moved away, if not at a trot, then at a quick walk. She was just slowing down when she came around the other side of the auditorium, where the landing again came into view. What she saw there brought her to a full stop.

There were two people standing on the landing. Not two streaks of color or two outlines of people, but two clearly defined and fully formed creatures. Facing her was a beautiful woman with white-blonde hair and a heart-shaped face that held unnaturally large sapphire-blue eyes. She looked more anime than human. Her 1950s-style, white swing dress added to that effect. Next to her was a dark-skinned man, tall and thin, but broad across the chest and shoulders. On his head he had an unusually tall but dingy black stovepipe hat with a maroon band. His trousers were black and tight with an actual codpiece on top of them. His appearance was unusual, but it was his movements that were completely out of place. As the woman tapped her foot, he reached out to caress her arm. His movements were slow and languid and yet occasionally jerky, as if frames had been cut from a film. Also, something about the way he stroked her arm made this innocent movement radiate with sexuality. The woman stopped tapping and gave him a small smile.

Dante, Amelie thought. *So that must be Kara with him. But how could I create her? How would I know what she looks like?*

Suddenly her brain shifted, and an image was pulled from her deep memory. An image of the woman that had held her close in the mental institution all those years ago. The woman who had helped her control her curse. The woman who had protected her from the staff and doctors. The woman who Amelie was sure had paid for her schooling.

This was the same woman. This woman had been her angel. Kara. The one everyone said was a monster.

"When did he contact you?" Kara asked Dante.

"Two days ago, just as I told you," Dante replied.

"Did he contact you before or after we had decided to come find her?"

"After," Dante said, "but I don't think he had access to that decision. I think it's just coincidence. I saw the girl in the library a few days before. I suspect she told him that she saw me."

"Why would he be interested in this girl?" Kara asked. "I wouldn't think high school girls were his thing. And why should I listen to anything he has to say anyway? He's dangerous and an outlier and we both know it. If he's this close, why don't I simply unmake him and be done with it?"

"I don't think you could catch him, my love," Dante replied. "We've tried to unmake him at close quarters before, but his thought patterns are simply too fast to latch onto."

Kara snorted.

"Well, one thing we know is that this place has a serious infestation," Dante said, pointing toward the back of the auditorium. Amelie followed the line of his finger and, near the base of the building, saw black shadows creeping and rolling.

Suddenly, as if out of nowhere, a third man appeared in front of them. Amelie gasped and immediately covered her mouth.

The creature in front of them was dressed like a high school boy, with a black T-shirt, khaki shorts, and black trainers. He looked about seventeen or eighteen, with pale skin and shaggy black hair. But that was where his similarity to any high schooler ended. The body of the boy was perfect. In fact, even from the back he was so beautiful that he was hard to look at. Amelie wasn't sure if that was how he appeared to everyone else, but it was certainly how he appeared to her.

Clovis.

"Looks like someone hasn't been doing their job," Clovis said with a laugh that was dark and mirthless. "This place is a viral pigsty."

"Those are not always viruses—not that this is any of your business," Kara replied. "I'm actually surprised you are concerned about it, given your disregard for hygiene or even safety."

As Kara spoke, she moved closer to Clovis. Her eyes were so blue that Amelie could see them at this distance. Or maybe that's because they seemed to have begun glowing.

"So why did you want to see us?" Dante said, placing a restraining hand on Kara.

"Come on, Dante. I know why you're interested in this little school. And you know that I know. You talked to Amelie, and you got enough information out of her to trace her back to me. So you know there is a connection there."

Dante nodded.

"So, what I want to know, is what you know about her, and what you are planning to do," Clovis said, crossing his arms over his chest.

Kara cocked her head and smiled unpleasantly.

"That's also not your business, is it? You must think very highly of yourself to think that you have any right to know anything about our actions."

Her voice sounded like tiny shards of broken glass falling on a metal plate. There was a murmuring sound in the air.

Clovis laughed as he moved to go sit on the railing of the landing. This was the first time his face was visible to her, and it took her breath away.

"I don't know about that, Kara," Clovis was saying, "but I do think highly enough of myself to believe that I can probably keep Amelie off your radar for the rest of her natural life, if it comes to that."

Suddenly the air was filled with flashing colors and symbols, mostly in languages that Amelie had never known or even imagined. She quickly clamped her inner eye shut but this only muted the symbols rather than stopping them. She could feel an electric tension causing her arms to goosebump.

"Yes, you probably can," Dante finally said. "But that begs the question of why you would want to and exactly why you are here."

"I'm here because I *could* keep her off your radar, but that would be tiring. And it certainly wouldn't be any fun for me," Clovis replied.

"And you are all about the fun, right?" said Kara. Her voice had turned flat.

"That's what you would think of me, so that's what I give you. But the reason I contacted Dante is because I think I can help you. You are searching for her because you think she is the source of the recent viruses, the dog flu and mouse virus, am I right?"

Kara's face became stony, and Dante smiled slightly.

"Yes, we do," said Dante.

"Well, you're right. She is the source of them, or at least some of them. But what you may not know is that she brought these viruses back directly from the hallway."

"What?" said Kara.

"Yes, she can get into the hallway. And she can bring things back from stories into our story."

"If that's true then you surely understand why she has to be unmade," said Dante softly.

"In theory, yeah," Clovis said, "but if you unmake her, what proof do you have that she will not be remade in exactly the same fashion eventually. And I know you will say that you will deal with that when it happens, but suppose you didn't have to? Suppose there was a way to fix it permanently, without unmaking her?"

"If such a thing were possible, we would know about it, and we would have already done it," Dante replied.

"Not necessarily. You wouldn't acknowledge it if it went against your perception of your world. You wouldn't know if it was alien to the structure of this story," Clovis replied. He was kicking his foot against the bricks of the landing but kept his eyes trained on Kara.

"And you know how to do such a thing?" Dante asked.

"Yeah, I do," Clovis replied.

"How would you know what we don't?" asked Kara.

"Because I can go places that you can't," Clovis replied softly, "and I remember things you don't."

Before Amelie could hear any more, everything around her began to pale. For the briefest of moments, Clovis turned and caught her eye.

Then the crown was lifted off her head and Camp's less than lovely face obscured her view.

Chapter Fourteen

Drooling and Coding

"I'm sorry, lamb, there seems to be a glitch in this thing," Camp said, peering at the headpiece as she moved it back and forth.

Amelie said nothing. She was concentrating on her breathing. This thing could pick up vitals and she was sure hers were all over the place.

She had just seen Clovis. He had been talking about her. She didn't know if that was real or not, but it wasn't a memory. She had never seen that before. How would she have access to it? Was it something she made up? No, she didn't have any of that information in her brain.

Camp had crossed the room and opened the control panel again.

"Sometimes these things can get a bit testy when we use them in the rooms. That's probably the reason that it didn't boot up," she muttered.

She thinks it didn't even boot.

"How long should it take before it boots up ... normally?" Amelie asked out loud.

"Well, usually it boots up in milliseconds, but I did give you a good thirty seconds, and nothing," Camp said.

"Nothing, as in no readings?"

"No, no readings, no displays of brain waves, no nothing. Wait, did you see anything?" Camp asked, face still in the control board.

"I saw white," Amelie said. It was true, so easy to say, even in her state.

"Yeah, that's what I thought. Oh, wait. Stupid me, the router hadn't been changed. You were on the wrong circuit." Camp pressed some buttons on the display.

"That was just me being stupid," she said, coming back toward Amelie, grinning sheepishly. But the grin did not sit comfortably on her face.

"If someone asks you, I'd appreciate if you didn't mention this little moment of stupidity," Camp said softly.

Amelie forced herself to smile and nod. "No problem."

"We really didn't need to start you today. I was just a bit overeager to show you the system," Camp said, trying for an embarrassed smile but ending up with something that looked much more predatory.

"So, tell you what, why don't you go out, do a bit of exploring, and we can start all this again tomorrow morning, when all the new recruits are plugged in?"

Camp said this in a bit of a jumbled rush. Her breath was coming quicker, and her movements were jerkier. She was clearly excited about something, but Amelie couldn't ascertain what.

She opened her inner eye and saw nothing. It wasn't really nothing, it was more like seeing things with a soft-focus lens. This jogged a memory for her. This had happened before recently. She scanned her memory quickly, but she couldn't find it. Her brain just kept jumping back to the visual of Clovis standing on the walkway.

"So I'll see you first thing tomorrow morning to set up again. I promise that I will have all the bugs out of the system before then. Okay?" Camp said, coming over to Amelie and patting her on the arm.

Her touch felt flat and dead. In the back of her throat, Amelie tasted metal again. She forced herself to smile and nod.

Camp smiled back at her then turned to walk out the door, but not before Amelie saw a strange green light drip from her downcast eyes.

Once Camp had left, Amelie scanned the room. She then stood up and began pacing. The image on the floor was now of sand. That sand looked mostly normal … mostly was the operative word. In spots, the image of the sand looked hard and cracked, but with mud and moisture leaking around the cracks. The visual might not have been quicksand, but that was where Amelie's mind went, and it was disturbing. She doubted this visual was accidental.

Despite the warm ambience and tone of the Director's welcome, none of the other parts of this experience felt welcoming.

But Clovis. I saw Clovis.

Suddenly, a sentence inserted itself in her head.

Get away from him now.

Amelie stopped in her tracks. She remembered where she had heard that voice in her head and where she had seen that soft-focus look before. It had been with Ossian Reese. He had had that muted energy pattern. She had also seen shades of green smoke dripping from his mouth.

He had been possessed—and he had come for her.

Amelie threw down her shields and took a deep breath. It was more important than ever to leave the room and check out her surroundings.

She suspected it would be a good idea to identify avenues of escape.

***

As she left her room, Amelie considered trying to find other members of her pod but ruled out that idea. It was easier to be anonymous if she was alone, even given her particular challenges with that. Over the years, she had perfected the art of draining her energy to the point that she could not only dampen her attractiveness to others, but she could also even dampen the recognition of her existence for short periods of time. She had done this exercise just as she left her room because it gave her a greater chance of moving unnoticed and unhindered through her new environment.

Amelie began her tour looking for what she was most interested in—avenues of escape. Her room was in a building that seemed to consist entirely of apartments. At one end of each corridor was a staircase, which led only to upper and lower levels. There was no roof access or basement access. The other end of all the corridors opened onto a large round atrium area that was eight stories high. All the walls in this area were windows, but right now she could see nothing but gray mist. Directly across the atrium was another corridor leading to the auditorium. To the left was a corridor with a sign next to it indicating that it would lead to restaurants, cafés, and other forms of entertainment. There were no emergency or fire doors anywhere in sight. Clearly this was a private, secret facility that was not being inspected by any health and security agency.

As Amelie descended the stairs toward the atrium, she reviewed the Director's presentation in her mind. Everything he said had been designed to make them feel special, elite, and cherished. Amelie didn't doubt his words. She was sure that he did consider them special and that he probably did cherish them, but this didn't mean that he had their best interests at heart. They had been injected with an experimental man-made virus without their knowledge or consent. According to the Director, they were injected with this virus to trigger latent abilities, but this didn't track with what happened to them. Caio's ability to talk to ghosts had not been latent, he had simply been hiding it from the Academy. However, it did seem to be enhancing some of her abilities, such as expanding her predictive senses from only visions to hearing, taste, and smell. The fact that the virus in question would also integrate them into the video game Verite was unnerving, to say the least. Then there was the fact, according to her senses and Majo's sight, that many of the people they had seen were not even people. What were these things, if not human? And were these non-people brought in with them, or were they already here? Did the virus they were given have the ability to change the spiritual nature of its host? Was the Academy planning to turn them into non-people as well? She couldn't process what that meant for them because she had too little information.

Amelie had always known that the Academy might decide to retire her at any given point. This wasn't hidden or questioned, so she had planned for it the best she could. She had money hidden in various accounts she had created over the years. Her missions with the underworld-type had given her access to people beyond her target. Without the Academy's knowledge, she had glamoured and groomed some of these people just in case things with the Academy took a bad turn. Even given this, she had never deluded herself about her chances of success. Hiding the Academy for any length of time would take all of her abilities and a flawless attention to detail at all times. Honestly, she had always given herself a fifty-fifty chance of surviving for five years. But escaping with her entire pod would up her odds. She was sure that the others must have done similar planning. If she added that to their collective abilities, she gave them a good eighty percent chance of surviving for five years. It would have been better if they had known of this and executed an escape while they were still in London. She had no idea what her chances of escape were from this place, but it was certainly less than it was before. So she would do her part and use her intellect and gifts to find out as much as she could about where they were before she met up with the others.

As Amelie walked through the corridors to the atrium, she discreetly scanned the people around her—and there were lots of people. People smiling, laughing, and talking and yet something was very wrong. Only about twenty-five percent of these people had normal energy levels. Amelie gauged this by the strength of the colors that came off them when she opened her inner eye. Most normal people were surrounded by colors that looked like a highlighter had marked over their bodies. But most of the people here had colors that were ridiculously pale, like watercolors with too much water. She also noticed that these pale people didn't smell right either, according to her new "inner nose." The people that she met who had normal color signatures had the same normal type of smell, a bit like a mix between warm bread and earth. It wasn't an unpleasant smell, if fact, it smelled like life. The people with the pale signatures also had pale smells. They smelled like flowers in hospital rooms. They smelled faint, sweet, and sickly.

Looking out the window, Amelie saw that all the buildings seemed to be connected via covered walkways or balconies. She moved easily from one area to another. There seemed to be no locked doors and no restricted areas. That being said, she also didn't find any exits. On the first floor of the atrium, she noticed a man dressed in navy overalls stepping out from one of one of the corridors with living quarters. He was pushing a cart filled with linens that looked like bedsheets.

Amelie followed him at a distance. Wherever he was going, it was unlikely that it would be through normal "guest" corridors. He rolled the cart through the atrium and then through a small, camouflaged door just next to the entrance to one of the restaurants. Amelie waited until he was through and then moved with purpose to the door. She expected it to be locked but the door opened with ease.

She stepped through the doorway into a long tunnel with hanging fluorescent lights. The walls were gray ceramic tiles, and the floor was concrete. It smelled of chalk and old water. She could see no one in front of her. The man she had been following was nowhere in sight. She walked quietly down the hallway, sending out runners of energy to feel for people, but she felt nothing.

As she approached a junction in the hallway, she slowed down. She heard no one but saw that there were elevators at the junction. They were large industrial elevators and instead of buttons to press to call the elevator, there was a spot for a key. There were also rooms that lined the wall across from these elevators. Amelie had learned that to raise the least suspicion, it was best to look like you belonged somewhere. So rather than skulking down the hallway, she strode purposefully, her eyes mostly forward, but scanning her periphery. All the rooms in this hallway had both windows and doors. Some of the windows were tinted black. The untinted ones revealed lab benches and equipment.

As she came to the end of this corridor, she noticed that one room on the right had a door that was ajar. She walked past it quickly. Her eyes told her that it was empty. Her colors and senses said the same, so she pulled up a large ball of energy and released it down the empty hall. This would make her as invisible as possible. While the room might not be occupied, there could be surveillance footage, so it was better to be unobtrusive. She could always say that she followed the maintenance man looking for help and got lost. It wasn't far from the truth.

Amelie then returned to the room and stuck her head in the door. What she saw was perplexing. While there were many of the normal accoutrements of a lab, computers, beakers, test tubes, and microscopes, there were things that she couldn't identify. For one, there were four or five lab benches that were covered with one of the strangest substances she had ever seen. It seemed to be some kind of gel, but it was a mostly transparent violet color. It looked like someone had found a way to capture clouds. Around the periphery of each of these benches were racks of test tubes.

Amelie moved slowly into the room, trying to avoid touching anything. As she examined the captured clouds, she noticed that some of them had streaks of light red. She examined the test tubes that were next to one of these. They were filled with a red substance that looked a bit like blood but was lighter. She leaned in closer to one tube that was facing her, so that she wouldn't have to turn it. On the tube was a number and the name J. Winston. Something about this made her skin crawl.

Suddenly, she heard a voice and froze. She moved quickly to an area of the room that wasn't in line of sight from the window. The sound of footsteps approached but, to her relief, passed the room and moved on. Clearly it wasn't safe to snoop much longer, and it wasn't likely she would find an exit without much more time to explore.

She was just about to leave the room when one of the test tubes caught her eye. Her inner eye opened and the test tube lit up like a flare. Amelie moved to it and leaned down to examine it. When she saw the name, she felt her blood run cold.

The sticker on the vial read S. Chappell.

Sophie Chappell

Suddenly, the memories of flying came crashing back into her head: Sophie on the beach, the woman with solar panels for a face, the mutated fish with human arms and the little girl thrown into the water to be eaten by similar mutations. Sophie being told that something "better" was waiting for her.

And the Director overseeing all of it.

Amelie's heart was slamming in her chest, but only amateurs gave in to fear. Professionals suppressed it. Academy operatives used it. Amelie took the fear that she felt and compressed it into a little ball. She buried this behind her eyes, which allowed her to see with greater detail and retention. She looked back at the red-tinged cloud. She could see that all the red streaks branching through the matrix came from one dot of red near the surface. It split into two, and then four and so on until the bottom of the cloud was thick with them although they were so dispersed by that point that it was almost impossible to distinguish them but for a slight change in color.

There were sixteen vials of blood, next to the gel matrix. All sixteen had Sophie's name on it. When Amelie looked at the counter across from the lab bench, there were many, many more, all similarly labeled. She suddenly remembered the host that she had been inside when she was flying had suggested that

Sophie might have "absorbed some pieces that would accelerate the overall substrate" or something like that. She had then told the Director that they should send Sophie to "coding." Looking at all the vials with Sophie's name on it, the word coding took on a significantly more sinister connotation.

Amelie had learned much more than she expected here. Not from her surroundings but from the fact that it triggered her own memories. She was now certain that they weren't safe here, and the danger was far worse than simple death. She needed to find a way to tell her pod. She turned quickly and walked purposefully out of the room and down the hall the way she had come. Just as she passed the elevator, it pinged, and the doors opened. Out of it came a man. This was not the man she had been following. He was only a couple of steps out of it when he saw Amelie.

At the sight of her, his mouth dropped open. He was a tall man with black hair and pale skin. His bone structure was fine and elegant, but his expression was not. He looked at her with flat brown eyes that didn't seem to blink.

"Hi, do you work here?" Amelie asked, preparing the details of her "lost" story in her head.

The man said nothing but began shuffling toward her.

"I'm sorry," Amelie said, stepping backward. "My retinal scanner to my room isn't working, so I was just trying to find someone to fix it."

She smiled and shrugged.

When she smiled, the man lurched toward her. Amelie turned to run but it was too late. The man grabbed her and shoved her up against the wall.

"Huuuuuhhhhh," he said, his flat eyes now completely trained on her face. His hands were squeezing her upper arms, but she felt no desire coming from him. Despite that, he pressed his wet lips to hers, and began grinding his crotch against hers. There was no passion in this at all. It was like she was being molested by a cardboard box. Disgust mixed with the anger Amelie was already feeling. If she had been in possession of her curare ring, she would have killed him. As it was, she pushed him hard with energy, simultaneously shoving her knee into his groin. He doubled over at the same time she heard a sharp voice from behind her.

"Roger, you leave that lady alone right now!" a male voice yelled.

The man, apparently an orderly named Roger, cringed when he heard the voice, dropped, and curled into a ball on the ground, covering his head.

Amelie turned to find herself face-to-face with a tall, pale man with gray hair, cut military short. It was hard to determine his age. He was wearing a white button-down shirt and gray slacks. His face looked like he was in his thirties, but the hair looked more like he would be in his fifties. He had a name tag that simply said *Monsees*. Amelie didn't know if that was a first or last name.

"You really shouldn't be here, miss," the man said, taking her gently by the arm and leading her back down the corridor. "This is a prohibited area."

"I'm sorry," Amelie said in a flurried rush. "My retinal scan didn't work, and I saw him. I thought he was maintenance and could help me. He went through this door. It wasn't locked, so I thought it was okay. Besides, the Director said to avoid the below-ground floors. This is ground floor, so I thought it was okay. I didn't realize ..."

She stopped and made herself shudder.

"Roger should have locked the door behind him," the man said. "And he should not have been fraternizing with agents. I will have a discussion with him about this."

Roger was apparently going to catch it. For a moment, Amelie felt a twinge of guilt but then remembered his soggy lips on hers and that guilt disappeared.

Monsees walked Amelie down the hall to the door, opened it and walked her out into the atrium.

"The quickest way to get your retinal scan reset is to ask at the reception desk," the man said. "The quickest way to get there is to go through the auditorium. The door on the far side opens to a walkway that leads to the reception building. Are you okay or do you need me to walk you there?"

His words were a bit patronizing, but Amelie suspected this was his definition of chivalry.

Amelie let herself pause for a bit. Then she smiled.

"No, that's okay. I've dealt with worse," she said.

Then the man actually laughed. It softened the hard lines of his face.

"Of course you are fine. You are an operative. I keep forgetting that. In my day, we—" he stopped, and his eyes widened. He ran his hand over his cropped hair. "Well, there were more fellas in this agency. I mean, we always had ladies, but they were usually—well, they weren't ..."

"It's okay. I take no offense," Amelie said, laying her hand on his arm. The energy that came from him was strong and real. But the colors that came from him were navy blue, and yellow streaked with red. This was a primary colors kind of guy. There would be no shades of gray with him.

The man's eyes widened a bit with her touch, then he nodded and turned away.

Amelie wondered what sort of mental gymnastics this man must be doing to justify what was happening here. Or was he kept in the dark about the sort of things she had seen on the beach?

One thing was for certain, the Director was the instigator.

This place was worse than evil. It was evil that fostered indifference within its ranks to anything and everything. So it could then get away with anything and everything. She had been a willing part of it for almost twenty years.

And she and her pod were stuck on an island with no way off.

Chapter Fifteen

Unwanted Reunions

Amelie quickly made her way through the auditorium toward reception. If there was a reception area there, then it meant they received people. It would allow her to both solidify her story of needing to get maintenance to fix her retinal scan, and search for exits to the building. Her head was reeling with the memories of the things she had seen while flying. She couldn't allow herself to think of that right now. She needed to stay in the here and now so that she wouldn't misstep. Instead, she focused on the more immediate, and slightly less horrifying, things she had just learned.

What the fuck is going on with a mentally disabled guy at an Academy base? Since when is the Academy an equal opportunity employer? Since never. The Academy is more Gattaca than ADA.

On the other side of the auditorium, Amelie came to yet another enclosed walkway but this one ended in a much different room. This was a large wood-paneled room that looked like a combination of a reception room and library. It had a vaulted ceiling, and the walls were bookshelves lined with books. The floors were waxed wood and would have been easy to slide on if her thin slippers had not had rubber soles. There were also numerous paintings on display. There were works by Pollock, Turner, Cezanne, and Goya. At least the paintings were in the style of these artists, but she did not recognize the exact works of art. She had been here before but not as herself. She remembered that during her flight she had momentarily possessed someone who had walked through this door with the Director.

"Can I help you?" a clipped British voice asked. Amelie turned to see an elderly woman with thinning, badly dyed red hair smiling at her.

"Yes," Amelie said, "I'm so sorry but the retinal scan of my room isn't working. Either that, or I am not standing the right way or something. I'm probably just being stupid."

The woman smiled. Self-deprecation always worked well with the Brits.

"Oh no. Those silly little machines can be so unreliable. Shall I have someone look at it?" the woman asked.

"Yes please," Amelie said. It was better to keep the lie complete in case the crew-cut guy told someone.

"Your name?" the woman asked.

It was at that moment that Amelie saw exactly what she was looking for—a door. More specifically, a door to the outside.

"Amelie McCormick, room 21b."

"Ah, yes. Let me send them a message."

Amelie walked over to the door. There were two swinging doors with frosted glass between her and the outside world. She could feel cold air coming between the cracks of the door. She had floated through this very door. Outside there would be—no, she wouldn't think about it just now.

"The Director said that we can go outside, is that right?" Amelie asked.

"Of course," the woman said. "There's not too much out that way but on a pretty day, you can walk around the building to the center courtyards. That's where they have the outdoor basketball courts and the track. Further behind the back buildings we have jogging paths and outdoor exercise equipment for training purposes. But that's something that you want to do when it's sunny, or at least not rainy."

"But I can step out to get some fresh air?" Amelie asked. "I feel a bit cooped up in here."

"Of course," the woman said. She was wearing a name tag that said *Eleanor*. "It will take a few minutes for the maintenance men to get to your room. And I doubt you will want to be out there for more than a few minutes."

Amelie smiled and nodded. Before Eleanor could engage her in any more conversation, she pushed through the frosted doors to the outside world.

The minute she stepped outside into her environment, her heart sank. In her mind, their odds of escape plummeted to less than ten percent.

They were indeed on an island. She saw the shoreline, wreathed in mist. This was expected, they had been told that this was an island. She remembered the environment around her; the cold, salty smell of the air, the pattern of the clouds and the colors that appeared when she opened her inner eye. Yes, she had been here before and it had not turned out well for the people she saw here.

121

The wind that hit her face was cold and rainy. The clouds over her head were moving fast and low. In fact, they were so low that she felt almost as if she would be able to reach up and touch them. Something about the lowness of these clouds and the speed at which they were moving did not seem natural. Clouds this low usually just appeared as fog. But not these, these were separated into individual clouds. They were also spaced out in such a way that she would have a clear vision of what was around her for one minute and then it would all be shrouded in gray the next.

In the one of the moments of clarity, she saw a few things. She saw a small white walkway in front of her that branched into three. Two paths led to the right and left and then circled around the back of the building. The third, a steep, winding path, led to a small beach. The beach was a cove that was surrounded on either side by rolling hills. Amelie walked a way down this path, the cold biting into her skin through the thin fabric of her game suit, even though she knew what was in those waters. The wind coming from the ocean that whipped at her hair smelled of salt and metal and something less pleasant … something rotting and putrid.

The island she was on was as small as it had seemed on her flight. During the clear moments, she could see to the end of it on both her right and left. There were no real trees that she could see but there was overgrown, bright green grass everywhere. The tiny cove in front of her looked almost volcanic in shape. The sandy beach wasn't much more than four car lengths wide and two deep. Where the bay opened to the ocean, there were buoys, as if the bay was netted.

Keeping things out and keeping things in, Amelie thought.

On either side of the beach, the coastline was rocky and menacing. There was clearly no way in or out of this side of the island without a boat. It was too cold to swim even a short distance to any anchored boat and even if they could swim, whatever was in the water was nothing she would ever willingly subject herself to.

Amelie turned to see the building from which she had just exited. It was not what she had remembered. While the inside of the building was of a modern design, the front entrance was far from modern. The structure of the building she had just left was of a Victorian design. The building's exterior was made of red brick, with white Gothic ornamentation. The building looked like something she might have found in Pennsylvania or Connecticut, but not in this wild and inhospitable island.

As she looked around, she discovered that the building was part of a larger anomaly. There were seven or eight buildings around this first building and,

122

although they were connected by covered walkways and bridges, none of them maintained any one sense of architectural pattern. These buildings were all clumped together in a jumble with architectural designs ranging from Modern to Colonial to Gothic to Bauhaus. The result of this mismatch of styles and themes was painful to both the eye and the brain.

Why would they do that? she thought. *Why would they bother getting all those different materials for such different styles? Is there any way to use any of this to help us get out?*

The buildings aren't made of the usual materials. They are made of bits and pieces of things, and they are reflecting the nature of their composition, said a voice from somewhere inside her.

It was a voice she heard in her head from time to time. She wasn't sure whose it was, but it was usually right and it had saved her on more than a few occasions at the Academy.

Amelie's teeth were now beginning to chatter as the misty rain began to strengthen into something significantly heavier. She turned to head back into the building, but not before she glanced back to the beach. For a moment, she thought she saw a large shape rise from the water in the distance, but then the clouds obscured her view just as a strong gust of wind struck her face. She ran back inside the building.

"I did warn you that it wasn't a great day to be outside," Eleanor said, smiling.

"Yes, you did," Amelie said, forcing a smile.

"Just a little tip, we don't get much sun up here, so when it comes out, you should get outside as quick as you can. It never lasts," the woman said, this time with an odd lack of expression. For a moment, the woman's eyes turned silver. Amelie forced herself to smile at whatever this thing masquerading as a woman was.

"Thank you for all your help," she said.

"Of course, it's no problem at all," Eleanor replied.

Amelie turned away from her and moved back toward the auditorium, but not before noticing that the woman was twitching ever so slightly.

***

Amelie tried to organize her thoughts as she walked back to her room. The Academy was experimenting on people here. Of course, she knew that. The Director himself had told them that they had been administered a virus to act as a catalyst to expand their abilities. The fact that they were experimenting on non-agents shouldn't surprise her. What had surprised her was the Frankensteinesque nature of the experimentation, and the needless brutality. She had always known that the Academy would do whatever it needed to further its agenda, but she had always thought it was done in a needs-based, emotionless sort of way. In all her assignments, she had always been able to see reason in what they were doing, even if it was cruel. When her job had required that she implicate or hurt people, the people in question had always been unquestionably bad, if not outright horrible. As a result, she had always believed that her actions were driven by a strategy, something logical and reasonable.

What she had seen in the eyes of the Director on the beach was not reasonable. Torturing civilians that they had tricked into signing up with that Evermore service wasn't reasonable. Experimenting on children wasn't reasonable. She didn't know if those experiments had some sort of long-term purpose but surely it could be done in other ways. She remembered again that the Director had said something about sending Sophie to "coding," and she had just found vials of her blood being subjected to some strange filtering process. Amelie felt that metallic taste hit the back of her throat again at the thought.

She was also convinced that a significant number of the people here were not actually people. Majo had said as much. She wondered if Roger, the drooling man, was actually a person or not. Initially, she had thought him simply disabled in some way but now she wondered. What if he had been possessed or something? And if he had been, what was he possessed by? Could a human possess another human? And if he had been possessed, was that why he had been behaving that way? She was sure that Ossian Reese had been possessed. She had seen more than one person with the same soft-focus look that she had seen on Ossian Reese just before he attacked her. She had seen the same soft focus on Camp today.

So could that soft-focus effect be a tell that the person had been possessed? Would that be possible? Amelie didn't know much about possession. No, that wasn't true. She didn't know much about demonic possession. But she had certainly had up-close and personal dealings with possession years ago, when Clovis had possessed people's bodies in order to be with her.

At the thought of Clovis, Amelie's knee-jerk reaction was to start shutting those thoughts down, but now she stopped herself. She needed to think about him now, because she had seen him in Verite and what she saw felt important. She had seen him talking to Kara and Dante, and they had been talking about her. This scene was nothing that was drawn from her memory. It was nothing that could have been created from her biological reactions. If she was creating something in the game, she should only be able to create what she could imagine. The conversation between Clovis and Kara and Dante on the landing was nothing she could have created. And even if her mind had somehow concocted

124

it, why would it concoct a scenario which left her with more questions than answers. The lack of answers to the questions that she had about that time in her life was one of her worst scars. She was sure she would not be poking at that scar, even in her subconscious mind.

So what were the other options?

One was that the Academy already knew about her history with Clovis and had already programmed that into the game. She doubted that because there was a level of detail there that they could not have known from secondary sources. That also meant that they would have had to have known that she had already met Dante and Kara. She had given them no indication about this. She had never spoken of them with anyone besides Clovis. So none of this seemed likely.

The other possible option was that the game was actually some sort of connection to the hallway. While that was highly unlikely, it did seem to fit with the experience. She had stepped through a door in the game to get to the scene at her school. She had also flown in those moments just before she woke up here. In that flying, she had gone into the hallway and had seen Caio. That experience felt like the hallway always had but the experience of seeing this place while flying was not in the hallway. She had been possessing people, which supposedly happened when she was in a story in the hallway, but she had never felt it. This time she did. And after that exchange, when she found herself here, Caio had been shocked when he saw her again, as if he remembered something. Since then, his behavior had changed. He was agitated in a way she hadn't seen before. She wasn't sure if that was connected or not.

Amelie was thinking all these things as she made her way back to her room. As she turned the corner, she saw a brown-haired man in a navy-blue jumpsuit standing at the door to her room. His back was to her, and he had a tool kit at his feet. This would be the maintenance man who was sent to "fix" her retinal scan.

"Hi," Amelie said, approaching the man. "Sorry to put you to so much trouble."

"No trouble at all," said the man, with an accent that was familiar to her.

When he turned around to face her, she felt the air leave her lungs. She forced a smile and concentrated on her breath to avoid becoming faint.

"It seems there was a bit of a crossed wire," said the man with a smile and a wink. His eyes were silver.

And with that, Ossian Reese picked up his tool kit, turned and left.

***

125

It took Amelie hours to settle down enough just to get into bed.

We are on the island of Dr. Moreau, kept running through her brain, bringing with it the urge to giggle.

When she finally calmed enough to lie down, she tried to make sense of what she had just seen. Ossian Reese was a famous actor. She seriously doubted that he was moonlighting as a maintenance tech, even if it was for the Academy. Thinking back on the encounter, she had seen no recognition in his eyes. Of course, they were silver, so might have been hard to read. Maybe they were cloning people or something. That idea sounded like science fiction, but most scientific breakthroughs started out as a crazy idea in a scientist's head.

Her brain circled this information from every perspective and every angle, over and over. She didn't even notice that she had dropped off until she heard a loud voice. She sprang up in her bed.

Chapter Sixteen

Majo's Scar

"Wake up, lamb. Time for a little pre-breakfast Verite exercise. It shouldn't take any time at all and then you can go find your friends for whatever your breakfast poison is."

Camp was already standing at the control panel next to her bed. Amelie had slept through the night without waking, which was abnormal for her as she was usually a light sleeper. She swung her feet over the edge of her bed. Her floor immediately shifted from a view of green grass to rolling clouds behind a church steeple. When Camp turned from the control panel, it switched to back to grass.

The steeple looked familiar. With a sudden shock she realized that it was the same church and the same skyline that she had seen when she had been fleeing Ossian Reese in London.

Great. She and her pod were trapped on this island, where they would most likely be experimented on, tortured, dissected for parts, or all the above. And, to add insult to injury, she was stuck in a room with bastard decor.

Amelie plastered on a smile and counted her breaths as Camp adjusted her headpiece and goggles. She didn't want Camp to realize that she was already agitated before she was even in the game. Although it would probably do her good if she was slightly agitated when they were setting the control readings. It would give her more wiggle room in case her body reacted before she could control it.

Like they aren't already tracking me through these stupid long johns?

The thought made her pause.

"Okay, pumpkin. We are all set. I've set your time in the game for thirty seconds and no more," Camp said with a smile.

"Thirty seconds? That's hardly time to get it on," Amelie said, with a forced smile.

127

"Well, I don't want to keep you from breakfast. I know how grumpy I get if I'm late for my morning coffee and toast," Camp said, with a smile that was less warm than it had been the day before. She placed Amelie's headgear on much more quickly than she had previously.

"Okay. Here we go," Camp said, as she turned and went back to the control panel. A few seconds later, Amelie's goggles faded to black for a moment, and then a world seemed to open up around her.

***

This time in Verite, Amelie found herself standing in a large, pale green space. She immediately shielded her thoughts with random clutter. She didn't want any of her past emotions clouding what happened now. She had been lucky that they couldn't read her biomarkers from the last time and god only knew what they had read from the suit earlier today. She was well aware of the dangers of letting anyone know too much about what hurts you and what scares you. They were here to be trained, so the Academy would certainly be probing for these things. She should mask her emotions and be hypervigilant from this point on-ward. She needed to close down all thoughts about the events of the day.

Yes, she should be careful, but the last time she was in this game she saw Clovis.

Don't think about him. Not here. Not now.

Amelie took deep breaths and focused her attention on the green space around her.

It felt cold and clear … it also felt strangely clean. It didn't have the potent feel that it had the last time she was plugged in. It actually felt more like the scenery she went through when she was flying. When she was flying, she felt like she could travel anywhere she wanted, across space and time. Here, it was less about space and time and more about creation. The space around her felt pregnant with potential—if she could harness it.

She looked around and saw nothing besides the green. There was also no smell and no feel of anything on her skin besides a faint cooling sensation. She tried to conjure the image of a flower in her mind, and sort of expected one to appear in front of her, but there was no such result. She concentrated harder but the green around her remained stubbornly green.

Amelie began walking forward in the green. Maybe she was overthinking this. The last time she was here, she had no expectations. Perhaps her very an-ticipation and anxiety was blocking things. She wished that there had been some opportunity to speak with her podmates, but she had to find a safe place to talk before she could even allow herself to think about what she had learned.

But Clovis had been here.

Amelie felt a pang in her chest, familiar but stronger than she had felt in years. She quickly turned her thoughts away from Clovis and to her pod. She focused on Majo instead. Majo, who she trusted probably as much as she was capable of trusting. Majo, who had found her and saved her when she had given up on herself. Majo, who had been her introduction to the Academy itself.

Suddenly, Amelie felt wind on her arms and in her hair. The wind carried the smell of jasmine tea and sugar. It also carried a sound that rose and fell in pitch as the breeze drifted by. Amelie turned and began walking in its direction. As she got closer to its source, she noticed that it had the pattern of keening. The tone and resonance of the voice sounded familiar. As she walked toward the sound, an open door appeared in the distance. Its opening looked dark in the field of pale green.

The sound was clearly coming from this door. As Amelie reached the door, she saw that it hung in the air with nothing around it. Peering into it, she realized that she was gazing into a room at night. After her eyes adjusted to the gloom, she saw that light from a half-moon was streaming in through a window and coloring objects in the room shades of gray. Just inside the door was a large space containing three hospital-style beds separated by chests, tables, and chairs into three separate living spaces. Amelie guessed that it was a hospital or care facility of some kind. As she touched the door frame, the noise stopped.

In the darkened room, Amelie saw a girl sitting on the edge of one of the beds. A man was lying in the bed that she sat upon. He was probably in his seventies or eighties with a full head of snow-white hair that was brushed back from his face, and a closely cut white mustache and beard. He was lying on a bed covered with crinkled, worn-looking sheets. Reaching from behind the bed was an iron rod that ended in a triangular support device dangling above the man's chest, which must have been to help him sit up. A very small table was jammed up next to the bed. It was crowded with cups of water and pill jars.

The girl sitting on the edge of the bed was Majo.

***

Majo had one of the man's hands in hers and was stroking his face with her other hand. She was wearing a light blue polo shirt and a jeans skirt. Amelie stepped closer to the door frame. As her eyes further adjusted to the dark, she realized that this Majo was much younger than the Majo she knew. She couldn't be more than sixteen or seventeen. Much of her face was hidden from view by her hair, but her bone structure was tiny, and her movements were those of a young girl. Amelie suspected, from the way that Majo was hiding her face with

129

her hair, that she had been crying.

Is this her father?

The room they were sitting in began to materialize more as Amelie looked around. Its walls were covered in aged, peeling wallpaper. But the wall space nearest the man was covered with posters of artwork. Most of it was art that had an ethereal nature. Amelie recognized a poster of *The Little Mermaid* by Sulamith Wülfing. As she leaned into the room, keeping one foot still outside the door, the smell of medicine and urine assaulted her nostrils. It was so overwhelming that Amelie instinctively stepped back and covered her nose. Majo and the man were not alone. To their right, an older woman was sleeping in a bed with way too many covers for any situation, outside of sleeping in the Arctic. To their left, a balding, middle-aged man hooked up to an IV seemed more unconscious than asleep. From what she saw in front of her, Amelie assumed this was some sort of nursing home or extended care facility for the old or disabled, and not a hospital. Hospitals didn't smell like this. Hospitals tended to smell of disinfectant products and not urine. A hospital would never have allowed the level of mess and clutter on display here.

"Majo," Amelie whispered softly. But Majo either didn't hear her or didn't want to acknowledge her. So, after a moment of hesitation, Amelie stepped through the door. Once inside, she found herself in a bigger room than she had expected. Neither Majo nor the man seemed aware of her, so she moved forward slowly. As she approached, she saw the old man better. His face was pale, and his skin seemed to hang on his bones. There were age spots scattered across his cheeks. His arms were frail, bird-like things resting on a dingy comforter. His fingernails were long and discolored. Despite this, his face was still fairly unlined, and his skin had that sort of translucent beauty that comes to the lucky with age.

"Why?" she heard Majo whisper to the man. "Why?"

Her voice hitched. She was crying.

Suddenly, the man on the bed sat up.

"Majo?" he whispered in a voice of desperation.

"I'm here."

"Where are we, my love?" the man asked.

My love?

"We're in the home," Majo whispered back.

"Our home?" the man asked with a beatific smile.

"No," Majo whispered. "We are … we are …"

The man looked around him.

"Oh, I see. I'm remembering our past again, am I not?" he said.

130

Majo nodded.

The man reached out and put his hand on her face. Majo's face came fully into view, and it was a horror to see. Her normally placid and calm face was being ripped apart by emotion. Her cheeks were flaming red, and her eyes wet and wide. Her mouth trembled and her breathing was fast.

"I'm afraid I won't be here much longer," the man said to her. "We don't have much time. And I want to make sure we meet again. I *need* to make sure we meet again. But we need to be closer in age, so we can have a life together. Do you want that?"

Majo nodded.

"Then you know what we must do. There is only one way to connect ourselves through lifetimes in love, without death or blood. But you know that already, don't you? You know our past."

Majo put her face in her hands.

"Don't be afraid, my love. It doesn't take long. Just the connection is enough. I won't hurt you."

The man then leaned forward and kissed her. The kiss was long and not a platonic one. Majo wrapped her arms around his neck. As they kissed, Majo crawled onto the bed with him, and he reached beneath her skirt to pull down her underwear.

Amelie began backing away. This was too intimate, too personal, and too disturbing. She saw Majo seat herself upon the man's body, his hands on her waist. Amelie turned to go back through the door, only to find that the door had disappeared behind her. Just like it had done when she had been in the hallway.

She was scanning the room, just in case the door had moved, when she heard a horrid, guttural cry from behind her. It wasn't that loud, but it echoed in the silence of the room.

Amelie turned to see the old man sitting up. He violently shoved Majo away from him. She lost her balance and fell to the floor.

"Who are you? What are you doing to me?" he yelled at her, pointing with his pale hand and dirty nails.

Majo stood up quickly and ran to him.

"Shhh. Shhh. You forgot again, darling. You will remember again in a minute," she cooed, reaching out to him.

He slapped her and she fell against the table next to the bed. Water glasses and medications crashed to the ground.

"My love," Majo said, reaching out again, trying to take his hands.

"Whore!" the man screamed and lashed out at her again. This time his long fingernails dug into her cheek, clawing and ripping. Majo cried out and fell backward, her hand covering her face. Amelie could see blood beginning to well between her fingers.

The woman in the next bed sat up suddenly and began screaming, and then the man on the IV on the other side followed suit. They were like infants in a nursery, following the lead of a crier without knowing why.

Majo was scrambling back from the bed, toward the door behind her, when a nurse ran into the room and threw on the fluorescent lights. The green-yellow light was unkind to Majo's broken and bleeding face.

"What is happening in here?" the nurse yelled. Then she caught sight of the old man, now standing, pantless and pointing at Majo, whose skirt was still pulled up around her waist.

"You—you—you are disgusting, perverted—" the nurse began, and Amelie could not bear to hear more. She ran forward and fell at Majo's side.

"Majo, come with me," she said. Majo turned to her, wide-eyed.

"Come on," Amelie said, yanking Majo to her feet. "We need to get out of here."

How do I get out of here? Here is inside my head, Amelie thought.

Or is it?

The thought popped into her head, followed by words she had heard before, years ago, a lifetime ago.

"*Just hold your breath,*" he had said. "*When your heart starts to run out of oxygen, your heart will default to one beat ... the beat of your world. Does that make sense?*"

Change the rhythm of your heart. *I need to change the rhythm of my heart.*

She grabbed Majo around the waist, turned back and ran as hard as she could, not in the direction that she had come from, but out of the room. She needed enough space to work up a run.

She began to hold her breath as they ran. She ran past a nurses' station and into what seemed to be a cafeteria. She was running away from the screaming man, the screaming nurse and the smell of sex and urine.

Amelie was getting lightheaded, and her lungs were burning. Majo was sobbing at her side, and Amelie was having to drag her. She was just about at the end of the cafeteria when she felt an explosion of pain in her chest.

In that second, she found herself back in the pale green place, still running, with Majo now ahead of her.

"Majo!" Amelie said, grabbing her and pulling her to a stop. "We're out. You're away."

132

At first the Majo that turned to meet her gaze was the girl from the room, young and recently destroyed. Almost instantly that face began to melt away. In seconds, the face in front of her was the Majo she knew, older and scarred but the mark whose birth Amelie had just witnessed was pale and tattooed. But this Majo's face still looked ravaged.

"I was there. I was there again," Majo whispered. "Why was I there?"

"We are in the game," Amelie said, taking Majo's hand.

"Why would that be a part of a game? Why would I go there? Why would I relive that? Why would it pick that? How could it know that? What sort of monstrous creation—" Majo began, but she stopped.

She sat down suddenly in the green nothingness.

"What did you see?" Majo whispered to Amelie, looking down.

Amelie considered lying for a moment, but this was Majo, and this was her pod. Even if most of her existence was based on lies, she wouldn't lie to her pod.

"I saw you make love to that old man," Amelie said, sitting down next to her. "Was that a memory?"

"Yes," Majo whispered.

"Do you want to tell me about it?" Amelie asked.

"No. I want to never think of it again, but as you saw it, I will have to explain it."

"You don't have to," Amelie replied, reaching out to touch her arm.

"Oh, actually I do," Majo said, with a sad, watery smile. "There are maybe only five or six people in the world whose opinion of me matters to me. And one of them just got to see the worst moment of my life. So, for my own sanity, I do need to explain that to you. I need you to know that I am not a pervert. Or not that much of a pervert."

Majo stopped and let out a shaky breath and put her head in her hands.

"So you knew him from a past life?" Amelie asked gently.

Majo laughed in a desperate, lost way.

"Amelie, I know everyone from a past life," she finally said in soft voice. "That's the part of me that the Academy doesn't know."

Chapter Seventeen

Training and Other Tortures

Majo sat up and turned to face Amelie. Her face was beginning to regain its composure but just beneath the surface, just below the skin, the muscles were alive and twitching.

"I think it's time to tell you about my past," Majo said, then gave a sad little laugh. "So I can explain what you just saw."

Majo delicately wiped her eyes with the back of her hand, as she took a deep breath and then exhaled.

"Okay. To start with, when I was a child, I thought that everyone was my relative because I remembered them," Majo said softly. "I remembered almost everyone I encountered. I didn't always understand my memories, as a child wouldn't, but I knew when I had loved someone or cared for them or missed them. I used to run up to strangers and throw my arms around them. And— well, I'm sure you can guess how people responded. The kind ones gave me a little hug and laughed. The meanest ones would shove me away. But all of them looked at me with that horrible discomfort and lack of recognition. I was hurt over and over and over. Still, I kept trying—well, I kept trying until my mother began beating me for it when my father was not around. She said that I was possessed by a demon. It was awful. So I never spoke of it again. I just tried to overlook what I felt when I met people. I learned to have the same expression when I met my old lover as when I met my old killer. I was okay because I was the only one who felt it ... who recognized it. At least until I was seventeen."

Majo stopped and dropped her eyes again for a moment. When she looked back up, there were fresh teardrops in her lashes.

"Then, when I was seventeen, I started working in the nursing home to make extra money. My mother wanted me to contribute to the household income and my father thought that working in a nursing home would suit me because I was kind. I had been working there for only a few weeks when they brought him in. I saw him, and of course, I remembered him. But this time it was worse because I remembered multiple lives together. We had been mates, lovers, friends, companions for lifetimes upon lifetimes upon lifetimes. I buried it, like I always did. I ignored it until one night, when I was doing rounds, he stopped me to talk."

Majo sniffed and looked down at her hands.

"Maybe it's because it was nighttime and he wasn't totally conscious," she continued softly, "or maybe it was because he was so close to death … but in any case, he remembered … he remembered me."

Amelie's heart twinged in sympathy.

"I started visiting him every time I had a night shift," Majo said. "He was incoherent in the day, but at night, he was who he was. He told me stories about myself. He shared memories of our past together. When he spoke of it, the memory of it would open in my mind. It was so wonderful to be with someone who remembered. It was even better to be with him, who had been my passion for so many lives. I didn't want him to forget. I didn't want him to forget me, and I didn't want to lose him. He told me that sex connects people across lives. I already knew this. I knew it was true. So, I … we … well, you saw what happened."

"I'm so sorry," Amelie whispered.

She understood. She, better than anyone, understood becoming a pariah for her sexual choices. She remembered all too vividly thinking that she would do anything to stay with Clovis.

Majo nodded.

"Well, at least after that, I was rid of my family. My mother always hated me and once my dad found out what I did, well, he supported her in kicking me out. I wasn't the freak that they thought I was, or at least, not in the way that they thought I was. I just loved someone and chose to act on it at the wrong time and in the wrong manner."

Majo sat up straighter, let out a long breath and squared her shoulders. "So, you know my story. But, outside of all that, the bigger questions are how and why that scene came up in a *training* video game."

"Maybe they added some chemical patches or something to increase your anxiety level and this is what your mind produced," Amelie said.

"Maybe," Majo muttered, "or maybe not." She stood up and began pacing.

"Oh, wait. They are looking for our gifts," Majo said, suddenly stopping. "Can they hear us in here?"

"No," Amelie said, looking around. "Not unless someone else is around."

"How do you know that?" Majo asked.

"I don't know how to explain it, but there are new things I can do now. I can taste it when they are reading me or trying to read me. It tastes like metal. No one is trying to read me now."

"So they can't read us here?" Majo asked.

"No, I'm sure that they can't, or not our words. They can only send things to stimulate us and record our body responses."

"Okay, good. How did you find me?" Majo asked.

"I wasn't trying to find you—" Amelie began and then stopped.

Hadn't she been? Hadn't she been thinking that she wanted to see Majo? No, not thinking but feeling a need to be with her.

"I think I have felt my way to you," Amelie said.

"Do you think that's something the Academy coded us to do here somehow? Do you think they are directing it?" Majo asked.

"No," Amelie said. "Someone asked the Director about how they plan to use Verite in the general population and he sidestepped the answer and began to talk about training. I think that's because they have created something that they don't fully understand how to use. Like people who create pharmaceuticals. Sometimes they know what the drug does, but they don't exactly know how it works. They don't know the full pathway."

Amelie didn't realize this was what she believed until she said it, but now that she had said it, it rang true.

"Maybe that's why you ended up where you did. I think maybe this place doesn't respond to directives but to images and symbols. Maybe that's why I could find you. I—" She stopped. An idea had come into her head.

"Wait a second, I have an idea," Amelie said.

She closed her eyes, and dropped her inner eyelid. She thought about the Director and what he wanted. She wondered about Caio and what he might already know.

"Amelie," Majo said in a tight voice. "What the hell is all this?"

Amelie opened her eyes to see that a world had woken up in the three seconds she had had her eyes closed.

Amelie and Majo were standing in a patch of earth in the middle of a tropical rainforest. They were surrounded by a hurricane of colors and symbols.

A giant curd-white worm burst out from the ground in front of them, vomiting forth a host of smaller worms that whirled and descended toward them.

"Enough," Amelie yelled and closed her inner eye hard. The landscape around them went back to pale green.

"What the fuck was that?" Majo asked.

"I think it was where Caio came from," Amelie replied.

136

"No, what were all those colors and symbols?"

"Oh, it's what I always see if I don't control things," Amelie said.

"I might have felt better about my own situation if you had mentioned this earlier," Majo said, raising an eyebrow.

Amelie smiled back, and then laughed.

"So what was that about?" Majo asked.

"I suspected that this place operates more like the visions I have, or like dreams."

Or like things I see in the hallway, Amelie thought but didn't voice.

"I think that's the way to effect it," she continued out loud. "I think we need to be in a state that is similar to the state between waking and sleeping."

"Like lucid dreaming?" Majo asked.

"Exactly. My visions are like that. I think maybe we can use that to feel our way to each other."

"Maybe not just that. Maybe we can use it to find out more. But let's see what happens when we come out of this. We need to know what they can read about this. If they can't, then it could be a real asset for us," Majo said. Her face was a flat mask when she said this, but her eyes told a different story.

Majo knew this place was evil.

"You are thinking that this is a place we can meet and talk if we can find each other here?" Amelie asked.

Majo nodded.

"You said something about assessing us to check for new gift," Amelie said. "You know, Camp said something when I first woke up about the Academy discovering gifts that people were trying to hide."

Majo scooted closer to her until their knees were touching.

"Exactly," Majo said softly. "For example, with me, they know I can read human versus non-human. But they don't know how I know that. My assistants have been watching me very closely to see how I respond to them."

"Are they human?" Amelie asked.

"I don't think so," Majo whispered. "What they don't know about my gift is that I know human from non-human because I can read past lives. Non-humans have continual existence. They don't have past lives, so when I encounter them, it's like static on a screen. No past lives."

"But you said that you see things that aren't human, right?" Amelie asked.

"Yes, now I do. Now the static that exists from the lack of past lives tends to form itself into the shape of the thing that the static belongs to. That part of my ability didn't really start until I was in the Academy."

"You said that people here aren't human," Amelie said.

"That's what I thought at first, but it's strange. It's not consistently one way or another. Sometimes I can read past lives, sometimes I can't. Sometimes I see entities and sometimes I don't."

"So some are human, and some are not."

"No, that's not what I mean. I mean, in the same person, sometimes I see their past lives and sometimes I can't. Sometimes I see other entities and sometimes I don't. And when I do read the past lives, they are weak. I only encountered that once before."

Majo took a shaky breath.

"Amelie, this place is bad. That's what I know for sure. It's a nest of something unclean and we need to get out of it as soon as we can."

"I know. It may be worse than you think—" Amelie began, but at that moment, a smell hit Amelie's nose. A smell like smoke and sulfur. With it came a noise, a buzzing, clicking sound.

She whipped around, scanning the pale green around her. Sure enough, in the far distance to her right, she saw what she feared—an open door. On the other side of the door, she could see a red and black landscape. She recognized the place instantaneously even from this distance. It was a place of monsters, sickness, death—and love.

Her heart began to beat wildly in her chest when she saw a wave of green and black moving toward the opening of the doorway. The clicking sound was getting louder, blown toward them by a gust of powerful acidic wind.

"We have to get out of here now!" Amelie screamed to Majo over the sound of the wind.

"Why?"

"Those things will kill us." Amelie was scanning around them, but she saw nothing.

"We're in a game," Majo yelled over the increasing wind.

"We're in a game that can affect our bodies, you heard what the Director said. If we die in here, are you sure we won't die out there?" Amelie yelled back.

Majo jumped up, grabbed Amelie's hand, and began to run in the opposite direction from the door.

Amelie took a deep breath and held it. Almost immediately she felt the searing in her lungs and her blood begin to pulse behind her eyes, still she ran, her hand clinging to Majo's.

The pain in Amelie's chest was excruciating. The constant green of their surroundings gave them no sense of how far they were getting, but the growing sound of the clicking behind them told Amelie that they weren't getting anywhere fast enough, and they weren't disappearing.

Amelie's legs gave out and she fell to the ground, gasping for breath. Majo dropped to her side, trying to help pull her to her feet. Something hit her head. Another something landed on her arm. Fear, memory, and instinct made her swat it away before she even realized it had landed on her. Amelie turned and her heart stopped.

The insectile hoard was now cresting like a dark wave. The swirling, buzzing mass rose up behind them, and then began to descend. Amelie could see the purplish-green bodies of the monsters come into focus. Everything around her slowed down. She could see the creatures descending on her in detail. Their horrible, mutated bodies with insect shells that also sprouted hair. The bulgy, bloated heads flanked by gill-like structures that were large and liquid-filled. The air around them was filled with the sounds of their buzzing and flapping. It had a cadence that sounded like the rise and fall of the wind, but it was as loud as a hurricane. Amelie saw them descending on her and Majo and remembered the unimaginable pain of their kiss.

Amelie screamed, threw Majo to the ground behind her and covered her with her own body. She covered her face with her hands and tried to focus her gift, to throw these things at something else.

And then, everything around her went quiet. She opened her eyes to see white. She looked around and, at first, that was all that she saw. Majo was gone, the mouse bugs were gone, and all was white. Then, in the far distance above her head, she saw something else. For an instant, she saw a door open and through it she saw space and an ocean of stars. As she looked the stars coalesced to become images: a room full of screens, Widget crying in a chair, Hudson bloody and lying on the ground near a pool, and then Caio.

Just his head, lying upon a pillow.

***

Amelie felt arms on her shoulders.

"Okay, that's enough," she heard Camp say.

The helmet was being removed from her head. Amelie opened her eyes and blinked. She was back in her room. Camp was looking at her face intently.

"Wow. What happened to you in there? Your biological markers were off the chart."

Amelie took a deep breath.

Don't give them anything. Nothing real.

"Look, you don't have to tell me details. I am guessing that something in there triggered a memory for you, and it must have been one hell of a memory."

"Why would you think that?" Amelie asked.

"Because your dopamine, serotonin, norepinephrine levels were all sky-high, but at different times. You also had ridiculously high levels of endorphins and oxytocin. I pulled you out because your heart rate was entering cardiac arrest zone."

Amelie forced herself to laugh, even though she felt her throat tighten and that metallic taste had reappeared.

"Well, I guess the game is doing its job. It's supposed to present things for us to react to, so it worked," she said.

"What happened to you in there was not the game, it was you," Camp said.

Amelie suddenly became aware that the pale, odd-shaped growths on Camp's face seemed to have disappeared. She blinked hard, but no, they were still absent.

"So most people don't react that way to the game? I mean, I thought the game was supposed to adapt itself to us," Amelie asked.

"It does, over time," Camp said. "But the game can't construct a complex situation on its own. It needs to take readings from you and use those readings to create the construct of your game. After someone has been in the game a dozen times or so, we start getting significant readings. It takes the game at least that much time to learn you. I have never had readings like this after the first visit."

Visit. That was an odd word to use to describe playing a video game.

"Actually, I have never seen readings like this, period," Camp continued. "There is something different about you, lamb. I can see why the Director is so keen to see you."

"Really?"

"Absolutely," Camp said, with a knowing smile. "Shortly after your biometric reads started coming in, I got a call from the Director himself. He had been watching the data stream live. He wants to meet with you and your pod this afternoon. You will be the first pod he meets. That's quite an honor."

Shit. What did they see? Choose your words carefully.

"I feel like I didn't see that much. But if something in the game is dangerous for me, will you be able to see it, so you can pull me out like you did this time?" Amelie asked.

"Oh, we don't see what you see. That is all happening between the game and your brain. We can't tap that interface because it's using neural networks and viral interfaces."

"So you won't know if I am in danger?"

"Of course we will know. We will know from your readings. If the game starts having a negative impact on your physical body, of course we will pull you out. As the Director says, you are our greatest assets."

Camp said this with a smile that she probably intended to look kind, and while there was no green smoke or weird lights around her indicating a lie, the smile seemed less warm and genuine than it had before.

"Oh, your poor face, lamb," Camp said, as she came over and gave Amelie a brief, emotionless hug.

"You must have had a very bad experience in there. I won't ask you about it, it's not my business." Camp paused for a split second before continuing. "But I suspect the Director might ask you about it."

"You mean he will grill me about it?" Amelie asked, purposely putting her index finger to her mouth and chewing her nail.

"Grill you? Of course not, pumpkin. The Director does not grill people. He might ask but he will only want you to tell him what you are comfortable with. Personally, I would love to spend a quality hour with that man," Camp said, dramatically putting her hand over her heart.

Amelie forced herself to laugh again.

"I can tell you like him," she said.

"Lamb, I love him, and if you knew his story, you would to. What woman doesn't love a man who can deeply, passionately love a woman? And what woman doesn't want to be the woman to fix a man who has been horribly wronged by an evil ex-lover?"

"Is that his story?"

"In a nutshell, yes, but it's much more complex than that. He still loves her. Everything he has done has been for her. Everything around you, he built to try and save her."

Camp then stepped back a few paces and put her hands up.

"Shut my mouth, I am talking too much!" she said with a little grimace. "You'll find out all this in time, but he should be the one to tell you when you have graduated from this level. But for now, even though I adore spending time with you, I have to get back to my desk to start analyzing all the data on this morning's recruits. Lynche will be here soon to take you to the game room for your meeting with the Director. Make sure you get a good eyeful of him."

With that, she laughed, winked, did a bit of a curtsy, and left the room.

The minute Camp had left, the walls, ceiling, and floors went black for a second and then booted up images of a night sky. While that might have been beautiful on her walls and ceiling, having it on her floor as well gave the horrible impression of floating through an empty void.

141

Amelie stood up and went to sit on her bed. By the time she sat down, she was already dizzy from the visuals.

Okay, what happened? I met Majo. I saw her past. Then I held my breath to get us out of that place. Then we went back to the green space. And then the horrible mouse bugs came. And holding my breath didn't work. Why? And what brought us out?

Thinking about it, Amelie realized that the question was why holding her breath had got her out of the room where she had found Majo in the first place. She had been in a video game. There was no reason for that to work. That had only worked in the hallway or, more particularly, in the stories that she got to from the hallway.

Unless …

Unless part of where she had been had not been Verite at all. When she had seen Majo, she had seen her in the nursing home, hadn't she had to walk through a door to get to her? Her memory was a bit fuzzy on it, but it seemed that she had. And certainly, her readings should have been high when she was trying to get Majo out of there, but Camp had not pulled her out then. Amelie had used the same trick that she used in the hallway to get out.

No, not the hallway.

The hallway was a gateway. She had used that trick to get out of the stories she had traveled to from the hallway. It worked in the room where she had found Majo. And later, when she was back in the green space and the bugs that came, that same trick had not worked. But the bugs had also come from an open door. Amelie had been terrified and that was the moment that Camp pulled her out.

What if Verite was somehow connected to the hallway? Or what if it was some sort of synthetic way to get into stories? Was the story with Majo a story from her actual life, or another story built on parts of that life?

And she couldn't forget that she had also seen Caio in the hallway. It was not when she was in the game. That had happened after they had been gassed in their apartment and before she woke up at ACID. She had told Caio that they were in a story, and he had said that they were in a vision. Later, when she saw him after the Director's welcome, he had seemed to see her differently. And his actions had become completely different. He had been a plant, that was what he was supposed to do, but he had put himself at risk for their pod.

And then … Clovis. She had seen Clovis talking to Kara and Dante at her old school after she had gone through a white door she had found in the game.

Somehow, she felt that all this was connected to what they were doing here, particularly what had happened to Sophie.

Amelie put her head in her hands. It was all too much to take in at the moment. She wanted to talk to her pod. She needed to talk to Majo, to see if she had actually been present with her in the game or if it was only the Majo from the other story.

Suddenly, the door to her room slid open and Lynche appeared. Her surroundings immediately changed to calming beach scenes, complete with sand at her feet and the sounds of waves and sea birds.

"Motherfucker," she muttered to herself.

"Hey there girl," Lynche said with a big smile. "It's time to take you to the game room to debrief with the Director. Rumor has it that you had a big morning on Verite, everyone is abuzz to hear the story."

The story. Shit.

"Right now?" Amelie asked, standing up.

"No time like the present," laughed Lynche, motioning her toward the door.

On the walk to the game room, she would need to come up with some very convincing lies about her time in Verite.

No pressure.

She didn't notice the small insect wing entwined into the threads of the fabric of her sleeve.

Chapter Eighteen

Déjà Wing

When they entered the main circular atrium, rather than heading toward one of the attached walkways, Lynche turned to his right and stopped at an almost invisible white door in the wall, next to a couple of potted plants. He took out a key that he inserted into an equally invisible slot to the right of the door. The door slid open to reveal an elevator.

"Is this the way to the game room?" Amelie asked as they stepped in.

"It's one of them. But we need to pick up one of your podmates before we see the Director. He wants to see your *whole* pod, you know," Lynche said, with a toothy smile. Inside the elevator was a panel with numerous buttons, none of them with any numbers or designations.

Lynche pressed one and Amelie felt the elevator begin to descend.

In mere moments, the descent stopped with a sudden jerk. The door in front of them opened into a long hallway. At first, it looked just gray, but at closer glance, Amelie saw dark gray symbols carved into the gray cement of the walls. She shook her head for a moment, but the symbols didn't disappear, nor did they glow. They were real, physical things.

On either side of the hallway, there were picture windows looking onto sterile white rooms. The first four of these were empty. The last one in the hallway was larger and contained several tables stacked high with all forms of weaponry—and Caio.

Caio was crouched in combat position with a piano wire stretched taught between his hands. Surrounding him were four other men, all of whom were roughly twice his size and twice his weight. Rather than the black bodysuit that she was wearing, Caio was dressed in a white variety of the same—and it was cut, and stained with blood.

Amelie had her hands on the glass before she realized she was doing it.

144

"Stop," said Lynche, pulling her back. "You don't want to distract him."

"Those aren't fair odds. They are twice his size," Amelie said.

Lynche smiled.

"Since when has that mattered with operatives?" he said. "You should know that better than most. Just watch."

Amelie watched as the men began to circle Caio. He didn't move but Amelie could see his eyes darting around him. For a moment, those eyes settled on her, but then quickly moved on.

"Did you know that your podmate trained with SMERSH in Russia, the Japanese Riot Police, Delta Force, the Navy SEALs and JW GROM from Poland? You know GROM, right?" Lynche asked.

Amelie nodded. She knew GROM well. One of her assignments had been to seduce and collect intel from one of their officers. Their nickname was "The Surgeons" for their incredible knowledge of human anatomy and killing technique. She had found out that they also used that knowledge of human anatomy extensively in the bedroom.

"They are so cool," Lynche said, rubbing his hands together.

The bigger men around the room had all collected weapons from the white tables located around them. Three of them picked up hand weapons—a halberd, a dagger, and an axe. The fourth had picked up an automatic weapon.

"Oh man, the gun is a huge mistake, why would he do that?" Lynche said, with a sigh. "Damn it. Weren't these people coached? Won't be much of a fight this time."

Amelie stared at Caio, so thin and frail-looking compared to the muscle-bound guys around him. If only the glass wasn't here. If she could get past it, she was sure she could glamour these idiots in a heartbeat.

A buzzer went off. After that, everything happened so fast that Amelie barely had time to process it. Caio jumped to the table and used it as a springboard to jump on the man with the axe. He used the piano wire and his own body weight to break his opponent's neck before using his body as a shield against the bullets. After that he rolled himself and the axe man's body toward the shooter, whose legs he entangled with more wire. Once the shooter was down, Caio grabbed the gun and shot both the shooter and the guy with the halberd. In less than sixty seconds, Caio was standing in the middle of the room, wiping his face. In a weird way, what she had just seen had been graceful and beautiful, if people hadn't died.

"He's fast, right? That's one of his strengths. That and the fact that people underestimate him," Lynche said with a shrug. "I knew the gun was a mistake.

If you don't use it fast enough, it just becomes a weapon in someone else's hands."

"They let him kill those guys?" Amelie asked. "They aren't operatives?"

"No, they are retired operatives. Besides, the gun used rubber bullets with spikes to anesthetize the target, so they aren't dead."

What about the guy with the broken neck? she thought, looking at the lump of a man lying on the floor with his head at a right angle to his body, but she said nothing. She had caught the "retired operatives" reference.

Someone stuck their head into the room and Caio nodded, dropped the gun, and walked out.

"Why is he doing that in the first place? I thought you were training us in the game?" Amelie asked.

"Caio is a special circumstance. This isn't so much about training him as it is about studying his blood and stuff," Lynche said.

"What does 'and stuff' mean?"

"It means he gets trained, and in the process, he gets hurt in combat. They observe how long it takes him to heal under various circumstances and with various injuries."

"He heals more quickly than other people?"

"Yeah, he heals unnaturally quickly from wounds. He also heals from poisoning, chemicals, bacteria, and viruses."

"How do you know that?"

"Oh, they've been testing him for years … at least as long as I've been here. He's here at least a few weeks a year."

"So he's a lab rat, then?" Amelie asked, before she could stop herself. No, she could have stopped herself, but she was angry enough to let the question slip out, and to let the menace behind the question leak out.

Amelie's tone must have been seriously acidic because Lynche turned to face her.

"Oh, you are thinking they are cruel to do this, right?" he asked.

Amelie said nothing. She just studied Lynche's perfectly chiseled face.

"But you know he agreed to this. He wasn't forced at all."

"People agree to lots of things for lots of reasons," Amelie said.

"Yeah, but Camp said that he agreed to it because he likes what they are studying by testing him. Imagine if they could figure out what causes him to heal faster? Or if they could discover how he can survive poisoning? Or how he can be immune to all bacteria and viruses? Think of all the lives they could save and pain they could eliminate. We wouldn't even need vaccines anymore."

"That's why Caio agreed to do this?"

146

"Yeah. He's doing this to help other people and prevent pain."

These words rang metallic in her ears.

Partial truth.

When Caio joined them, he had a large bandage on his neck, stained with blood. His right upper arm was in a sling.

"You okay?' Amelie asked. Caio nodded and shrugged.

"Why are you here again?" he asked Lynche. He looked at him like someone looks at the hairball just thrown up by their cat.

"I am supposed to accompany you to see the Director," Lynche said.

At these words, a series of expressions flashed so quickly across Caio's face that Amelie couldn't make sense of any one of them. There were probably twenty-seven different expressions in less than two seconds. A moment after that, Caio's bandages begin to glow. Lights seeped out from around them: red, green, yellow. In less than an instant, the expressions and the lights were gone. Caio face had returned to its placid calm.

Suppressed.

"Okay. Let's go then," Caio said.

"Cool." Lynche put his hand on Caio's shoulder. Caio immediately brushed it off.

"Damn. Cold-blooded, dude," Lynche said.

"At least I have blood," Caio said. Lynche's eyes widened for just a moment and he glared.

"Okay then, let's go. We don't want to keep the main guy waiting," Lynche said, chirpy attitude firmly back in place.

As they fell in line behind Lynche, Caio reached out and put his arm around her, rubbing her upper arm.

***

Lynche took them back to the elevator they had just come from but this time he pressed one of the buttons at the bottom of the group. Amelie assumed this meant a basement floor.

The elevator door opened to huge room that seemed to run the length of one or two buildings. The room was filled with rows of desks, chairs, and computers. The furniture looked to be of the typical, bland IKEA office variety but even at first glance, Amelie knew that the computers were neither cheap nor bland. They were also not run-of-the-mill PCs or Macs.

Lynche led them down the center of one of the rows. There were a few people in each row of computers, but the room wasn't even close to full. Probably only thirty percent of the chairs were filled.

"Where is everyone today?" Caio asked.

"Oh, it isn't peak time yet," Lynche replied. "Most of the gamers are still sleeping off last night and getting lunch. You are the only gamers here right now. A larger group will come in the afternoon, at a reasonable time. But the monitors are still monitoring, of course."

He laughed at whatever he thought the joke was.

"Some reason why we are here so early then?" Caio asked. Lynche stopped laughing.

"Dunno, man," he said.

Amelie noticed that there were darkened glass windows on all the walls surrounding them.

"What's in those rooms?" she asked, as they walked.

"Those are the gaming rooms. It's better if they are completely dark. It helps you sync with Verite easier," Lynche said.

Lynche's words had that metallic ring again, the one that was always followed by a bitter taste in the back of her mouth. She was learning that this pattern meant lies.

"Okay, here we go," Lynche said, as they came to the end of the room. There was a darkened window here that was large enough that it took up most of the wall space at the end of the room.

"This is the main game room." He held an ID card that had been hanging around his neck up to a card reader.

The door swung open. Amelie could see that the door was probably a foot thick and metal, which was ominous at best. But as she entered, nothing felt particularly ominous, at least for a gaming facility.

The entire room was painted dark gray with long white lights lining the walls giving the effect of highways circling the room. Interspersed between these highways at odd angles were darkened screens. Amelie didn't know what they were for, as Verite used suits and headgear, but perhaps there were other games used.

The floor was white marble and so shiny that it looked waxed. Amelie had learned to be suspicious of floors like these. It was hard to get rid of blood stains on carpet, but on this sort of floor—well, no one would ever be any the wiser.

At various points around the room were chairs of differing sorts. There were some basic, rolling, black plastic office chairs. There were also high-backed blue velvet chairs. In the center of the room were ten black and red padded leather lounge chairs. Each of these had a Verite headset sitting in it. There were chairs but no people.

She, Caio, and Lynche were the first ones in the room.

148

"Come on in and sit down. It looks like the big man is a little late," said Lynche. He then sat down in one of the rolling chairs.

"Where do we sit?" Amelie asked.

"Wherever you want," Lynche said.

"Right," Caio said, promptly sitting cross-legged on the ground. He looked for all the world like the surly teen that Amelie knew he was not.

He is avoiding places where he knows there will be sensors.

As Amelie felt it would be unwise to show the suspicion she currently felt, she simply rolled her eyes a bit for the benefit of Lynche and sat down in one of the plastic rolling chairs. She also began to run the chorus of "YMCA" in a loop inside her head for the benefit of mind readers, if there happened to be any.

A few seconds later, James and Majo appeared at the door with Camp. They were wearing the same black bodysuit that Amelie was. Caio was still in his white one, with the blood stains. Majo glanced at him quickly and then glanced at Amelie. Amelie shrugged. Then Majo lifted her hand and ran a delicate finger very slowly across the scar on her cheek.

Her scar ... the origin of which Amelie now knew.

Majo remembers. So she was there in the game with me.

James's face was stony all through this, and he was avoiding making eye contact. Majo moved silently to sit down, ramrod straight, in the recliner. James opted for a high-backed velvet seat.

"So where's the Director?" James asked.

"He will be here in a minute, pet," Camp said.

"You finished your work early?" Amelie asked Camp, forcing a smile, and hoping it wasn't too obvious.

"Well, it turns out that my data was already collected and is collating, so I have some time. I decided to use the opportunity to see your personal orientation with the Director," Camp replied, with tone that sounded bright and tinny to Amelie's ears.

At that moment, as if called by his name, the Director walked in—with Widget. Widget did not look well. His face was pale and there were blue-green shadows under his eyes. His normal posture, perfect and mildly geeky, was nowhere to be seen. Instead, his shoulders were slumped, and his head lowered. As they crossed the threshold of the room, he stumbled a bit, and the Director caught him. When Widget looked up, his expression was pained.

"What's wrong with Widget?" James asked, beginning to stand. Amelie noticed that both Lynche and Camp had tensed muscles and wary eyes.

"He's fine," the Director said, leading him to a lounge chair. "He is having a bit of a harder transition out of his Verite exercise last night. That happens to some people the first few times. The best thing to do is usually to go back in. It resets people."

"You okay, Widge?" Amelie asked, starting to stand herself, but Widget put his hand up.

"Steady," he signed. She was unsure if that was a statement or a warning.

With the Director's help, Widget sat down less than gracefully in one of the lounge chairs next to Majo. Majo reached over and placed her hand on Widget's thigh. He turned to her and nodded.

The Director pulled up one of the rolling chairs and straddled it, sitting with his arms resting on the back.

"So here we are," he said with a smile. "I am happy to see all of you here. I make it a point of holding these individual sessions with all the groups here, but I am particularly happy to see all of you. I have heard so much about you from my data analysis teams. They've been telling me about your potential for a few years now. After viewing the data we got from last night's Verite sessions, it seems like they were right on the money."

"So what were you tracking and what were you looking for?" James asked. He had returned to his seat, but his arms were folded in front of him, and he was stock-still. The disgust in his voice was mirrored on his face.

"Well, what we were looking for, and what we normally track in first sessions, is simply your baseline vital signs," the Director said calmly. "That is almost all we get out of most recruits in the first few days. In a few rare instances, some recruits begin to explore and travel through the different matrix elements of the game. In these cases, we begin to track the changes in your vital signs as it pertains to the areas of the game that you enter." He smiled. "Imagine our surprise when not one but two of you began to explore the game in your first few sessions. So we began to track your movements against the backdrop of the game, and we got quite a surprise."

The Director turned to Majo.

"Majo, you and Amelie found each other in Verite last night, did you not?"

Amelie felt a surge of energy coming from the center of her stomach, that she immediately focused on the floor. She purposefully raised her eyebrows slightly, to show a reaction but a lesser one.

Majo didn't bat an eye, she just nodded.

"How did you know that?" James asked.

"We can track the areas of your brain that have the most activity. The exact pattern of those electrical signals, their speed, their rhythm, and their resonance are like a musical phrase. And it's a bit like data from a GPS. We may not know exactly what's going on but the electrical signals we monitor to track you were exactly the same in Majo and Amelie."

"So you control what we see?" Amelie asked. She wanted to ask if they saw what she saw but didn't want to tip her hand.

"Oh no, we can only control what we present to you, not what you see. We aren't nearly that advanced yet," the Director said. "Someday, I hope. We also can't see what you see, but we *can* see what area of the game matrix you are in. We can also see how you are reacting to what you see through the sensors in the suits you are wearing."

Amelie opened her inner eye for a moment. The room around her began to shimmer and sparkle like glitter. Colors flashed everywhere in dazzling red, yellow, and green. There were strong emotions present, but there was no pattern of falsehood.

"We know that you and Majo were very close in the matrix and after you came together, you stayed together. But it was the coming together part that intrigued me most. Given the nature of your pod."

"The nature of our pod? Is there something particular about our group then?" James asked. James was not trying to hide his suspicion, and this worried Amelie. He was usually savvier than this.

"Actually, yes," the Director said, with a warm smile. "Your group has … what can I call it … synched … in an unusual fashion."

"How so?" asked Majo softly. Her face was so immobile that Amelie barely saw her lips move.

"Well, you know that we at the Academy test and track you. With your pod we discovered that, over a very short period, all of your bodies seemed to sync to each other. This showed in a multitude of little ways. If all four of you were in a room, your bodies impact each other. For example, if one of you was exhibiting a lower-than-normal body temperature, the bodies of the others heat up in response, and so on and so forth. But this is just what happened on a biochemical level. On a genetic level, what has happened is more shocking and unique. It seems that there has been some horizontal gene transfer, HGT, between all of you."

"How do you know that?" Widget signed. He was now sitting up a bit straighter on the lounger.

"Well, some of you have, shall we say, unusual genetic markers. These markers are unique and are likely a result of your different heritage and your particular gifts. So imagine our surprise when we saw that some of these markers had been

151

found in other members of your pod. Even the most recent members of your pod," the Director said, nodding at Caio.

Caio didn't move or flinch. His eyes were focused on the Director.

"That's not possible," Caio said flatly.

"That's what we thought," the Director said. "Or that's what we would have thought. In your particular case, we were sure that your natural virus would kill any invading protein strand. That is one of the many reasons we put you in this pod. But it didn't. You, like all the rest of the pod, have been adapted to this pod via HGT. We don't know how this has happened. Do you?"

Caio shook his head and then looked down. Amelie saw red, black, and yellow plumes of light rise from his shoulders, shiny and transparent.

The Director nodded to himself.

"So we set up a test to see how you would respond, to see if these new markers in you gave rise to any new traits or behaviors. We put Amelie under serious stress by setting her up with a mark who was known to be possessed by something unusually horrible."

He turned to Amelie.

"I am very sorry about that, Amelie darling. I know that could not have been easy for you, and I am sure it was quite scary, but the situation did produce exactly what we were hoping it would produce. We saw evidence of new ability and new behaviors."

"In all of us?" Caio asked.

"Yes. We already knew that Majo could see non-human things in human form. We knew that James was a soul stealer. We knew that Caio could self-heal. But we suspected you could do more so we set the stage and waited to see what would happen. And what happened surpassed our expectations."

The Director looked at Amelie.

"The first thing was that we discovered that Amelie could attract non-human things as well as human things. The creature possessing Ossian Reese was very far removed from human, and yet she was just as attractive to this thing as she can be to humans."

"It didn't work the same, though. I couldn't control him, the mark," Amelie said.

"Not yet. But my guess is that you can learn that. We can teach you that. But he was attracted to you nonetheless. This is probably a new thing for you that has come as a result of the HGT. Something of Majo's connection to non-human resonances combined with your abilities to attract."

Doubt it. Ossian, or the thing in him, wasn't the first non-human to find me attractive.

Camp suddenly turned to stare at her.

Amelie started listing popes in her head, on top of "YMCA," to better cover her thoughts. She was beginning to suspect Camp of being one of the mind readers.

The Director then turned to Majo.

"Majo, how did you get into the heavily guarded and heavily monitored hotel where Ossian Reese was staying?"

"I flirted my way in," Majo said softly.

"And would you say that flirting normally comes easily for you? It is a strength for you?" the Director asked with a smile.

Majo shook her head.

"No, it's not. Being invisible is something you can do well, but glamouring isn't your gift, is it? However, given your blood work, it seems that there has been some gene transfer between you and Amelie."

The Director turned to James.

"And James, did you get your hand mended? The one that you broke when you sucked the spirit out of Ossian Reese?"

"How did you know I broke my hand?" James asked.

"We were monitoring everything. And your hand was broken. But by morning, it was healed. I wonder how that happened?" he said, turning to Caio, who was wide-eyed.

"And Caio, you weren't with this pod for very long at all, yet you were willing to expose that you can talk to ghosts to save Amelie. That was an interesting little fact that you had kept from us for many a long year. People don't do that sort of thing unless they care, do they? Particularly if they know it might change the stakes for them."

Caio was stone-still. His face was placid, but his eyes flashed toward Amelie.

"I can't care for anyone that I met after I was infected." That's what Caio had said. But I met him in the hallway. Was that before? Did that mean he knew me when he saw me after that, in the auditorium? Or is the Academy right, has he been altered by one of them?

The Director smiled and held out his hands.

"I mention all of this simply to show that you have attached to each other in unique ways. We have never seen this before, so we suspect that it is something special about the interplay between the four of you."

He didn't mention Widget. Why didn't he mention Widget?

"What does this have to do with Verite?" Caio asked.

"Alert and direct as always, Mr. Silva," the Director said. "What we hope is that your connection to each other will allow you to both find each other, and eventually work with each other, in the matrix of the game."

He stood up and began to pace the room. "You see, Verite is a matrix that is both minuscule and infinite. It has been very difficult for people to navigate once inside the game."

"It's not much of a game if you can't interact with other users," James said.

"Oh. No. That's not exactly what I meant. In most ways, it's like all other games. You can invite your friends; you can connect with other people. But those interactions are triggered outside the game. You choose friends and people to connect while you are outside the game matrix. That input goes into the game and is transmitted to other people when they are outside the game," the Director said.

"Yes, but you said that everyone is connected to the Academy through the game, right? All data feeds back to the Academy? How does that happen?" Widget asked.

"It's part of the initial start-up for the game. They have to connect to us to get into the game, so that gives us access to them. But that initial connection originates from outside the game. Of course, it provides us continual biometric data but it's something else to locate a particular person once inside the game, from within the substrate."

"Substrate?" Caio asked, folding his hand together and rubbing his palm with his thumb.

"Yes, substrate," the Director replied. "And within that substrate, you can only find people who have agreed to be found by you from the outside."

"And why would it be useful for us to be able to find someone within the substrate who has not agreed to be found by us?" Majo asked.

"As a way to influence unseen," the Director said with a smile. "Imagine what could be done if we can get directly into someone's subconscious via the game. Imagine the influence you could exert if someone thought you were nothing more than a part of the game."

"Couldn't you just use NPCs for that?" Widget asked. "An NPC could influence via information dumping as well."

"NPCs aren't elegant enough to adapt quickly to all the different levels of data it will be receiving, or to respond and drive participants down all the different rabbit holes that this information can open up. Besides, the game's use as influence is just one level of interaction."

Widget was more alert and together now, and Amelie could read his body language well enough to know that the answer the Director had given didn't sit well with him.

"But what we might be able to do inside the game is speculative at this point," the Director continued. "We need to be able to navigate it better. So first, we need to discover how people can connect with each other inside the game, rather than outside the game. As we have seen that two of you have already done this, without input from the outside, we want to see if you can do it again and to measure exactly what is happening. Then maybe it can be learned or taught."

"So this will be your first official mission inside Verite, to find each other," the Director said, and then waved toward the lounge chairs with headpieces sitting on them.

"Please, have a seat, and let's get you plugged in," he said, motioning to Caio, who was still sitting on the floor.

Amelie sat in a chair that was between James and Majo. Caio stood up and moved to a chair just across from her.

"Your mission this time is just to find each other," the Director said, as Camp and Lynche moved between them, helping to adjust the headpieces.

As Amelie placed the headpiece on, all went black. She heard a door opening, and steps walking away from her.

"So find each other," the Director's voice said. "And defend each other."

Amelie just had time to feel moist heat on her skin and open her eyes to the white blankness of the game, when she was thrown to the ground.

Chapter Nineteen

No Heart in the Jungle

Caio was standing above her, a long, curved metal spear with razor-sharp edges in his hands. They were surrounded by a crowd of some of the most grotesque humans she had ever seen.

"Get up! Fight!" Caio yelled at her.

Caio stood in front of Amelie. Facing him, shocking in contrast to the normal blankness of the game substrate, there were twenty or thirty or maybe more people—or a sort of people. All of them were humanoid. All of them were deformed. And all of them looked like children.

As Amelie scrambled to her feet, James suddenly appeared next to Caio. Two of the creatures lunged for him but Caio jumped forward and sliced their outstretched, lumpy, mottled arms.

"They're kids!" James said.

"They're not kids!" Caio yelled, crouched, spear held out in front of him. "They're training. Think of a weapon, anything."

James held out his hand, and a long butcher's knife appeared there.

Amelie tried to think of something, but her eyes were glued to one small creature in front of her. It had the face and head of a boy, with dark skin, short dark hair, and big brown eyes. He was about five feet tall with thin legs, a thin trunk, and thin upper arms. But that was where normalcy ended. His lower arms were five times the size that they should have been and his hands twenty times the size they should have been. He had eight fingers on one hand and ten on the other. He smiled at her, but when he opened his mouth, maybe to speak, three tongues emerged from it, all layered on top of each other.

What did that to them? The game did that to them?

"If they are from the game, they can't really hurt us, right?" Amelie asked, as her curare ring appeared on her finger.

"Yes, they can. If building muscle in this place results in building muscle on our bodies, what do you think death in this place will mean? Or injury?" Caio was spinning around, slicing faces, arms, necks.

The boy with the deformed hands grabbed Amelie's arm, and she whirled and ripped her ring across his face.

James was fighting ferociously. He sliced the throat of a creature that looked like a cross between a human and a recliner in one move and then turned and immediately stabbed another creature resembling a bloated fish on legs in its eye socket.

Suddenly the sound of gunshots filled the air.

"Down," James yelled, pulling Amelie to the ground.

Creature after creature around them dropped, each shot in the head or face. They had barely had time to turn and begin shambling toward the shooter before they were all taken down.

Amelie saw Majo standing, gun in hand, in sharpshooter stance. When the last of the creatures fell, she stood for an additional moment. Sure enough, a couple twitched and Majo double tapped, securing her work.

"Knives? You guys chose knives when you were outnumbered twenty to one? I thought you were good at this," Majo said, rolling her eyes. "It's a good thing those things weren't quicker, or we might have had more trouble."

Majo walked toward them. She was still wearing her black game suit, as were the rest of them. Caio's suit was now black, no longer white with bloodstains.

"You think if these things killed us in here, we'll actually die?" James asked, panting.

"I don't know for sure, but I didn't think any of you would want to take the chance," Caio said with a shrug. "It's different for me. I'm hard to kill, in case you hadn't picked that up."

James poked at one of the creatures with his foot. It flopped over with a wet squishing sound. A moment later, the dead thing released gas that sounded and smelled like flatulence. It then deflated, its milky liquid insides leaking from it, and forming a spreading puddle beneath it.

"You'd think the geniuses who made this game would have created something a bit better formed. As adversaries, they aren't much," James said.

"That depends on what they are supposed to do," Caio replied. "Maybe they weren't supposed to kill us. Maybe it is a test of our weaknesses."

"Like sympathy?" Amelie asked, looking at the deformed childlike things around her.

"Yes, exactly. Or empathy," Caio said, looking a bit sternly at Amelie.

157

So they noticed. It was true, she had choked for a moment because she felt sorry for them. Operatives couldn't afford to choke. Operatives who choked usually died. She had never choked before, but she had never been attacked by mutated children before, either.

"Maybe it's a test of our psychological weaknesses, but I'm more worried about our physical weaknesses," Majo said. "As far as we know, those things could be contagious."

"Contagious?" Amelie asked. "But they are part of the game."

"For the record, I'm not sure those things were constructs from a game," Majo said, pointing behind them.

There, maybe fifty feet away from them, was an open door. Even from this distance, Amelie could see the green of trees on the other side.

Caio went pale.

"We need to talk, but not here," Majo said, nodding toward the door.

"I'm not going in that place," Caio said, taking a step backward.

"Why not? I don't think they can track us in there," Majo said.

"I know they can't, but I still won't go," Caio said.

All of them turned to look at him. His dark eyes were cold and his jaw set.

"Why?" Majo asked.

"It's a place from my past that I won't have you see."

"Then you need to get over yourself, mate," James snapped.

"And you need to stop acting like you understand things you don't," Caio replied icily.

James opened his mouth, but Majo held up her hand.

Instead, she walked to Caio and took his face in her hands. To the shock of everyone, she kissed him on the lips.

"There is nothing you've done, nothing we can see, that would be worse than what I have done and seen," Majo said, putting her forehead to his.

Caio closed his eyes, then pulled away. "Wanna bet?" he said, with a cynical laugh, but his eyes were shiny.

James suddenly raised his hand. He was smiling but it was off-kilter.

"Oh, I'll take that bet," James said, with an edgy laugh. "If we want to start comparing sins—you're all a bunch of fucking amateurs."

Majo gave him a sharp look then turned back to Caio.

"Be that as it may, that door is the best chance for a private space—" Majo began, but Amelie cut her off.

"The Director said that they couldn't hear what we said in the game, and that rang true."

158

"Yes, but he could still have people in the game that he can garner information from. Like those things, for example," Majo said as she poked at a sack of flesh at her feet. "I don't want to take that chance and we need to talk, and plan."

Caio's eyes turned to the door; rain was obscuring the green behind it now. He then looked around, catching all their eyes. When he caught Amelie's, she simply returned his gaze and remained silent. She had a good idea of what was on the other side of that door, and she was not about to push Caio to relive that.

Finally, Caio shrugged, nodded and without another word, turned and walked through the door.

The rest of them followed suit.

***

Amelie felt the heat of the place before she had even walked through the door— the heat and the moisture. The rain was tapering off now, and she could see a lush green forest in the distance.

It wasn't until she stepped through the door that her suspicions were confirmed. The place looked the same as the last time she had been there. There was the rain, the jungle, the cleared patch of earth, and the hole in the middle of it.

Caio had walked to the hole and was peering over the edge.

Please let him not be down there.

But it seemed that nothing was amiss, as he turned from it with a shrug.

"It looks exactly the same, minus the foreman—and the whips, and the crying, and the dead bodies," he muttered.

"You know this place?" Majo asked.

"This is where they kept me. This is where I was raped and thrown into that hole to die. That … that was where I should have died but I didn't," he whispered, looking at the hole.

"I can't describe to you what it was like in that hole … or what was in it. You don't want to know, and I don't want to remember. But I will tell you that there were worms everywhere. They burrowed into me. They changed me."

"How did you end up there?" Majo asked softly.

"My parents sold me. That was a different time and different place. Love between parents and children wasn't expected in that world. What I don't understand about what they did is that it wasn't logical. I was supposed to be of value. I could've worked. I could've found food. That was valuable, so why did they sell me into slavery? And not just slavery but a slavery that would likely be nothing but torture leading to eventual death."

They said nothing. Around them, it seemed even the jungle had gone quiet. Caio was still staring at the hole.

"What made it horrible was that I still felt things then. I felt the pain, and the anger and the betrayal that I wouldn't, couldn't, feel now. And the only break that I had from it was when I hallucinated. I kept having the same hallucination about this woman. She had light hair and freckles and she had the whitest teeth I had ever seen. When she came, the pain would go away for a bit, and I would feel less desperate and alone."

Caio's voice was flat and dead-sounding.

"That's horrible," Majo said, eyes on the hole.

Caio snorted and turned to them.

"Oh no, I was lucky. You have no idea what they did to people here. They stole children from their families. They forced us to work and only fed us enough to keep us alive. Most of us were whipped daily. When we died, our bodies were then given to the dogs to eat."

Amelie felt her stomach lurch.

"You know what they used to do for entertainment—the foreman?" Caio said, staring up into the trees. "They would grab children by their feet and bash their heads into tree trunks. They thought that was the height of humor. Oh—no, the funniest was when they set us on fire. That was apparently the funniest of the funny."

"How did you get out of the hole?" James, in a much softer voice than Amelie had ever heard before.

"Someone saved me."

"Who?" asked Majo.

"A local Indian tribe heard me moaning and pulled me out. I lived with them for two or three years. I healed. I was happy. I even met a girl who loved me. But that ended badly. The tribe found out about us and kicked me out."

"Because you loved some girl?" Amelie asked.

"No, because they realized that I wasn't aging."

"How could that happen?" James asked.

"I was infected with a bacterium or a virus that was missing the DNA for aging. Those cells then replicated in me. So I don't age, and I heal incredibly fast. I'm immune to other bacteria and viruses because I'm part virus."

Caio closed his eyes for a moment. Amelie felt a sudden urge to hug him, to protect him.

"The girl you loved?" Majo asked.

"I didn't say I loved her," Caio said, opening his eyes. "I said she loved me. That was the other problem."

He looked back at the hole. His dark eyes shining with something that might have been a buried rage. He sighed.

"From the time that they pulled me from the well until—well, now—I haven't aged but I also haven't really been able to care about anyone. Not really. I can be nice and polite. I can speak with people and have pleasant, shallow relationships. But I can't feel anything for them. There has only been one exception to that."

Sarah. Sarah Baker, Amelie thought, remembering the vision she had of him in the hole.

"I feel almost nothing about everything, actually," Caio continued. "I fail all the psych tests, so I guess I am a monster."

"You aren't a monster," Majo said. "The people who put you in that hole were the monsters."

"See, I told you that you would find things here worse than you have ever done," Caio said. "The worst part is that we are now working for some of the descendants of the people who did this."

"The Academy did this?" James asked.

"Early members of the Academy financed it," Caio said. "They were just looking for the money and looked the other way in terms of what was sacrificed for that."

"If that's true, how can you stand to be an operative?" James asked, his voice now significantly gentler.

"That was the past. This is the now. Sometimes you have to work inside the evil to prevent more evil," Caio said.

"That sounds like the end justifies the means," James said.

"Of course it does," Majo said. "And that's the basis for everything we do. It is the justification for the people we kill. It's the justification for the lives we destroy. That somehow what we do makes things better. Somehow things we do can prevent places like this. This is what I told myself, but I'm questioning it now."

"Well, my goals are much smaller than that now," Caio said softly. "But, if you don't mind, can we walk away from this exact spot where I was raped and tortured? Then we can talk a little bit about our current situation and what we should do."

***

All of them nodded, and Caio then turned and moved quietly into the trees. The others followed him. The only sounds around them were made by the jungle; the sound of crushed vegetation as they forced their way through it felt violent and invasive. The buzzing of the insects in the thick air, a sound that had seemed merely tropical minutes before, now filled Amelie's brain with images of blood and carnage. As Amelie let her inner eye open, she saw flashes of blood-red and bone-white lights bounce off the green of the trees. It seemed that the land carried a memory of horror and Amelie was afraid of how this memory might show itself in years to come. If only she could burn this place down.

Her thoughts turned to Caio. What must he have lived through ... and for so many years ...

"Okay, this will do." Caio stepped from the tree line where the forest gave way to a large lake surrounded by trees. In front of them was a small wooden pier extending into muddy green water. The surface of the lake near the shore was covered with giant lily pads, roughly the size of a garbage can lid. Buzzing on top of these were flies that looked about twice the size of normal flies.

Everything is big here. The vegetation, the insects, the crimes against humanity, Amelie thought, as she stepped out onto the pier. The planks were silvery and cracked. They groaned with their weight.

Caio came to the end of the pier and sat down cross-legged.

"This will do," he said again. "We can see from all sides. But don't put your feet over the edge. We have crocodiles here, you know."

James, who had just put his feet over the edge, quickly pulled them back up.

"Okay, so we are here, and we managed to find each other, but where is here? Inside the game?" Majo asked.

"No, I don't think this part is inside the game," Caio said. "This is something straight out of my memory and I don't think the game is that sophisticated yet."

"Yes, and about that, those things out there. The things we just killed. They weren't part of the game either. Not completely. I know that," Majo said.

"How?" Amelie asked.

"Because I could see them," Majo replied. "I mean, I could see how they really look. They didn't look the same as the things I had seen in the game before, you know, the first couple of times we went in. When I look at things made in the game, they look the same to me as I am sure they do to you. That's because they have no history. But those things, the things we just killed, they have a history of some sort. And that history makes me see them, maybe in a worse way than what you saw."

"Then you didn't see what we saw," James muttered.

"Yes, I did. For a minute," Majo replied. "And let me tell you, what I saw afterward was such an abomination that shooting them felt like an act of absolution."

"They were from here, not the game," Caio said. "They were from an earlier part of my story or my lineage. They were what happened when infected people like me tried to reproduce."

"Jesus," James said.

"Hardly," Caio said. "The virus eventually ate out the human consciousness in the host and tried to create its own. You just saw the result."

Amelie and the others stared at him. The horror of Caio's existence was becoming clearer the more he spoke.

Caio shrugged. "But Majo's point is right. Those things were not made by the game. But how did they end up in it, and how did we get here?"

"You don't think the Academy made this?" Majo asked, gesturing around them.

"This—no, the Academy didn't construct this," Caio said. "I think they simply constructed the white stuff, or green stuff that we usually wake up into. The first few times that I was plugged in, all I saw was very good video game imagery. I had a few fights with some orcs or something, and the graphics were good, but not like this. Not even like the things we just saw. Those things were an abomination, but a real one."

"That was true for me too," Majo said. "At least the first time. The first time I went in, I saw nothing but flowers and a park. I think it was supposed to be Japan, and it was nice. There were smells and I could touch things, but even the touch felt different, it didn't feel real. It felt like the natural extension of video gaming into 4D. I thought it was impressive until I ended up in my own history the next time I was plugged in and saw the difference. That was real."

"So what was different between those times?" Caio asked.

Everyone was quiet.

"I was what was different," Amelie said, surprised to hear her own voice. "I think I drew the real things to us."

"What do you mean?" Caio asked.

Amelie paused for a second. She had never shared this part of her life with anyone. But, looking at Caio's calm face against a backdrop of a place where he had experienced so much horror, she pushed aside her caution. What she had seen from Caio and Majo demanded an equal showing from her—equal vulnerability.

"I've been in places like this before," Amelie said.

"Like the Amazon?" Caio asked.

"No, I've been in … how do I explain it—" She stopped and took a breath. "When I was young, I used to be able to fly inside my head. I used to be able to find a hallway, and from there I could go to all sorts of places. Someone told me that they were other stories, other realities. The hallway seemed to come to me, or it used to."

James was up and had his hand over her mouth before she even saw him move.

"Shhhh. You shouldn't speak of that. Not here. Not ever. Not with anyone," he said.

"I already know about it," Caio said.

"How?" Amelie asked, after removing James's hand from her mouth.

"The Academy discusses the hallway at certain levels of clearance," Caio replied. "And that thing on your sleeve when you came to pick me up. I picked it off because I knew it was not right when I saw it."

"What thing? What did it look like?" Amelie whispered.

"It looked like a bug wing, but not of any bug in our world, it was hairy and sticky," Caio replied.

Majo turned to Amelie.

"Was that from those things that attacked us the last time we were here?" Majo asked.

Amelie paused, then nodded. There wasn't much else she could do.

"You brought that *back* with you?" James whispered.

Amelie nodded.

"Sometimes I can do that. I don't try, it just happens. What did you do with it?" Amelie asked, turning to Caio.

"I dropped it on the floor in the atrium. It was transparent and not very substantial, and it will be crushed by people walking through," he replied.

James shook his head.

"We can't talk about that. None of us can repeat that. Not out there and not in here," he said softly.

"I agree," Caio said. "This is something that we should keep an eye out for, but never mention. The Academy would be way too interested. In fact, that might be the reason we are all at ACID. They may think one or more of us can get into the hallway. It's incredibly rare so they are always on the lookout for people who can do it."

"Why?" Majo asked.

"I could guess but I don't know for sure," Caio replied. "What I do know is, if they are looking for it that hard, I sure as hell wouldn't tell them that I could call it, let alone do … other things."

He looked pointedly at Amelie.

"I know why they are looking for it," James said.

"Why?" Amelie asked.

James stood up and walked a little way up the pier, searching their surroundings. Then he came and sat back down.

"I am guessing that we have all heard bits about this," James said, facing them. "Our world is one of many. Our world has many universes or dimensions—those are all part of our story. But what I'm talking about is completely different stories, whole other existences. Like books sitting in a library are all different stories. The hallway is a gateway to those other stories. Some rare individuals can get to the hallway."

"Did you hear all this at the Academy?" Amelie asked.

"No, I knew about it before I even got here," James said, eyes down. "And I'm guessing that the rest of you did too?"

They all nodded.

I learned from Clovis. Who did they learn from? Were all of them involved with an incubus?

"I think this game may be their way to try to punch holes in reality and find a short cut to the hallway," James continued.

"Well, maybe that isn't working so well if we needed Amelie to get to the stories we have been in," Majo said.

"Maybe. Maybe the game makes it easier for people who can," James said.

"Or, as the Director was so interested in our gene transfer," Caio said, "maybe he thinks that if one of us can do this then the others absorbed some of this ability. The game might speed that up."

"How?" James asked.

"Like he said, time works differently here," Caio replied. "Also, as I'm sure you all noticed, at our assembly the Director said these suits had a viral interface. Viruses are designed to insert DNA into cells and then make those cells replicate the DNA. Maybe he thinks the game will speed up that process. Or maybe he's stealing bits of our DNA to experiment with other people or to use in the game. It could be lots of things."

"Jesus," James muttered again.

"You say that a lot. Did you know him or something?" Caio asked, then turned to the others. "But my question is why the Academy would be so interested in the hallway?"

"Probably because they think that if there are enough people searching the hallway, they might find the door that leads to the library," James responded.

"What's the library?"

165

The library. Amelie had heard that term before.

"It's ... it's ... I don't know exactly. It's like the office of god. You can change all existences from there." That's what Clovis had said about it. He had been afraid that Dante might think I could get there.

"I don't know exactly. It's supposed to be the place where creation is born. It's where the idea of new worlds become real. It where stories that authors create go to become real." James stopped for a minute. "But there is no record of anyone ever seeing it. In incubus legend, Psyche was supposed to have gotten there and made a world for herself and Cupid to live in."

"So why is the Academy so interested in this?" Amelie asked.

"Why wouldn't they be?" James replied. "The Academy is all about power and control. The library is the ultimate power. It's the power to control literally everything. Everything that was, everything that is, everything that ever will be. Everything across all realities."

"And they believe such a place actually exists?" Caio asked.

"The Director does," James said.

Caio rolled his eyes. "So that's the reason for his insanity then," he said. Amelie wasn't sure if it was a question or a statement.

"To be honest, I'm not very sure what is sane anymore," Majo said quietly. "Everything we have experienced here is outside the realm of what is normal and sane. We, ourselves, are outside the realm of the expected. But I believe Amelie when she says that she brought us here and that this might be the hallway she describes. Are we all in agreement on that?"

All nodded, including Caio.

"So the Director might be right," Majo said. "But for us, it means he cannot know this. He cannot know we have come here. He cannot guess that any of us can get anywhere besides the game construct."

"We need to get out, off this island as quickly as possible," Amelie said, thinking of the vials holding Sophie's blood. "They are torturing people here."

Amelie was expecting questions but all she got was nods.

"And we trust no one in this place," Caio said.

Who would I trust? My creepy troll nurse? Or my possessed handyman ... oh right.

"And we only speak about these things while we are in the hallway," Majo said. "In the meantime, we put all our energies into learning as much as we can about this place so we can find a way off this island. Any possible way."

"There's something else," Amelie said. "I saw Ossian Reese."

"What? Where?" This was James.

"He was the person they sent to fix my retinal scanner," Amelie replied. "He was dressed like a handyman."

"Are you sure it was him?" Caio asked.

"I'm sure it was on the outside," Amelie said softly. "But he didn't seem to recognize me or remember me at all."

"Right, we absolutely need to get out of here as quickly as possible," Majo said. "There is something going on with almost everyone I have seen since I came here, present company excluded. I told Amelie this already but most of the people here in ACID are probably not human."

"How do you know?" Caio asked.

As Majo explained her experiences since coming to ACID, Amelie looked around. She was beginning to feel something, as if something were pulling at her. She opened her inner eye for a moment, but nothing was out of place. There were no unusual colors or symbols. It was more like a void. It was like a silence.

Silence …

"Where's Widget?" Amelie said suddenly, jumping to her feet. "They hooked him into the game at the same time they hooked us in!"

How could we have forgotten him?

The others were getting to their feet when an image flickered on the pier just in front of them. It was Widget. His body was rigid, and his fists clenched. His face, normally so composed, was contorted, as if in pain. His lips were pulled back over his teeth and his eyes were closed.

"Widget!" Amelie called.

"It's him," Majo said, jumping up. "I see him."

Widget opened his eyes and held out his arms to them.

"Help me!" he said, in a voice he had never had, and they had never heard. "They are trying to take me!"

Caio, James, and Majo ran forward.

Amelie was on her feet but something invisible inserted itself between her and Widget. At the instant the other three touched him, the whole world around them cracked. Amelie heard an ear-splitting roar, and then reality exploded with a blast that knocked her off her feet.

Chapter Twenty

Plastic Cows

When Amelie looked up, the jungle was gone. She wasn't in the green game matrix either. Instead, she found herself lying on scratchy, cheap, burgundy wall-to-wall carpeting. It smelled of car air fresheners, rubber, and feet. Her ears were still ringing from the blast she had just been through.

She sat up, staring and taking in her surroundings. She was in the middle of a Western Steer on New Year's Day ... and the others were nowhere to be seen. This was not just any Western Steer. It was *her* Western Steer. The one that she had worked at during her teen years. The one with the giant plastic cow sitting in the parking lot and the chicken clock on the wall.

For the moment, everything around her was frozen in stasis but as Amelie watched, the colors of the Western Steer started to become more vibrant, or as vibrant as they were ever going to be at a Western Steer. As the color was returning, she began to hear sounds as well. The sound of a car outside. The murmur of the voices of people that she could not yet see.

Amelie stood up and turned around. The room was basically a large rectangle with brown faux leather family booths around the perimeter. The center of the room was filled with square faux wood tables paired with faux wood chairs on each side, designed for the classic American family of four. To her left, Gavin, one of the regulars, suddenly appeared, pale and unmoving, seated at a booth. She walked toward him and tried to touch him, but her hand went through his image.

Where is my pod? What had happened to Widget? Why have I come here, and where am I? Am I in the hallway or the game?

At the far end of the rectangle was the salad bar and cashier's stand. Behind those were the kitchens. The salad bar was filled with trays of iceberg lettuce, pickles, cucumbers, tomatoes, olives, and the other requisite foodstuffs for a

Southern salad bar. There were potatoes wrapped in foil next to tubs filled with butter, sour cream, green onions, chili, and some sort of meat gravy—because you could never have too many meat toppings. The kitchen behind this looked black and unfinished for the moment.

On one wall was the giant yellow chicken clock, which read 4:59. She had always hated the chicken clock with a vehemence. It was huge. It was ugly. Worst of all, it had no excuse to be there. It had nothing to do with steak, which was supposed to be the theme of this restaurant. It was simply a testament to the surprisingly rich owner's horrible taste in decor. On top of that, it was impossible to ignore, which meant that while she had been at work, she had watched it all the time, as the minutes had dragged by, in the same way that the proverbial watched pot never boils.

As if to prove her wrong, as she was looking at it, the chicken clock struck 5 p.m. and with it came the sound of crashing from the kitchen.

"Goddamn it!" yelled Bob, one of the cooks, from the kitchen.

"Hey, Amelie, how was your holiday?"

Amelie whirled around to find Gavin smiling at her.

"Fine. How about you?" she asked, walking back to him. She noticed that she was wearing her Western Steer uniform.

"Good. My mom came into town. She had to leave this morning, but it was nice to have her here for a few days," he said, taking off his coat and putting it on the booth next to him.

Amelie remembered that Gavin had died of heart failure a few years after she had joined the Academy. She had seen this in the local paper that she occasionally accessed online. But here he was again, a thirty-something single man, with no embarrassment or reserve about telling her that he had spent Christmas with his mother. She never really knew his full story, but she knew he had been good sort. Sadly, his treatment by others hadn't usually been what a good guy deserved. Maybe that was because Gavin had been an all-you-can-eat kind of guy, and that was very apparent. He was pushing 300 pounds if he was a pound. People tended to be nasty about things like that, even adults. Despite this, or perhaps because of it, he had always been extremely nice—tidy, respectful, and always left a large tip.

He was dead now but, as she was unsure of where she was, she thought it best to play along.

"Would you like a Diet Coke to start?" Amelie asked, remembering his habits instantaneously.

"Yes, thank you, Amelie," Gavin said. "Do you think you will get a lot of people today?"

169

"I think we'll get a few, but I doubt too many. How do you want your steak today?"

"Medium well," he replied, as if that needed to be said. It had always been the same.

As Amelie moved away, she wondered at herself. How many times a day had she uttered sentences like that, sentences that gave the impression of conversation but which relayed no actual information? Sentences that gave nothing and asked nothing. It was like she had been preparing to work for the Academy all her life. It had only been different with Clovis.

She had just sent the order for Gavin's steak to the back when she heard the bell on the front door jangle.

Amelie turned to see a man standing there with his wife and daughter in tow. They were all dressed like they had just come from church. Amelie felt the bile rise in her throat as she saw that the man was none other than Phillip Sawyer, the teacher who had tried to attack her and had later disappeared at the same time as her best friend, Hudson. The police had said that there had been "evidence of foul play" at Hudson's house and that Sawyer had been a suspect.

Right now, he looked like the model of a churchgoing man. He was wearing a plain, dark blue suit with an actual tie. It might have looked smart if there had not been obvious flakes of dandruff on the shoulders. His wife was a forty-something blonde who had probably been pretty when she was young, but who now had that puffy, bloated look of a woman who was paying for the sins of her youth. She was wearing a horrible floral dress that had no place showing itself in the dead of winter. Their daughter, whose name Amelie thought had been Shannon, was standing behind her parents wearing a plain black dress that screamed don't look at me.

"Hi, Mr. Sawyer," Amelie said, approaching them.

As she was here, she supposed that she would need to keep playing this role. Clovis had told her that this was what he had to do when he visited different stories. So Amelie thought that would be the safest thing to start with.

"Happy New Year, Amelie," Mr. Sawyer said, with a tone that sounded a bit whiny and accusatory.

"Happy New Year," she replied as brightly as she could muster, taking them toward their table.

"Is this one of your students?" his wife asked as they took their seats.

"Yes. Amelie has done quite well this year. I believe she will be getting accepted to some excellent universities. Am I right, Amelie?"

"Phil! That's her business," his wife chided, and Amelie saw his face turn pink.

170

"I'm Lisa Sawyer, Phil's wife," she said, extending a hand across the table for Amelie to shake. This required Amelie to lean forward right in front of Mr. Sawyer, and she could almost feel his breath on her arm. His wife's nails were pink, longish, and most assuredly fake.

"Pleased to meet you."

"You must excuse him. He doesn't mean to be nosy, he is just genuinely very interested in the well-being of his students."

Sure, do you still tell yourself that?

At that moment a few words from the menu began to light up.

Protein. Choice. Unlimited. She had no idea what that was supposed to mean, but then again, a steak menu wasn't a lot to work with.

A few more regular customers arrived at that moment, so Amelie used it as an excuse to extricate herself from the painful conversation, after dutifully taking the Sawyer family's order. There were now twelve people in the restaurant, and another family was getting out of their car. She became busy taking drink and steak orders and delivering said steaks and drinks. Everything else was done in buffet fashion.

"Excuse me, ma'am," said a deep, rich voice from behind her. She turned around to see a man sitting in a booth who had not been there seconds before. He had mocha-colored skin and the clearest hazel eyes she had ever seen. While his face was of the androgynous type with big eyes, long lashes and full lips, his body was far from androgynous. He was thin but tall and muscular. He was also wearing an army uniform. He was smiling at her.

The woman sitting opposite him had red hair, pale skin and crystal-blue eyes set in a sweet-looking face. She would probably would have been considered traditionally beautiful if she had been thinner, but she wasn't thin. Despite this, and maybe because of it, her beauty had more power behind it. She was staring at the man in front of her with a flushed face and adoring eyes.

"Hi, I'm so sorry, I didn't see you there," Amelie said.

"Ain't no problem at all," the man said. "But it would be nice if I could get a Sundrop."

"Oh, I'm sorry. I don't think we have that here. We have Mountain Dew, though," Amelie said with a smile. Something about this man just made her want to smile.

"Veronica, is a Mountain Dew okay for you, honey?" he asked, turning to the woman and taking her hand.

"Anything is fine," she said, in a soft Southern drawl.

"She just says that 'cause you're here," the man said. "I'll find out what she really thinks when you walk away."

He winked at her.

"Lazlo!" Veronica said, but she was laughing. Amelie smiled but glanced around her. This was North Carolina, and a black man with a white woman could still cause some nasty comments from the redneck type. But so far, no one seemed to notice them.

"Two Mountain Dews coming up. How would you like your steaks?"

"Just run mine through a warm room," Lazlo said. "My Veronica likes things a bit more done, so medium for her."

Veronica smiled and, for just a split second, she seemed to flicker. Amelie shook her head, but there was a sudden bang behind her that made her turn before she had time to think about it too much.

A gorgeous guy had just walked in, slamming the door behind him. Amelie cringed when she recognized him. It was Charlie Danos, the son of the owner. All the patrons of the restaurant turned to stare at him, in the uncontrollable way that people do when faced with unusual beauty. Yes, Charlie was extremely good-looking. He had short hair with natural, dark copper highlights and waves perfectly placed to frame his face. His eyes were a shocking blue against the tan of his face. He had full lips, thin hips, and the swagger of a rock star. He probably could have modeled if he hadn't fancied himself a musician. Yep, he was handsome, and he was carelessly cool. Unfortunately, he was also an asshole. The problem with Charlie had been twofold. First, he knew he was good-looking because people around him had always treated him with the deference that people give those who are freakishly gorgeous. Second, he was an awful musician who hadn't figured out the awful part yet. He treated everyone like they were just blurs seen from the window of his fast train to stardom.

He turned to stare at her.

"Hi Charlie," Amelie said.

"Hey. Don't get any ideas," Charlie snapped. "I'm not here to help. I'm just picking up something for the old man. I don't do this kind of work," he said, emphasizing the word *this* with a roll of his eyes. He then sauntered past her toward the office in the back, which suddenly came to life with light.

Amelie shook her head.

This was not a memory; it had not happened before. Okay, the Gavin conversation could have happened. He was a regular, but Charlie Danos was not. He actively avoided his father's restaurants, so she would remember if he had ever shown up, and he hadn't. She also would have remembered a biracial couple showing up in her little restaurant, in her little town in the South.

Why am I here? What is this place? And where are the others? she thought, and then someone called out for her, and she returned to her duties.

Just as she was returning for Gavin's fifth drink order at the bar, she saw another family enter and her throat closed up involuntarily. She had sort of suspected her brother might drop by—but this was so much worse.

Jack was standing there with his family. He was dressed casually, but casual with an effort. He was in jeans, a sweater, and a leather jacket. He caught her eye, smiled, and waved.

Great. Phil Sawyer. Jack. After this it would only take her brother to make this Dante's Inferno night at the steakhouse for Amelie, and an inferno night that had never happened.

Amelie squared her shoulders to greet Jack and his family, but at that moment Charlie walked out from the back office. Behind him, the kitchen suddenly lit up like fireworks in gold, red, yellow, and pink.

He casually grabbed a few menus and greeted the Turner family in a manner that was cordial, bordering on actually friendly. Amelie stood with her mouth open for only a fraction of a second. A family was waving her over for the bill, so she didn't have time to thank Charlie. She didn't know if he had a sudden attack of conscience or just felt like messing with Jack, who he would have detested as a jock.

She quickly bussed the table left by the family, as she noticed yet another family arriving. *What is wrong with you people, shouldn't you all be at home watching football?* She was about to greet them, but Charlie beat her to it. He had also refilled the drinks of a couple of tables.

At around 6:40 p.m., Lazlo waved for their check. Amelie walked over to find him and Veronica holding hands across the table. There was no doubt that these two people loved each other, and didn't give a shit what anyone else thought. Amelie wrote up the bill with a smile.

"Here you go, I hope you two enjoyed your meal," Amelie said as she handed him the bill.

"We certainly did," he said. "I had no idea it had gotten this late."

"Sorry to have taken up the booth for so long," Veronica said. "I hope we haven't lost you potential tips."

"No problem at all," Amelie said, touched by the fact that this woman even thought of such a thing.

"Can I pay this with a card?" Lazlo asked, holding up a credit card.

"Sure, let me get the machine," Amelie said, but Lazlo shook his head.

"No problem, I'll just walk up with you," he said, standing up.

"Lazlo, we should give her a better tip to make up for all the time we spent here," Veronica said to him.

"Of course, my love."

"Do you and Veronica live here?" Amelie asked, as they walked.

Lazlo laughed, but this was a different laugh.

"Here? What you mean by here?"

"I mean, in this town," Amelie said, as she walked behind the register.

Lazlo leaned on the counter.

"I think you and me both know that there ain't no town here," Lazlo said softly.

Amelie felt her heart double beat.

"Are you playing the game?" Amelie whispered, leaning forward.

"I ain't playing no game, and neither are you."

"Who are you?"

"I gave you my name, and it was true. It's Lazlo, but I'm guessing that's not what you are asking?"

He handed her his credit card.

"Speak soft, we don't know who is here," he said. "Most people around you are just constructs of some program they are using. Most of them don't know nothing and can't see nothing. But sometimes they're spies. And things are merging between both so you can't always know."

"Are you with the Academy?" she asked.

"Hell, no. I never got near that place," Lazlo said. "I was a ghost."

"A ghost? How did you end up here?" Amelie whispered.

"The angel that was supposed to take me to the upper winds took me here instead."

What sort of angel would put someone in a video game? Are there gaming angels?

"Where is 'here'?" Amelie asked. "I thought it was my story or my memories, but this obviously isn't a memory, because you wouldn't be in it."

"No, these ain't memories. At best they are borrowed, or stolen bits of memories taken from people outside, like you. Maybe they are stealing bits of your soul to make this. I don't know how it works, but it doesn't last long. Those of us caught in here move from scene to scene and story to story with no real consistency between them."

"You mean you can't get out?" Amelie asked.

"Yep, I'm stuck here."

"So, where is here?"

"I don't really know," Lazlo said. "When the angel brought me here, it looked like a dark light. But I think it was just the same as a black box that I saw take a human boy's soul. But who are you and how did you get in here?"

"I came through a game. They told us that all the other people in here were avatars of players or constructs of the game," Amelie said.

Lazlo snorted.

"In the room right now, there are at least four ghosts, including me. Three of us are trapped here, but I think the other one is here by choice and can get out. I'm not sure if you see all of us. There are a handful of—what did you say—game constructs. Things made by this place, like the room and the food. But there are also a few more things that are living things but I'm not quite sure what they are. You're the only human from outside."

"How do you know all that?" Amelie asked.

"I was—I am—a Cambion," Lazlo said. "I'm guessing you know the word." Amelie nodded.

"I was always able to see what someone or something really was, underneath what they said or what they looked like," Lazlo said.

"I know someone like that," Amelie whispered.

"Then I am guessing that person is pretty messed up," Lazlo said, as Amelie handed him his credit card receipt.

Suddenly a thought struck her. Lazlo said an "angel" brought him here, but that wasn't true. She knew by the way the word had rung metallic in her ears.

"You said an angel put you here?" Amelie asked. "Why would an angel do that? And if there is a ghost here that can get out, then maybe you can too. Have you tried?"

Lazlo shook his head with a wan smile.

"You caught me out, little girl," he said. "You're right. I'm not sure that the angel who brought me here was really an angel. Truth is, I got pulled away from the original angel by this dark light. That was when another angel appeared and offered for me to come inside. I guess she could have been a devil instead."

"Why would you do that? You said the dark thing was something that took a human boy's soul."

"Because of something the angel or demon told me before I was put in here. She said that I could spend eternities looking for my Veronica from life to life, and never finding her. Or worse, finding her and losing her all over again. Or I could stay here and be with her forever, with certainty. When I got here, I found her here, just like the angel said. So I stay. And I'm okay with it."

Amelie looked over at the booth. Veronica was staring at them with a strange intensity. As she did so, she flickered in and out, like an old movie projection.

"But, Lazlo, she may not be your Veronica," Amelie whispered, turning her eyes back to him. "I can see her flickering. I think she's just part of the game."

Lazlo turned around to look at Veronica and blew her a kiss.

"No, she's not part of the game," Lazlo said, turning back to Amelie. "And I know she's not exactly my Veronica. I also know that she's not part of this place. She's one of the living things that ain't human. You're right, they flicker in and out. The game things look more solid and normal here. The ghosts vibrate, and humans in the game move a bit slower than everything else. So she's something else."

Amelie touched Lazlo's hand lightly.

"If she's not your Veronica, why do you stay?"

Lazlo smiled and shrugged slightly.

"When I found her here, she was sitting in the dark with nothing around her, but she was a living thing. And she was alone and crying. When she saw me and I saw her, she came alive. Since then, she has been happy just to be with me. I am pretty sure that she was brought here, like me, but she don't know where she's from. She can't remember much. But she was lonely, like me, so that makes us the same. Also, I told you that I see things as they really are, so I know that there is a part of my Veronica inside her. I don't know how, or how much. And I don't know why but it's enough for me. I am happy."

At that moment, Veronica came up behind them.

"Is everything okay?" The question was directed at Lazlo, but she looked at Amelie. Her gaze was both intense and kind.

"Just trying to make you jealous, so you won't leave me," Lazlo said.

Veronica snorted and rolled her eyes, but Lazlo immediately took her face in his hands and gently kissed her mouth. She flickered again but then lit up like a firefly.

They then exited out the restaurant, hand in hand.

Amelie turned to look around the room. Was anyone else flickering?

Mr. Sawyer and his family were still eating. Mr. Sawyer was not flickering but she noticed his daughter blink out for a moment. Jack and his family were also still in their booths. Jack's eyes met hers and for a moment, she felt like she had felt in high school. Claustrophobic and trapped.

At that moment, she wanted nothing more than to get out of there.

How do I do that? Should I hold my breath? Will that work here?

When Jack started to move to get out of his booth, eyes still locked on her, she decided it was time to try. She was just turning to escape to the bathroom when she literally ran into Charlie.

"Hey, sorry about that," he said, putting his hands on her arms. At his touch, she felt an electricity slam through her.

"The family in the back want their bill. I'm a bit embarrassed to admit it, but I don't know how to do that," he said.

"Oh, that's fine. I can do it, I just need to take a pit stop. Thanks for helping. I don't know why all these people suddenly—" She stopped talking. Charlie was smiling and looking down at her with black eyes.

Black eyes. Warm black eyes that she hadn't seen since she was eighteen years old.

Chapter Twenty-One

Truth is Where the Heart Is

Amelie was staring up at Charlie's face, and the whirling black eyes in it that were not his.

The eyes that had saved her from the horror of her life. The eyes that had taught her to love. The eyes that had torn her soul apart.

"Oh, I ... okay," was all she managed to get out.

"Oh, you just now noticed," he said with a small smile. He then nodded to the family who wanted their bill.

"I'll get that," Amelie said quickly. She needed a second to think. She tried to calm her brain, but it was chanting in her head.

He's here, he's here, he's here.

Clovis. He is here. But is he really here? Or is this something the machine is reading from me?

As she got the bill, took the credit card, her brain refused to stop the feed-back loop.

He's here. He's here. He's here.

She tried to calm herself and steady her heart.

When she finished ringing up the family's bill and had bussed the table, she forced herself to walk slowly back to the bar where the person who looked like Charlie, but wasn't, was sitting on a bar stool with one leg perched on the foot-rest of the stool next to him.

"So did your arm heal completely yet?" he asked. "I couldn't see the 'real you' in the other place, so I couldn't see it."

My arm? What about my arm? Think!

She looked down and saw that she had three small pink scratch marks on her left arm that looked like they were going to remain permanent in some form.

"Let me see that," he said.

Amelie held out her arm for him to see. Clovis gently took her arm in his hands and examined the marks. Then it hit her hard enough to make her head spin. These marks had been from the time they had first met when he had been in the body of a werewolf and scratched her. This removed all doubt about who he was, or at least who he was supposed to be. This caused her heart and stomach to drop into her pelvis.

"Wow," Clovis muttered, running his fingers over the marks. When he looked up at her, his eyes were filled with a mixture of amazement and concern.

"These are going to scar. Sorry about that." His tone was casual, but he kept tracing the marks with his fingers until Amelie felt herself begin to flush.

"That's okay," she said brightly, taking her arm back to stem the rush of emotion she was feeling: joy, fear, excitement, anger, longing. She began to busy herself with the meaningless task of stacking clean glasses behind the bar. Anything that would keep her hands from shaking.

This never happened. I am living something that never happened. It's not a memory. But is he real? Is the game stealing something out of me? Or am I talking to a ghost pretending to be him? Or is he something like Veronica, a not-quite-human taking this form to please me?

When she looked up, she saw that Clovis was staring at her with a little smile on his face and for a moment, she found didn't care at all if he was real or not. Just having him here, with her, felt like someone had taken a boulder off her chest.

Get yourself together. You are an Academy operative, not some teenage girl.

No, actually, here, in this moment, I am a teenage girl. So it pays to act like one.

"So you decided to drop by because you saw I was doing so badly here that I needed help?" she asked, going for lightness and teasing.

"No. I decided to drop by because I was able to find you," Clovis replied matter-of-factly. "Probably because your creepy vice principal is thinking of you. I've been hoping you would come find me."

He said this not looking at her but at the countertop. He looked vulnerable, like any awkward teenage boy. But then again, not really, no teenage boy would admit to being vulnerable in the way he just had. She felt heat rush into her chest.

"I tried to find you," she said softly. "You have no idea how hard I tried."

This was true. She had spent months searching for him after he disappeared. Clovis furrowed his brow.

"Maybe I've been trying too hard to be places where I thought you might find me. Or that I thought you would like," he said. "Or places we had already been together, Psyche."

Psyche. It was the word to prove it was really him. No one knew this but the two of them. No one. How could a game replicate this unless it was reading her mind? It had to be reading her mind.

Just at that moment, another family came in.

"I got them," Clovis said, jumping to his feet and smiling.

"That's okay. I can do it," she said.

"No, no, I don't mind. It's fairly entertaining. And maybe some manners will rub off on this one," he said, pointing his finger to his temple like a gun and jerking his head to the side like he had been shot.

Amelie laughed, even as her heart ached. She had refused to admit how much she had missed him. His words, his syntax, his sense of humor, his little movements.

She watched him greet a family with two small children. He sat them at a table, said something to the mother, and then immediately grabbed a few pieces of bread from the soup bar and put them on a plate for the kids. She could see the mother beaming at him with gratitude all the way across the room.

He then took the order, and sent it back to the kitchen. As he came back to sit down behind her at the bar, she realized that she had just been standing there in the aisle in front of the salad bar, staring at him. At that moment, the back door slammed, and Julie popped her head round the corner. Julie, another girl who had worked with her, who should have been insignificant but was now here in this moment—this moment where she felt like she was awaking from sleep, or death, or worse.

Julie's pale blue eyes got wide.

"Oh, hey Charlie," she said, looking perplexed.

"Hi Julie," Clovis responded with a smile and then turned back to Amelie.

"I'll just get changed and I'll be right out, Amelie," Julie said.

"How did you know her name?" she asked.

"Oh. I have access to what's in his head if I need it," he said. "If he ever knew something, I can find it."

"It's amazing he ever actually heard her name."

"A real asshole, huh?" Clovis said.

"Yep. Good-looking but an asshole," she said, moving past him to stand behind the bar again. Somehow, being able to lean her belly against the wood stabilized her nerves a bit. She was trying to keep herself together and not throw herself into his arms.

"So you find him attractive?" Clovis asked, putting his elbows on the table, chin in his hands, looking at her with false innocence.

"No, not really. But I guess he's attractive to young girls who go for that whole bad boy thing."

Clovis laughed out loud.

"Bad boy? People think this guy is a bad boy? Really?"

"Yeah. He has a band and I guess he's kind of dark and brooding," Amelie said. Clovis snorted.

"Dark and brooding is usually just a euphemism for sullen and self-absorbed. Plus, he's quite a mama's boy, from what I can gather. *And* he writes bad rock music because he thinks he can use it to share his deep and original thoughts and get laid."

He said this with a crooked smile. "I understand the getting laid part, but god knows I hate having to listen to a litany of someone's 'deep and original' thoughts."

"Why?"

"Oh, maybe because I wouldn't know a deep thought if it came up and bit me," Clovis said with a laugh, "Or maybe because I think that people who claim to have them don't. As for original, well there are so few original thoughts as to make them virtually non-existent. Not that this is a bad thing. What bonds us as living things is our similarity and not our originality. Being truly original is usually dangerous, lonely, and painful."

He said this with a small smile and a slight shrug of his shoulders that spoke volumes.

"For someone who doesn't like deep, that was pretty deep," Amelie said softly.

Clovis shrugged again.

Charlie's body and frame were enough like the Clovis she had seen in those other worlds that it was easy to forget he wasn't really there. The restaurant was enough like the one that she had worked in that it was easy to forget that *she* wasn't really here either.

Suddenly, her heart understood what Lazlo had said. Would this be enough for her? If she was allowed to stay here with Clovis, even if it wasn't Clovis, would she be willing to accept this dream of him if she could have it forever? If that were offered to her, would she have the strength to walk away from him, if she was given that choice?

Looking at him, looking at his eyes coming from this different body, Amelie wasn't sure.

The restaurant had now thinned out to the Sawyers, Jack's family and a handful of other people in singles and doubles. But many of those left were openly staring at them. For a moment, Amelie saw an actual dark cloud forming over

181

Jack's table, but she quickly forgot this when Clovis leaned forward and put his elbows back on the counter.

"I expect my time will be limited, with your friend now on duty. So tell me about your Christmas," he said.

"Didn't you see me?" she asked, going for playful. She was having to playact in a big way. It seemed like this was early in their relationship, so she couldn't get too heavy.

"No," Clovis replied, his face suddenly serious. "For me to see you at your home would mean that I'd have to come through one of your family members, and I thought that might be too weird for you. And it's generally not a good idea, in case it leaves some weird residue inside them. That's why I haven't seen you until now. I think you haven't been out much."

Some weird residue? What did that mean? she thought.

"So you didn't answer my question, how was your Christmas?"

"It wasn't a big deal. My parents put up the tree on Christmas Eve. We opened presents on Christmas morning, and I volunteered to make Christmas dinner," she said. It was easy to make up because it had been what she had done every Christmas Day of her teenage years.

"Well, did you at least get a few nice presents?" he asked.

"My parents never had any idea what to give me, so they just gave me gift certificates or cash. My brother always gave me cash," she said, then froze. She had used past tense. But Clovis didn't seem to notice.

"Not very personal," he said.

"I don't really want personal from them," she said softly.

Clovis raised an eyebrow at her.

"Would you like something personal from me, then?" he asked, all wide-eyed and innocent again, but with a barely discernible lift to the corner of his mouth.

Yes. Just you. Only you, but forever, she thought, but then slammed a lid on those thoughts and blurted out the first thing that came to mind.

"Uh. No. I don't expect—" she began, fumbling over her words, but before she could anything out, she saw Jack approaching. The fact that she had been operating with very low shields became apparent as instinct caused her to slam them down painfully at the sight of him.

"Hey, Amelie. Can I talk to you for a minute? Alone?" Jack asked gruffly.

Clovis stood up, turned, and gave Jack a look that Amelie could not see but she saw Jack's eyes widen a bit.

He then turned back to Amelie and leaned against the bar.

"So this guy wants to talk to you, but he seems to have a poor grasp of basic manners, which would dictate that he excuse himself before he interrupts a conversation that was already in progress. So, do you want to talk to him?" Clovis asked, looking directly into her eyes.

No. I don't. I hate this guy. I don't want to spend a second away from you. But it might give me a moment to regroup. I have spent close to twenty years surpassing these feelings and now they are all coming back, and it scares me.

She didn't know what Clovis saw in her eyes, but he simply nodded, and moved behind the bar, drawing himself a draft.

"How do you know him?" Jack asked sharply.

Amelie was startled until she realized that Jack was asking about Charlie.

"Oh, his dad owns this franchise, as well as a lot of other restaurants in North Carolina."

"He seemed like he—" Jack started, then stopped and shook his head slightly. "Never mind. Hey, I wanted to ask you if you have plans for February. The dance is only a month away."

Wait, this was January. What was happening with Clovis in January? Was this before or after she knew he was an incubus?

"Actually, I think I will be working quite a bit—" she began. She just wanted to get rid of him as quickly as possible.

"Well, you need to take time away from that for a little bit of fun," Jack said, smiling and mimicking Clovis's earlier body stance by leaning over the counter of the bar, which had a sickening effect on her. "You need to give yourself some time to enjoy things. It's our senior year, after all."

At that moment, Amelie heard a laugh coming from just inside the entrance. The cavalry had come in the most unexpected form she could imagine—her "friend" from high school, Judith.

Judith walked past Clovis without a glance in his direction to come stand next to Jack, whose face was now tense and tight.

"Seriously Jack, are you actually trying to ask Amelie to the Valentine's Dance ... *Amelie*?? You know, the one who is into heroic yet damned fictional characters. That's the right way to describe 'Constantine,' right?" Judith asked, turning to Amelie.

Amelie nodded.

"So I don't think she is going to be into jocks with too much family money to spend," Judith continued with a tinkling laugh. As Amelie looked behind them, she saw that Judith was accompanied by two girls she didn't know. Amelie felt relief wash over her, accompanied by a novel feeling of gratitude toward Judith.

"Well, Amelie has a right to have some fun too," Jack said tightly.

"Poor entitled thing," Judith replied. "You're just not used to failing to get what you want but I'm telling you, she's just not into you. She goes to school and to work. When she's not doing schoolwork, she has her nose in a book. So, if you aren't from a book, then you've got *no* chance."

Jack's face turned the color of tomato soup.

"Come on, get a drink with girls who can appreciate you," Judith said, taking Jack by the arm and pulling him toward a table. She looked back over at Amelie and winked.

"Thank you," Amelie found herself mouthing silently at her before she realized what she was doing. She was shocked at herself, but Judith nodded. She didn't remember ever thanking Judith for anything. Of course, Judith had never done anything worthy of thanks.

Amelie stood there stunned for a moment before realizing that she was probably supposed to take the orders of Judith and her friends.

She did this quickly and quietly, avoiding Jack's eyes. When she finished, she returned to the bar and sat across from Clovis.

"That was a nice save by your friend," he said quietly.

"She's not a friend."

"I know," Clovis replied. "I've watched you from inside her before."

Clovis was staring at her, and then at the people at the tables.

She wondered if he saw the same things she did. Gavin was quietly working diligently on his fifth or sixth plate of food. Mr. Sawyer was eating in tense silence, as his wife and daughter argued with each other. Jack had left Judith's table and rejoined his family. There were few others scattered about. It was quiet but suddenly it felt dangerous, like a jungle. She could see little lines, like ropes, made of tiny shining particles, connecting Mr. Sawyer's table to Jack's table to Judith's table. These lines crossed and overlapped. Holes formed in the cross sections that reminded Amelie of crosshairs and oubliettes. It felt like a place filled with traps and nets to snare her. She closed her eyes and gulped. She needed all her shields now, everything was telling her that, but she didn't want them. She just wanted to talk to Clovis.

"Are you okay?" he asked.

"Yes, I … just … I don't know. I don't know why these people are here," she said finally, looking at him. She felt confused and overwrought.

"Really, you don't?" Clovis asked. "More than a few of them are here to see you. Your vice principal and Jack are definitely here to see you. That guy Gavin is also here to see you, but for cleaner reasons. You're one of the few people who is nice to him. Judith doesn't know why she's here. There's a blank there.

Her friends are here because she is. The others who are here now are here because they have no family left, they are avoiding time with a family they don't like, or they are lonely."

"How do you know all that?"

"Most people are pretty easy to read," he replied.

"And me? Am I that easy to read too?" Amelie whispered.

"Clearly you aren't most people," he said with a smile.

No, she wasn't. She knew that now. But she needed to know what he was. She needed to understand what this place could do. She owed that to herself and her pod. To Majo, to Caio, to James, and to Widget, who was hurting somewhere.

With a sort of shock, she realized that these people had become her family in more than words alone. What she had to do now was find out what this place was and how to get out of it. If they could move in and out of it, it might be able to help them escape. If anyone would know that it would be Clovis, the creature tricky enough to outthink Kara, Dante, and the Academy.

"I have to ask you something," she said, feeling sick before the words even came from her mouth. She didn't want to have this conversation. She just wanted to stay in this moment with Clovis.

"Where were you, just now, before you possessed Charlie?" she asked softly.

"I was—" Clovis began, then furrowed his brow. "I was watching you."

"Where? Where was I when you were watching me?" Amelie asked.

Clovis opened his mouth to speak then closed it. He shook his head a bit.

"It's weird. I would think that I was watching you at school because I do that. But that doesn't ... I can't remember that. My memories of watching you are like pictures of you, but they don't make sense."

"Like what pictures?"

Clovis shook his head again and let out a breath.

"Not good ones."

"Tell me," Amelie said.

"One was you crying in a motel room." He stopped for a moment, and his knuckles tightened. "Then you being strangled by some man in a different hotel room."

He stopped, then looked at her wide-eyed.

"And you, much older, shooting a girl in the head, in a white room."

Amelie's head reeled. She held on to the bar to steady herself.

"Are those things real?" Clovis asked.

"Yes. Those things happened, but afterward. After ... after ..." her voice gave out.

She stopped to take a deep breath and let it out.

"After?" Clovis asked, leaning toward her.

"After you left me," Amelie replied, looking up to meet his eyes. She felt so much that the confusion of it all deadened her. All she could do was turn inward on herself and keep the outside cold and sterile. Even to her own ears, her voice sounded dead and dry, like leaves scattered upon sand.

Clovis reacted as if she had slapped him.

"After I what?" Clovis asked.

"After you left me ... just after having sex with me, using the body of my teacher. Elodie found us the next morning. My teacher got fired, and I had to leave town. No, I had to leave the country. I never saw you again." Amelie's words hung in stagnant air.

"What? I would never have done that!" Clovis whispered.

"Rose said you did that sort of thing all the time," Amelie replied.

"Rose? You talked to Rose?"

"She found me in a dream after you had been gone a few weeks. She said that you had been leading me on and had left me because you enjoyed the pain it would cause."

"You believed *Rose*?"

"You LEFT!" Amelie heard her voice break. "You didn't come back. Now, you are just something I am making up in my head. I am recreating you because I ... because I ..."

"Because you ...?"

"It doesn't matter. You aren't real."

"I thought we already went through all that."

"All what?"

"The me not being real thing."

"That was in life. We are now in a game," Amelie muttered.

"I don't know what difference that really makes," Clovis said. "It's not like 'reality' is a binary thing."

"A game is *not* real life," Amelie said, wishing she didn't believe those words. People around them turned to stare.

"Let's get out of here," Clovis said suddenly, taking her hand and leading her out of the Western Steer. As the door opened, the scene in front of them was limited to the parking lot. There was nothing behind it besides a gray sort of mist. This lasted for less than a second before it flickered and the world expanded to include everything as far as her eye could see. The hurt was pounding inside her chest, but she didn't want to feel like this, not with Clovis. She didn't want to talk about this. She didn't want to waste her precious time with him. He was like Veronica. He wasn't real. So she should do like Lazlo and just enjoy it.

But how could he remember the guy who tried to strangle her? That happened after he had left her.

He remembers because I do. He is something I am creating here, somewhere.

"What did you mean when you said that we were in a game?" Clovis asked. Amelie sighed.

"This place … it's not real. It's part of a game that was created by the place I work. It's a video game."

"So you are saying that I'm character in some video game?" Clovis asked.

"No, it's not just any video game. It's designed to interface with people using a bodysuit that reads your reactions to stimulus," Amelie said.

"So that might be believable. What's not believable is that it could make up an entire person. Someone that you know and whose traits and characteristics you know. You think a game could do that?"

"I don't know."

"So let me ask you, am I acting like myself or some glorified version of myself that you made up?" Clovis asked.

Amelie was taken aback for a moment.

Was he acting like a perfect version of him? What would the perfect version of him do?

He would have explained the reason why he had left me. He would have given me a reason that made sense of all the years since. He would have already taken me in his arms and allowed me to cry it out. Then he would have promised to stay with me forever.

"No," Amelie said softly. "You aren't acting like a glorified version of you."

Clovis smiled slightly.

"So, for a moment, can we say that I am me. If I believe you, that this is a game, how did I get here?" he asked.

"Well, maybe it has some of your DNA or something. The game uses a virus to interface with our DNA."

"It uses a virus?" Clovis raised an eyebrow.

"Look, I'm not a science person and I don't understand all of it, but one of my pod thinks the virus is taking bits of our DNA," Amelie said.

Clovis stepped closer to her.

"It's doing what?" Clovis asked.

"It's taking bits of DNA from all users and analyzing them. But Caio, a guy in my pod, thinks that they may be taking bits of our DNA for the game as well. Lazlo, a ghost who was just in the restaurant, he said the same thing."

"Who are they giving it to?"

"What do you mean?"

"If the game is stealing bits of your DNA, the question would be what bits it's stealing and why," Clovis said. Then, suddenly, his eyes widened and he took hold of her upper arms.

"Ames, where are you working now?" he said.

As he said this, a gust of wind hit behind her, pushing her hair into her face. She started to turn her head, but Clovis took her face in his hands.

"Amelie, where are you working?" he asked, louder now. There was another gust of wind.

"I work for a secret agency," she muttered.

Amelie looked into Clovis's face. How she had missed his face, his expressions, even his annoyance and anger. Right now, he looked afraid. She had seen this look once before, in an English mansion, when he had told her about Kara and Dante.

"What secret agency, Psyche?" Clovis asked, as he moved his face closer to hers.

"We do things to try to right the wrongs of the world," Amelie whispered, turning her head away. Clovis took her chin in his hands and turned her face back to his.

"What's its name?" Clovis asked.

Suddenly, Amelie didn't want to tell him. She wanted nothing more than to just talk to him about stupid, unimportant things. She wanted to hear him laugh and watch him eat and to kiss him until she had no more breath. She didn't want to think about who she was, or what she had spent the past twenty or so years of her life doing.

She threw her arms around his neck. He put his arms around her and pulled her to him. She buried her face in the crook of his neck. Suddenly, she had a vision of the cold box that she had created sitting on a rooftop in Paris all those years ago—the one where she had buried all her past. In her mind's eye, she saw the ice surrounding it cracking.

"Are you working for the Academy?" Clovis whispered into her ear. She nodded. He clutched her tighter to him.

"Jesus, what have I done?"

The wind around them was picking up even more. Amelie heard a clattering sound as something metallic was thrown to the ground.

"Amelie," Clovis whispered in her ear. "Something's coming for you."

He let go of her and pointed up. The sky above her head was filled with dark, roiling clouds. As her eyes moved across the skyline, she saw the clouds racing across the sky away from her.

The force of the wind was getting stronger. As Amelie watched, a large plastic garbage can was lifted by the wind and thrown halfway across the highway. Clovis pulled her back against the brick of the building.

"This is a game, huh?" he yelled, pointing into the distance where the clouds were spinning in a circle, forming a pale white funnel.

Clovis turned to her.

"Amelie you need to get away from the Academy as fast as you can," he yelled.

Amelie nodded, her hair whipping around her face and getting caught in her mouth as she opened it to speak.

"I mean now, as soon as you get out. That thing," he said, pointing to the funnel, "that isn't coming from a game. I think it might be coming for you ... or from you." The funnel didn't seem to be moving, it was just getting larger.

If a twister seems to be gettin' bigger, it means it's comin' right fer ya

Her father had told her that when she was young.

Clovis turned and put her back to the wall, his body shielding hers.

"Clovis, don't leave me!" Amelie yelled into his ear.

At that moment, she saw the tornado pass through electrical wires, which sparked as they were ripped apart. The funnel then gave birth to a car. Amelie had just enough time recognize it before it was flung in her direction.

Amelie screamed and the world went black. She remained conscious just long enough to hear Clovis say.

"If you try to keep me in your thoughts, I might be able to help you."

Then she came to herself, gasping in the game room ... with Rose staring into her face.

Chapter Twenty-Two

The Hallway's Darling

"Pumpkin, thank goodness you've come back!" Rose said, reaching her hand out toward Amelie's cheek.

Rose was sitting in a rolling chair to the right of Amelie's recliner. She was dressed in a transparent golden gown, her beautiful red hair was floating like a halo around her face.

Amelie tensed for a fight, but the second that Rose's hand touched her, her beautiful ivory skin began to morph and mottle. Growths appeared on her cheeks. Her cornflower-blue eyes sunk into their sockets, surrounded by thick flesh and her swan-like neck stretched and bulged. Rolls of fat appeared all over her slender body, shoving against her diaphanous gown. Mercifully, the gown was also changing into an opaque white cotton. In less time than it took to breathe out, the face examining hers was no longer Rose's but Camp's.

This was why Camp's voice had always seemed so familiar. It was Rose's, simply in a different packaging.

How could I not have recognized it as Rose?

It seemed so obvious now. The choice of words, the movements, the tone. Clovis was right, she needed to get out of there.

Clovis.

"Amelie, are you all right?"

On her left, the Director was leaning over her. He took her hand in his.

He's reading me. She's probably reading me, too.

Amelie nodded as she began to recite "The Naming of Cats" by T. S. Eliot in her head. She shoved her memories of what had just happened to her to the back of her mind. She would examine them later when she could better erect a more powerful privacy shield around herself.

Amelie looked around her. She was the only one of her pod left in the gaming room.

"Where are the others?" she asked.

"There was a problem, dear," Camp said.

"Yes, there was a problem in the game." The Director pulled up another rolling chair to sit next to her.

"A problem?" Amelie started to sit up but noticed that her arms had been strapped to the chair with Velcro bands.

Images forced themselves into her brain. Widget had been screaming. Widget had spoken. That had happened just before she had been pulled out to the steakhouse. Where she saw that ghost guy, Lazlo … and Clovis. Clovis told her to get out of here.

She quickly buried these images beneath the sound of children singing "London Bridge."

"Yes. We had an event," the Director said, frowning. "There was a breach in our game matrix. We aren't exactly sure how it happened, but many of the people who were in the game at the time—well, they felt some distress."

The air in the room turned colder on Amelie's skin.

"Widget," she began, before she caught herself.

She could not give away anything that had happened inside the game.

"He was already sick before he went in, is he okay now?" Amelie continued quickly.

The Director blinked twice in quick succession.

"I am afraid that Widget was one of the people affected. He was one of a few who went into cardiac arrest," he said.

Amelie began pulling at the straps on her arms.

"He is fine and is being attended to," the Director continued quickly, putting a firm hand on Amelie's shoulder. "All the other members of your pod are also fine. They have simply been taken back to their rooms for rest, but they are fine."

"Why am I being held down?" she asked.

"A few other gamers had convulsions," replied the Director, leaning across her to unrip the Velcro at her wrists and waist. "When we couldn't get you out of the game, we restrained you just in case you had convulsions."

"The game can send people into convulsions?" Amelie asked.

"Not the game itself, but maybe what the game was showing them," Camp said softly. She was smiling gently, a smile out of place with the moment.

"So someone hijacked your game and reprogrammed it to show things that could put someone into a seizure?" Amelie asked.

191

"They didn't hijack the game per se. Our game was fine but—" said the Director, his hand on her arm tightening. "Well, our game was fine, but you see we only control part of the game matrix. That part of it we can program and monitor and control, but there is a vast area of the gaming matrix that we don't control, or not yet."

"So you put us into something you don't understand and can't control?" Amelie said, trying to modulate her tone as much as possible, but fury was building in her belly.

"Oh no, dear. We don't put people into areas we don't control. We will eventually control all of it, but for the moment we constrain our activities to the areas we can control. The problem is that an attacker came through the area we don't control."

"What attacker?" Amelie asked.

"We aren't sure, not yet, but whoever it was forced their way into a part of the game that exists outside our matrix. In doing so, they distorted the game. They also managed to hijack some people's consciousness, for a short time. There were a few other casualties, but none that would affect you or yours."

The Director looked away for a moment.

"This is concerning because it means our work here may have been discovered."

"What work? And who discovered it?" Amelie asked, scanning her environment for possible weapons. There was no way off the island, but if she was going to get stuck here, she would take a few people down before she was shackled.

The Director smiled, and then reached out to brush a strand of hair from Amelie's eyes in a gesture both tender and weirdly familiar.

"Things are going much faster than I anticipated. I had hoped to have more time to integrate and train you, but I believe we have been exposed," he said. "So I think it is time for a bit more truth between us, Amelie, my darling."

The Director's eyes found hers and held them. Colors that only she could see swirled in those eyes, whites and blues and yellows and greens. They spun, creating galaxies and nebula that danced across his irises. He was trying to glamour her.

"Amelie, my dear, we know more about you, and the incidents in your life, than we have let on," he said, taking a strand of her hair and twirling it in his fingers.

"Such as?"

"Such as your ability to get into the hallway. I don't know if you have always had this gift, or if it came from your dalliance with the incubus."

192

Shit, shit, shit, shit.

Amelie felt her insides start to freeze up. They knew about Clovis.

The closed cold box inside her, the one that had started to thaw when she saw Clovis again, reappeared and opened wide. She threw all the things she was feeling into its maw and refroze it shut.

"We have been watching you for years, since your childhood actually," the Director continued. "We sent Majo to you when it seemed you were finally at the end of your tether and brought you to the Academy where you could be safe and free to grow your talents. Since then, we have watched you—for years—to see if you would continue to have access to the hallway. Under our tutelage, you have grown your talent for attraction and influence more than we could have hoped but, if our brain wave monitoring is to be believed, you didn't have any unusual experiences at different levels of consciousness for all the years since—until recently. In the past year, we noticed that that some your podmates were beginning to demonstrate aspects of each other's gifts. On examination, we realized that you had all begun to exchange genetic material. That gave us hope that that some of the other members of your pod would pick up your ability to enter the hallway. However, we didn't really predict that your own ability to enter the hallway would return. But it seems that it has."

"What makes you think so?" Amelie asked.

"Because one of ours saw you enter the hallway," the Director said. "Starting from the first time you went in the game, I think."

Shit. How did they know that? They can't see in the game. They said so. Or that could be a lie. What do they know? It must have been someone in the game. Who did I see in the game?

"I have only been in the game," Amelie said out loud. "What does the game have to do with the hallway?"

"So that's the interesting part, my dear," said the Director. "And this is where I need to be more candid with you. We did create a game. But in creating the code for it, we used certain coding from—well, different sources. And in the creation of the matrix of the game, we used some elements that had particles collected from—well, other stories, not to put too fine a point on it."

"How did you get them?" Amelie began, but the Director held up his hand.

"That is for another time and another place," he said, as he glanced at Camp.

A taste of metal hit the back of Amelie's throat and she opened her inner eye. Camp was glowing pink and green … and something else. A color Amelie had never seen before and could not name. It made her head hurt. She shut down her inner eye and focused on the Director.

"You see, the game we created ended up being much more than we antici-pated," the Director said. "We had wanted a game that would help us influence people of power through their own subconscious minds. What we got was much more than that. Somehow, in ways we don't completely understand, the game has managed to link itself to a hallway between worlds."

"So, if the game already gives you access to the hallway, what do you need me or any of our pod for?" Amelie asked.

"*We* don't have access to the hallway," the Director said, "the game does."

"Once again, it's sounding like you don't control your own game," Amelie said.

"We control what part of it we made," the Director replied. "We know the parameters of the game we created, and we have a lot of historic information about the hallway. What we don't understand is how the game seems to have become connected to the hallway. Our best guess is that, somehow, what we made managed to punch a hole in our story."

"So you think you created a new story?" Amelie asked.

"Oh no, of course not, you can only create stories if you find the library," the Director replied quickly, and then, for the briefest of moments, his eyes went wide. Then he smiled.

"I think what we did was to create a hole that can give us an access point to the hallway, but that is just a guess." He shrugged. "In the end, how it got there is not as important as what it is and what it means to us."

"What does this have to do with our pod?" Amelie asked.

"Right, I didn't answer your question," the Director continued, tapping his head. "We need you because of your relationship with the hallway. For almost everyone we have sent in, well, let me say first that access to the hallway seems to appear in random places and disappear for no reason. For the few who have seen it and found access—well, when they entered the hallway, it didn't go very well."

"In what way?" Amelie asked.

The Director grimaced and shook his head.

"The best-case scenario was that they didn't come back," he said.

"*For most people, their first time in the hallway is their last. They either die or they go crazy. Or they go through a dark door and even worse happens.*"

That was what Clovis had said all those years ago.

"But apparently that doesn't seem to apply to you," the Director said. "The hallway seems drawn to you for some reason. Even more astounding is that you seem to be able to draw those who are in the same sector of the game into the hallway with you."

194

The room suddenly flooded with green light. In Amelie's ears she could hear footsteps, laughter, talking ... and then the ringing of a school bell. She blocked this with metal in her head.

"In fact, this is how we discovered that you had been in the hallway the very first time you were placed into the game," the Director said with a little smile. "It seems that you already had a ghost who was waiting to stalk you."

"How is that possible, you said that you can't find people in the game without their permission?" Amelie asked.

"You caught me," the Director said, with a shrug. "We did give him permission to try to find you in the game."

He took Amelie's hand again.

"I know this may sound deceptive, but a ghost came to us through a mutual acquaintance who claimed to have known you in life. He said that he would be willing to go into the game to keep an eye on you. So we inserted him in spots close to you whenever we plugged you into the game."

Who had she seen? Besides Clovis ... Kara? Dante?

Then a picture came to her head. A car in the teacher's parking lot. The balding head visible behind foggy glass.

Mr. Sawyer. Mr. Sawyer was now dead and a ghost that was watching her. A cool breeze with the smell of grass hit her. Things she associated with truth.

"How did he get into the hallway?" Amelie asked.

"He followed you once you opened the door. You just didn't see him enter," the Director said. "Ghosts are good at being invisible."

Amelie forced herself to keep a neutral expression and ran earworms in her brain. This was the Academy. Being spied on was something she should expect, it came with the territory. She could not respond.

"I understand that finding out you were being spied on must be unpleasant, but to be honest, this would be the gold standard Academy protocol for everyone going into the game, if we had the particular resources to do it," the Director said, as if reading her thoughts. "But we don't. We were just fortunate in your case."

"This ghost, did he experience what we did?" Amelie asked.

"As I wasn't there, I don't know," replied the Director. "But I would be happy to share his report with you, if you want to check for inconsistencies."

"I'd be happy to, if you think it would do any good," Amelie said, she hoped not too quickly. This was the smart thing to say.

"That's our girl," the Director said, patting her cheek.

"But I still don't understand the value of getting into the hallway for the Academy," Amelie asked, attempting to project authenticity with an authentic question. "To be honest with you, I only ever went there as a way to escape my high school life."

"Ah, but you met the incubus in that hallway, no?" the Director said.

Amelie nodded. They clearly already knew about this.

"Did he not explain to you that the hallway was the access to completely different stories?"

"Yes."

"You say yes, but have you grasped what that means?" the Director asked. He stood up and walked toward the wall with the darkened video monitors. He placed his hand against the screens. Then he sighed.

"Amelie, you surely have noticed that our world is on a downward spiral," he said. "You don't even have to answer that, I have read your mission reports. What you have seen over the years has already convinced you of this. It underscores every sentence, every word choice you have picked in every report you have ever written. You know this is the case, and I know you know it."

Amelie nodded slightly. The Director was not looking at her, but Camp's eyes were glued to her face. Amelie began to mentally list all the Beatles songs she could remember. She needed a lot of clutter in her head right now to block her thoughts.

"Our goal, at the Academy, is to keep the world from imploding," the Director said. "It's already difficult enough to achieve this, but we aim to achieve more. We want to make our story better whenever that's possible. But there is only so much we can do. The Academy has been around for a long time and this downward spiral has accelerated exponentially in recent years."

He turned back to her.

"And it's not just on our planet that things are in this downward spiral. Our microbiologists see it in the mutation of other planet viruses and bacteria, our astronomers see it in the movement of planets, our physicists in small shifts in the fundamental particles of our existence. Our story is degrading. We are trying to find ways to save us, all of us, but I'm not sure we will be able to keep up. If we can't even convince political leaders of basic Earth-based concepts like climate change, how can we hope to convince them of the broader concept of story degradation?"

"What does that mean, 'degradation'?" Amelie asked.

"Everything has a natural shelf life," the Director replied. "Isn't obvious that our story is coming to the end of its natural shelf life? We can do what we can to extend it, by eliminating physical threats, viral threats, people threats, but that will only work for so long. At the end of the day, there is the end of the day. I can accept that—but what I can't accept is losing all the good that exists here."

The Director came to sit next to her, and Amelie was shocked to find tears in his eyes.

"Would it surprise you to know that I have loved and lost? Would it surprise you to know that the one thing that I cannot bear, even now, is the thought that she might be lost to me forever? If our story dies, then she is gone. That is what I will not accept. I think maybe you can understand that?" he asked, meeting her eyes.

Amelie nodded. His words could have been spoken from her own heart. She closed down those thoughts before her eyes betrayed her.

"I won't bore you with my own story, but I wanted you to know that the reason I have to have a plan C comes from a place of love, not power," he said. "Plan A is to try to save this planet. Plan B is to try to carve out some element of our story that we can save, if we can't save all of it. But we need a plan in case our whole story is not savable. We need a plan C. The hallway is my plan C. If we could find a way to navigate it and map it—well, that is the first step to exploring it. And if we can explore it, then maybe we can find a way for others to explore it. And if we can do that, then maybe we can find a way to a new home. It is the ultimate escape plan."

"That's a lot of ifs," Amelie whispered. Her head was reeling.

"That's true, but I never thought we would find someone who could not only get into the hallway but call it to her. I never imagined finding someone who can transfer this ability to others. And yet here you are, sitting right in front of me." The Director smiled. "Can you see what a gift you are? Can you see why you are so important to us? In you, I see the capacity not just to save our world, but all worlds in our story. Not just those currently alive but all those who are, were, or ever will be. That's a miracle."

The Director's eyes were shining as he looked at her. So many different expressions danced across his face, it was painful to look at.

Amelie turned her eyes away from him and toward Camp. Her face was strangely stony. No, it looked strangely dead.

Dead.

"You said you wanted to save people who weren't here anymore," Amelie said, turning back to the Director. "How do you plan to save people who are dead? They are gone."

The Director blinked, then he laughed.

"You know better than that," the Director said. "You've been in the hallway. You know about spirits. And your incubus knew about human reincarnation. He told you that he had known you over lifetimes that night on the beach. So you know we all come back."

Amelie suddenly felt the world come to a stop. Her heart began to race with different beats in her chest.

"How do you know what Clovis said to me?" she heard herself ask before she realized she was speaking.

"I know because I know the people who killed him," the Director said, taking her hand and putting it to his chest.

"Who killed him …" Amelie repeated.

"Yes. He was killed, or he was unmade, by the same people who would unmake you if they found you."

"Kara and Dante?" Amelie whispered.

"Yes," the Director said. "You have heard of them. Of course, Clovis would have warned you. This is why we were so worried about you. We think that they may be the ones who infiltrated some of the outer layers of Verite. We also think they may be targeting you for unmaking."

"Why would they want to kill me after all this time? And why would they unmake Clovis?"

"For the same reasons … both of you could get into the hallway and both of you were not under their control. And you are now with us."

Clovis had been killed. He had not left me. He had been taken.

Amelie felt a surge of energy begin to circle at the base of her spine. It burned and began to twist its way upward toward her sex.

"I also believe that they suspected Clovis of being able to bring back things from other stories into this one, physical objects. For them, that's the greatest crime that a creature could commit. They would destroy entire civilizations to keep that from happening. No, they *have* destroyed entire civilizations to keep that from happening."

He didn't know this yet. Block it.

Amelie closed her eyes. She felt the energy begin to twist its way up into the pit of her stomach. She now recognized it. It had happened to her twice before. Once with her brother, and once with Jack outside the school. This energy was related to anger, but only distantly, in the same way an ocean might be related to a puddle.

Amelie opened her eyes to find Camp had turned and was staring at her. Camp's ugly eyes were also wet.

"Amelie looks a bit overwhelmed, don't you think?" she said to the Director. He looked up at Camp and then back to Amelie. His eyes widened slightly, then he nodded.

"Yes, this is a lot to take in," the Director said, giving her hand a squeeze. "Amelie, I don't ask that you agree to help us with this right now. If you do this there is the very real risk of being found and unmade by Kara. I just ask you to think about it. Who knows, there may be a story out there, or some version of our story, where Clovis lives."

He's reading this from me.

Amelie opened her inner eye. For a moment, she saw Rose again, standing at the opposite side of the room. She turned to look at the Director and, for just a moment, he looked like Mr. Roberts, her old teacher and one-time partial lover. When she blinked, this vision was gone, and he was the Director again.

"When can I see the rest of my pod?" Amelie asked softly.

"This afternoon," Camp said, coming back to her side. "But for now, I think you need to have a rest."

"Of course," the Director said, standing. "And we should keep you out of Verite until we know it is secure."

Camp helped Amelie to her feet.

"Camp can take you back to your room through the back door," he said, standing and moving toward a side wall. He pulled a badge from his belt, one that looked much the same as the badge on Camp's belt. He waved it at the wall, and a panel slid backward, revealing a gray corridor. He smiled at Amelie.

"Secret back doors. We are all a bit geeky here," he said with a little laugh.

Camp took her by the arm.

"If you get dizzy, just lean on me," Camp said. But Amelie suspected this was less about helping her than restraining her.

They haven't been able to get a read on me yet. They don't know how I am taking this.

This was a good thing. Maybe she was hiding it better than she thought.

As Amelie was about to step through the door, the Director put his hand on her shoulder.

"Get some rest, and we'll talk again soon," he said, with an expression that looked warm, but also something else that she couldn't put her finger on.

It wasn't until he was out of sight that it came to her.

When he looked at her, the Director looked hungry.

***

Camp was silent as she led Amelie through a series of ash-gray corridors that looked like a maze designed to torment and depress hamsters. Amelie wondered how many Academy hamsters were observing them through the walls of their rooms.

Camp suddenly stopped at another smooth spot in the wall.

"This opens into your room," Camp said, nodding at the wall.

"You have direct access to my room?" Amelie asked.

"We have back door access to all rooms, just in case there is a fire or other type of emergency," Camp said.

Oh, fire risk is what they are worried about, Amelie thought, suppressing a dark smile. But as Camp moved into Amelie's room in front of her, Amelie saw that there was another person at the end of the corridor. For a second, nothing registered and then when it did, her breath caught in her throat, and the smell of sea oats hit her nostrils.

"Coming?" Camp said from inside her room.

Amelie nodded, blinking hard, trying to control her heart, which was now beating wildly out of rhythm.

As she entered her room, the video monitors on her walls, ceiling, and floors showed a bubbling red liquid a lot like blood. This was immediately replaced by blue skies and puffy clouds.

"Son of a fucking bitch," Amelie muttered under her breath.

"Are you all right, dear?" Camp said.

"I'm fine," Amelie said. "Or as fine as I can be after someone just told me the fate of all realities could rest on my shoulders."

Camp laughed lightly, an odd sound in this room and in this moment.

"The Director does tend toward the dramatic, doesn't he?" she said.

Amelie's face must have registered shock because Camp held up her hands.

"Oh, don't get me wrong, I'm not saying you aren't very important and unique. I have sensed that from the beginning. But you are neither completely unique nor irreplaceable. I say that because I don't want you to feel like it's all up to you. There is always more than one person who can do a job. And there are always different ways to achieve one's end goals. Sometimes we can forget that."

Camp took Amelie's hand, patted it, and led her to the bed.

"You just lie down a bit, pet. You've had a lot dumped on you, and I am sure you need a bit of time to process it all. I'll be back to get you for dinner. For now, we are confining people to their rooms because of the security break with Verite. We just want to make sure no one accidentally plugs in until it is all fixed up and ready to go. So this gives you time to relax and maybe get a little nap in. You can join your podmates for dinner."

Amelie nodded and lay down.

"Ta," Camp said, as she wiggled her fingers at Amelie in a wave, and then left via the front entrance.

For a moment, Amelie laid completely still and kept her eyes closed. She was waiting. She wasn't sure if she had seen right in the corridor. The figure had motioned to her, but she wasn't sure she had read the correct meaning. A small scratching noise on her wall confirmed that meaning.

Amelie got up quietly, her heart still beating wildly. She went to her front door and put her ear to it. She did not go out because she suspected such activity would trigger an alarm, given their lockdown status. She left her ear there for a minute or so and heard nothing from the hall. No footsteps, no voices.

When she heard another scratching at the wall across from her, she moved cautiously to the spot where she and Camp had entered from the corridors. She gently knocked at the door. Almost immediately, there was a noise from the other side of the door and the panel slid back.

Standing on the other side of the door, blinking hard and drooling, was Mr. Roberts.

Chapter Twenty-Three

Pernicious Legos

Mr. Roberts pulled Amelie into the corridor and into an embrace, kissing her forcefully. Amelie started to fight but then heard footsteps to her right, followed by the sounds of moronic laughter.

"Girl!" a male voice said, and then whooped.

"Yeah, girl!" said another, followed by another whoop.

As Mr. Roberts's lips were pressed against hers, Amelie realized that something was wrong. He felt wrong. He held her tight in his arms, but his embrace was passionless. While his lips were on hers, he was not really kissing her. He was just drooling against her face. She couldn't really see him in this position, but for the moment that she had seen his face, his expression had not been that of the insightful teacher she had known in high school. It looked more like the expression of the mentally challenged workman who had attacked her earlier.

The sound of voices stopped as the sound of footsteps faded away. When it was silent, Mr. Roberts released her and Amelie jumped back. The person in front of her had the form of Mr. Roberts. He had the height, dark hair, slight build, and golden eyes. But where those eyes had once held intellect, humor, and laughter, now they were flat and dull.

"Mr. Roberts, is that you?" Amelie asked. The dull expression on his face flickered for a moment. His whole body twitched and then the dull expression returned.

"Mr. Roberts?" Amelie said, reaching out and touching his arm. His head suddenly jerked backward, and he made a low strangling sound in the depths of his throat. His body began to twitch and tremble, and he moaned. Then, suddenly, he threw himself against the wall and began hitting his head against it—hard. After three hits, Amelie saw blood on the wall.

"Stop, Mr. Roberts ... stop!" Amelie whispered furiously. To her shock, he did. He squeezed his eyes tight and gritted his teeth, using his arms to cover his head.

"Can't ... can't ... can't—" he began, stamping his foot on the ground. Then he grabbed at his own hair and began to pull it. He turned and once again began slamming his head against the wall. Amelie reached for him, but he stopped on his own. When he turned around again, there was a cut over his eyebrow, but his eyes were clearer.

"Amelie?" he asked. "You?"

"Yes, it's me, Mr. Roberts," Amelie whispered.

"Not ... Roberts," he said, pushing each word out with breath. "Not ... your ... Roberts."

Amelie had no idea what he meant. What had happened to him? Something had clearly incapacitated him mentally. For a moment, she had a horrible thought. What if she had led the Academy to him, and they had done this to him? What if she had led them to Sophie as well?

At this thought, she felt guilt, horror, sadness, fear, and so much more, but she didn't have time to wallow in emotions. She needed information from him, and she needed to be willing to use whatever power she had to get it.

"Mr. Roberts, do you know a way out of here, out of the building, using the corridors? Do you know a way off the island?" she whispered.

He looked at her and squeezed his eyes shut again.

"Mr. Roberts, we don't have long. Can you show me a way out?" she asked, taking hold of both his arms, and releasing a tiny, fractional piece of energy toward him. She felt it wrap around his middle.

He twitched in her arms, and his eyes snapped open. Then he smiled. It was probably a real attempt at a smile, but it sat horribly on his face.

"One ... way," he said.

The sound of a footstep came from one of the side corridors. At this sound, Mr. Roberts took her hand and began to run in the other direction.

For someone with obvious mental deficiencies, he ran quickly and quietly.

***

Amelie tried hard to memorize all the twists and turns Mr. Roberts took as they ran through one identical gray corridor after another. After the first two or three, she began to drop little rivers of energy behind her. She had never done this before, and she hoped that maybe she would be able to see them later and re-trace her steps. She suspected that this would probably be about as useful as Hansel and Gretel's breadcrumbs, but it was worth a try.

203

After what felt like fifteen minutes of running, they came to a hallway that ended in a huge, black rock wall. Embedded in the wall were several chrome and glass doors. Mr. Roberts approached one and put his card against the glass. The door immediately opened to a large industrial-sized elevator with glass walls and steel supports. There were no buttons or panels or any other obvious means of control, but the moment they entered, the door closed behind them, and they began to descend.

The elevator dropped quickly but smoothly. All around them, she could see nothing but black. The packed earth around the elevator shaft was dark, lumpy, and slick. It gave Amelie the ominous image of passing through some monster's intestinal tract.

So what does that make us? she thought with black amusement.

Mr. Roberts was leaning with his head against the elevator door, and drooling. Amelie just had time to note this when the elevator came to a stop and the door opened, spilling Mr. Roberts out into a room—and what a room it was.

The space in front of her was easily the size of four football fields, or more. She couldn't see the end of it. The floor was dark blue quartz for as far as she could see. Above her looked like a night sky but, on closer inspection, was a cavernous dome made of volcanic rock that easily rose a hundred feet above her head. The roof was embedded with tiny, bright white lights that looked like stars in a night sky, if you squinted and were of a positive disposition. Amelie herself thought it looked like eyes watching you from under your bed.

All of this would have been enough to astound the eye, but it was the contrast between the construction and the contents of the room that pushed everything over the edge of normalcy. Between the volcano sky and the marble floor were thousands upon thousands of giant, stacked, multicolored Legos— or that is what they looked like.

Amelie's eye took all this in as she darted forward, grabbed Mr. Roberts, and pulled him behind the nearest stack of Legos, where he promptly collapsed on the floor. Amelie crouched, waiting and listening. She could hear the whir and hum of machinery all around her and the air was cold and reconditioned on her skin.

She opened her inner eye and almost fell backward. The room was a dayglow wash of color, and this time smells came with the colors. There were smells of burned meat, lemons, garbage, flowers, fecal material, and cotton candy, just to mention a few. Even worse, the taste of metal hit the back of her throat harder than ever before. She had a mental image of swallowing liquid mercury. It burned her throat and made her gag, such that she had to cover her mouth to stifle the sounds.

She quickly closed everything down. This was too much to take in and it didn't seem accurate. Outside of her early days with Clovis, the only other times she had been subjected to this many colors had been when she was in the middle of a very large and agitated crowd of thousands. She was fairly sure that there was no one else in the room right now.

Amelie stood up slowly and looked around. There was no one within sight. She scanned the perimeters but saw no exits other than the elevator they had come down in.

"Mr. Roberts," Amelie said, shaking him. He was still lying on the floor next to her. He moaned slightly.

"Mr. Roberts, why did you bring me here?" She pulled him up into a sitting position. "Is there a way off the island from here?"

Mr. Roberts grabbed his head, using his hands to force his face around to look at her. He looked like a ventriloquist turning the head of his doll ... if his doll were himself.

"Bad," he muttered, "bad ... place."

"Yes, I get that," Amelie said, "but is there a way out from here?"

Mr. Roberts nodded and pushed himself to his feet. He began to wobble down the nearest row of Legos as Amelie followed him. He passed through a group of red Legos and into a group of black Legos. As she followed him, Amelie noticed a pattern of arrangement of these blocks. Each set of Legos was piled up eight high. Each individual rectangle was probably ten feet long, four feet wide and four feet deep. At the end of each stack of Legos, there was a large, white plastic container rising to a height just above the top of the top storage unit. It looked like giant water cooler and, like a water cooler, was transparent enough to see that there was light-colored liquid inside of it. The "water cooler" was segmented, and each segment had several plastic tubes leading from it and into one of the storage boxes next to it. The plastic of the boxes was opaque. Amelie reached out to touch one, but Mr. Roberts grabbed her hand and shook his head. He pointed to himself and then to a box.

"What are you saying?" Amelie asked, but at that moment, she heard a noise from behind her. She pulled Mr. Roberts to the ground. The elevator door opened and two men in white outfits walked out of it, rolling an empty hospital bed, complete with drip bags, IV and, of all things, a Verite game headpiece. Amelie was near enough to hear their voices and, as they walked further into the room, Amelie began to be able to make out their conversation.

"So, Simulacra or Shell?" one man asked the other.

"Shell, of course. That's what everyone wants," said the second with an unpleasant laugh.

"She is asking for a Shell, but do we know if her resonance is low enough to control a Shell?" replied the first. "I don't want to deal with another drooling, shitting, vomiting mess, like the one we had last week."

Amelie had her back to the Lego closest to her, and she now slowly and carefully glanced around it. Several rows over, the two uniformed men had their backs to her. Both were tall, but one was pale and redheaded and the other had skin that could be called caramel colored, and long, dark curly hair.

"Fair enough," said the redhead. "Simulacra should be good enough for her. I mean, Jesus, they are grown to be almost physically perfect—tall, fit, perfectly proportioned. I mean, have you ever seen a Shell that was near as hot as a Simulacra?"

"Yeah, but there is something sort of creepy about knowing it started out as a clump of cells in a test tube," the dark-haired man replied, shuddering.

"How is that any creepier than starting out as a sperm?" The redhead laughed.

"You always know the grossest thing to say. How many times has she been out? I mean the elemental that wants this body?"

The redhead grabbed the chart hanging from the hospital bed. "It says here that she's only been out a few times, so Simulacra should do her just fine."

"Is it mission or recreation?"

"Supposed to be mission, but you know how it is …"

"Does she have to do any speaking?"

"Don't think so, or it isn't in the specs," replied the redhead. "Why?"

"That new model of Simulacra is great." The dark-haired man pointed toward a group of green Legos a bit further down the row. "But we have a few out there that have been in circulation for ten years or more, and they are well known to have voice issues. The spirit connection to the vocal cords doesn't always settle. They haven't been able to work that out. The next generation should come out in ten years or so. Hopefully they will fix that."

"Well, talking is not really what most of us think about when we think about a stay in the Kingdom, is it?" laughed the redhead. The other man laughed and nodded.

The two had stopped at the top of one of the rows of green plastic containers. One of them engaged the brakes of the hospital bed, while the other moved to the far left side of the room. There was a sound of an engine starting and within minutes, a miniature forklift appeared at the end of the row with the redheaded attendant driving it.

"Which one?" he yelled to the other man standing at the head of the row, who then pulled a device from the pocket of his coat. It looked like a supermarket scanner. He then began to run it up and down the green plastic cartons as he walked along the row. After a few moments, he stopped.

"This one, this has the closest readings," he said, pointing to the plastic container at the top of one of the stacks midway down the aisle.

"You haven't scanned very many," the forklift driver said.

"She is a low-level elemental; she doesn't deserve a lot of my time," he scoffed. "Besides, it's the one on the top, that makes it easier for you."

The other man grinned and gave him a thumbs-up. He maneuvered the forklift quickly and efficiently to remove the top green Lego from the stack and place it next to the hospital bed.

"Your turn or my turn?"

"Your turn. I have to put this back," said the redhead, beginning to back up the forklift.

"I hate this part," the other one yelled, as he leaned over the box. He tapped on the top of the box and it burst open.

"Oh, Jesus that stinks. You can help me get this stinking thing on the bed. God, what do they marinate them in, urine?"

The redhead came up and made a face. Then both men reached into the box and pulled out the limp, wet body of a naked white woman.

They immediately dumped her onto the bed and rolled her over on her back. Amelie couldn't make out much from this distance except that the woman was pretty, very tall, blonde, and well-endowed.

"Do we hook it into the game already? Is the elemental ready to start making the transfer now?" asked the redhead.

"No, let's just wait till we get back to the room. We'll go through the tunnels so none of the new operatives will see it, in case anyone decides to question. Besides, sometimes they get all *convulsey* when they first start the transfer, and I hate having to hold them down. They're all wet and slimy."

The redhead laughed.

"Maintenance will pick up the box?" he asked.

"Yeah, probably put another one in it. No one comes down here besides us and them anyway, so it doesn't matter much." The dark-haired man took one end of the bed and began to roll it.

Amelie moved to the end of the row. The men had their backs to her as they entered the elevator. They were continuing to talk and laugh. But, just as the door was closing, the dark-haired man looked up ... and his eyes locked on Amelie's.

***

"Quick, Mr. Roberts, we don't have much time," Amelie said, turning to him. "Is there a way out of here that's not through the elevator?"

Mr. Roberts shook his head. Then he shuddered and nodded. He grabbed her and began to pull her along the row of black Legos.

"Are you one of those? Those Simulacra things?" Amelie asked Mr. Roberts as they ran.

He shook his head again and then pointed to one of the black boxes near them.

"You came from one of those?" Amelie whispered. Mr. Roberts nodded.

At the end of one of the rows, they came to a black Lego that looked like it had fallen from the stack. It was lying on its side, open, with a greenish liquid running out of it onto the floor.

"What is that?" Amelie asked. Mr. Roberts began to rock from one foot to the other and then shook his head. He grimaced and put his hands over his ears. Then, to Amelie's horror, he dropped to his knees and began banging his head on the floor.

"Stop!" Amelie hissed. "We don't have much time. How do we get out?"

He stopped.

"Pain …" Mr. Roberts muttered, looking up at her. "Pain … helps."

He pointed to the Lego. Amelie moved forward and Mr. Roberts followed her. She crouched down next to the box. Every muscle in her body told her to run. She needed to get out of there before someone was sent for her. She was sure that the redheaded man would call this in. But there was something about the box she needed to know. Her body was vibrating, and her arms and legs were tingling.

She turned the box around so that she could see the lid. On the outside of the lid was a metal plate. When Amelie slid the plate back, she could see a plastic sleeve with a typed card inserted into it. The card read:

Colin Roberts: Drug overdose, 01/26/1983. Evermore insertion date: 04/29/1983. Cognizance Level: 5/10. Match Found: 07/04/1983. Permanent Match Secured: 04/04/1985 Taylor Nathan Thomas, Use Level: Intermittent four. Priority 9/10.

"Taylor Nathan Thomas. That's the Director's name," Amelie said. Mr. Roberts nodded and pointed to himself. Then he stood and pushed the lid of the box fully open. On the underside of it, there were various tubes, wires and electrodes. Mr. Roberts pointed to an open tube, then he leaned down and inserted it into his mouth.

208

"Stop," Amelie said. "You were in the box?"

He nodded.

"Did the Director catch you after … after … after what happened between us?" Amelie asked.

Mr. Roberts shook his head again and pointed to the box, and ran his finger over the line that said Drug overdose, 01/26/1983.

"You had a drug overdose in 1983?" Amelie asked.

Mr. Roberts nodded.

"But I met you in my high school, much later than that," she whispered.

Mr. Roberts shook his head, then pointed to the box again. This time he ran his finger over the words, Permanent Match Secured: 04/04/1985 Taylor Nathan Thomas.

As those words sunk in, Amelie felt a wave of nausea. She reached out and touched the words written on the plate. Bright lights and bombs went off inside her head. Thousands of images, colors, and words flooded her brain.

Mr. Roberts at the dance, looking at her and Clovis, and saying, "Whoever *you* are, would you make sure that you leave Charlie Danos's body in reasonable condition when you go."

She heard her own voice saying, "Does he know what you are?" and Clovis's voice answering, "I'm not sure if he knows exactly but he clearly knows that I am not Charlie. He didn't feel particularly unusual the one time that I inhabited him, but something about him was odd tonight. He felt 'full' somehow. Probably not a problem but we should still be careful around him, you know. Don't give him too much information."

The Director knew conversations that she had had with Clovis that night on the beach. That night she …

Amelie sat back and put her head in her hands.

And the next morning, after being with Clovis, the next days, hadn't Mr. Roberts been extremely prepared to get her out of the country? He just happened to have plane tickets, and a place for her to stay.

All these years, a part of her had felt guilty about what she had done to Mr. Roberts, when it had never been Mr. Roberts. Instead, it had been the Director of the Academy using a body he had stolen from the real Mr. Roberts.

For what purpose would he have done this? To influence me? To get close to Clovis?

Amelie felt herself start to shake. That snake energy that had been sitting curled around her tailbone since she found out someone had killed Clovis— that energy now sparked again, burning in her hips and thighs.

She shook her head. And another thought struck her. Majo said that most of the people here were not human. Majo could see what they were inside, and what was inside was not human. The Director, an incubus, was walking around in a human body at least one of which had been Mr. Roberts's body. But what did that guy say about Shells? And Simulacra?

Amelie looked up. Mr. Roberts was standing above her, but he was now staring off into space, and drooling again.

"Mr. Roberts," she said. He did not reply.

"Mr. Roberts," she grabbed his arms and shook him hard.

His eyes cleared slightly.

"Are you—is your body—what they were calling a Shell?" she asked.

Mr. Roberts nodded, trembling all over.

"Did the Director take your body? Use your body? Does he take your body?" she asked.

Mr. Roberts grimaced and began to hit himself in the head with his fists. This time Amelie did not try to stop him.

Finally, Mr. Roberts looked up at her. His eyes were focused. "He ... I ... OD'd ... but ... not. He ... they ... trapped me ... there ..."

He pointed to the box.

"He trapped you in the box? You were buried alive in that box?"

Mr. Roberts shook his head again. He then pointed to the lid of the box and the wires attached there. The wires that were attached to sticky pads.

The game.

"He trapped you in the game?" Amelie whispered. "He trapped your spirit in the game? And used your body while you were trapped there?"

Mr. Roberts nodded.

"How did you get out?"

"Game ... gone ... wrong ..." Mr. Roberts choked out.

"Oh, the malfunction. Something broke you out?" she said.

He nodded and then shuddered.

"Ghoul ... came. Tried ... to ... eat ... me," he muttered.

Amelie didn't understand that bit, but she had bigger problems.

"Mr. Roberts, is there a way off the island?"

Mr. Roberts shook his head. And then he pointed again to the tangled wires in the plastic box.

"Game," he said.

Before Amelie could ask anything else, an alarm blared from the somewhere in the room. She was out of time.

Mr. Roberts screamed, fell to the floor, and put his hands over his ears. The sound of the alarm reverberated around the room, shaking the floor. It was making little waves in the tanks of fluid next to Mr. Roberts's casket.

"All personnel please return to their rooms immediately," came a familiar voice over some speaker system. It was the Director. His voice seemed to come from the little lights overhead, like the voice of god.

Mr. Roberts moaned on the floor. Looking at him, the energy snake slid upward from Amelie's sex and into her belly. Her legs were beginning to tingle.

"There has been a breach in our game security. There has also been a breach in sector G9."

Amelie stood up. The snake had moved up to her belly and heart and her arms were trembling, but not with fear.

"Amelie."

The voice coming from the sky was no longer that of the Director. It was now Rose's voice—Rose's voice coming through the body of whoever Camp was. Amelie wondered if poor Camp was stuck somewhere in the game while Rose was hijacking her body.

"Amelie McCormick, please remain where you are. Someone will be there shortly to escort you."

The voice clicked off. It didn't bother to tell her where she would be escorted to.

Mr. Roberts was cowering on the ground.

Amelie crouched beside him.

"You need to go hide. They are coming to get me now ..."

Mr. Roberts grabbed at her arm, shaking his head.

"No ... no ... no ... can't go ..." he blathered, spittle flying.

Amelie patted his head.

"Don't worry, I will be fine," she said. "Just hide yourself."

There was the sound of the elevator descending. Amelie stood up and backed down the corridor she was in, so that she would not be coming out of the same row that Mr. Roberts was hiding in. As she passed through the rows, she ran her hands on all the boxes she passed. She now understood why she had seen so many lights and colors when she first came in. At least some of these boxes were containing the bodies of people that the Academy had trapped in Verite. Maybe there were more of those Simulacra things as well. God knows what sort of horror those were.

She sent bursts of energy into each box one. She didn't know if it would do any good, but the anger rising in her was directing her.

As she walked past a row of black Legos, one of the boxes shot back the energy that she'd sent. It stung her hand, and she pulled it back. As she slid open the panel of the box, she heard the elevator gears in the distance stop.

She only had the time to see the words Simulacra, Cultured 2001, Body Fully Functional 2005, before she heard a familiar voice call her name.

"Amelie?" Caio called, from the direction of the door.

She turned and ran toward him. She found him standing just outside the elevator door, staring at his surroundings.

"Caio, thank god. But what are you doing here? Never mind, we need to get out now. The Director is sending someone to get me, and I don't think it's going to go very well."

"I know," Caio said. "I'm the one he sent."

He then raised a gun and pointed it at her.

Chapter Twenty-Four

Coming Clean

Amelie stopped where she was.

Caio was now in front of the elevator, in shooter's stance.

"The Director wants to see you," he said, gun pointed at her head.

"Why?" she asked.

"I don't know. I'm just supposed to bring you to the game room," he said, and motioned her forward with his gun. Amelie didn't move. Caio sighed.

"Look. Don't think I won't shoot you. You may think you know me. Whatever abilities you have may have given you a false sense of security. But you don't know me. You don't know what I am capable of."

"Well, apparently you are capable of betrayal," Amelie replied.

"Yes, I am," Caio replied. "I am capable of lying, cheating, stealing, killing men, women, children, and even infants. And yes, I have betrayed multiple pods over the years."

"But you're not going to kill me, because the Director wants me."

"That's true. But that doesn't mean I can't shoot you in the arm, or the leg, or the kneecap."

He motioned Amelie forward into the elevator.

"Do you know what they are doing in there, in that room?" Amelie asked him as the elevator doors closed.

"I've got a pretty good idea," Caio said.

"They are stealing people's bodies?" Amelie asked.

"Yep," Caio said.

"And everyone in this place is some sort of spirit possessing some sort of stolen body?" Amelie asked.

Caio turned his face to hers.

"You really want to know this? You might not like some of the answers," he said. His voice was soft, but his eyes were cold.

He had dropped his gun, but Amelie knew better than to start a physical fight with him. She would lose. She might have a shot at glamouring him, but he would be expecting that. She also suspected he had a defense for it, or the Academy wouldn't have sent him. But maybe, if she could keep him engaged, she might be able to find a moment of weakness.

"I don't know about you, but I'm of the school of thought that truth is better than living a lie," she said.

Caio laughed.

"Really? Is that how you really see yourself? Amelie, advocate of truth."

"Try me," Amelie said, coldly. His laugh had stung more than his words.

"Okay, then," Caio said, "but don't say I didn't warn you. Everyone in this place is either a spirit in a Cambion body, which is permanently in the game, or a spirit in a Simulacra."

The doors of the elevator opened into the hallway where she had come with Mr. Roberts.

"What's a Simulacra?" Amelie asked.

"Simulacra are soulless bodies grown up from human tissues. Most of them are Cambion human tissues," Caio said.

"And spirits go into them?"

Caio nodded.

"What sort of spirits?"

"All sorts." Caio shrugged, pointing her in the direction of the hallway on the right-hand side.

"So they are fake bodies?" Amelie asked, scanning the surroundings for any sign of an exit.

"No, they are real bodies. The only difference is that they have no soul inherently. Once a soul is inside them, you would have a hard time recognizing them from human," Caio said.

"Majo could," Amelie said softly, but Caio snorted.

"Apparently not," he said. Amelie turned to look at him, but he pushed her forward.

"Okay, then, what do they use these bodies for? And why would they steal Cambion bodies if they have these?" Amelie asked him.

"You'll have to ask the Director that," Caio said.

Suddenly, at Amelie's feet, she saw something flicker. When she looked, nothing was there. When she opened her inner eye, she saw that it was the remains of the energy she had left behind when she had been running with Mr.

214

Roberts. The glow stopped at a spot on her right. She could make out the outline of her apartment door by the glow coming from around it. There was a soft sound of flapping coming from inside it. God knows what her walls and floor were doing right now, while they were alone.

"Keep moving please," Caio said, pushing her forward. His touch was not particularly forceful, but it was full of energy.

"Where are the others?" Amelie asked.

"We are going to meet them," Caio said. "They are with the Director."

His voice changed when he said the word director. It hung in the air like a scythe above a stalk of wheat. Amelie felt the metallic taste again on the back of her tongue. Something about the Director triggered Caio. So, he might be more vulnerable in this moment.

Amelie concentrated and aimed the tiniest runner of energy in Caio's direction.

Immediately, Caio grabbed her and slammed her against the wall. Her head hit the concrete with a smack that resounded in her ears. For a moment, everything went sideways.

"Don't try that shit on me again," Caio snarled into her ear. "That doesn't work on me, and it's not like I care about you."

"Are you sure?" Amelie whispered back.

In her mind's eye, Amelie saw Caio's dark eyes as he looked up at her from the bottom of that well. She saw the despair in them.

He pulled back from her. He grabbed her by the shoulders and pushed her in front of him.

"Yeah, pretty sure. I failed all my psych tests. Psychopath is how I am categorized by the shrinks at the Academy."

"Were you a psychopath with Sarah?" Amelie asked.

Caio grabbed her arm and whirled her round.

"How do you know about Sarah?" he hissed. His grip on her arm was painful.

"You told me," Amelie whispered.

"I told you no such thing. Who told you about her?"

"You told me," Amelie said between clenched teeth. "You told me when you were in your hole. I saw you in the game."

"We didn't talk about Sarah when we went into the game," Caio said.

"Not the time when we went with the others. It was the time I saw you when you were trapped in the hole," Amelie said softly.

Caio let her go and stepped back. "You saw me ... in the hole? What else did you see? What did I say?"

"You were in the hole in the rain. There were worms there, going in and out of you. You told me that that was the reason that you couldn't age. The worms had exchanged DNA with you."

Caio's eyes widened. "I saw you. Wait. I remember. That's why it changed. That's why I felt ... it changed. I saw you there. You went back in time."

"No, it wasn't like that. I think it was a different story—" Amelie began, but Caio held up his hand. He shook his head.

"It doesn't matter. I still have to take you to him," he said, motioning her forward, but he didn't push her this time.

Amelie walked in front of him, she could hear him breathing hard.

"You also told me that you were working for the Academy to keep her safe."

"Yes," Caio said, his voice more of a breath than a word.

"I wanted to tell you that, no matter what happens, I will try to protect her if I can. I promised you that."

Caio said nothing but Amelie felt his breathing come harder.

"Here," Caio said, pointing to a spot on the wall on their left. The wall looked smooth, but Amelie felt a buzz of energy on the other side of it. She was pretty sure that it was the room she had left what seemed like years ago.

Caio stepped to the side and pulled out an identification card. A slot opened in the wall containing a bio scanner. But before Caio put his hand to the identification pad, he met her eyes.

"I can't help you in there. Whatever you do, whatever you try, I can't help. I'm sorry. I just can't. I can't take the risk."

Amelie leaned forward. Caio quickly put the gun to the side of her head, but she simply kissed him on the cheek.

"I know," she whispered. "But you need to know that my family is in there. And if I have to kill you to get them out, I will. I won't hesitate."

"I would expect no less of you," Caio said with a small smile.

He put his hand to the panel, the light flashed green three times and the door opened.

***

The first thing that Amelie saw when she entered the room was that it was indeed the game room she had just left. The second thing was that all the members of her pod were strapped into the lounge chairs, plugged into Verite. The third was that they were all in distress.

James was thrashing in his seat, veins popping in his neck and arms as he pulled against the restraints. His face was bright red and covered in sweat. He was breathing hard and grunting, teeth bared and clenched, in either pain or anger.

Majo was across from James. She was pale as death, sitting silent, rigid, and motionless in her chair. The only thing that marked her as living were the tears rolling down her face.

Widget was slumped sideways in his chair at the back of the room. His head was hanging down in such a way that Amelie could not see his face, but his body was limp.

The Director was standing at the front of the room, staring at three monitors on the wall. Each of the three was flashing various pictures and garbled sounds. Rose, hidden in Camp's body, was standing with her hand on one of the screens.

"What are you doing to them?" Amelie said, moving cautiously into the room. Caio grabbed her by the arm, but she yanked it back and quickly moved away.

The Director turned and held up his hand.

"They are in the game … not to worry though. People seem to have much more exaggerated emotions while they are in the game than they remember coming out of it," the Director said.

"Like twilight anesthesia?" Amelie asked softly, beginning to edge to her left toward Widget.

There were no weapons in the room—wait, there was one. On the other side of the room, near the unlatched outer door, there was a fire extinguisher behind glass. It wasn't much, but it was something. Perhaps she could use it to distract long enough to get out the door. If she could get out into the main game room, she might be able to find a weapon. It was a long shot, but she had to try.

"A bit like twilight anesthesia, yes," replied the Director, moving toward her. Amelie stopped and began reaching for the energy at the bottom of her spine. Could she pull it out if she needed it? She had done so before. Would it work on an incubus in a human body?

The Director stopped next to James.

"I'm sorry that we need to do this. It feels heavy handed to me, but I suppose it is important for you to know that your actions will affect not just you, but people you care about."

"Let them out of the game then. You've made your point," Amelie replied.

James suddenly screamed and Amelie moved toward him. The Director put his hand on James's head, and he went quiet.

"Yes, love, but your friends' situation is more than simply making a point," said Rose, "it's a source of motivation for you."

"I know who you are," Amelie said.

Rose's eyes widened for a moment, then she smiled.

"Listen, if you want me to do something, I suggest you tell her to keep her mouth shut," Amelie said to the Director. She was throwing anger on the outer layer of her energy. This is what she wanted them to read. Anger made some agents sloppy.

The Director nodded toward Rose, who stepped back toward the wall.

"What do you want from me?" Amelie said.

"Exactly what we already told you. We need you to go into the game for us, that's all," the Director said with a smile.

"Like all those bodies of people downstairs? You want me like that?" Amelie asked, moving slowly toward Widget.

"Yes, you have put me in a difficult situation," the Director said with a sigh. "I wish you had let me explain what we are doing here before you went wandering off on your own."

"You wanted to explain why you are stealing people's bodies?" Amelie said.

"No—well, not exactly. It would have been nice to explain to you that those bodies were not stolen. They were donated to us by their owners."

"I don't think Mr. Roberts donated his body to you," Amelie said. She was searching the room for the source of the game. If she couldn't get out, the backup plan would be to destroy the game somehow, but she couldn't see a console anywhere.

"I see, you found out about that from him, did you?" the Director said with a little shrug. "Yes, it was a bad coincidence that you happened to run into him of all people. But he does represent one type of body we have. When the Academy found him, his body was almost gone, and his mind most certainly was. He had been a traveler who made the mistake of ingesting one too many of the local drugs given to him by members of some indigenous tribes. Eventually, the risk of such behavior caught up with him. His brain was fried, and he was in an induced coma when we found him. So we took his body and put his soul into the game to try to help heal his consciousness. I took his body to use while this was happening."

"What are you, that you need to steal people's bodies?" Amelie asked, managing to make it to where she was standing next to Widget. She placed her hand on his wrist. It was still warm, and she felt a pulse.

"I didn't steal his body, I *borrowed* it," the Director said. "And to be honest, borrowing his body helps him. It keeps his physical form in shape while his brain is trying to heal, otherwise, his body would atrophy."

"You didn't answer the question. What are you?" Amelie asked.

"I'm surprised you haven't guessed," he said. "Particularly given the fact that what some of us want is what you yourself would have given anything to have only a few years back, when Clovis was still alive."

"You're an incubus," she said. The Director nodded with a smile. She had known but having him admit it solidified the anger rising from her spine. It was now sitting in her belly.

"Yes, like Clovis," he said.

"And like Rose."

"Yes, like Rose too."

"So the whole business about using the hallway to find another world was just a cover. You are just an incubus looking for bodies." Amelie moved toward Majo to her left.

"No, borrowing bodies is more of a sideline. Our goal is to get people into the game for all the reasons I told you. If there are people who love the game so much that they want to remain inside it, we offer that to them."

"So they stay in the game until their bodies die? Then what?" Amelie asked.

"Well, you've probably noticed that time runs differently inside Verite. A person could live a thousand lifetimes in there before their physical body would wear out, even if the body aged normally. But, with the soul gone but not severed, the bodies tend survive much longer than they normally would. For all intents and purposes, once inside the game you can live forever," the Director said.

"And what if you want to come out?" Amelie asked. "Is this what you are doing in the Verite game that half the world is using? Using it to steal bodies?"

"We are doing a lot of things with the game, actually. It's working great as a locator of people. We have access to the brains of millions, so if someone has been seen by anyone else who is a registered player in the game, we will know where they are. For example, Mr. Silva's partner and child were located somewhere in the Hawaiian Islands through someone who was playing the game. We don't know exactly where yet, but we will in time. So hiding any locational information from us will be impossible in the very near future."

Amelie looked at Caio, but his face was placid. He held his gun in both hands now and it was still lowered, but one thumb was twitching ever so slightly.

"Of course, I don't suppose that's what you were really asking about," the Director continued. "You were asking about whether we use the game to borrow bodies in the normal game played out in the population. Well, we don't. People don't leave their bodies long enough for that. So people come and go as they would in a regular game. Here, we can set up a more permanent arrangement."

"So you control when they come out?"

"For practical purposes, yes."

"And you let them come out, if they want?"

"Of course—if they are capable of functioning in our world," the Director replied.

The taste of metal hit the back of her throat with such potency that Amelie felt a rush of nausea.

He's lying.

"And what do you want of me, then?" Amelie asked.

"We want you to go into the game, completely," The Director said.

"Why?"

"There are a few reasons. The first is that we want to find and isolate the part of your genetic code that allows you to call the hallway. If you—"

"How does my being in the game help with that?" Amelie asked.

"We have all sorts of talented beings inside the game, let us worry about that," the Director said with a smile.

"Okay, what else?" Amelie asked.

"We want you to find the library," he said. Another metallic bomb went off in her throat. When she opened her inner eye, she saw clear blue streaked with shards of white and opaque pink light around the Director.

Truth and not truth.

"What's that?" she asked.

"The library is the hub of all creation. We want you to stay inside the hallway until you find it. Then you can come out. After you do that, you and your pod can then be on your way. You can stay with the Academy or leave, with no consequences for you."

The Director smiled and shrugged.

"And how would I find this place—" Amelie started, but at that moment the main door opened. Two men dressed in workers' overalls entered. These two did not look like the workers she had seen so far. They were strong and muscular, and both were carrying guns at their sides. They were agents, or soldiers—most likely soldiers. The first stopped just inside the door and stood with his legs spread slightly and his hands behind his back.

The second went immediately to the Director.

"So sorry, sir, but we may have the location of the recent game breach ..."

Rose stepped forward to join them.

Amelie stopped listening. She threw a large wave of energy at the man standing next to the door. The man's body shuddered, his arms dropped to his sides, and he turned to look at her with love.

220

"We think that some of the missing players have been intercepted by the office," said the other soldier.

Both the Director and Rose were completely focused on the soldier speaking.

Without another thought, Amelie threw herself forward, grabbed the gun from the smitten soldier's holster and crouched. She then shot the guard talking to the Director and Rose in the back of the head. His body was pitched forward into Rose. The Director turned toward her just in time for her to shoot him directly in the face. His head exploded in red. She then aimed upward and shot the guard standing above her in the groin. He crumpled to the ground, blood already staining the crotch of his uniform.

Amelie turned to Rose, only to see Caio standing in shooter stance, aiming at Widget. Rose had moved next to James and had her hands on his head.

"Drop it," Rose said to Amelie. "Or you will lose your friends."

Amelie hesitated.

Rose nodded, and Caio shot Widget in the head.

***

Caio just shot Widget.

Widget's body was convulsing in its restraints, and blood was gushing from the side of his head.

Widget was strong and healthy but even given that, surviving a head shot was highly unlikely.

Amelie turned to face Caio, who returned her stare. For the briefest of moments, a series of emotions passed across his face. Unbidden shades of color lit up the people in the room, as if each was in a spotlight. Rose was sitting in a halo of green and purple. Majo was in a gray light. James was bathed in shades of red and yellow. Widget was in shades of black and white. But Caio, Caio was a rainbow that she could not read. As he stared at her, a taste of peppermint touched her tongue. She had no idea of the meaning of all this.

"Well, you've made quite a mess, haven't you, lamb?" Rose said, her hand still on James's head. "So I suggest that we all calm down and you put your weapons away."

"Since when have you been a fan of calming things down?" Amelie snapped, throwing a blast of energy in Rose's direction.

Rose laughed.

"Nice try, precious, but your little gift won't work on me, and it likely won't work on Caio, psychologically twisted as *he* is. And it certainly won't work if you are missing your head."

221

Missing my head.

Amelie put the gun under her own chin.

"Unhook them from the game or lose me," she said.

Rose smiled inside Camp's ugly countenance.

"Go ahead, kill yourself, darling," Rose said. "That's no skin off my back. The Director is the one who so desperately needs you. But he is out of the picture until he can find a new host, so for now I am in charge."

"And how long will that last, then?" Amelie asked.

"Long enough," Rose said.

"Long enough to replace me with someone else who can do what I do? Can you manage that before he gets back?" Amelie asked.

"You have always been replaceable, dear," Rose purred.

"Okay. Let's test that," Amelie said, shooting Caio a look as she cocked the trigger of the gun.

"She'll do it," Caio said softly.

Amelie closed her eyes and projected fury.

"Wait," Rose said suddenly.

Amelie opened her eyes.

"Listen, lamb, if you're dead, you can't help your friends. In fact, I'll kill them just to spite you. They are completely replaceable," Rose said sharply but caught herself.

"But I'll make a deal with you," she said in a gentler voice. "And it's a much better deal than any deal the Director would give you."

"I'm listening," Amelie said.

"You and I will go into the game together. While I'm gone, I will instruct Caio to release your friends from the game."

"He won't do it, he just shot one of them," Amelie said.

"Him?" Rose said, pointing to Widget and laughing. "He's a Simulacra. He was never here."

"What are you talking about? He was in my pod," Amelie said.

"Yeah, and he was always a Simulacra," Caio said. "Whatever spirit was in him had nothing to do with the body he's in."

"I'm very surprised none of you caught that," Rose said, running her fingers through James's hair. "The voice problems were a huge red flag. Of course, maybe you can only know what his spirit knows, and his was quite amnesiac."

"So where is his spirit now?" Amelie asked.

"Still in this body, I suppose," Rose said, standing up and walking around the circle to Widget. "It takes a while for these things to die, even when severely

222

injured. I suspect in another hour or so whatever spirit was in him will be released to do whatever it does."

Rose poked Widget's body and it twitched.

"See," Rose laughed.

Amelie pointed her gun at Rose, but Rose just smiled.

"Listen, lamb, you can shoot me, of course. But you know it won't kill me. It will just destroy the body of the poor, sad, scientist woman whose body I am inhabiting. The one who sold her soul to be beautiful in a ridiculous game."

A mental picture of Camp, sitting alone and ignored at a high school dance, inserted itself into Amelie's brain. She lowered her gun slightly.

"Also, you know this room is monitored and I already triggered the alarm," said Rose. "There will be security here in minutes. Once they are here, I won't be in control and your friends will likely stay in the game, and in their current condition, until the Director can authorize a change."

"So if I go in the game with you, how does that happen?" Amelie asked.

"We strap you in and I will plug you into the section of the game where I can find you," Rose said.

"Why do you want me in the game?" Amelie asked.

"I want to show you something," Rose replied, moving toward her. "But we are running out of time to get your friends unhooked. It's only seconds before the cavalry shows up, and minutes to get into the room, and then only if you can manage to bolt it first."

"You know how to let them out?" Amelie asked Caio.

He nodded.

"And you'll do it?"

"Yes," Caio said, lowering his gun. His eyes met hers, unblinking. He folded his arms and began tapping his finger high up on his upper arm in a strange fluttering pattern ... fluttering, like wings.

Amelie's brain flashed to Caio putting his arm around her before their last Verite session. When he said she had brought back a mouse bug wing. She brought something.

They didn't know that I could bring things back ... but Caio did.

Maybe she could bring something back that could help them ... a grenade, ammo, reinforcements.

Amelie nodded and lowered her gun. Rose moved toward her, motioning toward one of the empty chairs. She held out her hand for Amelie's gun.

Amelie sighed and handed Rose the gun. She had no choice.

As Amelie sat down in the lounge chair, focusing her thoughts on raising the power in her belly, Rose pulled Velcro straps tight around her wrists, upper arms, thighs, and ankles.

Rose picked up the headpiece and lowered it over Amelie's eyes.

"See you inside, pet," she whispered.

Yes, where it will just be you and me, Amelie thought, before a red haze covered her sight.

Chapter Twenty-Five

Into the Blackest Rose

When Amelie opened her eyes, she found herself face-to-face with Rose. Not Rose in Camp's body, but Rose in all her beautiful, despicable grandeur.

Rose lunged at her, and Amelie threw herself to the ground and rolled out of the way before jumping to her feet.

She and Rose were standing in the pale green of the game matrix.

Amelie visualized a gun and one immediately appeared in her hand. She aimed it at Rose.

Rose laughed and raised her hands.

"Just a joke, pet," she said. Rose was wearing pants and a fitted white shirt—attractive, but far from the lingerie that Amelie usually saw her in.

"So what do you want to show me?" Amelie asked. "Or did you really just want to try to kill me?"

"Of course, I could kill you in the game, but why would I bother? I could just as easily kill you in the Kingdom, and more efficiently," Rose said with a shrug.

"What I want is for you to help me find Clovis," Rose said.

Find Clovis, did she just say that?

"How can I find Clovis? The Director said he was unmade," said Amelie.

"Yes, but you saw him in this game, didn't you? I saw that in your data, and in your face. If you saw him, it means a part of him was in the story where you found him."

"Is that what happens when something gets unmade?" Amelie asked.

"No. Not at all," Rose said. "Normally, the spirit has to re-attract the bits of itself. It does this over time, as it finds small bits of itself and gains mass. But this happens within one story. Clovis, as you know, was a creature that could travel in the hallway and therefore to many stories. I think his essence has been scattered across all of these. Without help, he may never make it back."

Rose looked down for a moment.

"When I first learned of his unmaking, oh, I was as distraught as I have ever been. I knew that he would be thrown to different stories. His father was from a different story, so it would have to be that way. I thought I had lost him for good. Then I realized that you had seen him. And it came to me."

"What did?" Amelie asked.

"For some reason, and certainly not because you earned it, you have been given certain gifts. We know that you can attract humans. We also learned that you can attract non-humans."

"You knew that before I came to the Academy," Amelie said.

"If you are referring to Clovis, that's not what I meant," Rose said with a sniff. "Incubi are attracted to humans as food. But you seem to attract all sorts of non-humans, and as more than simply food."

"Okay, so what?" Amelie said.

"Then we learned that you attracted the hallway itself. Every time you are in the game, the hallway appears, like it's drawn to you. So the Director began to believe that you might be a singularity."

"What is a singularity?"

"Something that attracts everything: people, things, inanimate objects, elements, everything."

Amelie shook her head.

"I don't attract inanimate objects or elements—" she began, but now Rose shook her head.

"Singularities don't start attracting everything, but they end up that way," she said. "Well, they attract everything they get close to."

"So what does that have to do with finding Clovis?" Amelie said. Her heart still skipped beats at the sound of his name.

Rose turned and looked around them. Then she turned back to Amelie.

"The Director has told you that he knows you can get into the hallway," Rose said, looking down. "He also told you that he knows about your relationship with Clovis. He knows that because he watched it from the body of Roberts. He knows that Clovis was unmade, because he saw it happen that night on the beach. He went into Roberts's body only after Clovis had been completely unmade."

When Rose looked up, Amelie was surprised to see tears in her eyes.

"It wasn't like Clovis to be caught off guard, or to be messy," she said with a little laugh and a shrug. "So I've come to believe that he let them find him."

"Why would he do that?" Amelie asked.

"To be able to leave a part of himself inside of you," Rose replied.

"How would him being unmade leave a part of him inside me?" Amelie asked.

"Well, to leave a part of himself inside you, he would have to be inside you when he was unmade," Rose said.

Inside me. When we were together on the beach. When I fell asleep, he was still ...

Amelie felt her heart begin to beat inside her chest with a different rhythm than she had felt before. The world around her began to spin.

He planned it, she thought, *he planned to unmake himself so that ...*

"Ah, I see your small brain has finally understood the implications of what my son did for you," Rose said, her eyes burning into Amelie's.

"Why would he do that? Why was it so important to have a part of him ... to ..." Amelie found she couldn't complete the sentence. She was keeping the horror of it at bay.

"He did that for you for the same reasons that I chose to keep my baby, even though he was born of rape by monsters," Rose said. "I knew that Clovis's father, despite the horror of what it was, would keep him safe. It would give him certain abilities including, among other things, a shield against viruses from other stories. I did all this because I loved him, more than I feared pain. Clovis seems to have chosen to leave a part of himself in you, to shield you from those viruses and thereby keep you off the radar of Kara and her demon lover."

A wind rose up around them. It smelled of cinnamon and sugar. It reminded Amelie of the Cinnabon at the mall. The mall where Clovis taught her ... well, that she could live a semi-normal life. Behind Rose, Amelie saw the matrix of the game begin to shimmer and warp.

"Even if all that is true, why the hell does it matter to you?" Amelie asked.

Rose laughed. It sounded annoyingly like tinkling wine glasses.

"Well, if all of that is true, then a part of Clovis remains in you. That one part of him will call to the other parts of him. With you, I can find all those parts."

"What good would that do?" Amelie said. "Unless there is a way to put him back together ..."

At that moment, the rippling of the matrix behind Rose arranged itself into a doorway. Rose either sensed this or saw Amelie's eyes move in that direction because she turned.

"You see, there it is. The hallway has come for you. Either it is drawn to you, or you have turned this space into a hallway. It doesn't matter either way. So, shall we take the door and see where we end up?" Rose said, motioning toward the door.

Could Clovis be alive? Would there be a way to put him back together?

She couldn't trust Rose, but she knew that Rose was obsessed with Clovis, so her wanting him back was believable, and using her as a means to get him back could also be believable.

Rose began walking toward the door, just before reaching it, she turned and motioned Amelie forward.

Amelie was afraid to believe what Rose was saying. Rose was crazy, after all. But she had seen Clovis in a story. He had seemed real enough then. Maybe …

Amelie silenced her inner critic, nodded to Rose, and strode forward. If there was even a chance that Clovis was out there in pieces … well, she would find a way to bring him back.

She saw that the doorway was a slightly darker green than the surrounding walls. It was inlaid with gold and silver patterns. There was no door handle. Amelie put her hand to the door, and she felt that sensation she had felt so many times before—a sensation of tugging.

Next thing she knew, she was standing in the hallway.

***

Amelie had been expecting to walk into a story. That had been what happened the last few times she was in the game. But this time, she was in the hallway … sort of. What she stepped into this time looked very different from the times she had been in the hallway before.

She was standing on damp cement in a never-ending rectangular hallway, which was lit by small red ceiling lights placed every fifty feet or so. The floors and walls were also cement and shiny with moisture. The doors themselves were large black metal things that looked more like garage doors than doors to a house. These doors were covered in droplets of water. The dim light bouncing off the wet doors, walls, and floor made the whole place look like it was covered in blood.

Despite all this, it wasn't the appearance of the hallway that disturbed her, it was the feel of it. In the past, it had felt comforting, exciting, dangerous, and even creepy in different moments, but it had never felt evil. What was in front of her now throbbed with malevolence.

"Well, well, well, it looks like something is up in the Kingdom."

Amelie whirled around to find Rose standing behind her.

"Why do you think that? It could be reflecting any story," Amelie said.

"No, this hallway has come through you, so its look and feel reflects your Kingdom," Rose said. "But it doesn't matter, as long as I can find what I need."

Rose began to walk toward her. Amelie immediately started backing down the hallway, keeping the distance between her and Rose far enough to prevent a lunge.

"So you asked how I could put Clovis back together," Rose said. "The answer is you. I can find him with you and integrate each piece of him back into you. You could be the vessel."

"I can't do that," Amelie said, but Rose laughed.

"Don't you see. You do that all the time. That is part of your gift. As an attractor, you naturally pull people in. But you are porous too, so you can keep part of them inside you. That's why weaker people get so obsessed with you, because they are not strong enough to keep you from stealing parts of their soul. I suspect you have incubus lineage somewhere in you."

"How do you know any of that?" Amelie asked, still backing away.

"That's part of my gift, sweetie. I have what the Director calls 'diverse' lineage," Rose said, still moving forward. Her blue eyes were wide, and her smile was too sunny.

Rose is crazy and getting crazier by the moment.

"Even if I can pull pieces of him, I can't put him back together," Amelie said.

"Oh, that's no problem. He will naturally come together inside you, if there isn't too much of you in his way. So I just need to hollow you out to your bare minimum, just the parts that allow you to attract and find Clovis. Then I think the parts of him will reassemble themselves."

Yep, officially crazy.

"I don't think I want to be hollowed out," Amelie said, moving backward a bit faster.

She was looking at the doors along the way. They could be an escape route but none of them looked particularly appealing.

"I know, lamb. It's terrible to be the sacrifice, but on the bright side, a tiny part of you will probably remain, a fragment. And that tiny part of you will be forever with Clovis."

Amelie turned to glance behind her. In this distance, she saw a soft pink glow. One of the doors was glowing, like doors used to glow when she traveled the hallway with Clovis. Glowing doors were good doors. Glowing doors were safe doors.

"I have to admit, when Clovis first chose you, I didn't think you were anything special," Rose said, cocking her head to the side. "But now, I see that there is something to you. I certainly see why the Director was so taken with you."

"About that, I was surprised to find you working *for* the Director," Amelie said, hoping to keep Rose talking so she had time to get to the door. "You didn't strike me as a follower type."

Rose scoffed.

"I don't work for anyone. I work with him because he and I have similar goals," Rose said.

"What goals would those be?" Amelie glanced back. Yes, there was a door glowing pink in the distance. "To find whatever the library is? Or to find a way to get physical people into other stories?" Amelie continued, keeping her eyes on Rose, and backing away slowly. Rose shrugged.

"I'm not even remotely interested in his little save the world plan and even less interested in his 'let's find a way into the library so I can create a new reality of worlds' plan. He's misdirected. His problem is that he is ridiculously obsessed with a creature who loves someone else."

Rose stopped suddenly, then laughed her Tinkerbell laugh.

"Oh wait, that's my problem too," she giggled.

"So you are both fucking with reality for some sort of unrequited love issue?" Amelie scoffed.

"Not exactly," said Rose, stepping forward. "The Director does what he does to win Kara back. He knows that as long as this world exists, she will feel responsible for it. For a while, I believe he may have thought that if the world was functioning well enough on its own, then she would feel free to come back to him. If he thought that, then he was a fool. What mother will give up on her child, no matter how badly her child treats her?" Rose smiled her crocked smile … the same crocked smile that Amelie had seen on Clovis's face. It seemed obscene on her lips.

"But even he had to eventually see that she was never going to let go of this place. And she will never let it die. So he decided that he needed to recreate the world and bring all of creation into a new world—a world that didn't belong to her. He knew this would take millennia. He believed that, in time, he would have a good chance of making that happen. But he could make it happen quicker if he managed to find the library. If he found that, he could simply remake this reality into what he wanted it to be within seconds."

As Rose said this, she began moving forward a bit faster.

"And what about you?" Amelie asked, backing away at a similar pace.

230

"Me? I don't need to couch my desire in some ridiculous nobility," Rose purred. "I love Clovis. I want him. And that's all."

Rose's blue eyes were drilling into Amelie's own.

"And I will get Clovis back," she said. "That's it. I know you are the key to this. I want a life with him, in a body, forever. I don't care if it means gutting out thousands of humans over the years if I can have this. Why should humans get the gift of physicality. You're horrible. You're stupid, filthy creatures that live to be in the muck. Why do you get to live over and over? Why do you get a jump start all fresh every hundred years or so? Why shouldn't we get a different body every hundred years or so, when we can enjoy the flesh so much more? There are a lot of my kind that would give almost anything for this."

There are more incubi as psycho as Rose? Goody.

Rose lunged forward. Amelie jumped back and felt herself run into something hard. She tripped and as she fell, she instinctively rolled. As she scrambled to her feet, she saw that she had tripped over something that looked like an animal carcass. It was hard and bloated. It looked like it might have been something in the deer family because it had horns.

Rose laughed.

"That's the door you need to go into," Rose said, pointing to it.

"That's not a door, it's a dead thing," Amelie whispered.

"It's not a door for normal humans to get into stories, no. But for other sorts of creatures, that's exactly the sort of doorway they would want and expect," Rose said.

Amelie stared at the thing and noticed it rising and falling in places, as if something were crawling beneath its skin.

"I can't go through there," Amelie said.

"You can and you will," Rose replied, stepping closer to her. "That's the place where they will make you what I need you to be. Don't worry, I'll go with you. Some of my relatives are in there."

Rose lunged forward again, reaching out and grasping Amelie's hand. As Rose began to drag her forward, Amelie saw the door in the distance again, it was now gleaming neon pink in the crimson light.

Amelie dropped to the ground on her knees, pulling Rose toward her. As Rose began to yank her in the opposite direction, Amelie used that motion to launch herself at Rose. Her head connected with Rose's stomach and Rose was thrown off balance. Amelie spun twice around Rose's arm and managed to free herself.

As Rose grabbed for her, Amelie jumped over the animal thing on the floor, cleared it and landed in a crouched position on the other side. A long green-gray mass erupted from the bloated creature. Amelie got to her feet and began running, just as she felt something hot and wet burn into her calf. She pushed forward, toward the gleaming door. She could hear Rose behind her, yelling something but she did not listen.

She made it to the door just as she heard wet scraping sounds behind her and Rose speaking in a language she didn't recognize. The pink-black door in front of her looked like it was made of tar. It was roiling and bubbling. A tiny strand of black substance reached out and wrapped itself around her arm. With no more hesitation, Amelie stepped into the black goo.

Chapter Twenty-Six

Pale Homecoming

The first thing Amelie became aware of was that everything around her was white. It wasn't a clean, pure white. It was a white with a tinge of yellow, like pus or foam in spit. This whiteness was relentless, oppressive, and everywhere. It was the air around her; it was the substance supporting her body. She was neither standing, or sitting, nor lying. She was simply suspended in this whiteness. It surrounded her body and invaded her brain, erasing her thoughts and memories.

After the awareness of the white came another type of awareness. It was a sense that she could not describe. It was not hearing, not smell, not sight, not feeling. It was something else. It was as if she were experiencing a layer of all these things, one on top of each other, creating a repellent sort of texture ... as if there were an extra dimension superimposed over the whiteness.

She tried moving but the substance around her clung to her and pulled at her skin, creating tiny bleeding rips if she so much as breathed too hard. Despite the pain coming from it, her body felt insubstantial. Or she felt insubstantial in what skin she had.

She wasn't sure why she had come here, or been brought here. But she was fairly sure that she had come here by choice. The one thing she was sure of was that this place was BAD. No, worse than bad. It was unnatural and she felt this in her body, in her nerves. She did not belong here. The very makeup of what she was did not fit here. She could feel terror-inducing hormones flowing through her.

Occasionally she could see things moving in and between the layers of this translucent white ooze. They had shape, and occasionally, one would come into focus but even when they did, she still could not really see them. She suspected that this was because they had a form that her brain could not translate into thought. It simply shut down the processing of the image so that she could hold on to her sanity.

She heard a sound near her. There was a crunch, followed by the sound of squelching, like the sound of crushing a cockroach underfoot and hearing its white guts spill out from the confines of its body. Then there was a moan, coming from her left, followed by a wet, squeaking sound, like rubber on wet concrete. She turned her head toward the sound, pulling rips in her face as she did so. What she saw in front of her made her forget anything as insignificant as pain. A large white bubble had formed in the sticky fabric of the air around her. It stretched and pulled and turned in space as it expanded outward. There was something inside it, pushing at its perimeters. Finally, and expectedly, the bubble burst with a sickly wet pop and something crawled out of the slime it left behind.

The something in question looked human, but only vaguely. It looked like something that might have once been human but had been mangled, twisted, stretched, and ripped beyond recognition. It was albino-pale and covered in welts and pustules. Its paper-thin skin was riddled with frayed holes. What was left of its head was malformed and twisted, with sprigs of pale-yellow mucus erupting from it like strands of hair. Its face was eyeless and mouthless, but it had darkened pits where those things should have been. It looked like an emotionally disturbed child's attempt at a Picasso.

The thing pulled itself from the slime that had birthed it and began dragging itself toward Amelie, making a mewling sound from somewhere in its body. Even amid all the horror, a new one inserted itself into Amelie's brain. The mewling sound that the thing was making had a tone that she remembered. A cadence that was familiar. Suddenly a face appeared in her mind. Sophie, whimpering on the beach as she saw children being torn apart by fish.

"There's something much more interesting waiting for you," Camp had said.

When Amelie turned her head to the monstrosity approaching her, her brain suddenly saw through the blasphemy of her current condition. Somewhere, stuck in that mess of mangled flesh, was Sophie Chappell.

Amelie screamed and tried to move, but no matter how she pulled, no matter how much she ripped her own flesh, she was unable to move more than a few inches in any direction. The creature was twitching and squirming as it crawled toward her, dragging tiny, deformed legs behind it.

She turned her head away, refusing to look at the thing, even as it touched her, as it grabbed her leg and began pulling itself up her body. Whatever horror this was, she would survive it. She would not be driven over the edge by this hell.

Hands with unnaturally long fingers grabbed her waist. She felt weight as the thing pulled itself up her body. If it tried to kiss her, she would bite its tongue out of its mouth. That might stop it. It might even kill it, as fragile a thing as it seemed to be.

She felt its hand on her breast and then … nothing.

She opened her eyes to see the creature had been pulled from her by something else … another abomination. This creature was equally as repellent. It was humanoid in form but distorted and pulled in the same way as the first one, if somewhat less. But this creature was tar-black, streaked with open wounds that leaked clear pink fluid into a gel-like substance around them. It had an almost normal-looking head but pools of red blood where its eyes should have been and a red gash for a mouth. It also had the anatomy of a male.

The tar man grabbed the remains of Sophie and the two of them tumbled together in the white. The muck surrounded them, and bound them, and yet they continued to fight each other, mad combatants wrestling in quicksand. Amelie turned her head away. She could hear them grunting and snarling at each other, but she shut her mind to these sounds. She needed to get out of there before these things finished their fight, because whichever one of them prevailed would be back for her.

She had escaped bad places before. How had she done it? She searched for the memory, but it did not appear. She focused harder on the bits of memories scattered like old leaves across the terrain of her brain, but it was almost impossible to sort them out. She flipped through memory after memory in her head, looking for one that would remind her, but her fear made her frantic and unfocused.

Suddenly, she realized that the sound of the struggle had stopped. She turned her head to see the dark creature in a sitting position with its head in its hands, cradled by the muck.

She closed her eyes again. Focus.

"*Hold your breath*," she heard a voice say. Who had told her that? It didn't matter, she felt its truth ring through her.

She held her breath. She kept the air inside her even as she felt the arms of the creature grab her and pull her down in the pale gel. Even as she felt her skin rip, she kept holding her breath. Her lungs were to the point of burning and her heart pounding when she felt the creature crawl on top of her. That was when she stopped holding her breath and began screaming.

She kicked out, punching and thrashing but the monster on top of her pinned her down, pushed her legs open. She only understood what was happening when the thing began to force itself into her. She screamed and screamed into the milky sick around her. She screamed until there was no air left in her lungs. Her heart was hammering in her chest, and she felt like she would vomit. The air around her was poisoning her—and the thing on top of her was stabbing her from the inside.

Then, in the midst of this nightmare, came an element of insanity. The creature on top of her began to stroke her face gently and to make noises. She couldn't understand the words. It was some guttural, barking language, but the tone was soft. Then, it began to sing. Even with the horror surrounding and filling her, she was overcome by shock. When she looked up into the thing's face, what she saw there was beyond her understanding. The creature now had a face. A grotesque, unimaginably horrible face. Scabs and bloody sores covered its skin. Pus dripped from the corners of its mouth. But what was leaking from its wounded eyes was neither pus nor blood. For all the universe, it looked like tears. What came from its pus-filled mouth was a melody. The more she stared, the more the face of the thing shifted and moved in her mind. However, she also felt the pummeling as it pushed itself into her more forcefully. The pain of it became searing. And yet, the melody coming from its obscene mouth was weirdly soothing. It sounded like words ... real words. In her head she heard *"we will never be apart, if I'm part of you."* Words that she recognized from somewhere ... words that stirred memories and longing. Clovis sang these words to her on that beautiful night at the beach so many years ago.

She remembered Clovis, and now she would not push these memories away. Instead, she would use these images to get her through this. She remembered his face, his touch, his black eyes burning when he looked at her. She remembered her longing for him.

Her womb was aching, and she was sore. The creature, despite its gentle sounds, was not gentle in its actions. Its thrusts were becoming harder, more violent. With each thrust, with each new violence, she felt the pain more. She felt more ... but she was also less frightened.

I am not afraid of death, she thought. *I am not afraid of this thing. I will find a way to kill it. That's who I am. That's what I do. No, first I'll make it love me. That's what the Academy wants from me. I can make anything love me. That's what I really do. I will make it love me, and when it does, I'll make it kill itself. It's what I do. I attract things and then I destroy them.*

As she thought this, the creature shuddered and a hot liquid shot through her. She used the moment. She kicked at it, pulling herself away from it. She rolled and scrambled to her feet. Suddenly she could see the world around her clearly.

What Amelie saw around her was insanity-inducing. The additional dimension of this place was now visible everywhere. Creatures, superimposed upon each other, moved and flopped in and through the fabric of space. Some seemed to be consuming each other, others seemed to be mating. Some searched with white, spectral eyes for movement, looking for food or a mate.

"Go," a voice croaked at her. It was the creature who had been molesting her. It spoke with words now.

"How?" she gasped. Searching around her for a path, a road, a door—anything that was different from the white, but she could see nothing. She could see no route out and holding her breath had not worked.

"How?" Amelie whispered to herself.

"Remember," the creature rasped.

Remember, she thought. Remember what? The sounds of the monstrosities around her were building up inside her head. She was leaking the seed of a monster, and all of this was threatening to nail her brain to the inside of her skull. She shoved her hands up to her head.

The creature groaned. It dragged itself upward, the sticky white substance around them pulled clumps of skin from its body, revealing bloody red tissue beneath. Still, it pushed itself forward and grabbed her again. She pulled backward but the goo caught her legs and held her. The creature grabbed one of her legs and shoved its hips against her, inserting itself into her again. She screamed and beat at it when its form began to shift.

"Remember," it whispered.

At that word, the creature in front of her was no longer a monster but a boy. A beautiful boy with black hair, pale skin, and onyx eyes. And tears on his face.

"Clovis," she said as she reached for him and pulled him into her arms.

***

"You gave me part of *this*? Why would you do that? Why would you die for that?" Amelie whispered, looking into his dark eyes.

"I gave this to you because the only way I could save you, protect you, was by being in your blood. That way, my blood could shield yours. The abomination that lives in my lineage could protect you from others with an alien nature, including viruses," Clovis said, touching her face gingerly. "Kara, Dante, the Academy, they were all watching you. Not what you do, but your blood. That's why I never wanted you to let anyone take your blood. But I knew that eventually one of them would get samples of your blood. They would start scanning your DNA."

"Why? They know I am Cambion. So is everyone else at the Academy," Amelie said, her face buried in his neck.

"My love, you have different DNA. Different from humans, different from even most Cambion. You have a different structure buried in you. I found this out when I learned who you were. You have this because you are a broken thing, and you are broken because I broke you. I wasn't there for you all those centuries ago when I was called, and you were broken by that. But my DNA is special too. So, by giving you this part of my DNA, I hoped to hide your alien nature with my own. My blood in yours is a red herring that I hoped would keep you safe until—"

"Until you come back?" Amelie felt hope bloom in her chest, in this most awful of places.

"Eventually, yes," Clovis said, kissing her nose. "But I don't know how long it will take me to re-find myself. It could be a very long time, my love, but a part of me is now in you forever."

Amelie felt the tiniest breeze brush her face, but it chilled her. She knew what it meant.

"You will be pulled home now," Clovis said, with a sad smile.

"How?" Amelie asked. "Why now, when I couldn't get out before?"

"I have given you life in your body, or potential life. The spark of life, in the form it takes in our story, is against the natural laws of this story. So, as it gets further inside you, you will be drawn back to your own world."

"I can't leave you here." Amelie clutched him tightly. "I won't leave you here."

"You have to, Psyche," Clovis whispered in her ear. "I'll be okay. I can take it. Suffering doesn't scare me. Forgetting why I was suffering was what terrified me. You coming here reminded me of who I am. I had forgotten that. But now I can remember it, I'm pretty sure I can hold on to it. If I know who I am, then I know all the places that the other parts of me might be."

Amelie shook her head, but he pulled back from her and took her head in his hands.

"I once told you that all you have to do is survive and thrive," he said. "I meant that. If you don't do that, then I don't have a chance. You have to be strong. I will do whatever I have to do to get back to you. But you have to stay strong, alive, and whole. You have so much more power than you know, or they can guess. Don't let them take you apart."

His black eyes were burning and swirling in that way that was dizzying and hypnotic. He was glamouring her.

Amelie shook her head again.

"No. No. There has to be another way," she said between clenched teeth. "Wait. No. Wait. I can bring things back. You can come back with me. I can bring you back. I can bring physical things back. Let me take you back."

Clovis pulled her to him and kissed her hard. She no longer felt anything of the monster she had seen and felt. Now it was just Clovis. He was inside her and he was all she could see, all she could feel.

Then he pulled back from her and shook his head.

"You can't bring me back, Ames. I'm torn apart. I'm not whole. I am just the part of me that belongs here. This part of me wouldn't survive alone in your world without the other parts. But you need to go, or this place will take you."

"You can exist inside of me—" Amelie began, but Clovis just shook his head and kissed her nose.

With this, he pulled himself out of her and away. She saw him shining in front of her for just a second before he morphed back into the monster who had invaded her minutes before.

She felt a sweet wind rush over her and between them. It pulled her upward and toward a door that had opened above her.

"Clovis!" she screamed, reaching out for him, as she felt herself being sucked away.

Chapter Twenty-Seven

Valentines for All

Amelie felt herself falling. She knew this meant that she was seconds away from being back in her body, but she was fighting it.

She had promised Clovis that she would be strong. Long ago she had promised to do whatever she had to do for them to be together. But all those words had just been words, dissolved away with a few miserable tears, like wet paper. In the best of times, Amelie's opinion of herself had always been one of wary ambivalence, but now she was beginning to stoke a real hatred. Clovis had looked like a monster in that other place, but she was the real monster here. She had abandoned him.

Her arms and legs began to tingle and burn as she felt herself settling back into her body, a body she would, for the time being, prefer to be without. She needed to settle herself. No matter what had just happened, she needed to survive now. Clovis had sacrificed himself for her well-being, to make rash decisions was to make a mockery of all that he had done, all that he had suffered. As her eyes became functional enough to see the black behind her eyelids, she heard a scuffle.

She opened her eyes to see Rose standing over her. Rose, with her hungry eyes peering into her own from inside Camp's body. At the sight of her, Amelie's grief was completely washed away by a tide of fury. And this fury now had a target that was outside of herself. Rose, who had stalked Clovis but had failed to know when he was in danger. Rose, who was a powerful incubus and his mother, but who hadn't used her power to protect, but instead to injure him for her own deviant desires. Amelie felt energy rise in her, the energy that was awakened when she was threatened and that had temporarily taken the mind of her brother in her youth. This energy flared and twisted in her, winding its way further upward and into her belly, her heart, the throat, and finally to her eyes.

Rose was suddenly pulled away from her.

Amelie tried to sit up, but she was still tied down to the chair. She was still in the game room, but the situation had changed. Majo was standing next to Camp, with her gun to Camp's head. James was now awake and standing in shooter's stance, gun aimed at the door. The room around them was sprayed with blood and littered with bodies.

Caio was standing facing the wall, feeling the surface of it.

"See, she's fine. Just like I told you," Camp said to Majo, holding her hands up.

Caio suddenly stood back and shot a round of bullets into the wall. Sparks flew in all directions.

Majo whirled and Rose jumped back away from her.

"Found the interface for the game," Caio said, turning to face the others.

Rose's eyes were burning as she turned to glare at Caio.

"That piece of technology was more complicated than your primitive little brain could imagine," she hissed.

Caio ripped a computer cable from beneath one of the Verite chairs, grabbed Rose and wrapped it around her neck with such speed that she barely had time to turn before Caio was twisting the cord in the back and tightening it. Rose snarled and struggled, but Caio was much stronger than he looked. He kept the pressure on the cord until Camp's body went slack. Caio dropped her to the ground.

"Why didn't you shoot her?" James said.

"I didn't want to add to the ridiculous amount of noise you just made. Another group will be down here soon enough to check on things as it is," Caio said. "Besides, I didn't want to kill her. It wouldn't hurt Rose, in the long run, and she would just find another hapless victim whose body she could steal."

"But you had no problem shooting Widget," James growled, turning his gun on Caio, and looking at Widget's now lifeless body in the chair. "I was semi-conscious when you did that, you arsehole."

"Widget wasn't a real person," Caio said. "He was a Simulacra body holding some other spirit. After seeing him screaming in Amelie's hallway, I assumed that spirit was being held against its will. So killing the body was doing him a favor."

James and Majo both looked at Amelie. She nodded at them.

"Why did you change your mind?" Amelie asked Caio, as he undid the ties of her chair.

"I'll tell you as we walk," Caio said.

"Where are we walking to?" James asked.

"There is no way off this island," Caio said, walking to the door and peering into the next room. "The island is surrounded by genetically altered wildlife, and it's covered by a chemical cloud bank that repels radar. It also messes with electrical signals, including biological ones. That means if the animals don't kill you, the air will. If you tried to go in or out by aircraft, the controls wouldn't work once it entered the cloud. And whoever was piloting would be likely to have cardiac arrest."

Caio walked to the door and stuck his head into the outer room briefly. "It's empty for the moment but backup will be down here in a minute. We should go through the maze."

"What's the maze?" James asked.

"The pathways behind walls and rooms that run all through this place," Caio said, moving back across the room and to the door he had brought Amelie through earlier. He put his badge up against the door and it opened.

He motioned them out with his gun.

"There is a harbor, why can't we get out by boat?" Amelie asked. "Surely they have some boats here, right?" The moment the question was out of her mouth, she knew the answer.

"Oh yeah, sure, they have boats," Caio said, as he began walking quickly down the hall. "The water there is just like everything else on this island. It's filled with genetically modified fish, algae, even microbes. They've been modified to view human flesh as the preferred food source. And the least of the things you will find in that water."

"Then how do they get supplies in and out?" James asked.

"Simulacra," Caio replied. "Simulacra bodies are close enough to human to pass as human, but not with predators."

Amelie walked faster to catch up with him.

"Why are you helping us?" Amelie asked.

"You want to know my motivations?" Caio asked. "You think I might betray you again? That's smart. But you don't need to worry. I won't betray you."

"Why?" Amelie asked.

"Because of what you said earlier," Caio replied. "I've been trying to find ways that I could kill the Director for years. If he is alive, Sarah's in danger. He's a nutjob and if he knew more about her, she would be in even more danger. So I kept his attention focused on me, instead of her."

"But he's an incubus in someone's body," Amelie said, as they turned into the hallway that held the back entrance to her room. "You can't kill him."

"You *can* kill incubi, but it's very hard," Caio said. "You have to unmake them, and I don't have that power. But when you told me that you would keep

Sarah safe, I realized a few things. First, I had thought that she was hidden and safe, but the Director just threatened me with his knowledge of where she's living. If he is willing to do that, then he will eventually send people after her. I thought that having me stay here was keeping her safe, because I would know if they found her. Well, now they have, so I need to find a way to get back to her and protect her. But I'm not stupid and I know I might get killed in all this. Second, I think you have some power, some leverage with the Academy and others in power that I don't have. You weren't bullshitting me when you said you would keep my wife safe, were you?"

"No," Amelie said, and she meant it. She was no longer going to make promises that she wouldn't keep. Nor was she going to take the simple way out by not making promises. She had done that for years, and Clovis had suffered for it. No, she was done with all that.

"I promise I will do what I can to keep her safe," Amelie said.

Caio nodded.

James caught up with them.

"If we can't get off the island, then where are we going?" James asked.

"You can't get off the island, but you can get out of *here*," Caio replied, as they turned a corner.

Amelie found herself standing in front of the elevators that led to the basement and the Lego room—that horror room filled with man-made flesh vehicles and bodies of real people whose spirits were in video game hell.

Amelie turned to stare at Caio. He held her eye.

"The only way you can get out is to go into the game," Caio said.

"No, I'm not going back into that nightmare," Majo said, face stony. "There is nothing—"

Her words were cut short by the crack of a gunshot.

Majo crumpled to the floor.

"I said 'don't fire,'" said a familiar voice.

The body of Mr. Roberts walked from around the corner that they had just passed.

***

Amelie dropped to the floor. Majo was lying motionless on her stomach and blood was seeping out from under her. Amelie looked up to see the Director, in the body of Mr. Roberts, standing twenty feet from her, as guards, maintenance men, admin staff and operatives began filling the corridor they had just passed through. As she watched, more and more appeared from doorways hidden in the walls.

James and Caio both had guns out, pointed at the Director, who was smiling, hands raised.

"Certainly, you know now that bullets won't hurt me. You will just hurt the body of Amelie's poor high school teacher."

The Director moved forward and Caio trained his gun on him as he did so.

"We can slow you down though," Caio said.

"Ah yes, Mr. Silva. You seem to have grown a conscience. Did Amelie get under your skin?"

Caio said nothing. His face was cold and expressionless.

"I'm sorry." The Director raised his hands again. "That was an unnecessary comment. I am just very distressed and frustrated at how quickly things have devolved. And I'm also sorry about the entourage. I had to put out a general alert, you see. It took me a few minutes to call my alternative Shell. I chose this one because I think Amelie likes it. You do, do you not?"

He smiled and Amelie felt sick to her stomach, but that simply added to her spiking rage. She turned her focus to Majo, putting her hands on Majo's chest. She was still breathing, and her heartbeat was still strong. Even if it wasn't, there wasn't much they could do in this moment without the Director's help.

"I'm not angry that you shot me," the Director continued. "I am angry at myself. I should have spent more time with you. I should have told you that you had not been abandoned by Clovis. Of course, your anger at him, and therefore at men in general, helped you do your job, but it hurt you. I should have seen that coming and explained what happened to him earlier, before it prevented you from trusting anyone else and before it did you so much harm. I also should have helped you understand what we were doing before you found the Shells and the Simulacra. That is the least important part of what we are doing here. It's the least meaningful thing. Amelie, I should have started by telling you the full story of Clovis's death."

Amelie felt a metallic taste hit the back of her throat. She wasn't sure if this was an indication of a lie or just a result of her anger and disgust.

"You already told me that. You said he was unmade," she spat out.

"Yes, I did," he said. "I saw Kara and Dante unmake him. They did it even as he slept in your arms. The thing I didn't know back then was why. I probably mentioned one possible reason—that he could go into the hallway, or that he might even be able to bring things back from the hallway. Of course, that would be enough for them to want to kill him, but I have long suspected much more."

"You're talking a lot of shite about a creature who never said more than three words to you," James snarled, stepping forward.

244

"That's an interesting observation, James, and exactly how would you know how many words Clovis had said to me?" the Director said cocking his head. "You might not be as clever as you think."

James visibly blanched and the Director turned his attention back to Amelie.

"You know that some rare creatures can enter the hallway. Rarer still are those that can bring things back into our story from other stories. But rarest of all is the ability to find and enter the library. I'm convinced that Clovis had this gift."

The Director crouched down, so that he was eye level with Amelie.

"I believe this because if he hadn't found it, he couldn't have saved you all those lifetimes ago. Your soul was destroyed then. To remake your soul, he would have had to remake the entire story and the library is the only place where stories are created. Our story was changed that day. It was rewritten. You will find no records of the event in history. Even years later, you would find no one who would remember it … even those who took part in it."

"How would you know what happened to Amelie's soul hundreds of years ago?" Caio asked.

"Thousands, actually." The Director threw a hostile glance toward Caio. "But it is an astute question. I know because I was there. I know that the story has been rewritten because there are signs of the rewrite if you know what to look for. One of our more talented Cambion who was once able to get into the hallway claimed to have found a story like our story in another door in the hallway. When a story is rewritten, it exists in two forms, or three or four, depending on how many times it is rewritten."

Next to her, Majo let out a tiny puff of breath. Just enough to signal that she was alive to someone sitting very near her.

"So, I believe that Clovis rewrote our story to keep you alive." The Director's eyes were back on Amelie. "So that means he could get into the library. Kara and Dante would consider someone who could do this a threat to them and their very way of life. Kara views this world as canon. She will allow no changes to it. So, if she found out that he had already done that, he would have to be destroyed. I am just surprised it took them that long to find him and unmake him."

"What the hell does that have to do with us being here, your bloody game, or anything else?" James asked.

"I felt that it was worth mentioning and that I should have mentioned it earlier, because I don't think Clovis would have been caught or unmade if he had been a part of the Academy," the Director said. "He didn't trust us."

"Imagine that," said Caio.

"I understand why he distrusted us. His history hadn't given him much reason to trust anyone. But he was wrong to distrust us. We are all the same. We Cambion are all scarred things. All of us are marked and branded in some way by this thing, this thing that we are. But there is something beautiful that lurks in those brands. Something strange and magical. We have been marked by a single remnant of the beginning of everything. Some of us, the most spectacular of us, still have that single spark inside us, that tiny bit of code from our creator. That singularity. It is a tiny thing that we may not even know we possess, but the right bit in the right person could destroy us all or pull us all back together after we have broken apart. And that's worth looking for."

The Director was staring past Amelie now, his eyes misted over.

Amelie put her hand to Majo's neck. Her pulse was still strong, but she would need to be looked at soon.

"We should probably have Majo seen to," the Director said, noting Amelie's movements.

"*I'm okay,*" a voice said in her head. It was Majo's voice. Amelie looked up at the Director.

"How can I trust that you will take care of her and not just plug her back into that machine?" she asked, to distract him as she turned her focus inside her own head.

Majo? she asked in her head.

"*Yes, it's me. I'm not critical, but I will need this sewn up before I lose too much blood. The bullet got my arm but there's a lot of blood, so a vein might be nicked.*"

"Trust is something that is always built on faith and risk, is it not? Besides, you may not have much choice," the Director said.

How can you be in my head? Amelie asked Majo, in her head.

"*My non-human father was a demon. Demons possess things. I have some very limited ability from that, but I think it's been enhanced by my time with James,*" Majo said quickly. "*We need to get out of here, and you are the only one who can make that happen. You need to use your energy, and use it fast.*"

Use my energy? How can that help in this situation?

The Director's eyes were on her. Amelie looked down toward Majo's form.

"You, yourself, never belonged anywhere until you came to us," the Director continued. "You aren't like other people, and you shouldn't have to try to be. So for almost twenty years we have kept you safe and provided you a home ..."

He kept speaking but Amelie wasn't listening—or not to him. She was listening to a chorus of voices that now filled her head.

"*You have so much more power than you know, or that they can guess.*"

"*You can attract humans and non-humans.*"

"You did this to your brother. You made him want you. You made him crazy. You took his brain."

"Those two guys back there are probably going to have an ill-fated love affair. That one was a bit too hard."

"You can bounce attraction from one person to another. But be careful, orgies are frowned upon at the mall."

Then, in less than a moment, Amelie's life became clearer. She had always thought that what she had done to her brother's brain after he attacked her was something different than her ability to attract. But now, in this instant, she realized it was all part of the same thing … just a matter of extremity. Lust, taken to its extreme, could be brain-destroying.

Amelie directed her thoughts back to Majo.

If I use my gift, what about all of you? What if I hurt you? she asked.

"You won't," Majo said. *"We've spent years in a pod with you. What with our shared DNA and proximity, we are immunized."*

Amelie smiled, then looked back up at the Director.

"Well, one thing you said was right," James was saying. He examined his gun, twirled it quickly, and then returned to shooter's stance. "We aren't like other people, and we should stop trying to be. But we don't have to fit in anywhere. Not with 'normal' people, and not with the bleeding Academy either."

Amelie stood up and met the Director's eyes.

"You shot Majo," she said softly. "That was a mistake."

"Yes, it was a mistake. We didn't mean to—"

"Oh, you absolutely meant to," Amelie said. "That was a none-too-subtle threat. What I meant was that it was a strategic mistake."

The Director stood back up. His smile was no longer warm, but cold and acknowledging.

"You don't want to set yourself against us, Amelie, dear," he said. "There are a lot of us."

"Us meaning what?" Amelie asked. "Agents? Cambion?"

"There are very few conscious Cambion here, and we are the only actual pod of new recruits in the building at the moment," Caio said. "If a pod is special enough to be brought here, it takes the whole building of special ops to brainwash, subdue, and reprogram it."

"So everyone here is like Ossian Reese?" Amelie asked the Director. "What is he? A demon? A possessed Shell?"

She let her energy mix with the rage snake that was coiled around her belly. The resulting flood of chemicals inside her was joyful in its intensity.

But was it enough?

"Yes, Amelie. Ossian Reese is Simulacra, one of the earlier models of Simulacra, actually. You might have noticed that they have trouble maintaining normal eye color."

The silver eyes of Ossian Reese flashed across her brain along with the memory of him striking her. This added an even hotter rage to her energy mix.

"Mr. Reese is only one model of an entire army of Simulacra and Shells we have here and around the world," the Director said. "This whole building is filled with Simulacra containing the souls of killers, monsters, and demons. Creatures that can be just as beautiful as angels and gods, if they are on your side. But you don't want to set yourself against them. And why would you? You are one of them."

The Director held his hands out toward them.

"All of you. We are all the same inside," he said softly, his eyes becoming shiny with emotion. "You are more of our world than this world. A child of a demon. A walking virus. A universal attractor. An incubus condemned to human form. What part of the regular world would take you in? Where do you have to go? You belong here with us."

"I wonder if you even know how much shite you talk," James said softly.

Amelie stepped forward. The build-up of energy was now coursing throughout her body. She felt it begin to seep from her pores, like sweat. This combination of energies was different from any she had brought forth before. It was neither focused nor coming from any particular centers of energy in her body. It was more general, like it was coming from inside her cells. It felt wicked, glorious, and sexual.

As she met the Director's eyes, she dropped all her shields. She felt the energy burst out of her and fill the room, the hallway, the elevator behind them. It pushed at the ceiling and seeped under the invisible doors. She knew that this time it would fill the building, and maybe even cover the island. She wondered if it would cover continents if she simply let it go for long enough. She breathed into this energy and felt a surge of joy that she hadn't felt in years. It was bliss, but a dangerous bliss. As it coursed from her body, she felt like she was an overburdened electrical wire, being consumed as it transmitted.

The Director laughed lightly.

"Very nice, but your power won't work on these creatures, you know," he said. "The Simulacra and Shells aren't being filled by human spirits."

"And?" Amelie replied, a grin dancing on her lips. "As you so intelligently told me, my power to attract seems to transcend attracting only physical beings."

"My dear, don't tell me you are trying to convince me that you have honed that skill enough to make it a weapon. You can barely control it."

"Maybe you should look behind you then," said Caio flatly. He and James had both lowered their guns. James's mouth was hanging open, but Caio was smiling.

As the Director turned, he saw what Amelie's energy had unleashed.

Behind him, his little army had broken ranks. Some were now on the floor, others up against the wall, but all were coupled ... and coupling. Clothing was either already gone or being ripped off and bare flesh was exposed everywhere. There were men with women, men with men, women with women, in all positions and combinations imaginable. There were even a few people experimenting with inanimate objects. The air was heating up around them. The only sounds were moans and the slick sound of lips touching, tongues meeting, and bodies connecting. The air was thick with the smell of salt, sweat, and chlorine.

"Love's a bitch, isn't it?" Amelie said.

The Director turned back to her with a look of shock, and possibly admiration.

"Ah, I see you have learned to control your abilities a bit more than I might have expected. Well done, but there is still an entire compound full of people—"

"Who are all now out of their minds and humping whatever is closest to them," Amelie said softly. "If you doubt me, then check. Try to call someone."

The Director paused, then smiled.

"What would you like from me then?" he asked her.

"I want you to have one of your skin things take us out of here on a boat." She sounded calm but she felt like a wire burning up as lightning passed through it. Her body was beginning to tremble, and she didn't know how much longer she could bear the intensity of the energy radiating from her. She could feel her consciousness beginning to slip sideways. She needed to end this before she passed out.

"I'm afraid I can't do that," the Director replied, shrugging his shoulders. "So I'm afraid we are at a bit of an impasse."

The sound of a shot ringing out coincided with the right side of Mr. Roberts's face exploding in a mess of blood and bone.

Amelie turned to see James, smoking gun in hand.

"I was sick the fuck of listening to him," he said. Then he turned to Caio.

"So, you have some of idea of how to get us out of here?" James asked.

"Yeah," Caio said, walking over and picking up Majo in his arms. "But first, let's get Majo downstairs and patched up. My plan has two parts ... and she's not going to like either one of them."

Chapter Twenty-Eight

The Other Way Out

Amelie's felt goosebumps rise up on her arms as soon as the door to the elevator opened onto the Lego room. Her legs already felt weak, and returning to the Lego room didn't help. Actually, now that she knew what it was, it was less of a Lego room and more of a zombie room. The place was filled with bodies just waiting to be possessed by something evil. So maybe it was a zombie waiting room.

Caio gently laid Majo on the cement floor.

"In the back corner, you'll find a cabinet with some medical supplies," Caio said to James. He pointed to the right of the elevator. James nodded and trotted in that direction.

Caio then walked to a panel on the wall to the left of the elevator and opened it. Inside it was a mass of buttons, switches, and leads. Caio studied it for a moment, then began flipping switches and disconnecting leads.

"How are you?" Amelie asked, sitting next to Majo.

"I'm okay. It's just my arm. The problem is that it might have nicked a vein, 'cause there's a lot of blood. So it will need to be sewed up," Majo said, her bleeding arm raised above her head to slow the blood flow.

"Damn, I wish Widget was here," Amelie said. "I'm terrible with field dressings."

"I can do it," Caio said. "Give me a second."

Caio turned, pulled his gun out, and aimed three shots at the elevator, then turned back to them.

"For a bunch of spirits, and computer technology geniuses, these people here are totally crap at electricals," he said, as he sat down next to Majo. James had appeared and dropped an oversized emergency kit next to him.

James was examining Majo's arm.

"The bullet passed through, so that's good," he said.

Caio took a brown bundle from the emergency kit.

"More good news is that they actually have a suture kit in this thing," he said, opening the bundle to reveal needles, forceps, a scalpel, and twelve braided sutures with needles.

"The bad news is, no local anesthetic," he said with a sigh.

"Didn't expect it," Majo said. "I've been through this before, and with a little luck, I will live through this day so I can go through it again at a later date."

Caio cleaned and sterilized the wound as James paced.

"So what's your plan?" James said. "It won't take them long to get down here."

"Longer than you might think," Caio replied. "Like I said, they suck in terms of electrical engineering because they think things like that are beneath their superior intellect. So it could take them an hour or hours to figure out how to reroute electricals to turn the elevator back on … but we need as much time as we can get."

As Caio threaded the first stitch through Majo's arm, she winced.

"I'm not going back into that monstrosity of a game," Majo said. "Not after—" She winced again.

"That's okay," Caio replied. "My initial plan was that I would stay behind, but it's just as easy if it's you and me. I will put James and Amelie into the game."

"Why us and for what purpose?" James asked.

"Amelie has to go in, because she can get into the hallway. As James is the only other one of us who has any useful experience with the hallway, he is the logical choice to go in and help her."

"James has experience in the hallway? How?" Amelie asked, turning to James, who had colored.

"Because of his heritage," Caio replied.

"What heritage?" Amelie asked.

Caio looked between the two of them, then shook his head. "If you don't know, that's not a discussion for right now. For right now, what you need to know is this. I can get you hooked up into the game from here. If I am the one who puts you in the game, I can use the tracking system down here to be able to find you."

"And do what with us?" Amelie asked.

"I will bring your spirits back into Simulacra bodies," Caio said.

"Why the hell would you do that?" James asked.

"There is only one way out of here, and that's by water," Caio said. "Way at the opposite end of the room, there is a door. That door leads to the harbor and boats. We leave that way and take our chances."

"Then why don't we do that now?" Amelie asked.

"The boats aren't docked. You will have to swim to them, and what is in the water would eat a human before you got halfway there."

"Are you sure we have no shot with swimming? Maybe we can make a makeshift raft to get out to the boats," said James.

"No, there is no chance to survive the water. As I said, normal algae, plankton, and fish have been genetically modified to recognize humans as a food source. I've seen what happens to people who have been used as test subjects in the water. I've also seen people try to escape. The algae and plankton bury into your skin, covering you and dragging you down, where you will drown, and they will eat you. The bigger fish are all active human predators and the smaller fish act like piranha. The bigger fish would knock us off whatever makeshift thing we could find. They can think, you know, these fish and microbes. They are learning."

"Why would the Academy do that?" Amelie whispered.

"It's part of the Director's ongoing experiments to insert higher consciousness into lower consciousness organisms," Caio said. "Listen, you have no idea of all the shit that the Director is doing here. I have a better idea than most, but I don't have time to explain it. But I can tell you that inserting you into Simulacra is our best chance out, the fish and algae don't recognize Simulacra as human. That means I will need to put you in one of the newer Simulacra."

"What will happen to our bodies?" Amelie asked.

"We will take them with us in their pods. I can bring the transfer unit with me, and I should be able to pull you back once we get somewhere safe. Simulacra bodies are a lot stronger than ours, so that makes the carrying of your pods easier," Caio replied.

"How do you know how to do all this?" James asked.

Caio sighed. "I convinced someone to train me on it."

"How?" James asked, eyes narrowed.

"Spirits coming into Simulacra or Shells for a short time are interested in as many physical pleasures as they can experience in a short time. Someone who looks like me is really appealing to some of them," Caio said.

James snorted, but Majo shook her head.

"So you can get Amelie and James in, and you can get them out. That's great, but what do we do to get it started?"

"'Cause if we are doing this, we need to do it fast," James said, standing up.

252

"I can make the connections and do the transfer in less than an hour," Caio said.

"Then let's go," James said, reaching for Amelie and pulling her to her feet.

"Wait, what I just told you was the easy part," Caio said. "Majo and I can get you in a body, but the hard part is staying alive while we are setting that up. While you are in the game, you are vulnerable to every single spirit, agent, virus that is associated with the Academy."

"Why is that a problem? You said we could do it in less than an hour," Majo asked.

"Less than an hour *our* time," Caio said.

James sighed and put his hand to his forehead.

"Time runs differently in the game," Caio replied, turning to James. "And the Academy has a bit of control on the time rate in the game itself. They have just begun experimenting with that. It's possible that they could speed up the time of the game in relation to time in our world to keep you in it for as long as they need to find you. So you will need to go from the game into the hallway. Once you are in the hallway, in a story, wait until an hour has passed of our time and then go back into the hallway."

"How the hell will I know when it's been an hour our time? I don't know that. I've never been able to assess that," Amelie said. James closed his eyes, his jaw clenching.

"James can do it," Caio said. "Incubi, well some particular incubi, have the ability to gauge time across different stories."

"Incubi?" Amelie said turning to James, who was looking down.

"Was I wrong in assuming you can do that?" Caio asked.

"No, you weren't wrong," James muttered.

Caio nodded.

"They'll send people searching for Amelie immediately," Caio said. "I suspect some assets in the game have already been alerted. Will you protect her, while she is in the hallway, until we can bring you back?"

"Yes," James said, looking away. "I always have, haven't I?"

Amelie's inner eye opened, and she saw those words hanging in the air above James's head: *I always have*, in glowing pink and gold, outlined in red.

Amelie looked at him, but he refused to look at her.

"What if something goes wrong?" Majo asked. "What if the Academy reaches us before we can get Amelie and James into a body? Or what if they pull them out before we do?"

"Yes, that is a possibility. So if you come out of the hallway and into the game in an hour and you are not almost immediately brought back into our world, then something has happened to us, and you go immediately back into the hallway. You will have to find another way out. If you are pulled out and it's not us, but the Academy, then I am afraid you will need to fight your way out."

Caio looked at James and he nodded.

"Majo, for you and me, if it looks like they will get through the elevator, we have three options. One is to go into the game ourselves, but we won't have a way to come out. Second is to fight our way out and try to kill everyone here. Last, is to brave the water."

"I'm willing to try any combination of two or three but I won't go back into that game," Majo said.

Caio nodded.

"Okay, we all know what we have to do," Caio said. "First, follow me. I need to put Amelie and James in a bed, and Majo needs to know where that is, in case something happens to me."

Caio began walking toward the opposite end of the room. Amelie caught up with him.

"Isn't there a problem here?" she asked. "If all these things around us are Simulacra and Shells, then can't they just possess them and attack you here?"

"I thought of that," Caio said, "but making the transfer of a spirit consciousness into one of these requires energy—specific electrical energy that they only have here in the room. It's true they could theoretically do that remotely, because all the electrical equipment is in the beds and all the beds are connected via the interface to the mainframe. That's why I disconnected the electricals from the interface. Like I said, they suck at electricals, but it won't last forever, and they will find a way to work around it eventually, but it should hold for long enough to do what we have to do."

The world around her turned shades of lavender and red.

"What if that doesn't work?" Amelie asked.

"Then Majo and I will kill whatever comes out of those boxes," Caio replied.

"What if they all come out?"

"Then we'll kill them all."

"All of them?"

"Yes. I have some experience in this area," Caio said, with a slight smile. "They had me train against Simulacra. Spirits just inserted into a new body are slow, and I'm not. I am also hard to kill. This is why I needed to be one of the ones to stay."

As they were talking, they entered an area containing Legos that looked different. First, they were not stacked, instead they were laid out individually on the floor in rows, like coffins in a cemetery. They were the same shape and size as the others, but they were multicolored and they looked metallic. They shimmered in colors of gold, pink, blue, and green. Amelie blinked and closed her inner eye, but the colors remained the same.

"These are different," Amelie said, as Caio walked up to one at the end of a row.

"Yeah, these are the Evermore beds that are made of bismuth," Caio replied. "It is diamagnetic."

"Meaning?" James asked, coming to stand next to them.

"Meaning it repels magnetic fields," Caio replied. "This has the benefit of creating a barrier between spirits inside it and outside it. It also shields against most external scanning, so it keeps them hidden. That's important to the Academy—and it's very stable. That means you will be harder to find if they try to find your bodies."

"You know a lot about this," James said.

"Yes, and it came at a great price." Caio turned to face him. "The Evermore pods are for Shells or Simulacra that they hope will last almost indefinitely," he continued. "They are made different, they are prepared different. Very few spirits are allowed to use these because they are also experimental. So your average lowly worker wouldn't come back here, and you will be safer that way too."

Metallic taste in the back of Amelie's mouth.

"Also, it uses the Verite platform, but it resonates at a higher level. It exists above the dream state," Caio said to James. "That should make it easier for both you and Amelie to navigate."

"Okay, let's get this over with," James said. Caio nodded and motioned James forward to the bed.

"Whoa, what is that?" James asked. Amelie stepped forward and peered into the box. Inside the box was a cloud.

"It's aerogel," Caio replied. "It's ninety-nine-point-eight percent air, so is less harmful on bodies that will not be moving much for long periods of time. They also use it as a drug delivery system and as insulation."

James nodded.

"All right. Best get it done then," he said, then he walked to Majo and gave her a kiss on the forehead. "See you when we get out."

He gave Amelie a quick hug and let Caio help him into the pod.

"You might feel a bit suffocated at first, but that will fade quickly," Caio said, attaching sticky pads with leads to his neck and forehead. Then he stepped back.

James gave a weak little smile, and then a thumbs-up.

Caio closed the lid and locked it. He quickly opened a panel on the top containing an electronic panel. He entered a few numbers and then stepped back. Amelie felt her throat close up.

"Majo, I entered 334428 as an entry zone at 4:44 p.m. Can you run back to the desk near the elevator and log that on a piece of paper, so I don't forget it when I enter Amelie's info."

Majo raised her eyebrow at him but nodded and turned to walk swiftly back down the row of Legos.

Caio took Amelie to a pod three up and four over from where James had been placed. When he opened the lid, Amelie looked at the strange mass of wires and spongy liquid and felt her throat constrict again.

What choice did she have? If there was such a thing as evil, this place was the definition of it. This place that was the hub of the Academy.

Amelie looked into Caio's earnest face. He had committed horrors, but he had done them to save someone he loved. She had no such excuse. She had also committed acts of atrocity in the name of the Academy. She had killed, maimed, destroyed people's reputations and worse. She had often been sent out to destroy people's faith in the beliefs that guided them, in the things they held most dear. She had done this without question, and why? Because the Academy offered her a potent drug—distraction. It gave her things to do while she hid herself from the world. And in return she had used the power of her abilities for whatever purpose suited them. She had done what she had done not to save anyone but because she was weak and lazy. Now, she realized that she had abandoned everything for this distraction. She had abandoned her family, she had abandoned Hudson, and, in the end, she had even abandoned Clovis.

"Are you okay? Are you ready?" Caio's eyes darted across her face, reading each small movement.

If this had just been about herself, she might have stayed here and fought, and accepted her death. But now, she had more lives than her own to save. She had broken promises to fulfill. She had also promised to find Sarah if something happened to Caio. She promised to put Clovis back together and she had promised, among other things, to keep herself safe.

"I'm ready," Amelie said. Caio took her hand and helped her into the pod. The cloud was much denser than she expected and took her weight easily.

Caio then attached the sticky pads to her shoulders, neck, and forehead. Then he leaned down and put his face near hers.

"Despite what I said, there is a chance that I will die in this room," he whispered.

"I know," Amelie said.

"If that happens, you will have to get yourselves out. Maybe you can even bring help."

"How would we do that?" she began, but Caio shook his head.

"How have you done any of the things you have done? Normal people excuses don't work with you. You're not normal," he said. "Besides, you promised me you would keep Sarah and my child safe. I am holding you to that."

"So you *do* have a child?" Amelie whispered. For the first time, she saw tears in Caio's eyes.

"A girl," he said softly. "Keep her safe."

Amelie nodded.

Caio leaned over her and slipped something very tiny into her hand. It was a flash drive the size of a penny.

"This is all the information I have collected about the Academy. If things go wrong, you might be able to use it as a bargaining chip with whoever might help you. They are likely to help you more if they know that you can provide them with insider information."

"Who might help us?" Amelie asked.

"You can't trust anyone completely, but the enemy of your enemy is your friend," Caio said, with a sad little smile. "At least for a while."

"But what can I do with this?" Amelie asked, holding up the flash drive. "It's not like I can take it into the game."

"Let me see it," Caio said, taking the drive back from her. He reached into the back of the Lego and pulled out what looked like a glue gun. He then inserted the disk into a slot on the top of it. "They use trackers a lot to keep track of the Simulacra. Hold out your arm."

Amelie held out her arm and winced as the tracker was swiftly inserted under the skin of her arm, and the wound burned closed.

"I don't know how this helps. Just because it's in me now doesn't mean it will go into the game."

"No? Why not?" Caio said softly, then leaned down again and whispered in her ear. "You brought things out, didn't you? Like the bug wings. Don't try to bring the physical thing in. Bring the thought that the thing is now part of your body. The thought of what it does and what it means. I suspect the physicality of it will follow."

As Amelie looked into his dark eyes, a taste hit the back of her tongue. This was a new taste ... it tasted like blood.

"Caio, I think they are coming," she began, and at that moment, there was the sound of banging from above them, and drills.

"Sssshhhh, no more," he said. "Do what you have to do, and I will do what I have to do. Keep yourself safe. I care about you, all of you, and that's a miracle to me."

Amelie raised herself and kissed Caio's cheek.

"Come back to me, sister," whispered Caio.

With that, he pulled the cover down over her cloud coffin.

When Amelie opened her eyes, it was not to a game matrix but to a vast sky stretching out above her.

Acknowledgements

As always, my deepest thanks to those who helped in the creation of this book.

A big thanks to my constant and supportive friends and beta readers, Addie, Myra, Valerie, who took time from their incredibly busy lives to read my books. Also hugs to Ian, Hassy, Tessa and Leo for all their friendship, insights, help and support.

Most of all, thanks and love to my family. Everyone in our family always seems to be "running" with our own individual passions and projects, not to mention more global moves than might be considered sane. Despite this, they have always taken the time to be very involved in my writing. So thank you to Sebastien, my unnaturally gifted developmental editor, treatment author, and the one who helps me make my stories visual; Lucas, scientist and creative dream weaver, who asks the right questions to help me build worlds ; and Julien, my husband, my partner and now my translator, who is my cheerleader and keeps me smiling through our crazy life.

For Those Who Enjoyed this Book

Amelie, Lazlo, Hudson, Kara and Dante will return in "Limerence".

***

As most people know, reviews make or break authors, so if this book made you feel anything, do please share it, and connect with me at the following:

Webpage: *Lsdelorme.com*
Tiktok: *@lexyshawdelorme*
Insta: *ls_delorme*
Twitter: *@lexyshawdelorme*
Facebook Page: *Lexy Shaw Delorme*

BV - #0059 - 120924 - C0 - 229/152/15 - PB - 9798987488065 - Gloss Lamination